SING CODA
The Submission Series Book Three

CD Reiss

*everafter*ROMANCE

The Submission Series

EverAfter Romance
An Imprint of Diversion Publishing Corp.
443 Park Avenue South, Suite 1008
New York, New York 10016
www.DiversionBooks.com

For more information, email info@diversionbooks.com

First Diversion Books edition July 2015.
Print ISBN: 978-1-68230-020-6

Contents

sing.

The Submission Series
Book Seven

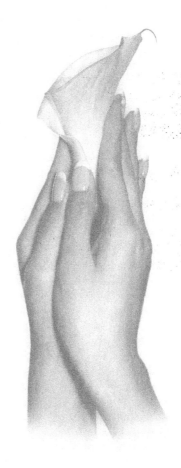

Take my hand, my love.
On sinews of air we tread
Aught but distance our guide
With no tempo to our gait
No endpoint drawn
Neither plot nor plan
By the thorns of a compass rose
We bound toward the horizon

Chapter 1

Monica

Dr. Thorensen had put up his Christmas lights on December first, two weeks ago, decorating his wood detailing and redwood fence with tiny multicolored dots. No fat inflatable snowmen. No Santas. No elves. Just classy little spots hanging around the edges of his property like a joyful fucking aura.

It was too early to ring Dr. Thorensen's bell. He was a single guy in his mid-thirties, and it was Tuesday morning. He was probably at his office or the hospital. Maybe nuzzling one of the women I saw come around periodically. But I was losing my shit. I couldn't wait another minute, and I'd noticed he kept odd hours. I saw him through the glass in a polo and jeans, carrying a coffee cup. When the door opened, he looked grave.

"Monica, am I blocking your driveway?" Then he looked at me. I must have been a sight. "Are you okay?"

"Not really."

"What happened?"

I felt silly, as if I'd become a story he'd tell his friends. I'd become the annoying girl next door. He'd told me once that he didn't put an MD license plate on his car because he wanted to avoid random advice-seekers and neighbors with a sniffle. I laughed with him over the story of the Montessori mother two doors down who wanted him to look at her son's scraped knee. So I'd avoided ringing his bell for five long, lonely, friendless days.

But he was a cardiologist, and when Santa brought me a gift, I figured I shouldn't try to cram it back up the chimney. One long sentence poured out. "I didn't want to bother you—I mean, it's not like he can't afford the best doctors in the world—but I'm afraid to tell them what I think or that I'll look crazy, so I was wondering if you had privileges at Sequoia Hospital?"

"I do." I feared his next words would be something like, "Sorry, I'm not working right now. I deserve to be at home in peace as much as the next person, and the fact that I spent a quarter million dollars on school doesn't make me public property." But he stepped aside and said, "Come in."

I'd never been inside his house. Though I'd always been curious about it, when I finally did see it, I barely noticed anything. I'd been blind to details for a week. My brain had somehow narrowed down to what it thought were the only important things: breathing, worrying about Jonathan, and desire to kill Jessica. But when I passed the living room, flashing lights caught my eye. Three huge flatscreen TVs were up with a leather chair set positioned to see all of them. I recognized the steampunk settings and those particular burnished brass and wood finishes from a party I'd attended before Jonathan. In another life.

"You play *City of Dis*?" I asked. The online multiplayer game was highly competitive, complex to a fault, and if a player had the brain power to keep up with it, more addictive than crack.

"Yeah." He seemed a little embarrassed. "Need to wind down sometimes, you know."

"I know this guy who wears Depends when he plays so he doesn't have to get up to go to the bathroom."

"I'm potty trained, even in character. Coffee?"

I followed him to the marble and glass kitchen. "No, thanks. I'm more of a tea person."

"So," he refreshed his cup, "if it's not the driveway, and you're asking about Sequoia, must be a medical call?"

"I'm so sorry to bother you."

"You're fine. Sit." He pulled out a tall chair by the marble kitchen bar.

I sat, feet wrapped around the legs, a coiled tension in my hips. "You did the place nice. It's probably the best house on the block."

"It's an investment." He put a pot of water on the stove. "Could have gotten something in Beverly Hills or Palisades for twice the price and half the aggravation, but where's the fun in that?"

"It's quieter and cleaner?"

"No potential, though. Nowhere to go but down. This neighborhood's going to be Beverly Hills in ten years, and I get to live next to people like you. Interesting people. It's all lawyers over there." He glanced at me as if checking on me. "So what brings you?"

"You're a cardiologist. I'm sorry, but—"

"Stop apologizing."

"My...I guess you'd call him a boyfriend? He's at Sequoia."

"A patient, I assume."

"They say he has a heart problem. That he damaged his valves when he was younger and he..." Was I betraying a confidence? People had been talking of his suicide attempt so often that it seemed like old news, but the talk had been within the confines of his family and doctors. Dr. Thorensen waited, leaning on the counter, his cup warming his hands. "He took too much Adderall once when he was a teenager."

"This is Jonathan Drazen?"

I felt a tingle of shock, like an adrenaline rush. He knew, and he mentioned his name right there in the kitchen, as if Jonathan's condition and how he came to be so sick was public knowledge.

He must have seen the confirmation on my face. He put down his cup and opened a chrome canister on the counter. It was full of teabags. "That explains the car."

Was I just being sensitive? It sounded as though he thought I couldn't possibly have bought a Jaguar without fucking someone. I didn't have time to decide if I was mad because Dr. Thorensen continued as if he knew he'd implied something that could twist my knickers and wanted me to forget it.

"We have a weekly meeting on the high-risk cardiology patients," he said. "Just to check diagnoses and make sure we're on the same page about treatment. I've seen him." He held up a hand as if to reassure me. "I'm not his doctor or anything. Dr. Emerson is with him. He's highly qualified."

"And you agreed a sixteen-year-old overdose gave him a heart attack? That makes no sense."

"Adderall is basically legalized speed. Taking a fistful will damage your valves, and the slightest blockage will give you a heart attack. No question. It's a miracle he made it this far."

He handed me my cup. I didn't want it but found my hands clasping it anyway. "Are you sure?" I asked. He raised an eyebrow but said nothing. "I don't mean to question you. I'm sorry. I didn't go to medical school. But before it happened, we were at a party, and he was gone a long time. I think..." I felt so stupid even saying it. I'd told Margie my theory, and she'd dismissed it. "I think he was poisoned." I stared into my teacup.

"That's a pretty broad accusation." He said it softly and kindly, but under it all was a hint of condescension, as if what he really wanted to say was that I was crazy.

"He has enemies," I said.

"Yes."

"His ex-wife was mad at him."

"Okay."

"He was fine just before."

"No, he wasn't."

"I was there, you weren't. I'm sorry, but he was fine."

He put his cup down, and I felt the weight of my intrusion. He was playing a video game at eight in the morning, getting a moment's peace from a high pressure job, and I was dragging his work into his kitchen. And he didn't believe me. I wanted him to believe me, even though I felt crazier and crazier.

He said, "There was nothing on his tox screen. I sat with his attending for two hours looking at EKGs. He had a massive coronary event. There's a pretty good chance he'd been having small heart attacks in the days previous. His valves are shot." He stopped his sentence as if catching himself. He'd been talking about a man's heart like it was a carburetor.

"I should go."

"He has a very good prognosis."

"Thanks for the tea." I put it on the counter.

"Monica, listen—"

"Dr. Thorensen—"

"I'm Brad."

"Brad, it's been a rough five days. He's got seven sisters and a mother and they...most of them...act like I'm no one to him. I'm on his list, so I'm told everything, but I'm surrounded by strangers. Seeing him like that, with the IV and the tubes and just waiting to get cut open... Everyone's worried, and no one wants to listen."

"I understand the desire to blame someone, but he wasn't poisoned. I promise you," he said.

There had been no evidence of poisoning, and Jessica had been in my sights, or in the bathroom, most of the time. I was looking for a ten-second interval where she could have...What? Fed him something? Slyly injected him? Did I think I was living in an Agatha Christie novel where conceptual artists moonlit as chemists?

"Yeah," I said, "I guess."

"Tell you what. Why don't you play *City of Dis* with me for a little while?

I'm in the eighth circle. I'll build you a character from my profile. You won't get an opportunity to play at that level anywhere else. All your problems go away." He snapped his fingers. "Magic. Come on."

"I can't."

"An hour."

"I haven't done laundry in two weeks, and I have to go to work."

He put down his cup. "Rain check?"

"Yes, and thank you, Brad." His short name sounded both overly familiar and coldly detached in my mouth.

"Any time."

He walked me out, and I went home to wrestle the laundry. Maybe I'd hang out a Christmas light myself. I found a letter taped to my screen door. No envelope, just an open sheet.

NOTICE OF PUBLIC AUCTION

The rest was legal bullshit, but I scanned the page for the handwritten parts. My address. Thirty days. Non-payment.

"Shit." I looked at my house as I might find an answer there, but it was just a dark wooden box with a crumbling foundation. I still hadn't gotten the papers signed to fix it, but if the permits had been opened, my mother had gotten the notice in the mail. So she knew something was going down. The notice must have been the result of my failure to send her a check two months running.

I had to call her.

I didn't want to call her.

I stared at my phone. The number was right there. I'd missed rent twice before, once when Kevin and I broke up, and once when Gabby had tried to commit suicide. Both times, I'd sent two month's (months') rent in an envelope with a thank you note. So when Gabby died and I was short, I just figured I'd make it up. I could have, except I was in Vancouver December first and forgot. Then I stopped working when Jonathan collapsed. Honestly, even if I'd had the cash, I was too preoccupied to manage any practical aspect of my life.

That's what I got for living in her house. Really, how long could I mooch off someone I wasn't speaking to anyway? How old was I? I hit her number while I unlocked my front door. It was easier to do difficult things if I multitasked through them.

My house was exactly the same every time I went into it to shower or grab something. Nothing moved. The blanket on the couch was rumpled in the shape of an opening rose. The curtains draped over the back of the chair like perfectly-trimmed bangs. The dishes in the rack were filed and waiting for archiving in the cabinets.

The phone stopped ringing, and there was a click. Mom's voice still had the slight Brazilian accent that had been carefully chipped away but never smoothed off. My heart skipped a beat, an adrenaline rush in preparation for the confrontation. It was her voice mail.

"Hi, Mom. I got a notice the bank is auctioning off the house? Should we talk about it?"

God, that was stupid. I hung up. Should've paid the fucking rent. Should've called her to let her know I was in a pinch. Should've had Darren move in. One more stupid shit thing in a long line of other stupid shit things. I folded the notice and wedged into the corner of my notebook. Fuck the Christmas lights.

Chapter 2

Monica

I was nearly out of gas. I had five dollars in my pocket, one maxed out credit card, and a checking account dangerously close to scraped clean. I could get to work and make some cash, but without that eighth of a tank, I'd be taking the bus to the hospital and paying the fare with change found between couch cushions.

I didn't dare tell Jonathan things had gotten that bad. I went to him every night with sunshine in my voice and rainbows in my pocket. When I wasn't at Sequoia, I let the panic come. Slamming my locker closed, I painted on a customer service smile for no one in particular.

"Monica?" Andrea came up behind me, her hair dyed blue. It was always a new color with her, and I seemed to have missed that change. The color was already fading back to green.

"Hey, how are you? Love the color."

"What are you doing here?" she asked.

"It's my shift."

She rolled her eyes and twisted her mouth. "Uhm, we're kinda in the habit of swapping you out. So I'm working."

"No," I heard the squeak in my voice, "I need the cash." God, I hated sounding like that. I hated whining about money. She shrugged and walked out to the floor. I went to Debbie's office.

"Come in," she said after I knocked. She was alone, behind her desk and shuffling through God-only-knows. She looked up as if she was pleased to see me. She stood and put her arms out for a hug. "Monica. How are you?"

"I'm fine. I came to work, but Andrea says she's got my shift?"

"You've missed five shifts. And you were out the week before. I need to run the floor."

"I need my shift."

She put her hand under my chin. "You're in no condition to work. You lost weight. You have circles. A little lipstick?"

"Please."

"What's happening? Sit. Tell me."

I lowered myself into the leather chair. Debbie sat on the arm of the one next to it. The nightly mist that descended on Los Angeles dotted the window. It was the wettest year in history. The bar would be slow and tips scarce. Just tourists who had nowhere else to go and regulars who came out of habit. The Hollywood hitters would be in clubs downtown or Silver Lake venues.

"They're trying to stabilize him so they can do a valve transplant and open up his arteries," I said. She looked at me blankly, as if she was waiting to understand. "He damaged his heart when he was sixteen—" I stopped abruptly. I knew Debbie and Jonathan had been close, but I couldn't be sure he'd told her about the fistful of drugs he'd taken. He hadn't known he was broken until the stress of the past weeks broke him.

"Here," Debbie said, handing me a tissue. "Go ahead."

"They have to replace parts of his heart." I felt strongly that I didn't know what I was talking about because I didn't. "He hasn't been stable enough for the surgery." I pressed the tissue to my eyes. It came back with blobs of mascara. I really couldn't work the floor. "I go in every night and talk to him, but I need to work tonight."

"No, you need to go in to him."

"I need the money. I'm sorry. I know it seems gross."

"He can't give you money?" She seemed shocked, as if he *wouldn't*, which wasn't the case. Asking for money would sully the sunshine and rainbows.

"I don't want him to worry."

"What about his family?"

"Outside of Margie, they tolerate my existence. Which is fine. But I'm not asking."

"He hasn't given you something you can sell?"

The title for the Jag, which was my only transportation, had been in the glove compartment when Lil drove it to me. The platinum lariat that symbolized our bond twisted around itself on my dresser, binding sea and sky. The diamond navel bar was where he'd put it when he committed to me. "No. I have nothing to sell."

Debbie got up and walked behind her desk. Bending at the waist, she opened a drawer and pulled out her wallet. "I don't usually do this."

"Don't. I'll manage."

She took a pile of bills out and folded them once, coming around the desk. "We can cover your shifts another couple of days before we have to put you on personal leave. That's unpaid." She picked up my hand and slapped the bills into it. "Figure it out."

I squeezed the money. I couldn't refuse it. Taking it meant I could see Jonathan. "You're very nice to me."

"Jonathan helped a friend of mine through a rough time. You make him happy. So helping you is helping him. Now go. I have work to do."

Chapter 3

Monica

One hundred fifty-seven dollars in smallish bills. God bless Debbie. I loved her. I put gas in the car. Then I bought a container of cubed cantaloupe at Ralph's for dinner. I parked three blocks away so I wouldn't have to pay for the lot and walked. Night was falling, and it was getting cold. I was bundled in a scarf and light coat, having forgotten a hat in my rush to get to work.

Sequoia was huge. Half the babies in L.A. were born there, and everyone else managed to die there. The charge nurse in the cardiac unit knew me by sight and nodded at me and my cantaloupe.

"Hi," I said when I walked into Jonathan's room of bland pinks, beiges, hard edges, and the smell of sickness and alcohol. I'd gotten him a little light-up Christmas tree for the table by the bed, and every night, he made sure it was on.

"I thought you were working tonight." Jonathan was sitting up, reading by a single lamp. I'd seen him in that bed every night for the past week and a half, and he'd gotten better and better. I couldn't believe they wouldn't let him just walk out.

"It's raining. Debbie didn't need me." I sat on the edge of his bed and took his hand while trying not to disturb the IV in it. Machines beeped and hummed. A stylus scratched on paper, tracing the lines of his heartbeat. "How are you feeling?"

"Like I want to punch someone. You?"

I smiled. "The contracts are signed. Margie was a hero. Seriously, I couldn't have done it without her. I'm finalized to record tomorrow. I'm singing 'Collared' with full production value."

He took the cantaloupe container from me. "They're getting the L.A. Phil in?"

"I know you're joking," I said, compulsively starting to help him open the container. But in the past couple of days, he hadn't needed me, so I pulled back my hands. "But yeah. Fifteen pieces. String-heavy. Like, real. Next week, we're doing 'Craven.' I laid down some scratch on a few others, and they're going to pick two more for an EP."

He plucked out a piece of melon and held it up. I leaned forward and opened my mouth. He brushed the juice on my bottom lip before letting it touch my tongue. "Orchestras cost a lot of money," he said. "They must believe in you."

I took the cantaloupe gently and closed my lips around it, catching his fingers and sucking them on the way out. "We'll see."

"Is this what you brought for dinner?"

"I ate stuff at home," I lied. If he knew my fridge was empty and I didn't want to spend Debbie's money getting takeout, he'd worry. Or he'd lose his shit all over the hospital room. He'd already had a Code Blue over his mother trying to shut me out.

"You're supposed to have dinner with *me*." He wasn't mad or scolding. During the day when his family visited, I hung around in the shadows. That was the deal. I didn't have to be front and center with his sisters and mother, but I came to him at night, alone.

"What did the doctors say? Will you be out for Christmas?" I changed the subject away from dinner, which would lead to talk of my financial distress. "I have no idea what to get you, by the way." He paused, picking through the fruit, eyes cast down. "Well?"

"Not yet." He held up some cantaloupe. I took it, but I sensed he was hiding something. I chewed slowly. As if sensing my recalcitrance, he said, "I'm strong enough, but the arrhythmia's still there."

"It was gone yesterday!"

He shrugged. "Eat. I want that body ready for me when I get the hell out of here."

That was Jonathan. Focused on getting the hell out of what he perceived as a prison.

"This body's always ready for you." I parted my lips for his fingers.

He pulled the fruit back an inch, and I followed. He let it touch my tongue, then pulled it back. We played cat and mouse with the melon until he popped it in his mouth, grabbed me by the back of the head, and kissed me. Our tongues tasted of cold fruit. I kissed him as if I'd almost lost him. I pushed into him as if he was a delicate creature living only by the grace of

God and modern medicine. His tongue wove around mine as if he was as healthy as ever. As if an elevated heart rate wouldn't kill him or, at the very least, send nurses running in with paddles and carts of beige machines. He could deny what was happening all he wanted. He was getting stronger, but if his doctors were to be believed, every day without that surgery brought him closer to another heart failure.

"Goddess," he whispered, "I have to have you."

"No fucking way." We'd tried two nights previous, and the word "disaster" would be used if we were underplaying the results. I'd gotten an earful from Nurse Irene and had cried for hours from the stress and the scolding.

He pushed his finger under my waistband. "Undo these."

"No."

"Open your jeans and pull them down." He spoke as if I hadn't just refused him, and the command sent waves of lust through me. "I swear to God I won't get my heart rate up."

"I'm scared."

"I'm not. Come on. Trust me." His face was inches from mine, his hand on my cheek and stroking my lower lip. Every night, I curled up next to him and slept for a few hours before I was asked to get in my chair. Every night I wanted him, and every night I worried. He'd gone from distraught, to annoyed, to depressed, to this. He felt as though he'd lost control, and he was using me to feel as though he had it back for a minute. I just didn't know if I could trust him to take care of himself.

I unbuttoned my pants. He sighed and put the container on the table. His eyes stayed locked on mine as I straightened my hips, put a knee on the bed, and pulled down my pants.

"Straddle me."

I was restricted by the waistband, but I got a leg out and wiggled around the instruments and tubes to get myself on either side of him. I made no move to shift the sheets away or touch him. I only did what I was told. "The door's ajar."

"The curtain's closed," he whispered, feeling my ass. "You're wearing this cotton shit again." His left hand, the one without the IV, stroked my lower back and found its way under my panties.

"It feels silly to waste the good stuff when you won't see it."

"You miss the point." He pulled me forward. "Put your hands behind me." I placed them on the wall behind him. With his left hand, he reached between my legs, caressing me through the fabric of my underpants. "The idea is that during the day, I'm present where no one can see. You dress for the world, but under that, you dress for me. I own your softest places, and what touches them is mine."

"How can I think about that when you're sick?"

"I need you to. Knowing I own you even from here is the only thing that gets me through the day. Can you do something for me tomorrow?"

"Anything."

"At three o'clock, when you're in the studio, at exactly three, put your fingers on your lips and think of me."

"Yes. I can do that."

He brushed his thumbnail over the crotch of my panties. My clit throbbed, and I gasped.

"Remember the office?" he whispered. "On the desk?"

"How could I forget? You were cruel."

He stroked four fingernails over the cotton he so hated. It was damp already. "I wanted you so badly."

"You could have had me."

"Anyone else, I would have just fucked. Not you." He brushed one finger under my panties, stroking my opening. "You were so wet. So responsive. A quickie on a desk would have been such a waste."

His finger ran circles around my wettest part, and his thumb touched my clit gently. When I thrust forward, he pulled it back.

"You were a bastard." I spoke through gasps as he teased me. "You could have let me come and fucked me later." He pushed two fingers in me. I closed my eyes and groaned.

"Look at me," he said. I put my nose to his and tried to keep my eyes open. "I wanted you before my trip. I needed you motivated. I had to have you."

"Have me," I gasped as he put only the lightest pressure on his thumb while rotating his fingers in my hole.

"You were fantastic that first night. Unforgettable." Pulling his fingers out, he slipped them up my cleft, stroking my clit slowly, barely moving. Every millimeter of movement sent a shot of sensation from my cunt to my knees and waist.

"Oh, God."

His right hand went to the back of my head. I knew he had his IV in that hand, but I wasn't thinking about that. I only thought about the excruciatingly unhurried motion of his fingers. "Do you want to come, Monica?"

"Please let me come. I want to."

He grabbed my hair. "I don't believe you."

"Please. Jonathan, please. Don't let me walk away like this. Let me come for you." My begging could not have been more sincere. The pleasure and tension between my legs was so intense, so heavy, it was almost painful.

"No." He dragged his fingers over my clit then lodged them back in me. He pulled them out, rolled around the outside, and then pushed them back in again. All the while, he kept my head still by holding a fistful of my hair.

"Please," I whispered.

"Why should I?"

"You love me."

"I do." But he didn't say anything more.

"And I love you."

"So?"

"I miss your body. I want to come for you. Please."

He pulled the tips of his fingers over my clit. It was just enough to take me to the next level. I couldn't speak as the pleasure soaked my body, yet it wasn't a full release. "When you sing tomorrow, wear something that reminds you of me."

"Yes." I would have promised him the World Series, but that, I meant. Under my clothes, he owned me. "Please."

Rubbing my clit in earnest, he held my face close to his. "Who do you belong to?" Like a glass of water on a hot day, my cunt drank him in. I was getting what I had craved, every inch of wet skin receiving the touch it wanted like the answer to a prayer.

"You. I am yours. Oh. I'm—"

"Come, darling."

I bit back a cry as the orgasm ripped through me like a fire hose had been turned on. My hips thrust forward and bullets of pleasure shot through my nervous system, squeezing the air from my lungs, shutting out every sense except the sensation of his fingers between my legs, his breath on my face, his eyes on mine.

He slowed but kept his hand on me, stroking me down until I felt as though I could think again. "Again, goddess. And quietly." He pushed in me, gathering juices, and put his fingers to my clit again. The waters rose like a flash flood.

"Fuck." I groaned, clenching and thrusting. A grunt stopped in my throat as I came for him again. My eyes closed involuntarily as I released, the fireworks between my legs taking up every sensory input.

A machine beeped. We froze. It double-beeped once, twice, then stopped. He patted my ass, and I knew what that meant. I scurried off him and pulled up my pants. I got them buttoned just as Irene Szabó , RN opened the door.

"Mister Drazen," she said in her thick Hungarian accent, "you are okay?"

"We're fine."

"I didn't know if I should be getting the crash cart again," she joked, shuffling in on her clunky padded shoes. Her hands, like risen dough, pulled Jonathan to a sitting position so she could mess with his pillows. Her grey hair was cut short, and her lower lip seemed to extend a good seven inches from her face.

"For two beeps?" Jonathan said. "I'm going to start thinking you want me to live."

"When I started to nurse, we had rules. No girlfriends in the room alone with door closed. Now patients can make request. Request is like *law*, so I have machines beeping twice all night."

"I don't think it'll beep again," I said meekly.

She went to the computer and tapped away at it with two lightning-fast fingers. "You ready for tomorrow, Mister Drazen?"

"Like any other day in paradise, Irene."

She took his blood pressure, and I sat by and held his other hand. "What's tomorrow?"

"Wednesday," he whispered back.

Irene snapped the belt off his arm. "Okay." She tapped his IV bags. "You're fine." She looked at me over her plastic trifocals. "You be a good girl."

"Yes, ma'am." She scuttled out. "I love how it was my fault."

Jonathan shrugged and held out his left hand. His left side didn't have IVs or tubes, and it was the side I'd slept on since the third night of his stay. I slipped onto the mattress next to him. I couldn't move much, but I didn't want to. He turned the light out, and I rested my head on his shoulder.

"I'm selling my house," he said.

"Why?"

"I bought it with Jessica. It's not relevant anymore."

"I have some nice memories of that house."

Curled up against him, I felt his smile. "Me too," he said, voice heavy with those same memories. "We'll make new ones somewhere else."

"Where were you thinking?"

"I don't know. Where would you like to go?"

The machines whispered dreams of a future I'd given little thought to, blinking lights of hope and trepidation. "I live in Echo Park. If you stayed close, I'd like that."

He turned his head, pressing his lips to my hair. "I'll stay in the basin. More or less. Not the west side. Too many people I know, and it's far from you."

I didn't think he could get up and walk me down the hall without collapsing, but he still managed to make me feel protected. That hospital room, that bed, his body next to mine had become my world. I came at night, and when he turned off the light, he was my beautiful, healthy Jonathan again, and I his goddess. The troubles of the day melted away.

Over the past week, with only the light pollution of Los Angeles coming in through the windows, he'd told me about a losing game he'd pitched at Penn, walking in a run in the ninth. He'd told me about the out-of-control years before his suicide attempt, about his friends and him drifting their cars on rainy nights in the Valley, breaking into schooners on the piers of Seal Beach. He'd told me about Westonwood, where he got into a fistfight over a French fry his first night and, over the next months, learned to maintain the tight control over himself he still exhibited. I exchanged stories of my father, who couldn't play a note but made sure I had everything I needed to make music, his gardening, his lust for life, and my mother.

"Why don't you talk to her?" he'd asked.

"She doesn't approve of me, and I won't change into something I'm not, to please her."

"You live in her house. You could say hello."

"It was by default. I was already there when she called Kevin a seducer and a slimeball. I just kept paying the rent, and she kept cashing the checks."

"It's unlike you to be so passive." Every word expressed in that bed was said and heard without judgment, an unspoken rule I'd been able to obey without trouble until Jonathan implied I should see my mother. He'd felt me stiffen and tightened his arm around me. "It's true." Back then, just a few days before, his voice had been weak and breathy. He'd had oxygen tubes in his nose, and talking was difficult.

He sounded so much better now. Almost like his old self. Soon, they'd give him the surgery he needed, and he'd walk out with a healthy heart. I could go back to work. He'd fuck me blind as often as I let him. Our nightmare would be over.

Chapter 4

Monica

Another nurse came at the two a.m. shift change. She took Jonathan's blood pressure and tapped on the computer. That happened every night, as if he didn't need a full night's rest. I slid off the bed, kissed him good-bye, and left.

My studio time started at eleven a.m., and I wanted to be fresh. I tried to pick up another hour of sleep, but I only succeeded in two things: Worrying about Jonathan's arrhythmia, which would postpone his surgery yet again, and thinking of new ways to add percussion to "Collared." It needed some kind of thump with the stringed hum. So freshness was a fail, but punctuality didn't have to be. I decided to conserve the gas by getting ready early and taking the bus.

That was considered a major faux pas, unheard of and even shocking to most of my friends. One simply didn't *take the bus*. But it was a straight shot across Sunset, and I found looking out the window while someone else drove meditative enough to make it worth my while. It wasn't rush hour, so I wouldn't be late. I didn't need to bring anything but my vocal chords and my viola. Just me, and my thoughts, and Los Angeles lumbering by my window.

I imagined Jonathan naked as I tapped my thumb to a song without words. The tempo was an expression of his curves and edges, the notes colored by the flavors of his skin, and the dynamics became his voice when he commanded me for his pleasure. My mind curled into itself, conjuring a song as the bus lurched and heaved to its own time, drawing me into a state of melancholy contentment.

My phone rang. I considered letting it vibrate until it went to voice mail, but it kept ringing. The protective coil around my song shattered, leaving me with the music but not the mood. Might as well answer. It was Margie. Up until the day before, I didn't know if she was calling about my contract with Carnival or Jonathan. I spoke to her more often than I spoke to myself.

"Hi," I said.

"Where are you?"

"Santa Monica and Canon."

"I'm sorry." Her voice was taut. "Did you guys discuss you not coming or something?"

I sat upright. "What's going on?"

"He's in surgery today, and I thought you might want to be here when he got out. Unless something changed with you two."

"No!" Fuck. I rang the bell to get off at the next stop. If I picked up a connection, I could make it in an hour.

"What was that?" Margie asked. "Are you on the *bus*?"

In my haste to get off the bus, I dropped the viola case. It popped open next to the driver, who yelled at me. I scrambled to get it together before my viola got stepped on, while the phone was pressed between my jaw and shoulder. I didn't have a free hand to pick it up, so I had to listen to Margie have a fit over my location and circumstance, which irritated me enough to shoot back at her. "Lot parking is fifteen dollars and it's permit parking on the street over there at this hour. I don't need to blow gas money when the bus is fine." The bus dumped me in front of the Beverly Hills Police Station. I headed across Santa Monica, scuttling to make the light.

"Wait," Margie said, and I regretted blowing off steam at her. "Did you know about the surgery today or not?"

"I was on my way to the studio, but I can make it there in an hour if I get the Rapid at Beverly."

"Stay where you are. Lil is coming for you."

Chapter 5

Monica

I sat in the back of the Bentley, wanting to absolutely die. The idea of being in the studio when Jonathan got out of surgery was unacceptable, yet the thought of not showing up to sing for any sickness besides my own seemed ridiculous. Cancelling studio time would cost Carnival a fortune. Everyone would still have to be paid. An orchestra full of people. Assistants. Session guys. Whatever executive felt like showing up to see Miss Taking-The-Bus cut her debut EP. I was a complete career fuckup. Who would set up another session after this bullshit?

Margie met me in the hallway as soon as I got out of the elevator. "They just wheeled him into the OR. He didn't ask for you which tells me he knew you weren't coming." She walked me down the empty corridor.

"I told him I was laying something down for Carnival this afternoon. He knew if he told me he was going under the knife today, I'd cancel."

"Is it important? The studio thing?"

"Not as important as being here."

"Spare me the emotional comparisons." Her impatience was a sign of how tightly wound she was. Her words were clipped, and her intent unmistakable. I felt compelled to give her any answer she asked for. She must have been a magician in a courtroom.

"It's going to make my career," I said. "But not today."

"First of all, you don't ask my brother ever again about his condition. He's a notorious liar of convenience."

"No shit."

"Secondly"—she stopped and stood in front of me—"how broke are you?"

"I'm fine."

"You two are so sweet together. Really. He lies so you'll go to the studio, and you omit your destitution so he won't worry about you. It breaks my fucking heart to see this level of well-meaning duplicity."

We stared at each other for what seemed like a minute and a half. She had that Drazen thing where she looked perfectly put together even though her family and her work were eating her alive. Her hair sat up in a copper bun, her skin was luminescent, and her lavender business suit looked as if it should still be in the dry cleaning bag.

"How broke?" Margie asked.

I took a deep breath. I didn't want to tell her. It was shameful, but I couldn't avoid it any longer. "I haven't had a roommate in months. I haven't worked since before I left for Vancouver. I bought clothes I shouldn't have. I fixed a car I didn't need to. Here I am."

"Is he not taking care of you?"

"I'm not his whore." I said it in a sotto whisper, but it seemed to amplify and echo against the hard walls and floor. Margie took me by the bicep and pulled me into an empty room. I followed because I didn't want to make a scene, but by the time she closed the door, I was livid. "Is bossiness a Drazen thing?"

She held up her finger. "Don't posture with me. No one who ever saw you together would call you his whore, so stop it. How much do you need?"

I held up my hands. Taking gifts from Jonathan was one thing; having his sister write me a check was viscerally offensive. "I'll figure it out."

"How? What's your plan to stay with him and go to work at the same time?"

I didn't have one, except closing my eyes and hoping I'd wake up at the end of it with a healthy Jonathan and an undamaged career. The signs did not appear to be in my favor. I was pretty sure I'd wind up unemployed, ten pounds lighter, and evicted by my own mother. My EP wouldn't get cut, and I'd have a reputation as a flake.

"I'm going to be there for him," I said. "If it makes me broke and ruins my career, that's the deal. I'm not taking a dime from you or anyone else. If you have a problem with that, you can take it up with him when he comes around."

"You're a real pain in the ass."

"Don't hold back. Tell me how you really feel."

"Welcome to the family," she said, as if I'd ever been welcomed. "Speaking of, we have good attendance today."

"Can I have a roll call?" I leaned on the foot of the empty bed.

"Theresa's calling, but she can't come in. Deirdre's in chapel. Leanne is here but running off to some Asia backwater in three minutes. Fiona's in and out with her entourage. Sheila's ripping paper. Carrie's still not coming."

"And your mother?"

"Fully medicated. I spoke to her."

From what I could see, Margie and her mother had a sisterly relationship. The elder Drazen was only fifteen and a half years older. "I spoke to her" meant Margie had reprimanded her own mother over how she'd treated me, which included stone cold silences, saccharine kindness, and blatant disregard when she was tired.

I nodded. "Will she ever say more than two words to me?"

"She and Deirdre love Jessica. That's not going to change."

"I don't expect it to."

"Good. There's something else." She glanced at the door as if making sure it was still closed. "Jonathan hasn't spoken to our father in fifteen years. He's here. You might not see him, he and Mom are on the outs, but he's in the building. If he meets you, whatever he tells you, grain of salt, okay?"

"I don't know what he'd have to lie to me about."

"He'd say something just to see how you react. My brother thinks it's evil. I think it's just a shitty hobby."

"Can we go?" I collected my things and stood up straight, ready for the door.

"I'm not done. About the money—"

"You're done."

Chapter 6

Jonathan

When I first felt as if I was dying, I stood in a doorway at the L.A. Mod for half an hour, trying to control the tightness in my chest. I focused on my breathing, sat down, tried to think about anything else, but it kept getting worse. I kept sitting there, thinking I had to get to Monica before my father did, and I really started panicking. It had tumbled down from there to that ridiculously long hospital stay, to getting wheeled into an operating room for surgery at thirty-two.

When I woke up, I had the feeling something had gone terribly wrong. I swam to consciousness feeling as if I was being choked. I panicked the same panic I had felt in that doorway. I couldn't control my sensations, my body, my thoughts. I couldn't see clearly. I couldn't move my arms. I was bound like a prisoner. My voice was dead. My face itched. Was I warned it would feel like that?

Or was I dead and in the hell of everything I'd ever done to every woman I'd tied down and fucked? I thought of Dante. His hells were the excess of our desires and, in the deepest circles, the pain of our victims. There I was. Fuck. I was terrified. I didn't think I could stand it for eternity. The blackness, the crippling paralysis. No control. Utter submission to emptiness. I was breathing, but the pressure on my throat was enormous. I'd never choked a sex partner because I never believed I could control the results. How could my hell include that? I never believed life was fair, but was God so unjust?

"Jonathan."

A voice. Female. I recognized it as Sheila's. She always had a way about her that seemed as though she'd given birth to the world and loved it to maturity, even when her words cut deep and rage twisted her mouth.

I realized I could open my eyes if I chose to. The whisper and beep of machines broke the silence of my anxiety. Okay. Not hell. Not dead. But the choking feeling was real, and I panicked again.

Sheila's face blocked out the light. "You're intubated. The machine is breathing for you. Keep still. It's okay."

I chose to believe her. I waited. It was five minutes to three. I couldn't speak to ask her to unbind my wrists, so I stared at the clock. At three o'clock, I closed my eyes and imagined I could touch my lips.

Chapter 7

Monica

Three p.m. came unexpectedly. I figured it would, since I was supposed to be in the studio, so I'd set my phone alarm to remind me. It dinged as I listened to Eddie launch into a diatribe. I closed my eyes, shut out Eddie's aggravation, and touched my lips, thinking of nothing but Jonathan. The warmth in my chest and the smile on my face didn't last.

His voice was tight enough to shatter my reverie. "Are you fucking with me?"

"He's your friend too. It's not like you can pretend to think I'm lying." I was in the third floor stairwell, avoiding the mob in the waiting room. It was nice that Jonathan had so many family members who cared about him, it was also overwhelming.

"We got the contract signed in a week," he said.

"I know."

The fourth floor door smacked open, and Leanne Drazen tore down the stairs. Theresa's Irish twin, she was two years and ten months older than Jonathan, but she looked and acted as if she was in her mid-twenties. A tote bag flew behind her, and her red cowboy boots clopped down the steps. She looked tattered and slovenly, strawberry-blond hair falling out of a ponytail and her bag open.

"That's fucking unheard of," Eddie said. "We had to send twenty-two people home. Do you know what we paid to get them in there on two day's notice?"

"No."

Leanne grabbed the bannister and swung around, inertia and centripetal force taking her to the top of the next set of stairs. She grabbed my shoulders. "He's out!"

"A fucking *lot*," Eddie said into my ear.

I put my hand over the receiver. "How does he look?" She put her thumb up and smiled then took off down the stairs with a wave. Sweet girl. Too bad she was never around. "I have to be here, Ed." I bounded up to the fourth floor.

"I'm not saying I don't understand. I was at the show. I saw it. What I'm saying is, I don't know if I can herd these cats again."

"Tell me what hoop I have to jump through to get a reschedule, and I'll jump it." I strode through the waiting room, past two sisters and a mother. Margie indicated a room, and I went in. Sheila, the most vulnerable-seeming of the bunch, was with him. With wild, wheaten hair and four children born close together, she was the one most visibly upset about her brother. Jonathan was there, lying on his back arms on top of the blankets and tubes everywhere.

"When can you do it?" Eddie asked.

"Next week. I think he'll be better then."

"I need a guarantee."

I touched his arm, and Jonathan opened his eyes. When he saw me, he winked. "Guaranteed." I hung up the phone. To Sheila, I said, "Well? It went okay?"

"Yeah. They just pulled a tube out of his throat and unstrapped him."

Jonathan picked up his hand and flicked his fingers to Sheila. The international sign for *shoo*. She started to object, but Margie grabbed her arm.

"Come on. The kids need you," Margie said.

"Onna has them."

Margie pulled her out, but Eileen, Jonathan's mother, strode in. "Ma," Margie said, "you were just here."

But Eileen ignored her. "Jon, how are you feeling?"

"Tired."

"Should we go?" She put her hand on my arm as if I was going out with her.

"Yes. I mean, let me talk to Monica for a minute."

She smiled the biggest, fakest thing I'd ever seen in my life. "Of course."

"Oh, ma?"

"Yes?"

He pointed at me. "Spot for Christmas Eve. Okay? Don't forget."

"Of course." Eileen looked at me. "You're free?"

"You bet." I put on my customer service smile. Once she was out,

I sat next to him. I didn't say anything, but somehow he intuited what I was thinking.

"That's just how she is."

He looked as pale as death, and his body was flat under the sheets as if he could have just sunk into them. His face looked slack, inactive. His eyes were unfocused, and the lids didn't want to stay open. That wasn't Jonathan. He was some other, powerless man who didn't yank my head back by my hair as he pounded me from behind. Someone who didn't fuck me in such a slow, controlled way I felt every inch of my orgasm. He wasn't the man whose name I'd cried into the night; the man to whom I entrusted control, to whose dominance I submitted. He was another man entirely, and I loved him.

I took his hand. "You look like shit."

"You look like an angel." His voice crunched like gravel under a tire.

"I should tie your elbows behind your back with a belt and spank you until you scream. To get your voice back. Works every time."

A smile curled the side of his mouth. He croaked so low I had to put my ear to his mouth to hear him. "A week. I'm going to do unspeakable things to your body."

"Really?" I kept my face to his and my voice low. "Like what?"

I realized I'd asked too much of him when he licked his lips, paused, and said, "Secret." He'd love to tell me, I knew that, but between having his chest cracked open and the tube down his throat, it probably hurt to speak.

"I know already," I said. He raised an eyebrow. "I can read your mind."

"Not this. It's filthy."

I reached over until my body bridged his and touched his ear with my lips. "The great and powerful Madame Monica will predict the future with utmost certainty. Are you ready to hear your destiny, young man?" I was so close to him that when I looked into his eyes, I could see the blue flecks.

"What's this gonna cost me?"

"Everything."

"Worth it."

We're in your house. The living room. I'm naked from the waist up, and you're in jeans and a polo shirt. You're looking at me like you want to eat me alive, but you don't. Yet. You're waiting. You're thinking. You're constructing the next minutes of my life like a movie director blocks a scene.

You tell me to take off my pants, and I do. You watch. You like my body. The way my breasts hang when I bend over to release my feet. My ass when I bend at the waist.

When I step out of my jeans, you step toward me in your bare feet. I look nervous. You tell me to stop my hands from twitching, and when I cast my eyes down and say 'yes, sir,' you feel power surge in you. Everything's under control. Everything's going to be all right, unless it's not. What you have planned can go terribly wrong. The worry bothers you.

You ask me my safe word, and I tell you to shut up and fuck me.

'Oh, goddess,' you say. Then you take the hair at the back of my neck and pull until I'm looking at the ceiling. My lips part, and I sigh.

'Say it. Or you can put those jeans back on and go home.'

I mouth 'tangerine' but don't use my voice.

You look down at me and you say, 'Say it.'

I whisper it so softly you can barely hear it. You spin me around and shove me into the kitchen. I start to turn back, but you bend me over the butcher block. You're sharp and violent, and when you see me cringe, your dick gets hard. You want to see me scream. You need it.

You.

Need.

It.

Your dick is out, a throbbing piece of meat aimed between my legs. There's wetness emanating from me. It would slide in so easily. You'd be sucked into my cunt so fast, and you'd forget everything.

'Say it, or you go home.' You feel me quiver under you. You think you might just have me put my jeans on and leave. That would be the right punishment for making you uneasy. You slap my ass, and I yelp as if I didn't expect it. Your hand stings, and you're poised to do it again when I speak up.

'Tangerine.'

The word is barely out of my mouth, and you're fucking me, pressing my cheek to the butcher block. Thrust after thrust...you know you're pushing the countertop against the sensitive part of my hip. I'm yours to hurt, and you know it. The things on the counter rattle as you fuck me. Salt and pepper grinders. A canister of utensils. Fancy bottles of condiments. You pull my ass cheeks apart with your free hand so you can go deeper, gripping hard enough to bruise, watching how your fingers indent my skin. My feet come off the floor, you're pounding me so hard. I gasp and grunt.

You take a bottle of olive oil and smack it against the edge of the counter, breaking the neck. I'm startled, but you push my head down hard. The glass is everywhere. Oil splashes on the floor. You run your hand down my back as you fuck me. Slowly, you pour oil on my back. You rub it all over me then pour more until a river of oil falls into the crack of my ass. You feel it on your cock. You pull out then slide in again. Hard. Once. Twice. Olive oil coats us. You slap my butt again and again. I cry out in pleasure, your name on my lips.

Then without breaking your rhythm, you jam your cock in my ass.

I scream.

You're halfway in, and you feel two things at once. You're incredibly aroused... aroused enough to lose control. But there's also the worry that in losing control, you'll hurt me. You ask me how I am.

I say through my teeth, 'Is that all you got, Drazen?' My face is red. My fingers are clutching the edge of the butcher block.

You put down the bottle and take my jaw, turning it until I'm facing you. You bend until you're so close you can smell green tea on my breath. Then you push the rest of the way into me, the skin of your dick sliding against the olive oil, stretching me without friction as a barrier.

I grunt. You know it hurts, you see it in my eyes. But you don't stop. You whisper words of encouragement, pulling out, then slamming into me. We're mouth to mouth as I whimper and you fuck my ass. Sliding in and out with the olive oil. Balls deep. I'm tight. You're getting squeezed. I'm getting ripped apart.

But my whimpering is turning into gasps and moans. I'm looking at you now with something besides agony. You go faster, pounding. Pushing deeper with every stroke. You pull me up until we're both standing. You slide your hand across my breasts and down my stomach. There's oil everywhere. Your fingers go between my legs and find my clit right away. It's hard to the touch. When you circle it, you slow your thrusts. You slip over it, reaching for my hole. Then you drag four fingers over my clit. You do this over and over, until I beg.

'Let me come. Please.'

You want me to come while you're in my ass. You want me to want it after it hurts me. That's the victory, to have us both love my pain.

I'm whispering 'please' like a chant. Your fingers move in the same circles. You have me at the edge. You own me. 'Please, please, please, please.'

You say, 'Come.'

I thrust my hips into you, burying you in me. There's a moment of nothing, then you feel my orgasm on your dick, pulsing around you. Gripping you. Milking your cock until the fullness in you is too much to bear, and you have to let it go. You slam into me and come. You lose control, forgetting your hand is gripping my cunt. You bite my shoulder, and I scream for the second time. You lose yourself. You forget everything.

Chapter 8

Jonathan

I felt her.

We spoke. I wanted to possess her, but I couldn't find the strength to move my arms. I smelled her canned peaches scent and heard the warm caramel of her voice. I answered her in short sentences, because I felt as if I'd gulped a handful of driveway and forgot how to swallow.

She tapped my arm as she described what I would do to her. Even in my state, I got hard because it was an epic fuck coming from her sweet mouth. I didn't even know if she noticed, but with that tapping finger, she was keeping a rhythm as she told the story. I strained to listen as unconsciousness tried to invade again. I heard her words, but what I felt when she talked about me hurting her was the connection created when her pain turns to pleasure, and she is under me, a piece of the world I control completely.

"You're good at this," I said. "I'm taking mental notes."

"When did the doctor say you could enslave me again?"

"As soon as I was up to it."

"I predict day after tomorrow."

"You're selling me short."

"I'll be at your service tomorrow if you want. But you're in here for five days, and you need to be alone tonight."

I grumbled deep in my throat. She was right, of course. The drugs hadn't even worn off. I had no idea how I would feel about sex once the pain kicked in. All I knew was I wanted to be inside her. "Go sleep in your bed tonight, then."

"If I'm up at three a.m., I'll think of you." She stood straight and got her bag. "Actually, if I'm awake any time, I'll think of you." She leaned down to kiss me, and I touched her lips.

Chapter 9

Monica

On my way out, a song hit me. I ran into the cafeteria to write it down. I texted Lil and asked her to meet me out front in fifteen minutes, and I got myself tea.

I'd been in that fucking hospital forever. What had looked sparkling clean the first day looked dingy, dirty, and worthless on day four. I spotted the black scratches on the pink cafeteria tabletops instantly and the little dust bombs sticking to the legs of the chairs. I hated the tea. It was too hot, the Styrofoam made the liquid acerbic, and Jonathan was sick. I hated the greasy eggs and potatoes. I hated the stink of vinegar that seemed to be on everything. I hated being kicked out of Jonathan's room because too many people were in it.

But on the day of the surgery, the cafeteria sparkled again. The Christmas lights were the most cheerful shades, the tinsel and garland was festive and joyous, and the fake tree in the corner, with toys for sick kids under it, made my heart swell with pride for human generosity.

My god, what do you get a man like Jonathan for Christmas?

I got into the chair I always sat in, and I took out my little notebook and clicky pencil. Everything about the hospital had sucked, but I was writing. A lot. I didn't even know if half of them were songs or opera or part of something so much bigger, but I couldn't stop the verses or the tapping of my foot as I laid them down. In the days I'd been at the hospital, waiting for the hours I could see Jonathan, my tea usually went cold before I gulped it down.

I moved the Notice of Public Auction to the front of my notebook so it wouldn't be in my way, and I wrote. Another Styrofoam cup appeared at my side when I was still neck deep in a song about an imaginary ass-fuck that was disguised as a poem about something else entirely. I looked up at a six foot four man who had hit his sixties in a movie-star kind of way.

He smiled at me. "We meet again."

"I'm sorry?"

He held out his hand, and I knew that even though I didn't know him, I did. "My daughter told me my son's girlfriend was often down here. I thought it might be you."

J. Declan. Shit. Jonathan wouldn't like me being with him. And just when I was getting used to that hateful table. I shook his hand briefly then stood. "Yeah. I was just going."

He sat down. "Looks like you were in the middle of something. Can you just ignore me? There are no other seats."

I looked around. Every other table was full. I was a single person taking up a four-seater. In the middle of writing, I hadn't even noticed. "I'll make room for the rest of the family."

He laughed to himself. A silent chuckle. No more than a breath.

"What?" I asked.

"If my boy is the sun, I'm Pluto. Smallest. Farthest. Still in orbit, however. Have you seen him?"

"Yes."

"How does he seem?"

"The same."

"And his mood?"

"Hard to tell through the wisecracks."

He nodded, looking around the cafeteria. Kids screamed. Mothers yelled. A mop slapped against the edge of a yellow bucket. To our right, a man wept while a much younger woman comforted him. I glanced at Declan. He looked far away, and I felt sorry for him.

"You should talk to him," I said. I hadn't seen the outside world in too many hours, and Lil would be outside in a red zone in four minutes.

"I should," he said in a way that implied that he would if it were an option. I wanted to say more, but I remembered what Jonathan had told me and what Margie had said about his shitty hobbies. I excused myself to go home to try to manage my life.

Chapter 10

Monica

It was night by the time the Bentley made its way slowly down my hill. I'd called Debbie to let her know Jonathan was okay, and I told her if any shifts opened up, I'd fill in. Then I left a message with Darren, who had offered me the moon and stars, the food in his kitchen, the gas in his car, and the surface area of his shoulder should I need it. But unless I asked for something specific or called during an unpredictable sliver of time, he was unavailable. I had no idea what he was doing. When I did catch him long enough to ask after him, his "fines" and "greats" seemed sincere. So I left him alone.

"What time are you going in tomorrow, miss?" asked Lil as she opened the back door for me.

"I'm hoping for an afternoon shift," I said. "Can I call you?"

She stepped aside as I got out. "I expect you to. I don't mean to be disrespectful, but it's my job to drive. I don't want to hear about you taking the bus again." She slammed the door.

"I'm a poor girl. It's not a big deal to take the bus."

"To me it is. No more." She wagged her finger once and walked around to her side. When she opened her door, she waved, dismissing me.

I fingered the extra bus token in my pocket, went through my gate, and ascended my porch steps. There was no notice on the door, which reminded me I hadn't heard from Mom. I checked my phone. Nope. Nothing.

"Hey, Monica," Dr. Thorensen called over the fence.

"Hi."

"You all right?" He blooped his car. The lights flashed.

"Sure."

"Because you're standing on your porch staring at your phone. Is your boyfriend all right? Did the surgery go okay?"

"Yeah."

He didn't move. He just looked at me under my shitty porch light, which would be auctioned off with the rest of my house. Except my stuff. The bank couldn't auction what was mine. I'd take the light bulbs, the furniture, the fixtures, and anything that could be unscrewed, unbolted, or pulled off.

"Dad's tangerine tree," I said out loud. I didn't mean to do that.

"Excuse me?" Dr. Thorensen asked.

"Nothing. Just thinking out loud." I snapped my keys out of their little pocket.

"Have you eaten?"

I hadn't expected an actual question, so I answered honestly. "No."

"I have some pad thai from last night. It reheats like a solid brick, and I don't want to suffer alone."

I wanted to slip in during the dead after hours and fall asleep next to Jonathan again, but if there was one night I should let him rest, that was probably it. A twisting disappointment pinched my chest when I realized I wouldn't go see him. I'd have to sleep alone in my stupid shit bed. But though I could be lonely and depressed and worried, I didn't have to be hungry. "How are you reheating it?"

"I put the cardboard box in the microwave. It ain't open heart surgery."

"You have to heat it covered with a little water." I put my keys back in my bag, glad to be of use to someone. "A glass container is best. Let me show you."

Chapter 11

Monica

"Magic" was too mild a word for *City of Dis* as Dr. Brad Thorensen played it. Extreme might be better. Intense. Powerful.

The idea was the player was in hell. Not just a block character of pixels. Not some person the player made up from die rolls and categories, but...*you.*

Meaning, the player created a character based on himself. Plenty of people created characters whole cloth, but the point was to create their own personal self and send it through hell. The player struggled to exit each circle, but he knew the next one would be worse, the stakes would be higher, and his missions would be harder. That being the case, when he stopped, he found his sin. His flaw. He discovered what would send him into the inferno.

Dr. Thorensen taught me how to use the controllers then went to reheat the pad thai as I instructed. The game started with a fifteen-minute questionnaire. Except it should have been a two-hour questionnaire. It should have required thought and rumination. The basics—gender, age, education, family structure—came slowly. Then deeply personal questions had to be answered so quickly I didn't have a second to think twice. Multiple choice. Choose the closest answer. Rapid fire.

—do you cook your own dinner how long does it take you to eat it how long do you chat with friends after dinner do you have a mirror in your room do you wear makeup every day is your nose big are you fat do you have enough money how much does a pound of feathers weigh where was your car made price of the most expensive bag you ever bought if you found a wallet what would you do someone hits your car on the freeway what do you do how often do you shop do you reconcile your checkbook does your thumb hurt right now how many cups of coffee or tea do you drink a day how many moving violations have you gotten what color is the red hat when was your last felony arrest did your parents spank you are you worthless what is your political affiliation do you believe in legal abortion are you on birth control how many sexual partners have you had this month how much is too much are you hungry right now do you own a firearm are people generally bad or generally good what time do you eat dinner what time do you go to bed do you dream—

::—PLEASE BE PATIENT WHILE WE
CREATE YOUR AVATAR—::

"It'll take a few minutes," Dr. Thorensen said.

"I need a nap after that."

"You walked in here looking like you needed a nap." He put down two plates of moist, delicious pad thai that had been reheated to perfection. I felt a mentally overwhelming need to eat it. I sat at the kitchen bar and placed a napkin over my knee. When was the last time I'd eaten a hot meal? Days ago? I would take those noodles slow. I would make love to each one as if it was the first time.

"I'll try not to be offended by that," I said. He offered chopsticks and a fork. I could use chopsticks, but my hands had started shaking, so I took the fork.

"I see a lot of people who don't take care of themselves when a loved one is sick." He said it in a doctor voice, as if it was a professional opinion, and thus something that could not cause offense.

I wondered what it would be like to date a doctor and deal with that voice all the time. Did he use it when he wanted to tell a woman she needed to pay attention to his feelings, or she shouldn't rehearse on Tuesday nights? Was he a professional when complaining about the in-laws?

"Yeah, well," I said, spooling a single noodle onto my fork, "he's going to be out soon. Then I'm going to be fat and happy."

"I peeked in on his surgery. Everything seemed to be going fine. He's young. You guys will be tooling around in your new Jaguar in no time."

I think I turned a little red. "I just want to get back to work. They feed us. Nothing like a free lunch."

"He doesn't take care of you?"

I must have burned black, smoking holes in his face because he pursed his lips shut and looked at his plate as if he'd just stepped in my personal daisy patch. "I will allow you to take that back," I said. "A show of gratitude for the thai."

He laughed, and it didn't sound professional. Thank god. "I'm sorry. I take it back. I shouldn't have assumed."

"Got that right, doctor."

"Brad."

"Fine."

A singsong bell rang from the stereo speakers. Naturally, an audio monolith had been connected to the system to make *City of Dis* a three-dimensional aural experience.

"Your avatar's ready," Brad said. "I'm dying of curiosity."

I swallowed the last noodle and bean sprout and went to find out who the game thought I was.

Chapter 12

Monica

I pulled a last-minute brunch shift, which was such a relief I think I giggled all the way through it. I'd played *City of Dis* with Brad until midnight, so I was tired which made me punchier. The game was all-encompassing. He'd started me on the eighth circle, where he was, and we cycled around to see if I'd get caught in the trap of my invisible sins. We solved puzzles, interacted with hellions, ate virtual food, and imbibed radioactive-colored drinks that made the screens blurry and shaky. The game was alternately frightening, sweet, intense, dramatic, and funny. I actually forgot about Jonathan for seconds at a time.

The call from Debbie that morning was like the clouds opening up to heavenly light. I'd texted Margie that I wouldn't be in to see Jonathan until after my shift. She responded right away.

—He looks better. Already demanding your presence. I told him to hold his horses.—

—Do NOT tell him I need the money you'll give him another heart attack—

At break time, I rummaged through my bag for my phone and found my mother had called me. Funny how I'd forgotten all about that. Not ha-ha funny, but you-are-a-pussy funny. I had ten minutes left of my break, so I had a time limit to how long the pain could last. I stood in front of my locker and dialed my mother's number. Eight minutes of break left.

"Hello?"

It was amazing how her voice could sound so familiar and so strange at the same time. "Hi, mom. It's me. I've been calling."

"Are you all right?" She broadcast panic, and the rawness of her emotion sent a welling in my chest and brought moisture to my eyes.

I hadn't shed a tear of stress or worry over Jonathan because I wanted to be strong. I didn't want to show weakness in front of his family. They were all so freaking stoic. But with my mother's tone telling me that *Hi, mom. It's me* was enough to panic her, I almost lost my shit. I remembered my mom then. I remembered the things that put me over the edge, the drama, the constant emotional storms. One such storm had led her to fling names at Kevin and me, sending me out the door permanently, my viola forgotten in his trunk.

"I'm fine. I'm sorry I missed the rent twice." Silence. "Mom?" Sigh. "I got an auction notice on the door."

"Oh, I've been meaning to call you." I heard the rustle of sheets, and I looked at my watch. It was noon, and to all indications, she was still in bed. Fuck. "It wasn't just that. There were other things. I talked to the bank. They don't care about your problems. All they care about is money."

"They're banks, mom." I rubbed my eyes. "How long has it been since you paid the mortgage?"

"Oh, I don't know. I should ask how *you* are."

"It's complicated. I have only a minute left. What should I do about the auction? Should I move?"

"If you want."

"Okay, then. I'd better get going."

"Can you come up some time? I'd like to see you."

I cringed. I didn't want to see her. I knew something bad was going on out there, and whether I'd spoken to her in years or not, I was obligated to at least figure out why she wasn't paying the mortgage. But another responsibility was the last thing I needed. I tried to remove the dread from my voice. "Sure."

"I'm free most days. Today, even."

"I'll let you know."

In typical Los Angeles fashion, I left the call without making any definitive plans.

Chapter 13

Monica

"I hate you seeing me like this." Jonathan's voice had a little less gravel, but he sounded as if the effort involved in speaking was unbearable.

I wasn't allowed to sit on the edge of the bed, so I sat in the chair next to him and put my elbows on the railing. "Then you shouldn't let me in here."

"I need you. Deal with it."

"Okay, well, I'm not going anywhere."

"You look thinner."

"These are my skinny pants. You like them?" I was sitting. He couldn't even see my pants.

"I can see your cheekbones."

I touched his face, stroked the stubble on his chin, and brushed his lip, dry yet yielding under my touch. Was it wrong to want him even in that horrible place with him cut open? Was it wrong to want his arms around me when he could barely lift them? I wasn't feeling lustful but greedy, ravenous, ardent. He took my hand away and held it. Obviously, he wasn't *that* weak.

"Let me ask you a question," I said. "If I was in a hospital bed for a week waiting for open heart surgery, how much would you eat? How well would you sleep? I'm not complaining. I'm just saying don't try to deflect away from what you need by making yourself worry about me. I'm fine."

"When I can get up—"

"You can give me the spanking I so richly deserve. Until then, I'll be the one doing all the legwork around here."

"Tell me about it."

"Oh, I will."

• • •

There's a chair in your bedroom.

It has red leather cushions on the seat, back, and arms. It looks antique and probably is, now that I'm thinking of it. You tied my ankles to the place where the arms meet the seat. You tied me gently, stroking between my thighs, kissing my legs, but in the end, I'm naked and spread-eagled, tied to your antique chair. Though your hands were gentle, the binds are tight. I can't move.

Then you tied my hands above my head, looping the leather straps around the sconce above me. You kiss my breasts until my nipples are so hard they're the size of dimes. You make sure I feel safe and loved. You don't want me to be scared. I'm not scared. I'm so turned on I'm pretty sure I'd come if you breathed on me.

Then you undress. You do it slowly, not sexy and camp, but methodically. You put your things away and spend a minute in the bathroom. You don't let me speak. You threaten to gag me if I make another joke. You need control over me. This is how you feel safe.

So I wait, my cunt getting wetter every second. I feel it dripping down the crack of my ass. Then you're naked and magnificent. Jonathan, darling, you are utterly spectacular. But you don't want to hear that.

You look at me. Your eyes eat me alive. I feel you between my legs even though you're half a room away. If I could draw you closer with my desire, you'd be on me. I'm hungry for you.

You step toward me and put your hands on the back of the chair, leaning over it. My arms stretch above me. You put the tip of your tongue inside my elbow then draw your tongue down until your lips touch my breast. You circle my nipple, caressing it with your lips. It's so hard, pointing up like it wants to be millimeters closer to you. You kiss it, making it wet, then release. I feel the cold air. It's so sensitive, and you glance at me like you know it. You suck it again and release it to the cold.

Then you warm it with your mouth, and you bite. I arch my back. I thrust my hips into you. I moan your name.

'Behave,' you say, pushing my chin up so I can only see the ceiling. 'Don't move.'

You roll the wet nipple under your fingers, then move to the other and do the same. Suck, release. Suck, release. Suck, bite. I'm on fire.

You kiss my belly, my legs, and I feel your fingers inside my thigh. You're brushing your fingers toward my cunt. It quivers. You flick my clit like it's a crumb on your pant leg. You do it hard, and I bite my lip. It stings. Then it fills up with pleasure.

You do it again and again while kissing inside my thighs. I'm trying not to wiggle, but everything in my body wants to arch toward you. You hurt me with your fingers then stroke. I burn with the pain, but it only makes the pleasure more unbearable. It's not enough to make me come.

I want to beg, but you told me not to speak. I'd take you anyway you'd give yourself. I'd have you in my mouth, my ass. I'd crawl on the floor to have you. You're barely even touching me, but you have complete control over me. Just with your fingertips.

And when you draw your tongue over my cunt, my toes, eyes, and fingernails feel it.

Then you do that thing. With a flick of your wrist, you undo the knots at my ankles. You stand up and tell me to get my clothes on. We're going out.

"You're fucking with me," he said.

"Turnabout's fair play."

He smiled then caught his lips between his teeth. "It hurts when I laugh."

"I wasn't joking."

He put his hand on my cheek, brushing the skin. Even sick as he was, the feel of his body on mine was electric. "Can you stay?"

"I have something to tell you."

"You love me."

"My God, Jonathan, I'm crazy with loving you."

"Feeling's mutual. Now, what were you going to tell me?"

"I need to go see my mother. In Castaic. I'll be back late, but I'll come right here." I wrinkled my nose to let him know the trip wasn't a vacation away from him or his hospital room.

"Lil can drive you."

"You bought me a car."

"Let me take care of you. You can rest in the back. Put your feet on the seats."

I turned and put my lips to his palm. "Go to sleep, darling."

"It's a long drive." I kissed his mouth. His lips were dry but responsive, and his face scratched mine. He put his hands on my face and pulled me close. "You trying to shut me up?"

"Yes."

"I hate being like this."

"You can boss me around when you're better."

I put my head on the mattress next to him, and he stroked my hair. I watched the clouds move across the sky, humming a tune that may or may not have been "Collared." When I knew he was sleeping, I slipped away.

Chapter 14

Monica

I took a white-knuckled drive up the 5 freeway past all signs of civilization, past subdivisions, up a bifurcated mountain and back down it. The bestfuckingthingever drank gas like a frat boy drank beer at a kegger. Everything was dead, flat, dry. Then it hit. Castaic.

All the garage doors faced the street like mouths stretched into a closed grimace. Front yards that had not been flattened by concrete were neglected and brown or tamed and green with sad blowup snowmen and fat, jolly Santas. Everything in the unforgiving landscape was scorched by the sun. Even the mountains ringing the town looked compacted under the weight of the sky. Or maybe that was just me.

Big girl pants.

Maria Souza-Faulkner had two settings: Park—which meant she was passive, sweet, and slept seventeen hours a day—and fourth gear—which meant she was in full-on rage with an eye to wiping the world of sin. Kevin had suggested she was bipolar. I'd laughed not because he was wrong, but because she'd never do something as sensible as see a doctor to figure out why she was crazy. Dad had loved her through all of it, so obviously she saw no need to fix what was functioning just fine.

Her house, a one-story beige box with a two-car garage and a front door set back twenty feet behind it, had fallen out of repair. Dad wouldn't have allowed that. He'd spent his time in the States painting, plastering, and gardening. The young citrus he planted had a few leaves on the twiggy branches, and the front lawn looked like an infield. I didn't know how long she'd been stuck in park, but judging from the look of the place, it had been at least through the beginning of the summer.

My mother answered the door in a long polyester thing that fell over her curves in a way that was modest but sexual. Like me, she had a body that was hard to hide, and unlike me, she kept trying. She was a Brazilian beauty my dad had met on some unholy peacetime mission. She was five eleven, in her early fifties, and she had darker skin than mine but the same dark eyes and hair. She was Catholic as only a South American girl could be, and that was the rub. She believed in the infallibility of the Pope and the virginity of Mary long after anyone else with a brain had moved on.

"Hi, ma."

She hugged me, and after a second, I hugged her back. She held on longer than I thought she would. Maybe the visit wouldn't be so bad. We'd just forgive each other. She moved out of the way, and I stepped inside.

She saw the car. My immediate reaction was to make excuses for it. It was borrowed. I was returning it. I didn't ask for it. Then I decided to shut up. I didn't come to fight, and I didn't come to lie. She closed the door without saying anything.

The house was hermetically sealed against the desert heat and dust, and the artificially cooled air was stale and thin. Everything was beige. Dad had hated beige, but my mother insisted. When she insisted, she got what she wanted.

Well, everything *permanent* was beige. Whatever had been moved in was a color, and a bright one. African masks and Mexican blankets. A hand-carved teak partition blocked a window draped in Ikat fabric. Stacks of travel books stood in front of the stuffed bookcases. It looked as if my mother had gotten the shit stamped out of her passport.

"You came," she said.

"Yeah." The couch had a pillow on one end with a case that matched the bed sheet balled up at the other end. She was sleeping on it, probably regularly.

"I don't think we can save the house," she said.

I had a speech prepared, so I spit it out. "I didn't come because of the house. It's not that I can't move or get an apartment or whatever. I just find it hard to believe you'd let the place go. I got worried about you."

"Oh, Monya," she said, calling me by my grandmother's name. "All this way for nothing." She put her hand on the doorknob.

That was her. She'd kick me out and waste away rather than admit there was a problem. Though she seemed healthy, if older, I could tell sunshine and butterflies weren't the order of the day. "Come on, Mom. I'm here. Make me some tea."

Her hand slipped from the knob. She glanced out the window at the white Jaguar as if she didn't trust it and didn't like it. As she walked me to the kitchen, I saw more third world knicknackery and clean, beige rectangles spotting the walls as if old pictures had been removed.

It wasn't until she indicated my seat that I realized what those rectangles represented. They were where the pictures of Dad had been. She'd kept them up after he died three years before, but now they were gone.

As she put a copper pot on the stove and got out a mug with I LOST MY HEART IN BELIZE scripted across it, everything became clear. The tchotchke. The missing pictures of Dad. The depression. The multiple mortgages.

"Still waitressing?" she asked.

"Yep. You still doing the books for the church?"

"What's his name?" she asked, not answering my question. "You didn't buy that car on a waitress's salary."

"I don't make a salary. I make tips." What kind of answer was that? That was the answer of a woman ashamed of who she was, and I'd given that up. "His name is Jonathan. I hope we're not going to argue about it."

"As long as it's not that other guy. I didn't like him."

"Does yours have a name?" She didn't answer, just dicked with some floral canisters that may or may not have been full of expired tea. "Mom, is there anyone out here you can talk to? The priest? Someone in the choir?"

"It's not that easy."

"Is it the rector that dumped you?"

"For the love of all that is holy, Monya, that is—"

"A totally reasonable assumption. Except for the obvious world travel that's happening. You're sleeping until after noon, so I know you're not working for him. You can't talk to anyone, and all your friends are there."

"I don't want to." The teapot whistled.

"I'll be gone in a few hours. So you might as well tell me."

She put the mug of hot liquid in front of me and left the room. I started to follow, but I saw her open a door in the china cabinet. She crouched down, rummaging through old dishes and cookbooks, until she came up with a brown paper expanding file. I sat back down, and she slapped it in front of me.

She said, "This is what you came for. All my paperwork. Take it. No, I don't want to lose the house. I love that house as much as you do. If I didn't love it, I would have sold it and kicked you to the street for being an insolent, disrespectful bitch two years ago."

"Don't hold back, ma. Tell me how you really feel."

She didn't say anything else, but she didn't laugh and forgive me either. That was it. That was what she'd wanted to say. It wasn't as bad as I'd feared. I didn't get crushed under the weight of her disapproval. But she was right. Despite my initial protestations, I wanted to save the house.

"I'm sorry about whatever-his-name-is," I said. "It looks like you guys had a good time together."

"I don't want to talk about it."

"Okay." I unspooled the string from the felt disk and flipped open the envelope. I don't know anything about finance. Numbers only interested me insofar as they related to sound vibrations, but once I spread the papers across the table and stacked them into a narrative I could get my head around, one thing was abundantly clear.

My mother had blown about three quarters of a million dollars traveling the globe.

The house I lived in had been purchased for ninety-five thousand in the mid-nineties and paid in full twenty years later with my dad's life insurance. But Echo Park had been in the nascent stages of a renaissance when my parents bought it. Since then, more and more people like Dr. Thorensen had moved in next to artists, Hispanic families, and gang members.

According to a bank located in Colorado, my little house on a hill was worth six hundred fifty thousand dollars. I knew that because my mother had cashed out every dime, and then some, piggy-backing mortgages and loans. She'd attempted to squeeze almost another hundred grand in equity out of the thing when I'd had those permits opened. As if there would be actual improvements.

She'd bailed on her job in February. She'd been at that church since I was in high school and had a salary good enough to cover all her obligations. Without that job, it had all tumbled on her. I imagined the gentleman in question was the cause of her slide.

"You're a goddamn genius, ma."

"Watch your mouth."

"You know you'll never pay this back?"

"They won't miss it. It's a bank," she said.

"It's about four banks. Mom, Christ—"

"Mouth."

"I can't even get my head around what to do." I collected the papers. I wanted to slam and bang them to illustrate my annoyance, but they only made shuffling sounds. "Can you just tell me what happened? You didn't raise me to do stuff like this."

She put her fists on her hips. "Like what?"

"Stealing. This is stealing."

"Not if I let them have that house."

"It's not worth seven hundred thousand dollars."

"The appraisers said it was, so it is. Things are worth what experts say they're worth. People like us, we're nothing. Our opinions don't mean anything. And you agree. In your heart, you know it. You think the house isn't worth anything because you love it, and if you love it, it's garbage, right? Well, how much would you pay for it? Huh? How much for your father's trees? How much for the porch your father and I sat on after you were in bed?"

"Mom—"

"How much for the kitchen where I cooked for you? How much for the side door you snuck into after curfew as if I didn't know? Or the bathroom where I miscarried two babies? How much is it worth, Monya? Even that cracked foundation your father promised to fix a hundred times before he shipped himself across the world. That house was where I waited for him. Where he *wasn't* when I found out I had cancer. How much would a stranger pay for those years? If my life there wasn't worth seven hundred thousand dollars, what was my life worth?"

I couldn't take it any more. Her face was red and strained. Her voice hit a crescendo, and I had been a neglectful, indolent (do you mean insolent? Because I don't see how indolent would fit) bitch. I bolted from the chair, put my arms around her, and let her cry. "It's okay, ma. We'll fix it."

"I can't. I tried everything."

"I have friends who are lawyers. I can—" I stopped myself. I could have them look at the paperwork, maybe explain the situation. But Jonathan would offer to buy the house, no doubt, and I didn't want him to. I didn't want to go down a road where he bailed out my family, then my friends. I didn't want him to trade Jessica's financial distress for mine. I could soothe my mother for the moment, but in the end, we'd have to let the house go. I'd tell Jonathan I was okay with it, pretend as though it wasn't a big deal.

A call came in. Still holding my mother, I slipped the phone out of my pocket. Margie. I missed it by a second and put it back in my pocket while it went to voice mail. "Let me see what I can do."

She sniffed and stood up straight. "There's nothing to do. I'm sorry you have to move."

"I'll live." I waved it off, but I knew I wasn't convincing. "I should have been here for you. Come around more often."

"Yes. You should have."

"I'm sorry." A text blooped on my phone. My mother and I looked at each other.

"This the man with the car?" Her tone did not bode well for an intelligent conversation. If I had just learned to stop calling myself a whore, my mother hadn't. She was in park, but that could change on a dime.

"No, it's his sister, probably." I looked. It was a text from Margie, as I expected.

—*Where the fuck are you?*—

The next one came immediately after.

—*He's bleeding into his chest. Bad*
   suture ripped tissue—

It took me sixty seconds to say good-bye to my mother, promise I'd do my best for her, scoop up the papers, and get in the car.

Chapter 15

Monica

I texted Margie that I'd be there in two hours. It was getting dark already, and I'd hit Los Angeles right around rush hour. That would literally double the time it would take me to get to Sequoia. The hospital was inside a knot of traffic arteries that made it hard to move toward or away from during peak hours. It was poor planning for the sake of the ambulances and women in labor, but for a central, urban hospital accessible from the five points of L.A., it was prime real estate.

Jonathan was in the middle of the best cardiac unit in the country, if the internet was to be believed. Whatever happened, I was sure it would be rectified in no time at all. I worried that he might face unpleasantness and that I wouldn't be there for him, but he'd be fine. I was sure, positive as a matter of fact, that it wasn't a big deal.

I finally got into the waiting room at seven p.m. and was redirected to intensive care. I didn't shake, nor did I panic, because in ten years, the visit would be funny. When I got to intensive care, it didn't look as though anyone was laughing.

Fiona blew past me without greeting. Deirdre smiled at me, but she couldn't hide her concern like the rest of them. Sheila, who always came off as motherly and kind, was talking to Margie as if she wanted to bite off her head. Doing my own roll call, I counted off. Carrie wasn't coming. Leanne was in Asia. Theresa hadn't been around in days. Eileen stood by Margie, twisting her diamond ring. Her pumps had been traded for sneakers days ago when her medication was upped. She waved to me but didn't call me over. Margie's presence made me bold. I walked forward.

"This is unacceptable." Sheila spoke in clipped vowels and hard consonants, her finger pointed at Margie's throat. "And you treat it like another day in the park. This hospital fucked up. They as good as killed him."

I gasped, and the three of them paused, glanced, ignored.

"Thanks for the drama," Margie said to Sheila. "It's exactly what we need."

"You need to start a filing a malpractice suit immediately."

"Like hell."

"You're losing your guts."

"I want us focusing on Jonathan. Not legal battles. Let them do an inquiry—" Margie said.

"And start the cover-up."

"This is not TV—"

"I'll hire my own counsel."

"Exactly what he needs."

"You—"

"I agree with Margie," I said. Six light eyes turned toward me, and I got my first ever case of stage fright. "It's going to take years to sue. A week won't make a difference."

Sheila turned her head but didn't commit the rest of her body to face me. She'd been kind to me from the minute I met her, but I had the feeling that was about to change. "Who are you?" She knew goddamn well who I was. Nobody.

I walked away and wasn't followed. Good. Fucking Drazens, all of them. Except the one. I didn't know the nurses in the ICU, so I put a harmless look on my face as I approached the dark-skinned woman with an armful of charts. "Hi, I'm looking for Jonathan Drazen's room?"

"He's down in X-ray. Come back in an hour."

I had two choices: Go back and try to find out what I needed from the Family Drazen or wait in the cafeteria until Jonathan came back. I knew Margie would tell me everything once she shook Sheila, and Sheila might even calm down enough to be nice to me. But I saw no reason to stand there and be abused while I waited.

As I walked into the cafeteria, I saw Daddy Drazen sitting with a long-haired man in sandals who had a toddler on his knee. The man was talking fast with his head down. Declan leaned in to hear and put his hand on the man's shoulder. Declan didn't seem like a sociopath, which didn't mean much of anything. I wasn't an expert on either Declan or abnormal psychology.

I got in line for a cup of tea. A song percolated in my head. I went to get my notebook, but dig as I might, it wasn't in my bag. I must have left it at home. Damn it. I took out a Sharpie and got ready to write it on my arm.

"Monica?"

I heard my name as I spaced out to the music in my head, trying to get words and rhythm to match. "Dr. Thorensen. I mean, Brad. Hi." He had a white lab coat over his suit with a nametag clipped to the lapel. "I've never seen you at work before."

"What are you doing down here?"

"Getting something to eat. I just got in." He took me by the elbow and sat me down at an empty table. "What?"

"I just had to open a transplant assessment of Mr. Drazen."

I don't know what I must have looked like. Maybe blank, because a sort of vacuity took hold of me. Or maybe I looked puzzled. "I don't understand. It was a bad suture. I know Sheila's pissed, but…" But I'd assumed she was flying off the handle. But I thought he got X-rays all the time. But I thought it was a complication, not ruination. But I was hanging on to my optimism because I missed it.

He glanced around then back at me.

"Say it," I said. "I don't want to hear it from anyone else."

"It was a suture inside his heart. The tearing's very bad. He's bleeding faster than they can pump it out. If they go in and patch him up… Well, they can't. There's no room. And the tear has moved into his left ventricle."

"Are you going to fix it?" I panicked the panic of someone whose anxiety was a show because I knew everything would be okay. For sure, there was an easy fix for all this, and Jonathan and I soon laugh about how silly I was to worry so much. I couldn't wait for that laughter. I told the story in my head over an imaginary Thanksgiving dinner, describing the goose bumps on my arms, the dry feeling in my mouth, the sudden breathlessness in my lungs. I'd wax dramatic about holding back tears, and Jonathan would laugh that laugh from deep in his chest, and tears would stream down his face.

"I don't know," Brad said.

"What do you mean you don't know?"

"We're still doing the assessment. I have a lot of forms to fill out. I have to talk to the rest of the cardiac team. It's tricky."

"What's fucking tricky? You're either fixing it, or you're filling out fucking paperwork."

"Take it easy."

"I'm not taking it easy. I will burn your fucking house down if you don't tell me right now why you assholes can't fix it immediately."

He took my wrists and held me in place. I knew he wouldn't have done that unless he knew me. The privilege of whatever information I'd already gotten was courtesy of a few hours of *City of Dis*. "There's a good chance, and I don't know for sure because I need to review everything with the committee, but I'm pretty sure he'll need a transplant."

"Okay." I breathed, which I'd forgotten to do. That was a thing. It was a course of action. "Then give him one."

"We need a heart, and his blood type? AB negative? It's rare. He needs to get on the list. Monica, I hope I'm wrong. If the surgical team believes they can go back in and fix it, then this whole conversation is moot." His eyes, deep blue and a little bloodshot, as if he'd been up too many hours, did not waver from mine. He had the confidence of a man who had held a human heart and made it beat again. He had made life and death happen, and Jonathan was just another patient, another puzzle to solve, another career challenge.

I slipped my hands down to hold his hands. I squeezed them and closed my eyes. "I want you to understand something. That man? He's not some boyfriend in a line of them. He is my alpha and omega. He is the sky over me. Without him, I'm lost. There's no one else, no one whose soul balances mine the way his does. I've waited my life for him, and when he came, I didn't recognize him. Not until recently. If I lose him, I swear, as God is my witness, I will be alone. No man can match him."

When I opened my eyes, Brad was looking at our clasped hands, head down. "I didn't know."

"I only live next door."

He looked back up. "I'll do my best. I can't promise anything. If he needs a new heart, I want you to be ready for a rough time. He doesn't have forever to bleed into himself, and healthy hearts don't come all that often. You need to sleep and eat and live your life while you wait."

I smirked. "My life is with him. That's how I live it. The rest is unnecessary complication." I felt like Jonathan was there with me when I quoted him. We sat like that for a few seconds, and I tried to transmit my seriousness. It felt good to just sit with someone and *be*, even if it couldn't last.

His cell phone beeped. He didn't look at it but let go of my hands. "That's my office. I have to go."

"Will you let me know?"

"You'll know, Monica. You'll know." He stood. "Just the sleeping and eating. Do those. Okay?"

My tea was cold. My granola bar looked more and more like a slab of pressed shit. "After I see him. Then I'll go home and go to bed."

He looked at his watch. "Come with me. Hurry." He waved and walked off, hand in his pocket for his phone before he'd even turned around completely. I scuttled behind.

Examination rooms inside offices inside suites inside wards, around corners and up secret stairs, I followed Brad to X-ray. While texting, he spoke to a lady in a pink smock, and Pink Smock gave him the name of yet another space I never would have found on my own. In that space was a gurney. On it was Jonathan.

I assumed Brad said good-bye, because by the time I was standing over my lover, Brad was gone. Jonathan was either sleeping or unconscious, pale as death, an altar to IV tower gods. I took his hand, pressing my palm to his. He didn't respond. It was just warm enough to indicate he wasn't lost. I stayed until Pink Smock and an orderly came to push him away. I went with them, just to make sure he was okay.

Chapter 16

Monica

I slept in a random waiting room despite promising Brad I'd go home. I woke up aching everywhere, went to the cafeteria, and wrote a song on a napkin. Something moved on the table. I snapped out of it. My notebook, with the NOPA inside, slid toward me. Declan stood over the table.

"I thought you might want this," he said. "You left it here the other day."

"Thanks." I stuffed it in my bag. "You're like a regular here these days. Piece of furniture."

"Like fiberglass and cheap chrome?"

"The Drazen sense of humor is genetic, apparently."

He sat down. "Not so apparent. I haven't heard my boy crack a joke in twenty years."

"He's funny." My voice cracked. I put my head down. I couldn't look at him because I had been about to say "he *was* funny." My eyes stung, and my face got red. I didn't want a man made of fiberglass and chrome to see me cry over his prodigal son.

"Margaret told me," he said.

I sniffed and tried to get my shit together. I clutched my tea, letting it heat up my icy hands. "Why aren't you ever upstairs with them?"

"This is as close as I'm allowed. They don't want me there. My wife, at least. We sleep on opposite sides of the house. Decades of neglect will do that."

"I'm sure it was purely benign." My raw emotions made my feelings hard to hide, and in that unguarded moment, my voice dripped with inappropriately rude sarcasm. I wasn't being a woman of grace.

But he seemed to take it in stride. "I had a very, shall we say, *intense* mid-life crisis."

"You shared a mistress with your son. Pretty intense."

"Is that what he told you? I guess he could have seen it that way. She was a manipulative girl, but yes, I did plenty I was pleased with at the time, but now... Well, now I need a golf cart to get to my wife's bedroom and my son won't see me." He massaged his coffee. "Would he be upset if he knew you were at a table with me?"

"Yeah." I felt guilty for being there. Jonathan wouldn't like it. Not one bit. If he was going to get well, he needed to know I was safe, and I was sure he didn't think of me as safe around his father. I put the granola bar in my bag. "I should go upstairs. It was nice talking to you."

"Yes, it was."

Chapter 17

Jonathan

I'd already tried to take the fucking little tubes out of my fucking nose. The room lit up like Griffith Park at Christmas, and it was Jingle Bells all over again. I'd be okay with it if I never got defibrillated again. Odds were not in my favor.

I had a hard time staying awake for long. My exhaustion came from lack of oxygen and a body worn out working for nothing. It pumped blood that went down a tube and sucked up more blood from a bag. There was medicine too. Bags of it going into my hand. And a bag of blood that kept getting replaced like a pot of coffee.

I remember one of them saying I was a lucky man. I had no idea what he was talking about, but I thought it didn't have a damn thing to do with my health. He was blond, Nordic looking, and I asked him what he meant. He just went on with another battery of questions that seemed like every other battery of questions every other white lab coat had asked me or the person next to them. If I had a dime for every doctor who walked in and talked about me as if I wasn't there, I could buy and sell myself. The non-entity of me. The skin bag of pain and discomfort. I didn't feel as though I owned my body any more. I felt like a piece of meat being kept alive until something happened. Some miracle. Or some news.

"I'm not here to make you upset."

I felt lucid when Margie said that, my brain snapping to attention at the thought that there was something I should, but shouldn't, be upset about. "Oh, good. You're here to tap dance."

"I love that you have the energy to joke but not give a shit about your condition."

"I give a shit." The effort speaking took was monumental, but contact with someone wearing real clothes and not wielding a needle was too welcome to not answer in full. "Guy came and told me I'm in a world of trouble. There's just nothing I can do about it."

"They called us into a meeting. This must be what it's about. What did they say?"

"Let them do their jobs. I can't..." I drifted off. I couldn't repeat what the guy with the silver hair had said. Dr. Emerson. Like the poet.

As if understanding, she put her hand on my shoulder. "I took care of something while you were down. It's going to create drama."

"Okay."

"Okay, you have no problem with it?"

"Okay, tell me what it is."

"Monica's broke. She hasn't been going to work because she's been hanging around Sequoia Hospital like she works here."

"Fuck." My life spinning out of control was bad enough, but I was taking Monica with me.

"I'm giving her money and saying it's from you. You're going to back me up."

"Yes."

"Good."

"Margie?" I raised my hand a little, and she took it, coming closer so she could hear me.

"What?"

"You're my new favorite. Thank you."

"I'm keeping tabs on every dime because you're going to get better, you little fuck. I don't know how, but this isn't how it ends. Do you understand me? It's not ending like this."

Chapter 18

Monica

The closer I got to Jonathan's family, the more I understood where he came from. His ability to laugh through anger and tears, the happy face he put on over his worries, and the Oscar-worthy show of confidence came from his mother. The deft manipulations of people and situations, the sadism, the raw hunger, and the social charm came from his father. The passion and protectiveness were learned through his sisters.

Margie had handed me five thousand dollars in an envelope and told me if I didn't take it, she would tell Jonathan. That would upset him enough to give him another heart attack. She was exaggerating, but I got the point. He'd arranged money and refusing it would cause him stress.

"I told you not to tell him," I'd said, holding on to a shred of pride even as I clutched the envelope.

"I ignored you. Tough."

"I hate this."

"Take it up with God."

"Well, thank you," I said. "I don't want you to think I don't appreciate it."

I needed the money. Badly. After spending a morning on the phone, I found I had long odds of saving the house. I could rescue my mother's finances by arranging a short sale, but I'd still have to move. One of the banks was adamant about the current resident vacating the premises. I could have waited for an eviction and then fought it, but I had too many balls in the air already. I needed to find a place to live and a place to store my stuff. I needed to rent a truck and pay a security deposit and first month's rent. Five thousand would just about cut it.

I had other business to attend to, as well. Accepting five grand from my lover's sister was something I never thought I'd do. The day would be a day of firsts. I dialed Eddie's cell phone. He picked up. Oh, the privilege of being me. Six months ago, he wouldn't have returned a voice mail from me, much less taken a call on the second ring.

"What's happening, princess?" he answered over a wave of ambient noise. I didn't like the nickname. It was too close in concept to "flake."

"I can't do a session," I said. "Jonathan... He's...it's bad. I need to be here."

"How bad?" The ambient noise disappeared as if he'd closed a window.

"Something went wrong. He's bleeding. He needs a transplant. Maybe. Probably."

"*What?*"

"If you have a heart lying around in the next few days..."

"*Days?*"

My head was screwed up. I was a monster. I'd thought Eddie would care that I was cancelling my recording session, but Jonathan was his friend. Why the hell would Eddie care about my fucking EP? "You should come and see him."

"Fuck."

"Are you all right? I'm sorry. I've been dealing with this for days. I should have broken it to you better."

He didn't answer right away. I thought I'd lost the connection, and then he spoke up. "When I banged up my dad's Maz, Jonathan took me all over L.A. to get it fixed. We got it home before my parents got back from Maui by, like, minutes. He drove like such a dick."

I sniffed. "Don't eulogize yet, please." I had the sudden need to see Jonathan, to stop wasting time in a cold stairway when I could be taking up space with him. I pushed through the stair doors into the hall.

"Sorry, I..." Eddie caught himself. "Tell him he's an asshole for me. All right?"

"Sure thing." The elevator dinged as I hung up, and I blocked traffic by standing there looking at my phone. I wondered why I didn't give a shit about the blown opportunity.

"Monica," came a voice in the crowd.

I turned to the source. "Jessica."

"I'd like to speak with you."

"Sure."

We stepped into a corner by a six-foot tall potted plant that looked too fake to be real, or too real to be fake.

"What?" I said.

She raised her eyebrows. "You've got no business being sharp with me."

"Thanks for letting me know my business."

"I didn't come here to fight with you. I came to see him."

"Why? To upset him? I'm sick of this. I've never seen anyone crush a man so hard then try to get him back like it was her job. For Chrissakes, I wish he'd just give you your money so you'd leave him the fuck alone."

"He will." Her face darkened like a desert under rare clouds. "This is a long-term hospitalization. The trust will move to irrevocable in a week. He'll be here."

It hit me then, her motivation for being there. It was sick. Unbelievably venal. "Unless he's dead, right? If he dies while the trust is revocable, you lose." I started to walk away, but she grabbed my elbow. I looked at where her fingers dented the fabric of my shirt then at her.

"You listen to me," she said through her teeth, "I loved him. Make no mistake. He wasn't for me, but I loved him. That doesn't go away."

"He. Is. Mine."

"Under the circumstances, he's everyone's. He needs all of us. We can have this fight now or after he's dead. Would that suit you?"

Something seethed in me. Something hot and black and angry, bubbling to the surface and settling in.

Before Los Angeles was a place, it had a tar pit. I'd gone on three field trips to the La Brea tar pits. In prehistory, an animal got stuck in it, and a predator came to eat the animal. The predator, even as he ate, got stuck. Carrion came to feast on the weakened bodies, and all were stuck. The number multiplied as more, driven by instinct and hunger, fell into the trap. Masses of mammals, winged creatures, and crustaceans came to feast. The black goo pulled them down to their deaths in a years-long chain of seething, building, predatory hunger. Ripping throats, blood-covered-fur, a routine orgy of violence and death, multiplied by an order of fear, melted into the tar and added to the organic mass of boiling, black pitch.

On La Brea Avenue, there's a park. In the park, the tar pits bubble underground, leaving puddles of sticky black goop in the grass. They come up where they want, and everything sinks into them.

When Jessica suggested Jonathan would die, I wanted to claw out her eyes and pull out her hair at the roots like one of those animals. I felt as if I'd put a lawn of sweet words over an aquifer of tar-sticky rage, and her presence had triggered a bubbling geyser of anger. I wasn't angry at Jessica, and I wasn't angry that she had the gall to bring death into the conversation like a threat.

I was angry at death. I was angry that it dared to black the light from the window, that it should come between Jonathan and me. We'd overcome so much together. What did it want? What was I supposed to do? And life? How dare life bring him to me just to take him away.

The elevator doors opened with a *ding*, but Jessica and I stared at each other as if guns were drawn.

"It's nice you kids are getting along," Margie's voice cut in.

Jessica let go of my arm. When she did, I realized something. I didn't like her. I didn't trust her. But I couldn't pretend I was angry at her. As if shunned, Jessica ran into the elevator at the last second.

"Cute, you two," Margie said. "Almost like you could stand being in the same room together."

"She's just going to upset Jonathan."

"No, she's not. He refused to see her. She's a little pissed off." Margie headed down the hall, her gait quick and sure.

I chased after her. "You look pretty pissed yourself."

"I got big news from the Department of Bad Shit. They can't get in to fix the suture. It's a transplant or nothing."

Chapter 19

Monica

He was lucid. I knew because he smiled when he saw me.

"Goddess."

"Sir."

"I'm very upset with you."

"I'll skip the spanking joke."

"You need to ask for what you need." He was talking about the money.

"Thank you," I said. "But I couldn't ask."

"I can't read your mind."

"Can we have this discussion when you're better?"

"Did anyone explain the odds of that to you yet? Because—"

"Stop it." I held up both hands, and he took one.

He was going to talk. He was going to tell me what I already knew from Margie and Brad and any doctor I happened upon in the halls. But I didn't want to hear it. I especially didn't want it from him because he would be Mr. Control. Hearing it from him in that measured, shredded voice would make me either scream or run out.

"Tell me what's happening with you," he whispered. "I hear about me all day."

"Eddie asked about you."

"Tell him he's a douchebag for me."

"I will," I said.

"Did he get you a new date to record?"

"Not yet. Christmas is coming, so it's dead."

My face was close to his. He was close enough to own my attention, shutting out the scritch of the stylus and the hissing of the oxygen tubes. Close enough for him to look at me long and deep and see the contents of my heart.

"Don't lie, goddess."

"Carnival has to wait. A four-song session will take all day. If something happens, I need to be here."

A machine beeped. He pressed his lips between his teeth. He'd used that expression when he was healthy, and it made me want to beg him to take me.

"I need you to do your work," he said.

"I won't do it right if I'm worrying about you."

I felt his hand on my waist, a light touch through my shirt. It slid up to my rib cage, bringing memories of everything we'd been together when his hands were forceful and cruel, responsive to desires I didn't even know I had. He fingered the black Bordelle bra I'd worn at his command.

"You've come so far," he said. "You're not the same woman I met. You have control. You can take it and channel it into the work. If I promise you that, would you believe me?"

"I can't."

"You don't know your own power. Please. Go sing. Sheila will watch me."

"I'll think about it."

He nodded as much has he could, and I pressed my lips to his. I kissed him like I kissed him every time since he fell into my arms—like it might be the last.

Chapter 20

Monica

I'd gone home to shower and rest. I shouldn't have. The Drazens had a suite at the hotel across from the hospital, and I should have eaten humble pie and gone there. But I couldn't ask Sheila for the key. I didn't have a change of clothes or the resources to buy new. Fucking pride. Now I was stuck in traffic ten blocks from the goddamn hospital. Another hour lost.

Sitting in traffic in thebestfuckingthingever was far better than sitting in traffic in the Honda. It beat the bus by a mile. But traffic was traffic, and sitting still in a Jaguar while helicopters beat the air was infuriating. Having grown up in Echo Park—before it was a real estate investment opportunity waiting to happen—I was familiar with that situation. The police were sealing off a perimeter so every car could be checked. Usually, a cop-killing created that kind of chaos. Or a gang assassination. Maybe a child abduction. I ticked off the list then closed the windows and sang a couple of the songs I'd prepared for the EP. I belted them out in the shitty acoustics of the car.

I flipped on the news. Music was just messing up the rhythm in my head, which I needed. Talk talk talk, and I half listened to the clipped chat about a mob shooting outside the golf course. No child abduction but a typical drive-by. I felt as though I knew the details without even hearing them, and I internally restated my belief that penalties should be harsher for crimes committed during rush hour. I would be there a while. I sang to the leather dash, letting the news drift away.

> *Yea, though he stands in the fear of the dark*
> *I shall walk at his right hand*
> *I have drawn rod and cudgel*
> *In his defense*
> *I shall lead him to the gate*
> *And if he seeks his end*

My heart shall keep him safe

I can walk
  Without it
I can work
  Without it
I can sing
  Half a woman

Surely goodness and mercy
Prevail in a city of sin
As barter for a life
Beats for beats
Breaths for breaths
Trade a heart for what's mine

I can breathe
  Without it
I can see
  Without it
I can sing
  Half a woman

I was leaning my forehead on the steering wheel when I finished. I couldn't get out the rest of the song. I couldn't breathe. I couldn't see through my tears. He didn't have long. I saw it in the doctors' faces when they spoke as if their careers were on the line. The inconvenience of his death would be epic for them.

Meanwhile, I'd die with him.

The phone rang. Fuck it. It wasn't as if I was moving. I picked up Margie's call.

"Hello?" I realized how snotty and blubbery I sounded when the last vowel came out in a froggy croak.

"Are you okay?"

"The love of my life is dying, so no."

"Well, I called with a little something. Some mafia kingpin just came in with half a brain and a working heart. We're fighting our way up the list, and they're checking for a match. But he's the same blood type."

"Oh, God. Really?" My face exploded in prickly happiness, and tears sprung into my eyes.

"Top secret, okay? This is not public knowledge, as a matter of fact, me knowing is illegal. But don't get your hopes up. The guy's family's going to be an obstacle. Donor cards don't mean anything without a living will, and his family has more hope than Jonathan has time."

"Is it evil to hope he dies?"

"Yes. You and I both."

"See you in hell," I said, with a little less despair in my voice.

"I'll buy the hand basket."

The traffic broke, and I was waved through the blockade on Beverly and Rossmore.

Chapter 21

Monica

"I sold the house. Thank God, Monya. Cash. At market price."

My mother had called just as I stepped into the elevator with nine other people. I was about to tell her I hadn't made any headway, nor had I found an opportune time to ask for Margie's help, when she blurted out her news like a kid blowing the date of a surprise party.

"That's great, ma," I whispered so I wouldn't annoy the three people pressed up against me. "Did they say when they were moving in?" I was happy for her. I really was. But the bank would have to put all my stuff in a Dumpster because I couldn't leave Jonathan long enough to move out.

"That's the good news! They're okay with a tenant. Okay with your rent and everything. You have to make your checks out to an investment company. ODRSN Partners. The address is 147—"

"Can I get it later? I'm in an elevator. I'll call you back."

We hung up, and I molted a few layers of anxiety. I must have bounced into Jonathan's room because he smiled when he saw me. The oxygen tubes were gone from his nose. The sun shone through the window. Yes, he had that auto-squeeze thing on his arm, and yes, he was in that god damn hospital bed, and yes, his heart was ripped up, but he was in a half sitting position and he looked as glad to see me as I was to see him.

"I don't have to move!" I announced, kissing him.

"Good?"

"Oh God, you missed the whole thing!" I blabbered. "My mom put the house into foreclosure. I thought I was going to have to move out really fast, which is impossible—hello, I have twenty years of stuff in that house—but some investor bought it."

"Ah, who beat me out?"

"Crap, she told me." I wrestled with the granola bar until he took it from me and got it open in one move—with a bad heart and IVs sticking out of him. "It's such a load off. I can't even tell you."

He broke off a piece of the bar and held it. "Was it Ganten Investments?"

I took the piece in my mouth. "No, it was a bunch of letters, like DRM... But five letters and not that. I made it into a word in my head, but I can't think of it."

"Doesn't matter, I guess."

"You have to move faster next time if you want property in Echo Park." I took another chunk of granola bar from his fingers. I felt light as a feather, waving at him to indicate I wanted another piece. "Oh my God, this thing tastes so bad. It's, like, stinky."

"Stinky?"

"With a touch of dredgy." Then I remembered, as I chewed, the rhythm of the letters. The taste of the stale barley malt brought it to me. "ODRSN. That was it. It sounded like odorous. ODRSN Partners."

He was looking at the bar, breaking another smelly piece, when he froze. "Did you say ODRSN?"

"Yep."

"Are you sure?"

"Yeah, why? Is that the competition or something?"

He put the bar on the side table then closed his eyes and took a deep breath. It wasn't deep at all though. He breathed as if he didn't have room for air in his lungs.

I took his hands. "Jonathan? Should I call someone?"

He shook his head, but I didn't believe him. I believed the machines, which were silent. But for how long? He was struggling, if not with his breath or his heart, then with his mind.

"I need you to marry me," he said.

"What?"

"Marry me."

"Are you insane?"

"If anything happens to me, I want to make sure you're taken care of," he said.

"I refuse to believe you're going to die. My God, we've maybe been together a few months."

"These are extenuating circumstances. I could leave you swinging in the wind."

"No." I shook my head as if I was trying to get a fly out of my hair. "This is crazy. This is not how I want it. I don't want you to get better then regret it. It's not your job to make sure I'm financially stable. What's come over you?"

Midway through my little speech, stuff started beeping and lighting up. By the time I was done, I was being pushed out by a woman in a blue facemask and gloves. I landed in the hall, back against the wall, trying to stay out of the way.

"What happened?" Eileen asked, standing close to Theresa as if her daughter held her up.

"I don't know," I said. "We were talking about something."

He asked me to marry him and I said no. I put my hands over my mouth when I realized what had happened, and I ran down the hall without looking back. Even when I passed the cafeteria and saw Declan in his usual spot talking to Jessica, I didn't stop. I just kept running.

Chapter 22

Jonathan

That went poorly.

I hadn't intended to ask for her hand, but then she said the name of my father's investment shell. He'd bought her house to save her when I couldn't or wouldn't. Whichever. I simply *didn't,* and the reason I didn't was I didn't know she was in that kind of trouble. I could only know and see what she brought to me. If she chose to protect me, I was impotent to protect her. I was stuck inside four walls with things sticking out of me, tied to a bed as much as I'd tied her.

By the time the smoke cleared, she was gone, and I couldn't explain. I didn't want to talk on the phone. I couldn't, actually. My body betrayed me with exhaustion, long breaths, and lost consciousness. I needed to be in her visual field to see what I was too tired to intuit. She needed to experience the long spaces between sentences that would seem like anger or petulant silence on the phone but were just me trying to breathe around my goddamn damaged heart.

I loved her. I wanted her. She felt right in ways no other woman ever had. Of course I was going to marry her one day, when I was out of that shitbox and untied from that bed. After more dinners and late nights. After more boundary leaping and fighting. More touching, kissing, laughing.

Just not now.

Except that it had to be now. I felt myself failing. My dips into unconsciousness came with less warning. The effort to exist was such a task, I couldn't imagine surviving. Was I scared? Fuck yes, I was terrified. The only thing that kept it at bay was the thought that I could make her life better than it had been, that I could save her from her chronic penury, keep her safe from the manipulations of men like my father. If I could die knowing I'd saved her, maybe I would have served my purpose. It wasn't like my money had anywhere useful to go, anyway.

Theresa sat in the chair Monica usually occupied, leaning forward with her fingers knit together. I wanted to explain all of it to her, but I didn't have the wherewithal to do it right. I had to explain my fear, my need to know Monica was all right, to keep a slice of control. I gave her the shortest version I had.

"I don't blame her for saying no," she said. "You need to get better first."

"What if I don't get better?"

"She'll be a widow."

At twenty-five. When was her birthday? She'd told me she was a Cancer, but if she told me the exact date, I couldn't recall it. I realized we'd never celebrated a birthday together, neither mine nor hers. I wanted to get her something extravagant six months early to make up for the time we'd never have. And Christmas, of course.

"What's today?" I asked Theresa.

"The nineteenth."

"Merry Christmas."

"What do you want under the tree? Besides a 'yes'?"

"I want her," I whispered. "I asked for the wrong reasons, but I want her."

She put her elbows on the bed and her hand on my shoulder. "Do it for the right reasons. Don't do it because it's convenient. Don't do it because you're scared. Marry her because you love her and your life wouldn't add up without her. Can you do that? Can you promise me you're not forcing it? It would break my heart to see you propose because you wanted to give yourself a reason to live."

I rarely saw Theresa so impassioned. She was more like Jessica in her refinement and grace than any of my sisters. She seemed broken down that day, slightly shattered and holding herself together with chicken wire.

"What's wrong, Tee?"

"I don't think love should be taken for granted, and I don't think you should keep on a path of least resistance."

"This is hardly—"

"Can you honestly say that if you were healthy, you'd marry her?"

"Yes. But we'd have a proper engagement." I thought about all Jessica and I had had together, and I wanted to give it to Monica but couldn't. A party, a ring, a wedding. I wanted to see her smiling as she came down the aisle toward me for the last time before we folded into each other's lives forever.

Theresa pressed something into my palm. It was hard and scratchy and oddly shaped. "Give it back when you can buy her her own."

I lifted my hand. It was her engagement ring, a two-carat sapphire cut that was totally Theresa and utterly wrong for Monica. "Daniel won't be happy."

"He'll tell himself he cares. But we cancel each other out. We add up to nothing. Trust me when I say I'd rather break up for the right reasons than get married for the wrong ones."

"I'm sorry."

"Don't be. I can't explain why I feel okay about it, but I do."

I held the ring in my fist as if I was afraid to lose it. "Thank you."

"I'll try to come back, but you might not see me for a while." She kissed my forehead and left.

I fell asleep with the ring in my hand.

Chapter 23
Monica

Jonathan was out of his room. More tests, more prep. More shit piled on top of shit. A hundred thousand checklists to make sure he was worthy of whatever heart came in. My mother texted me the address to send the rent check, and a quick internet search revealed J. Declan Drazen owned ODRSN Partners. Anger and gratitude swirled together inside me like a marble cake.

Dr. Thorensen was in his office looking at four computer screens. "Monica, come in." He stood. "Close the door."

"Thanks. I got your text, but I was driving."

"Sit." He stood in front of a little counter with a sink and poured water into a pot, leaving his screens unattended.

"You're playing *City of Dis*, aren't you? Where do you find the time?"

"This job doesn't afford the time for a dazzling social life, so video games it is. I have UNOS up on a screen right here." As if responding to what must have been my baffled look, he continued. "The transplant list."

"Ah. I heard someone came in..." I didn't know if I should continue. It was surely privileged information, yet once I started talking, I could hardly stop. "He's brain dead is what I heard. I don't mean to be creepy, but—"

"I think that's going to be a no-go."

"You telling me more or Jonathan getting the heart?"

"Yes."

I looked at my lap. Margie's text had given me enough hope to get in the door. When it dropped out of me, nothing replaced it. We were back where we had been that morning, except I was one day closer to the end.

"How are you holding up?" Brad asked.

I shrugged. "I guess I'm all right."

"You're never home."

"Doctor, my presence at home is hardly under your purview."

"I'm not asking as a doctor. I'm asking as your friend. How are you doing?"

"Fine. I feel like I'm waiting for him to either die or be saved, so the regular events of my life aren't so interesting right now."

He leaned back in his chair, eyes glowing in the screens' light. "I've lived next door to you for a couple of years."

"Three, I think."

"I wish I'd gone to your door with something besides the leaves falling on my car or the new fence. I should have known you better, sooner." His hands were folded over his tie, and his feet pushed his office chair back until the corners of his white lab coat dragged on the floor. Besides the hands, it was an exposed position. Even if he didn't intend to send the message he did, I understood the meaning in his heart.

"I'm too upset to give you a thoughtful response. I'm sorry."

"I understand. If you want to go up, he should be back any minute. Irene's at the desk. Check with her if he's okay to see. I'm watching this screen."

I stood up and touched the doorknob. "I'd give him my own heart if I could."

He sat up straight and put his hand on the mouse. "I hear that all the time." He glanced at me, his expression sucking the sarcasm out of the comment. He was just stating a fact. Death was hard, and people loved one another.

Chapter 24

Monica

Police milled around the hallways with radios squawking, belts laden with black leather geometry, swaying hips from the weight of the instrumentation. I leaned on the nurse's desk, peering at Irene's Russian newspaper.

"Hi," I said. "What are all the cops about?"

She waved her meaty hand and shook her head. "Security. You feel safe? I feel safe. Like in middle of street."

"I'm going in." I stepped away.

"No, you don't." She picked up the phone and hit one of the buttons on the bottom of the keypad. "Wait." The person on the other side must have answered because she muttered something in Russian, listened, and hung up. "Come with me."

She shuffled from behind the desk and went toward Jonathan's room. I didn't know why I needed her to guide me. My world revolved around that room and going to and from it. The door was closed. She knocked. A deep, powerful voice that couldn't have been Jonathan's made some sort of affirmative noise. Irene opened the door.

One lamp was on, a warm one I hadn't seen before. The room smelled nice, like salty sea air and clear water. I located a squat blue candle burning on the windowsill that must have been the source of the scent. A huge bald man stood by the doorway—one of the regular orderlies who didn't talk much. His nametag said Gregory. Irene babbled something, and he babbled back in the same language. He stepped out of the way.

Jonathan sat on the edge of the bed. I hadn't seen him actually sit up since the Collector's Board show, and I must have gasped a little. He wore a suit jacket over his hospital gown. He also had on pants and shoes. Tubes stuck out of his sleeves, and the effort it took for him to sit up was visible once I got over the initial shock.

"Jonathan," I said. "I—"

"You sit," Gregory interrupted, pointing at a red antique chair in front of Jonathan that I recognized from his bedroom. I'd described that chair and its place under a sconce one night, back when I thought I'd have him back. I glanced from Gregory to Irene, and then to my lover, who waited patiently.

I sat. "What's this about?"

No one answered. Gregory and Irene stood on either side of Jonathan, facing me.

"You ready, Mister Drazen?" Irene asked.

"For a long time now."

They did something that made me hold my breath and clutch the arms of the chair. They put their hands under Jonathan's arms, slid him off the bed, and lowered him to the floor.

"What—?" When they let him go, I was too stunned to finish the sentence. He kneeled before me. I heard his labored breathing, the rattle of the IV pole, and glanced at Irene and Gregory. "What are you doing? This is crazy."

I was ignored. Gregory said something to Jonathan in Russian, and he answered in kind, along with a wave of his hand that indicated, "I got it."

Jonathan, with great effort, pulled up a knee until he was on just one and glanced at me. "I'm going to lean on you a little."

"Sure?" He put a forearm on my knee and reached into his jacket pocket, pulling out a small black box. "Oh, Jonathan..."

He opened the box and handed it to me. It had a ridiculously huge square-cut diamond. "Thank Theresa if you see her. I'll get you one that suits you when we're up to it."

"You don't have to do this," I said.

"Shh. Behave, would you? For once?"

I pressed my lips together to keep from laughing. One side of his mouth curled in a smile, and then he laughed gingerly. I wanted to kiss him deeply and for a long time. I wanted to breathe him into me, but I knew he didn't have the breath to spare. I settled for a fraction of the kiss I wanted, just brushing my lips against his. The softest parts of our faces melted together for a second, half a gasp, a tease of desire.

"Goddess," he said, his breath on my mouth, "have me, please. I was wrong. You're not the sea under my sky. You are the sun I revolve around, the stars that mark me, the moon rising through me. I'm lost without you.

If you won't have me, I'll break, I swear to God. I know it's selfish, and I'm sorry. Let me serve you. Have me as yours. Let me live under you."

I held his face, running my fingers over his stubble, his jaw in the heel of my hand. I felt him leaning into me as if this had taken everything out of him. What could I say? What could I say to being loved enough for that monumental an effort? Did I ever, in my wildest imaginings, think I deserved that level of devotion after I'd rejected him the first time?

After I'd left him, cursed him, and denied him? After lying to him, drugging him, disobeying him, using him, could I justify letting him make such a mistake even if it was the last mistake he made? I was ambitious, venal, antagonistic, impoverished, and arrogant. I was unworthy by a mile and overcome by the circumstances that would lead such a man to beg to be bound to such a woman.

So I said the only thing I could.

"Yes."

Chapter 25

Jonathan

Her hair fell across our fists, which were balled together around a found box holding my sister's ring. My hands shook as I removed the ring. My rib cage ached as if it was being stretched by an ever-expanding balloon. With the tube out my chest, it was filling with blood, drop by drop. I was sure the feeling of expansion was air or my imagination, but fear made it hard to get the garish thing on her finger. The size was right, but the stone was wrong. All wrong. I wanted something else for her, something more original, a ring that could only belong to a goddess.

"I won't disappoint you," I said.

"I'm not worried about you being the disappointment."

Irene's voice cut in. "I declare you engaged. Time to go." She put her hand on my shoulder.

"I want to tell you what you do to me the night I agree to marry you," Monica whispered.

"They have to put me back in. I don't want you to see it."

"Jonathan, please—"

"Time to go," Irene said more firmly.

"Go," I said to my fiancée. "Please. Come back in an hour. Then you can tell me about our wedding night."

Her head tilted a little, and her eyes widened. Yes, it was quick, but wasn't that the point? She kissed me a second too long. When we ended, I was grimacing. She must have known it wasn't about her because she got up and walked out without looking back. Good woman.

I submitted myself to Irene and Gregory, who had broken a hundred rules or more to give me five minutes to ask properly for Monica's hand. Rules were good. They were there for a reason. I couldn't handle five minutes of kneeling. I felt as if I'd just run a marathon that ended in a dark alley where

I'd been beaten with baseball bats and cut into small pieces with a serrated knife. Or something that made me too weak, too pained, too outside myself to manage my own body.

They got me out of my clothes, then reinserted, realigned, and recalibrated the devices attached to me. They accepted my gratitude for as long as I had the wherewithal to express it, which was an eternity but probably about five minutes in the real world. Then I fell off the cliff of consciousness. It might have been because of the drugs or just my body giving out like it did a few times a day. Even then, I didn't have the energy to feel angry, though there was a cord of that in my spine. Mostly, I felt fear. I was responsible for her now. Though the unknown was bad enough to face alone, in the dark and unprepared, I felt as though I had something to live for tomorrow.

Chapter 26

Mlonica

I crouched on the stairwell. It was late. Jonathan couldn't see me for an hour after he'd given me the ring, or the hour after that. Sheila had come and gone, her lips pressed together in a line of rage. Eileen called to see if I was there, and if I was, was he lucid enough to see anyone. I didn't tell her we'd gotten engaged. I figured if Jonathan had wanted his family involved, they would have been involved.

I called Darren. "Do you have something blue?"

"Technically, yes." He stepped out of the studio to finish the sentence, and I heard the rain and traffic behind him.

"Something pretty and blue?"

"Okay, what the fuck?"

"I'm getting married, and I have this ring that's borrowed and this belt is, like, a hundred years old."

"What?"

"Can you just bring me something blue, please?" I asked. He started a sentence but didn't finish it. He took a breath, started to say something else, and stopped again. "Darren?"

"Jesus. I didn't...I don't know what to say. I haven't been there for you, have I?"

"Be here for me tonight. Something reasonably attractive. And blue. And new, if possible. I'm stretching the definition with what I have here."

Chapter 27

Monica

Darren arrived just as Irene was telling me to do something with my hair then come in. He handed me a CVS bag with four blue hair clips.

"Thank you," I said. He grabbed me and hugged me. It was the only real hug I'd gotten all week. It was warm and perfect, without expectation or promise. I chose a little rhinestone hairpin the color of the autumn sky and let Darren put it in. "You're the maid of honor and the best man."

"I'm not making a toast."

"He won't have the energy. He barely had it in him to ask me to marry him in the first place." We walked down the hall.

"I wish you'd told me...asked me for something," he said.

"You never pick up. I feel like I'm bothering you."

He shrugged, and we turned into Jonathan's room. It was lit only by the reading lamp over his bed. I felt Darren stiffen. Jonathan was halfway sitting up but bedridden and pale, connected to machines and IV bags of medicine and blood. The last time they'd seen each other, Jonathan was hale and Darren was threatening to send out wedding invitations if we had another breakup.

"Hi," Darren said. Jonathan held his hand up in greeting. "You look like fucking hell, man."

"Darren!" I cried.

"And I can still get a knockout wife," Jonathan said.

"Tough to be you," Darren said.

People came in behind me. I didn't see them; I only saw Jonathan. I kissed his lips for the last time as his lover and turned around. Irene and Gregory were at the foot of the bed. On the opposite side of the bed from me, in the chair I usually occupied, was a short woman in horn-rimmed glasses and clerical collar. She was a few years older than me and had a mop of curly hair held in place with a vintage clip. Darren stood behind her.

"Hi," she said brightly.

"Hi," Jonathan and I chanted. I straightened and held his hand. It was cold.

"My name is Sona, and let me tell you, this is not the kind of call I usually get when I do the hospital chaplaincy. I had to dig around for the right prayer book. But happy occasions are worth the trouble. So what do we have? Both Catholic, I hear?"

"Kind of," I said.

"I hear the groom has a big family? They aren't here?"

"I'll tell them tomorrow," Jonathan said. My sigh of relief must have been audible because he squeezed my hand.

"Sona," I said, "Jonathan isn't up for anything long and involved if that's okay. I don't mean to be disrespectful."

"Nope!" She smiled with big, white teeth. "You have rings?"

"Crap." I didn't. I glanced at Darren. He shrugged, holding up his palms.

"Can we make do with something?" she asked. "People do like the rings."

"Yes! I have it." I rummaged through my bag and came up with my keys. Car. House. Front gate. Locker at work. I clicked through them.

"Clever goddess," he said. "I owe your fingers some jewelry."

My eyes hurt again. The odds of him repaying that debt got smaller with each day. I focused on loosening as many keys as possible into the bottom of my bag.

"Let's do some paperwork while Monica does that, okay?" Sona smiled again, extracting a little clipboard from a leather case. She asked our full names, dates of birth, addresses, and had us sign on the dotted lines while I untwisted as many silver rings as I could. Darren showed his ID and cracked a joke about being licensed to witness weddings. By the time she was done, I'd released two smallish key rings. I adjusted one for Jonathan's hand and found another for myself. I pressed it into his palm.

"Okay," said Sona, standing. She was all enthusiasm and light as if our wedding wasn't the most depressing situation ever. "Groom goes first. You ready?"

"Yes," he said and pulled me toward him.

"Can you repeat after me?" she asked.

"I got this." He was talking to Sona but looking at me. His big, tired green eyes were serious, committed. I hoped to God he lived even if it meant he lived to regret it. "I, Jonathan Drazen, take you, Monica Faulkner, to be my lawfully wedded wife." He paused.

"You sure you want to do this?" I asked. "You can back out. I'll still love you."

"Shh. Behave." He smirked at me and took a deep breath. "Left hand, goddess."

I held it out, and he continued as he slipped the key ring on my finger. "To have and to hold, for better or worse, for richer or poorer, in sickness and in health, to love, cherish, honor, and worship all the days of my life."

"Excellent!" Sona said. "Monica? You want to do it the same? Or do you want to repeat after me?"

I didn't want to repeat anything. I wanted to spill my guts onto the sheets. I wanted to take my heart out and put it into his chest. If there was ever a time to hold anything back, it wasn't then.

"Jonathan Drazen," I said, squeezing his hand, "you're a manipulative bastard, a brazen liar, and a sadist. You've brought me to my knees. You've dominated me. You've told me who I am and then challenged me to be it. If you made me strong enough to stand up to the world, let me stand by you. If you completed the woman I am, let me be that woman in your honor. Every part in my body is dedicated to you. Every note I sing. Every breath in my lungs. My pleasure and pain. Take me. Let me serve you. Let me be yours."

He put my hand to his cheek. I was going to kiss him before I was told because it seemed as though it was taking Sona forever. When I looked from Jonathan to her, she was holding her phone.

"Sorry," she said, pocketing it, her good mood gone. "Gotta go do a 'Last Rites'." She cleared her throat and held up her hand. "You have declared your consent before the Church. May the Lord in his goodness strengthen your consent and fill you both with his blessings. What God has joined, let no one tear asunder. I now pronounce you husband and wife."

Irene and Gregory clapped a little, but I didn't pay attention to how wan they sounded. I was kissing my husband.

Chapter 28

Monica

Sona and the staff had cleared out. Darren hugged and congratulated me. He fist-bumped Jonathan, promising him a wild night of beer-slinging and barhopping in Silver Lake. He kissed me on the cheek and left, promising he'd call.

Irene had warned me, while ignoring Jonathan, that nothing was to go on behind the closed door that might bring a heart rate up. Just in case I didn't know, he was being monitored from the nurse's station, so no "funny business."

We laughed when the door closed. I wanted to lie on top of him, press my thighs to his, and tuck my head into the crook of his neck, but that was impossible. I sat in the adjacent chair and kissed his cheek.

"Do you regret it?" I said.

"I feel relieved."

"I'm glad."

He said, "I wish I could give you a wedding night. Throw you over my shoulder, dress and all, and carry you over the threshold. We wouldn't even make it up the stairs."

I made a satisfied purr. "I can just imagine it. Whose house?"

"Our house."

"Is there a porch?"

"More than one. I'll have you on all of them, regularly. Breakfast in the back. Lunch on the side. After dinner, we'll drink wine on the front porch, and I'll make love to you in the night air."

"Can I still call you sir?"

"I expect no less."

"Thank you, sir." I kissed his hand, letting my lips linger on his skin.

"Here we are," he said, "married, and we've never even talked about children."

"Can we pretend we had them?"

"Four," he said with a slight smile.

"Don't be greedy."

"Three. Can we settle on three?"

I should have agreed to ten children because there would be exactly none. There would be no house, no porches, no family.

"Can I admit something to you, my beautiful wife?"

"Yes."

"I'm scared."

I squeezed his hand and laid my head next to him. That was when the machine's beeping was replaced with a high, constant whine.

Chapter 29

Monica

I stood in the hall staring at his door.

They'd done CPR. Changed the tube. Pumped more drugs into him. Assured me there wasn't a spare heart with his blood type anywhere but Paulie Patalano's chest.

What the hell were we made of? Sausage casings and prime cuts to be wrapped up and swapped out as needed. I felt ill. The twisting in my gut told me to run to the bathroom and bend over the toilet, but nothing came up because I hadn't eaten in Lord knew how long. When I returned, panicking, he was alive, stable, and unconscious.

All the wrong things seemed definite and secure. I knew he loved me. I knew he was right in my life. But the life that fit mine so perfectly was going to end soon. Tomorrow. The next day. Didn't matter. Too soon. The house of our love would crumble under a cracked foundation.

I found myself outside Dr. Thorensen's office. He'd have answers, or at least different questions. "You're here," I said.

He was in the dark again, shades drawn, screens flashing. "Come in. Wanna play?"

"I can't believe you get away with this."

"I'm waiting to hear about something."

"Jonathan?"

"Sit."

"Is there a heart somewhere?"

He sighed. "I'm getting him put on the emergency list. I'm pretty sure it'll go through in an hour, but I don't want to leave until I see it. Come on. Sit. Your avatar's on the cloud. We can start you from the beginning." I hesitated. He patted the seat of the couch behind him. "Come."

"Fine." I sat, kicking off my shoes and tucking my feet under me. He rolled his chair back until the back of it pressed against the couch. The cushion was already indented from his hours of play.

He said, "You ready? There you are. I made you look like you."

"Jesus, I don't look like that." My avatar was ravishing.

"Yeah, you do. Okay, so we start out in the woods. Forest all over, and we're lost. We have to solve this puzzle before our guide comes. Hold on there! Get them!"

We shot down a leopard, a lion, and a wolf. We avoided shooting a blind guy. As a reward, he set us a puzzle to solve. We had that sorted out in no time, and I saw something I recognized.

ABANDON ALL HOPE, YE WHO ENTER HERE

"Such a cheerful game, Brad. Don't you have something with bunnies?"

"You can come over and play that next week."

There won't be a next week, Dr. Thorensen... I had no time to make that into a joke. We had to navigate a parade, and a flag, right, left, left, right, and still get to our destination, a boat on a black river.

"Tell me something," I said. "What are the odds of him getting a heart in time?"

"Can't say. Hit left, left. Nice."

"Do I duck the guy in the Pope hat?"

"God, yes."

"Can't or won't?"

"Can't or won't what? Just don't let him touch you."

"Can't or won't say about the heart. Fuck."

"Oh! Nice move. Both. His blood type's rare, so a good heart is hard enough but...okay, see that opening right there? Hit your blue button and the joystick at the same time."

"Is there any way to speed it up? The heart thing? Shit! Wait..."

"You got it... No, only what I'm doing—pushing him up the list." His shoulders slumped. "We're in. River Acheron. Good job. You earned the coins, so give one to the guy in the hood."

I clicked my buttons. "He won't take it."

"That's weird." He took the controller.

"What about the mafia guy? The brain dead one? If he died, would Jonathan get his heart?"

Brad was focused on the controls. "I can't promise anything. Crap. I heard this happens sometimes."

"What?"

"You're stuck in the vestibule. That's your sin. Wow. I guess we can make you a new avatar."

"My sin?" I asked. "Which one?"

He threw down the controller and kicked his feet up on the couch. "The vestibule is where you go when you don't take sides on an issue. Like when you could have taken action but didn't. Or, look, I'm not going to pretend to be a philosopher. You were probably just feeling passive when you answered the questions. Wanna do it again?"

I thought for a second. Did I want to sit in Brad's tiny office until sunrise, waiting for Jonathan to get bumped up a list, or did I want to make a decision about helping him? "I'm going to brush my teeth and find an empty waiting room couch."

"Suit yourself."

"When you know something, can you tell me?"

"I will. You tell me if you need anything, okay?" he said.

"Sure, and thanks." I was pretty sure he didn't know what I was thanking him for.

Chapter 30

Monica

Jonathan was still sleeping when I got back. I sat in the chair by his bed and looked at his hand in the moonlight and the little light-up Christmas tree. His fingers were set in a relaxed curl, the key ring wedding band half falling off. I knew those hands. They were strong. They were his instruments. I couldn't see past his elbows, but I knew the rest of him. I read his body like a book. The velvet of his skin. His scent when his cologne had worn off. The warmth of his touch, its perfect pressure on me. The tones and cadences of his voice, rising and falling, clipped to command, breathy to soothe, chopped fine to laugh.

I put my palm on his cheek, and in my mind, his eyes close for a second before he turns his head and kisses my hand, my wrist, the inside of my forearm. His stubble scratches, lips awakening, tongue taunting, fingers closed on my wrist like a vise. I feel bound, secure, safe. My tingling body is an exploding cage of sin.

He is before me, dressed in his business clothes, and I'm naked. We're in the hotel room where he spanked me the first time, the night I tried to hide my navel from him, and he gave me back my voice. He'd told me to be naked, and this is how I imagine it would have gone if I had been obedient.

He tells me to put my hands behind my back then kicks my legs open. He tells me that he won't fuck me until he hears my voice, and I whisper my doubts that it will work. He smirks in that way he does and runs his fingertips across my shoulder and down my chest to my nipple. He strokes it until it's hard. He bends it down, then circles it. He switches on the light and turns me toward the windows.

It's night. We're on a high floor, and Los Angeles is covered in a blanket of lights. I see myself naked, reflected in the windows, a ghost over the city.

"Put your hands on the glass," he says. I do. The basin is spread before me, a checkerboard of pinpricks, exactly as Mondrian had envisioned. Squares of light, blinking

signs of life create a haze in the distance. Above it all, my body, leaning into the window, stretched across miles of Los Angeles, bent at the waist as if I was about to fuck it.

"Anything that sounds like 'no' or 'stop' is effective. But you have to say it." He draws his palm across my ass in a hard slap. At that point, he hadn't spanked me yet, so my surprise overwhelms the arousal. I am immediately angry and defensive. "You have to use your voice. Do you understand?"

He puts his left hand on my rib cage, fingertips brushing my breast, and slaps me again. I'm not surprised the second time, nor am I angry. The raw tingle is arousing, as is the stroke and grab that follow. But what really arouses me is letting him do it. I submitted to it, making myself beneath him, under his command and control. I want it. I want every sting, every brush of his fingers against my sensitive skin. He slaps the back of my thighs, and I gasp.

"Monica, was that you?" he asks. I see him in the window, just behind me, his dark suit nearly invisible. I want him to take me, use me, fuck me like a whore. He reaches between my legs and jams two fingers in my cunt. My knees nearly buckle under the weight of my arousal. "You're wet."

"Yes," I whisper.

"You want me to fuck you?" He slaps my ass again, hard.

"Yes, please," I reply in breaths.

"Say it."

I can't. I can't engage my vocal cords. I can't make sounds. My voice kills people, I am convinced of it.

He takes his belt off and loops it once. "You don't know the power you have." He whacks me with the belt. God, it hurts. I'm more aware of the presence and place of my cunt. I feel it hanging between the raw singe of my ass cheeks. It's heavy, bloated, engorged with desire. He hits me again, lower, the leather kissing my wet opening. "Say it."

"Please fuck me."

"With your voice." Whack. The sting is definite, lingering, burning as if I'd sat on a hot stove. "You don't know the power you have." He hits me repeatedly on the word power until my ass is on fire. My clit is so engorged the belt touches it when it snaps, and I scream.

"Monica, was that you?" He's breathless himself.

I can't make the noise again until he drops the belt and slaps my cunt twice, hard and fast. The sting then the rush of pleasure pulls one long vowel sound from my throat.

"There it is. That beautiful voice." Behind me, he takes out his cock and places it at my opening. "Say it."

"Fuck me. Fuck me please." The air from my lungs vibrates my vocal cords, and I hear myself cry out as he rams into me. His hips touch my raw behind, making me feel *every thrust as pleasure and pain. I'm filled with the spectrum of sensations, every thought, every cell, every warp of my soul feels him move inside me.*

He pulls me up. My hands leave the cold glass, and I stand again, draped over the city, Jonathan fucking me from behind. I see him in the window, and he knows I'm looking at my giant self over the basin.

He whispers in my ear, "You're not the same woman I met. You have control."

I realize I'm hearing him say it the way he said it to me yesterday when he was trying to convince me to cut that EP. That same weak, enervated voice that I'd infused with muscle in my mind. I had stolen it and pasted it into the scene like a collage.

His fingers slip between my legs. I'm sopping for him, my clit a hard knob under his touch, and I watch my face in the window as I open my mouth to yell with pleasure as he whispers in my ear.

"You don't know your own power."

I put my head by his shoulder and fell asleep for a few hours.

Chapter 31
Monica

I went to the cafeteria aching from sleeping like a pretzel. I felt like the ghoul of Sequoia whenever I walked in there—until I saw Declan. He was the ghoul, of course. I was an amateur.

He sat with a young woman who was twisting her long dark hair, making a single, lacquered curl. They spoke earnestly, emotionally, much as he and Jessica had spoken the other day. To be more accurate, she was talking and he was nodding in the way a therapist might. He understood. He heard every word. He had answers posed as questions. He'd go home and forget it all.

I sat at my usual table. I could have gone back up to Jonathan, but I had business in the cafeteria. I was perfectly willing to sit and work on a song until that business came to me.

Take these rolling hills
Shorn grass and dewy mornings
Dump a street on them
Shove a house, then ten times ten

Take this starry night
Clean air and sparkling skies
Spray paint it with poison
Send up bleating sirens

I'm gonna rise through
My jawbone on your throat
Gonna get black tarred again
My heels dug in

Feasting under the surface
Death on life, me on you
Claws dig, teeth cut
Locked in a forever fuck

I was considering changing the last verse to a chorus when I felt someone above me. I knew who it was without looking up. "Mister Drazen."

"Miss Faulkner, or should I call you by your new name?"

"How do you know my last name?" I leaned away from my notebook, closing it so he wouldn't see my anger spit up on the page.

"I could start with you next to my son at the Eclipse show. The journalists had you figured out by publication. My daughter Theresa still speaks to me sometimes. She told me about you. May I sit?"

"Sure. Could it have been the notice you pulled out of my notebook?"

"Shouldn't leave it lying around if you don't want people to see it."

"You bought my mother's house," I said.

"Both of them. I didn't actually want property in Castaic, but—"

"You almost sent Jonathan over the edge."

He folded his lips between his teeth, a move so like my lover's I had a quick vision of what Jonathan would look like if he was ever allowed to age. "That wasn't my intention."

"Maybe." I paused, dunking my teabag repeatedly. It had no effect, but it gave me something to do with my hands. "What do you do down here all the time? You're a fourth-generation billionaire, for Chrissakes. Can't you pay someone to wait around here for you?"

He laughed. I didn't know what it was with the Drazen men. Every time I mentioned their money, they thought it was hilarious. He twisted and put his back to the wall, stretching out his feet. It was a gesture for a younger man, a man who wanted to take up a lot of room. "It's always amazing to me not what people do for money or revenge, but what they do for love. That woman I was just talking to?"

"Yeah."

"Her husband just got beaten nearly to death in a parking lot two blocks away. They wanted his car, but he had worked for it, so he wouldn't give it up. She said they only got the keys away from him when they threatened to rape her."

"That's awful."

"It wasn't even that nice a car," he mumbled, flicking a crumb off the table.

"But why's she down here talking to you?"

"That's the interesting thing. See, he was in surgery, getting his internal bleeding sewn up. But it was so bad, and it was taking too long. Two doctors came out to talk to her every hour." He held up two fingers to make his point. "They said, 'We're working on it. He's stable.' Then, on the fourth hour, three doctors come out." He held up three fingers that time. "She knows, from when her father had cancer, that three doctors coming out after surgery means bad news. If one doctor is attacked by a violent family member, the other is there to hold him down and the third is to call security. So she saw three and ran down here before they spoke to her."

"And like a shepherd with a lost lamb, you found her."

"If my son won't see me, at least I can do some good down here."

"Like buying my mother's house," I said.

"You're getting the idea."

I didn't trust him, not one bit. I didn't believe he stayed in the cafeteria to be in the same sphere as his estranged child. I didn't believe Jonathan had misconstrued a lifetime of manipulation and bad deeds. The facts didn't drive my mistrust; it was simply that I had to pick someone to believe. I chose my husband. Yet, if I was going to do what needed to be done, I would have to trust him enough to keep his word.

"He's dying. That suture tears a little more each day. He's bleeding into himself. A couple of days is all he's got. Tell me you're down here to do some good, and we can talk about something."

He shifted in his seat until he faced me, elbows on the table. "Go on."

"I'm a distraught wife. I might just suggest things I shouldn't."

"Grain of salt taken. Congratulations, by the way."

I ignored his glance at the borrowed ring. "There's a heart with the right blood type in this hospital. It's connected to a dead fucking brain. I want it."

"The Italian. Patalano, I believe? Paulie Patalano?"

"He filled out a donor card, but there's no living will. His family's keeping him alive with machines and prayer. It's time for the machines to give the prayers a chance to work."

"And?"

He wasn't going to give me anything. If he intuited what I was asking, he wouldn't step up and verbalize it. I had to do all the heavy lifting.

"And I think that if someone could arrange an opening in security, that heart could be available real soon."

He studied me as if seeing me for the first time. The depth of his stare made me uncomfortable, as if fingers were rooting around my insides, knocking around corners and dark places. I stayed still. Let the fucker try to figure me out. I didn't have all that many corners, and at that point, I didn't care what he turned up.

"Who would go through the opening?" he asked, an eyebrow lifted.

"Me." I said it without question or lilt in my voice.

"I admit, I thought he cared about you because you were beautiful," Declan said. "But I was wrong. You're loyal to the point of martyrdom."

"I'm tired of praying for miracles."

"You might need a miracle after the deed is done."

"I'll take my chances with him alive," I said.

He smirked, and I saw Jonathan's face in his one-sided grin. "You think because Patalano's brain dead already, you can get off. If you play the distressed woman, of course. Who would doubt you? As his wife, you have more to gain from him dying than living. And with the Drazen machine behind you? How could any judge even send it to a jury, much less convict?"

Murder. It was the word he'd avoided.

Despite the conversation, I was struck by a thought I couldn't get out of my head. I hadn't even wanted to date Jonathan, and there I was ready to commit murder for him. "I'm sure it won't be that easy. For you, maybe. You're Teflon."

"More well-seasoned cast iron," he joked. "What's in it for me?"

"There's nothing I can offer you but Jonathan's life."

He nodded. With a slight twitch of his hand, he indicated the entirety of the cafeteria. That twitch told me that Jonathan's life simply spared wasn't enough. He would still be relegated to the cafeteria at Sequoia Hospital. "I'm no martyr. My relationship with some of my family is painful. I don't want any of them leaving this world a stranger."

"I don't know if anything I can say will change his mind."

"Let me know when you figure it out."

That was it. That was the deal I was offered. Get Declan in to see Jonathan, and give him a heart attack that'll kill him. Don't get Declan in, and watch Jonathan die while some brainless mobster down the hall kept a heart alive for someone else.

Chapter 32

Monica

I stood outside Jonathan's door, listening to the symphony of instruments that kept him alive. I hated them. They intruded, bullying me into remembering my place when we were alone together. He faced away from the door, the tendons of his neck and the line of his jaw pale in the morning light. He turned when I tiptoed in, and he held his hand out for me. I kissed it, then his lips.

"Goddess." His voice was shredded, his breathing audible. I'd die if I had to watch him deteriorate.

"How do you feel?"

"With you here?" He touched my cheek. His fingertips were electric on my face, even in his condition. "Like fucking, but that's probably a bad idea."

"I have a headache anyway."

"How does it feel to be Mrs. Drazen?"

"You didn't need to marry me to protect me from your father."

"He's destroyed everything of mine he's ever touched. And look, he's already stepped in to get control of you."

How could I bring up seeing Declan? He'd be convinced his father was a puppet-master pulling my strings. "I married you for the right reasons. Not out of desperation," I said.

"Desperation's all I have. There's something unfinished in my life, and it's us. I needed you bound to me in front of heaven and earth. I'm glad we did it."

"I'm afraid I gave you permission to die."

"I don't need your permission." He seemed so collected when he said that, as if he was totally okay with leaving me, and marrying me was just him tidying up his affairs.

I felt a spark of rage and clenched my teeth. As his thumb stroked my jaw, the anger melted into irritation, then mild annoyance, and then into a liquid place that had been the base coat of my anger all day. The rush of sadness felt physical as it washed over me, pulling me into an undertow of grief. He was dead already. He knew it. It was a simple fact I hadn't come to terms with, holding out ridiculous hope. A dead man stroked my cheek, and the awakening between my legs from that touch was a ghastly perversion. I wanted a corpse. He looked ready for a coffin, peaceful at last, hands crossed over his chest, left ring finger bulging and swollen around his key ring band.

I broke as if an egg had been cracked behind my face, leaking yolk and clear albumin. My eyes fell apart under the weight of my tears. My nose clogged, lungs kicking air in hitched gulps. He touched my tears, but couldn't do anything else. He could barely lift his own head. I turned my wet, ugly, twisted face onto his palm and let him feel my sobbing contortions.

"Goddess, please," he said.

I was past the point of reason. "I'd kill for you, Jonathan. If I could—"

"Shh. That's enough."

I couldn't finish speaking anyway, my breathing was so charged with sobs. I swallowed a pint of gunk that had collected in my throat and squeezed my eyes shut until I'd stopped crying long enough to get out a sentence. "If I can, I will. You mark my words."

"Okay. Just hush."

"I'm going to suggest something. I don't want you to have a heart attack over it." I snapped up tissues and wiped my face. My eyes felt swollen and pained.

"Funny girl."

"Your father has been in the cafeteria for a week to be near you."

"Fuck, Monica. No. What did he say to you?"

I put my hands on either side of him and leaned over his face, blocking the light from the window. "I'll make a deal with the devil to save you."

"Don't. Whatever it is, don't do it."

"I'm giving you a reason to live."

He swallowed hard and stared past me at the ceiling. "*You* are my reason to live. Fuck." His lips moved in a litany of *fucks* that had no sound. They were made of breath and panic. I glanced at the machines. They seemed okay, not that I knew what that meant. They weren't beeping or honking. The stylus that kept track of his heartbeat was making the same scritchy noise it always did.

"It's okay," I said. But was it? I had no guarantee I wasn't being royally fucked with. I had no idea who I was dealing with. Declan seemed to be a different person to everyone who spoke about him. Who was he to me? Would I find out the hard way?

"I'm stuck here," he said. "I can't do anything but trust you, can I?"

"No. You can't. I love you, you have to know that."

"I know it. But your decision-making..."

"I decided to wait you out when you left me. I decided to ask you for exclusivity. I decided to let you kiss me on Mulholland Drive. I could go on."

"Maybe later," he said weakly.

"Will you do it for me? See your father?" I put everything into the question, and that was a mistake. He shouldn't see any emotion from me with regard to Declan. I should have played blithe or irritated. But I played it honest. I didn't realize my error until the machines whined and Jonathan's eyes closed.

Chapter 33

Jonathan

Fiona had gotten kicked in the chest once at the riding academy when she was making a token attempt to learn to check a hoof for splits. The thoroughbred had gotten annoyed, and Fiona, who never listened to a damn thing anyone said, had been sitting in the wrong spot. She went flying. Two broken ribs and a bruised ego later, she quit riding. I'd probably never see Fiona again to tell her getting defibrillated repeatedly felt the same as getting kicked in the chest by a horse looked.

Monica stood in the corner, wringing her hands as if she wanted to break a bone. She was terrified. I must have gone into arrest at some point in our conversation. I forgot what I'd said.

"How are you feeling, Mister Drazen?" asked the doctor, a young guy I'd seen a couple of times. He looked at his chart and barked orders after the question. The number of people in the room had doubled in the minute I was unconscious.

"Like a newlywed."

"Congratulations." He listened to my heart, eyes on an instrument panel. "You've taken quite a beating. I don't know how many more times we can do this."

"What's the world record? I want to break it."

"Stop trying to be funny," Monica said from her corner.

"Joking in this situation is common, miss," the doctor said as he scribbled something on the chart. He spoke medicalese to the nurse before and after his statement.

"What situation is that?" My wife was about to verbally cross-check the doctor, I saw it in the fact that she wouldn't look at me. She only had laser-hot eyes for the guy in the scrubs.

As if he could feel her seething, he stopped mumbling nonsense to the nurse and turned to her. "He needs a heart, miss."

"Or what?"

I could see the thrust of the conversation a mile away, even while feeling like a bag of shit with the hiss of oxygen tubes drowning out much of what was being said. If the doctor mentioned, implied, or thought about my death, she would go ballistic and get escorted out. I didn't want her to have to negotiate reentry. Every minute without her was a minute wasted.

"Goddess?" She didn't answer. "Monica." I tried to put dominance in my voice, and I know I came up short. As if hearing the intention and not the result, she turned toward me. "Go get my father for me, would you?"

Chapter 34

Monica

Any shadow of a feeling resembling doubt left my mind when those machines went crazy. I was in empty panic when they all rushed in. When they put the paddles on this chest and he convulsed, the empty panic turned to something else. Something like... When I felt pressure in my bladder, I went to the bathroom. I may stop and do other things, but my ultimate goal at some point was to release that pressure. Everything else is either a distraction or a means to an end.

When I walked out of Jonathan's room to get his father, I had absolutely nothing on my mind but making sure some motherfucker put a new heart in him. I did not ever want to see that again. I never, ever wanted to get used to it. If I went to jail for killing someone who was already pretty much dead, fuck it. I could be cool with that.

Declan paced the lobby, phone pressed to his ear. Even as exhausted as he must have been, he looked clean, energetic, and calm. That must be a Drazen thing. Only Leanne in her general slovenliness and Sheila in her constant backbitten rage ever seemed a tick to the left of perfect. Theresa, who looked buffed and polished when I'd met her, had looked as if she'd run a marathon in pumps when she came to the hospital. Maybe they were all human after all.

Except Declan of course. He had been described as less than human, yet somehow he had only shown me a vulnerable face. He saw me and held up a finger. I didn't have time for him. I scribbled—*Room 7719 NOW*—on one of the last blank pages in my notebook. I tore it out, slapped it in his hand, and walked away before he had a chance to answer. I had to assume he'd go up. I didn't have time to baby him, and I certainly didn't want a verbal cat and mouse.

I took the stairs to the fourth floor and strode to Dr. Thorensen's office.

He would assure me Jonathan was at the top of that list, and I wanted an update on Paulie Patalano's health. A cleaning cart stood outside the open door. He wasn't in his office, but his screens were flashing and blazing some twisted circle in the *City of Dis*. It was frozen, characters halted mid-action, a puzzle half-done. On the smallest screen, off to the right, was a blinking text box with nothing in it. Above that was a list.

I couldn't help myself. I looked. Each item on the list was the word PATIENT followed by a long string of letters and numbers. A location. A gender. A blood type. A colored box. Red. Orange. Yellow. It was all red at the top of the list, and the number two patient was in Los Angeles, California. He had AB negative blood. Jonathan. A fucking alphabet soup string with a red box at the end. My lover. My husband. Patient KJE873BP7988. M. LA, CA. AB-. Code red.

"Excuse me?" A short lady in soft shoes and maintenance gear stood in the doorway. Her hair was pulled back in a tight ponytail, and her hands were covered in yellow plastic gloves.

I didn't belong there. "Sorry. I was just leaving."

I walked past her before she could ask me what new horror I'd seen.

Chapter 35

Monica

Brad was home. What a nerve. Sitting in his house on a hill with his manicured garden of native plants and refinished wood porch. He'd been sorry he hadn't gotten close to me sooner? Well, let's just see how he felt about meeting me at all. I banged on his door with both fists, not caring if I woke him from a dead sleep or mid-video.

"Monica," he said when he opened the door in sweatpants and a T-shirt.

"Is he going to die?" I demanded.

"Can you come in?"

"No. Tell me. Is he getting a heart or not?"

"I have no way of knowing that."

"Why is he second on the list?"

He held up his hands as if he was fending off an attack. "What are you talking about?"

"I went to your office and saw the list. He's second. Which means he gets the second heart that comes."

"First of all—"

"Yes, I'm sorry I went into your office. I was looking for you, but to be honest? Not sorry."

He stiffened as if he'd been hit. "It's Sunday. You can call my Doheny office after nine a.m. to make an appointment, but I'm booked until January."

He didn't exactly slam the door, but he closed it. I looked through the leaded glass windows and saw him go out to the backyard. I stood still for a second, maybe ten, before I walked over to my house. Not my house. Not my mother's house. Not the bank's house. J. Declan Drazen's house.

It looked as though I would have to move anyway. If I lost Jonathan, and that looked more likely with every passing hour, I couldn't stay. He'd married me so I'd have the means to avoid his father. The foolish manipulations of a sick man.

I passed my car and walked up to my porch. I didn't go in the house, though I could have used a shower and the love of a toothbrush. I walked the floorboards where we'd stood as he put his pussy-soaked fingers in my mouth. I sat on the swing where he'd left me to protect me from ruination. Looking into the street, I thought only of what I had to do next. Jonathan was talking to Declan, a stressful situation I'd put him in. Then Declan would create an opening for me to murder Paulie Patalano. But what was the use if he was second on the list? If they were shipping that bloody muscle mass to someone else, what was the point of committing murder to save the wrong man?

I could have implored Brad to do something, anything, pull a string or ten, but I'd invaded his privacy. I should have known better. My own heart pounded as I wondered which of my fuckups would kill Jonathan. I played with the rings on my finger, both heavy with commitment to my course and my love.

A curtain moved in Brad's house. He could see me, I knew that much. I also knew I didn't want to be seen. I was thinking evil things. I might as well have been naked and in ready position on the porch. I was thinking evil, desperate thoughts, and I knew they were all over my face. If Paulie's heart went to someone else, at least I'd move Jonathan to the top.

I got in my car as Brad opened his front door, taking off before he could catch me.

Chapter 36

Jonathan

I felt him come into the room. Even through the doctors and nurses running around, poking, squeezing, and barking orders at one another, his presence was a needle at the base of my spine.

"Son," he said.

"What do you want?" I didn't look over. My scenery was the ceiling. If I lived, I would start a fund to put art on hospital ceilings for patients who were too fucked up to turn their head. No one should die looking at crusty paint and vinyl venting.

"I wanted to talk to you. To, ah, how do I say it?"

"Before I die. You want to live in peace."

"Am I that selfish?"

I swallowed. I felt myself slipping into the shattered state of semi-consciousness that so often overtook me. Getting married had required more energy than my body had reserved. The last thing I should be doing was speaking to my father. I guessed if I got to complete one act as Monica's husband, it should be to make her happy. I wished she'd picked something easier. Like swallowing an elephant.

The room quieted, and a nurse whose voice I recognized said, "We're monitoring you closely, Mister Drazen. Is there anything you need?"

"No."

"We'll be in and out." She patted my shoulder before leaving me alone with my father for the first time in ten years.

"Mom's going to be here soon," I said.

"That was what I wanted to bring up."

"Do it quick."

He sat in Monica's chair, and I didn't have the energy to tell him to get the fuck up. "I know what you and Carrie think of me. I know you think

I'm a monster. Maybe, I don't know, maybe I am. I've always known I was different, but I want you to consider this. I've never done anything in a rage. I've never been ruled by what I don't understand. I've never deceived myself into thinking my actions were anything but self-serving. However, I do *want* things. I do *need* things."

I reacted. It was half laugh, half groan. I was so focused on staying together I thought nothing showed on my face. But everything must have been there. Disdain. Disbelief. Disgust.

"You don't believe me," he said.

"Oh, I believe you."

"In my life, I know I've done everything I could to keep this family together. Nothing is as important to me. When I see it breaking, it...troubles me." Even dad had a safe place, apparently.

I knew I smiled at the thought, but I felt out of myself. "And me here reminds you of how you fucked it all up?"

"Not exactly."

Lettie bustled in, checked my tubes. "You have visitors. Do you want to see them?"

"Five minutes."

She took her time, tapping into a computer, taking notes. When a man came in—doctor or nurse, I couldn't tell—they spoke briefly in medicalese, the one language I didn't know. They left soon after.

"You're close to the end, you know," dad said.

"See you in hell." I was being obstructive because it was easy.

"You're making this hard for me."

"Just tell me what you want."

I heard him shift, a flash of movement from the corner of my eye. "I want your mother. She's entrenched in her position. She can't forget the past. I need what's left of this family to work before...well, before."

"Your philandering isn't her fault."

"I need you to talk to her. She won't ignore your request."

I wanted something from him, something big, but I had nothing to threaten him with. I had nothing to ensure he'd keep his promises. What was I supposed to do? Plead? I was already flat on my back. "Stay away from my wife."

"I don't know what you mean."

"Sell that house. Hello and good-bye. That's it." I couldn't go into longer explanations of all the things I didn't want him to do. Touch her. Tell her jokes. Communicate with her unsupervised. Entangle her business. Go to her second wedding. Breathe her air. Exist on her planet. "Promise it." I felt the futility of my demand. What would I do? Hold my pinkie out for a good twist or make him swear on a stack of Bibles? What was the devil's promise worth without a blood guarantee?

"You'll speak to your mother?"

"Yes."

"If you convince her, you have a deal."

"If not?" I asked.

"Then not. I'm sorry. My promise is contingent on the actions of a third party."

"I despise you."

"What if I told you I loved you?"

"You don't have the capacity." I may have said that or something else. The space around me fell into a dream of disembodied voices and floating lights. Just a touch of pain kept me from sleep.

Chapter 37

Monica

I waited in the cafeteria alone. I wrote a little, some verses about murder that could probably be used against me in court, with the judge unmoved toward leniency by the fact that they were atrocious, puerile, on-the-nose.

Whatever was going on, it was taking too long. I went up to Jonathan's floor and found Deirdre staring at a magazine that couldn't have been of interest to her. Sheila was pacing as if she wanted to carve a ditch in the floor. His mother stood, as usual, next to the chair closest to the hall leading to his room. She was the closest to the elevator, so she caught me first. I thought of something I hadn't before. She was my mother in-law. I wasn't calling her mom. No way.

"Hi, Eileen."

She smiled a smile so fake I could have bought it at Nordstrom's on the sale rack. "Monica. I hear congratulations are in order." She indicated my left hand with its borrowed engagement ring and jury-rigged wedding band.

"Thanks. How is he?"

Her face darkened. "They're constantly in there..." Her eyes got wet. The coldness of her expression had hidden the fact that she was breaking apart. She cleared her throat and straightened her neck. "A heart will come. I know it. I can feel it."

"I can too."

Her hand slipped into mine, and I squeezed it. All our bullshit fell away for a second. He was her son. We loved the same person. She wouldn't be easy to deal with, but we were bound by him whether we liked it or not. Then she smiled a couture smile; it was even kind of warmish, as if something had happened between us that had meaning to her.

I promised myself to never again forget that her goal was to protect him. That was worth something. I gave her hand a squeeze and sat next to

Deirdre. "Hi."

"Hi," she replied. "You got married last night."

"Yeah."

She nodded.

"I would have married him anyway, you know."

She flipped through her magazine. "I do."

"I think your mother's pissed about it."

"There wasn't a pre-nup. Jonathan doesn't believe in them. Neither do I."

"Ah, I hadn't thought about that."

She shrugged, still mindlessly going through the magazine. "Neither does God."

I'd never engaged Deirdre for such a non-antagonistic string of sentences, but that was all I was getting from her. She settled on an article and, for all intents and purposes, read it. I cupped my tea and gave the television my attention.

It was set too low to hear, but the talking head with perfect hair had a floating box next to him. In it was Paulie Patalano—mob boss, philanthropist, and murderer—drinking wine in a picture captured in happier days. The ticker described him as brain dead, as if I needed the reminder, and placed him in an unknown location. The picture flipped to three mug shots. I recognized one face, the brown-eyed man who had come in with Theresa. Even in the mug shot, he was handsome, angry, with a knowing grin that frightened me.

My newly minted mother-in-law didn't see the television. Her gaze stayed in the middle distance. Sheila was on the phone threatening someone, and Deirdre was into her magazine. Declan was either seeing Jonathan or making arrangements for me to kill someone. I'd need to be ready. It was time for me to see Paulie Patalano in his undisclosed location.

I excused myself and took the elevator to the second floor. I scoped out the stairwell, wondering if I should take it next time. Then more complications presented themselves. First being, how would I find him? How would I do it once I got there? How could I be sure Declan's job was done? Who did I think I was?

In pacing and beating the hell out of myself, I rounded a few corners, trying to look for something I'd never defined. I only found ignorance and a lack of expertise in the simple skill of murder. I had a scattered entry plan and a slight hope I'd only get caught when it was too late to do anything but harvest Patalano's organs. After that, I'd just confess and let Jonathan's family talk him into annulling our marriage. But he'd be alive. I could deal with the rest if he lived.

The squawk of a police radio made me look up before I crashed into the uniformed cop. He was in his thirties and seemed to take up more space than humanly possible. A female counterpart stood nearby.

"Staff only," he said, blocking my way to the narrow hall.

"Uh, okay?" I peered past him. The hall looked like every other one except for the lack of flitting staff and the presence of three old Italian women in black. That was the hall. I made note of the location and walked away.

I knew Brad had said he'd be in his Doheny office, but I checked anyway. He was just my neighbor and he meant nothing to me, but I'd stepped on him in a way guaranteed to offend him. I didn't want to leave things like that. He was on his way out the door, clipboard in hand. He slowed when he saw me, which I took as a good sign.

"I know you're busy," I said. "I just wanted to apologize."

He kept walking. "I want to explain how serious what you did is, but I have a meeting."

"I know. I have reasons but not excuses."

He pulled me to the side, out of the hall traffic. "I only have a second. I don't want to make you feel better because I'm still pissed off. But first of all, the list doesn't work the way you think. Geography is important. The state of the patient. The gender. It's not like a line for coffee. But second, you're not getting away with it. When this is over, you're sitting down with me and I'm explaining to you the ten ways you fucked up." He was taller than me and used to being in charge. He had the arrogance of a cardiologist and the authority of a man not called by his first name. But when he looked at me, I knew he wasn't half as pissed as his words let on.

"All right."

"Over dinner." He must have seen me turn to ice. "Platonic. If you knew me better, this wouldn't have happened. That's all I want."

"I guess I owe you."

"You do." He walked away. Had he just asked me out? Yes and no. Jonathan wouldn't be thrilled, but Brad didn't expect Jonathan to be around, did he?

Chapter 38

Monica

I had to see him once again before I did it and they dragged me away. I just had to put my fingers on his lips before I faced what I had to face. I wouldn't tell him what I was doing because he'd be an accessory if he didn't stop me and suicidal if he did. I would stand with him clean, as his mate, if even for an hour.

I got out of the elevator on Jonathan's floor and made a right instead of a left to check the placement of the stairwell closest to Patalano's room. I stopped at the turn as if a brick wall was in my way.

Margie and Will Santon stood in a corner, too close for friendship, too far for intimacy. Their hands were up, Margie pointing and accusing, Will in supplication. Their words were inaudible, but their faces shouted rage, hurt, and frustration. I'd have to check the placement of the stairs on the little map by the elevator because I couldn't just stroll past them. I turned and walked away.

I got two steps before I felt a hand on my arm. Margie slowed me down. She looked drawn and upset. Though I didn't know her well, I was sure she didn't want me to ask her what was going on with Will.

"I was just—" I started to explain exactly nothing and was grateful for her interruption.

"Forget it."

"Where have you been?"

She said, "This family's a full-time fucking job. Congratulations, by the way. Well done. One less pre-nup to argue over."

"It didn't even occur to me."

"Him either, I'm sure. But I want to tell you, if he doesn't make it through tonight, I have your back. I'll do what my brother wanted."

"He's not dead yet."

She grabbed my shoulders and put her eyes square with mine as if she wanted to tell me something, something critical and painful. Instead, she threw her arms around me and held me so tightly I thought my ribs would break.

"I envy you," she said. "You know that?"

"If something goes bad, like if I do something wrong, would you represent me? No matter what?"

She pushed me away, holding me by the shoulders. "What are you talking about?"

"Stuff. Life. Say yes."

"Fine." I saw Will out of the corner of my eye. Her gaze flicked to him then back to me. "Go see him. I'll be there in a minute."

Chapter 39
Monica

There were doctors and nurses everywhere. Clean white sheets and sage scrubs. Trays of uneaten food and plastic detritus in soothing, meaningless colors. The lights were pinpoint and dull as if that would help him sleep with all the human traffic in the room. The doctor wasn't much older than I was, but I knew her from the way she asked questions instead of answered them.

"Hi," I said.

"You're the wife?"

The title still hit me like a bag of flour. "Yeah. I'd like… I don't know. Time. A little."

"You got it."

She hustled everyone out, and it was just me and him. He looked as if someone had painted him white. If I thought it was hard to see him after his disastrous operation, well, that was worse. That night came down to me accepting the situation for what it was or me living in a fucking illusion.

"Good evening, sir," I said.

"Get over here." His voice was no better than a whisper breaking through a stone wall. It took too much effort, as if he carried me uphill.

I put my elbows on either side of his head and touched my nose to his. "Jonathan, I—"

"If you have never seen beauty in a moment of suffering—"

"Oh, I remember how that goes. Schiller was the poet. I looked it up."

"I always thought it was the object's suffering. But I think it was the viewer's, now. I think seeing you, I've seen beauty for the first time."

"You've made me so happy. I wanted to tell you that."

"I played with you in the beginning. I wasted too much time lying to you."

"That's over now."

"Actually..." He paused, and I knew why.

"You're kidding," I said.

"The night of the Eclipse show, when I went to Jessica's—"

"La la la, I don't hear you."

"There was more than kissing."

I let my neck release the weight of my head. My forehead dropped to his shoulder. "Go ahead."

"Second base."

From the way he stroked my arm and nuzzled my hair, he must have thought my shaking shoulders and hitched breaths were signs that I was crying. But when I picked my head back up and he saw that I was laughing, he smiled.

"So it's okay?" he asked.

"Yes, it's okay. Is there anything else? I mean, seriously. Something that matters?"

"No. But my brain's not working well. So something might come up later." I put my cheek to his because he spoke about later as if it would happen. He felt cold already. "You never told me about our wedding night. I carry you into our house over my shoulder."

I bite my lip. He doesn't want sad. He wants to have a life in his mind. I could give that to him. "I'm laughing because Lil can see us, and the whole caveman thing is hilarious. I know you have something planned, but I have no idea what. The house is on a hill in Beechwood Canyon. Can we do Beechwood Canyon?"

"For the sake of this conversation."

"It's a modernist masterpiece in the hills with walls of windows looking over the city. You close the door and carry me through the dark house out to the backyard. It's lit with tea lights, and the pool has lights in it. Everything shimmers like it's under water. You get me to my feet, and say, 'Take your hair down.'

"I raise my arms to pull a hundred pins and braids out of my hair. My arms are out of the way, and you use the opening to kiss my cheek, my neck. Your hands follow, landing on my collarbone. You drag your thumb across it and down. You find the zipper to my wedding dress on the side and pull it. I'm still not done with my hair. I admit I'm going super slow, but it's falling out of its arrangement. You pull the dress down until it pools at my feet. Your hands find the edges of my underwear. It's all straps and rings. My hair falls totally. You step back and look at me. I feel beautiful. You've made me feel like that all day, looking at me like that in your black tux. I say, 'What do you want, sir?' And you say—"

"I say this," he interrupted. Even with his rasp of a voice, I stopped. "I say, 'Tomorrow I'm going to destroy you. I'm going to mark your body and ruin your mind. By noon, you won't know whether to laugh or cry. But tonight? Tonight, I will revere you. I will build an altar of myself. I will frame you in stars.'"

"God, you make me crazy when you talk like that."

"There's a blanket on the grass. I lead you to it. You lie down."

"The night is clear. The stars are out."

"My lips on your body trace the story of my love."

My eyelashes fluttered on his cheek. "I try to touch you, but you won't let me. God, you're still in that tuxedo."

"I took it off."

"When?"

"When I say, goddess."

I sighed, going with him. "You're perfect. Shaped for me."

He swallowed thickly. "I kiss your ankles. Pull your legs apart. I draw a map to your sex with my tongue. I feel overtaken. In my guts, I need to yank you, pound you with my dick, make you scream and beg. But I hold back. I kiss behind your knees. I control myself for you."

"I want you. You're all I can think about."

"I'm losing steam."

His eyes filled my vision, red rims and pale skin. He was soaked in exhaustion, but he needed me to create the story for him, for us. I took a deep breath and kissed his cheek, letting my lips linger on him. "Your lips inside my thighs. Your tongue finding its way to me. You kiss my clit. You finger my nipples. You're touching me just enough to drive me crazy. Your mouth works between my legs, sucking and twitching. I arch my back. I'm so close when you stop, and you know it too. You pull me to you. We kiss. I taste my pussy on you."

"Wait."

"What?"

"I turn you around. We're both on our knees. Your back is against me. I push you up, spread you. I put my dick in you, and you push down."

"You're so hard, and I'm so wet. It's so easy isn't it? Wasn't it always so easy for you to put your cock in me? Like you were meant to be there."

"I pull your head back until you're looking at the sky. I hold your face up. My hand is on your throat."

"Your other hand slips between my legs. You touch where we're joined."

"I look at the stars with you."

"I move with you. I'm safe under the sky. I feel you everywhere on me. I'm filled with you. I tell you I'm coming."

"I say, 'yes.'"

We stayed silent for a minute, deeply joined as if he were inside me, expanding together, into each other, fully unified, merged, consciousness where our bodies should have been.

"I love you," I whispered.

"Please stay with me."

I didn't answer for a long time. I kept my face buried in his neck and listened to his breathing. At some point, I would have to leave and meet with Declan. If not to get the whens and wherefores, then to kick his ass for not holding up his end of the deal. "Your family's going to want to see you."

"You ever want sisters?" he asked.

"Always."

"You're welcome."

I laughed. He smiled. "They're outside. I'm going to take care of some business and come back, okay?"

"Stay."

I kissed his cheek. It felt warmer than it did before our pretend wedding night, and I lingered there. "I'll be back."

"Stay."

"I can't. I promise—"

"Stay."

I backed up and let his hand slip from mine.

Chapter 40

Monica

When I walked out, I must have been a sight. The bright hall lights hurt my eyes, and my hair was a rat's nest pressed in the shape of Jonathan's fingers.

Eileen approached. "How is he?"

I didn't say anything. Doctors would report facts to her. All I could say was something like, "He can barely tell me how he's going to fuck me because he's dying." But that wouldn't be helpful, least of all to me. Eileen passed me, then Sheila, then Margie and Deirdre. Leanne in Asia. Carrie far away. Theresa in some kind of trouble. Fiona, entourage-free for once, scuttled down the hall and blew past me.

Declan drew up the rear and whispered in my ear, "Fifteen minutes to a fire drill on the second floor. They don't move brain dead patients for drills. He'll be alone. Staff's been arranged. Cops are a wild card. Good luck." He winked at me with real élan, as if the situation was just delicious. As much as I'd doubted Jonathan's fear and hatred of his father, in that moment, I knew it wasn't completely unfounded.

Chapter 41

Monica

I had fifteen minutes.

I felt far away, my body a borrowed suit, my mind a blunt instrument, my soul in a room full of family curled up next to a dying man. Fifteen minutes to kill. I couldn't sit still. I went to the vending machines and stared at cheerful paper packets of synthetics, crisp under the unappetizing blue light. At a refrigerator-sized box of cola containers, eleven buttons all yielding the same drink, I felt like an alien standing in front of something new and unknown. People about to commit murder in movies seemed so sharp and aware. They could kick and punch with lightning reflexes. I didn't feel like that at all. I felt more as if I was walking under water.

Ten minutes.

More than anything, I wanted to rest. The thought of finding a waiting room and falling asleep on a couch seemed appealing. I'd sleep through my opportunity, and none of it would be my fault. Jonathan would die tomorrow or the next day, but I'd be okay. I'd go to work on Tuesday, and go on like I had before. Except for never touching him again, or hearing his voice, or kneeling before him like the slave I was. All the other chunks of my life would be the same.

Ultimately, I was being selfish. I wanted him to live for my sake. Because knowing he was there soothed me. Because I didn't truly believe I had any control over myself or my life if he wasn't there. Because without him, things were *wrong*. The wrongness was my perception. The world would be fine without him. Really. He wasn't Mother Theresa.

Five minutes.

Are you talking yourself out of this?

Calm yet somehow panicked, like a wheel moving so fast it appeared to be still, I went up the stairs. I knew where I had to go physically, but mentally, I felt as if I'd painted the floor from door to corner in blood. I pushed open the door with my fist and walked into the second floor. It was after two a.m. Skeleton crew. No visitors. I made eye contact with the cop reading the paper because anything less would make me out to be suspicious before I did this thing. And this thing needed doing.

Three minutes.

I went to the bathroom. The mirrors were streaked with cheap cleaning fluid, and my face looked poorly-wiped, tired, too fucking thin by a lot. I didn't look strong enough to do it. I looked like a wax doll.

One minute.

No. I couldn't do it. I would have to just deal with life without him and everything we could have been to each other. I would have to let him die. I couldn't rescue him. I wasn't strong enough. It wasn't the consequences that would break me but the act itself. I didn't have the spine for brutality. I was a child in over her head. A spineless coward, and an exhausted, hungry, stupid child.

A light flashed, and a squeal cut the air.

I would stay in the bathroom and watch myself fail. When they came to evacuate me for the drill, I'd run out with the crowd in a nice, orderly, single-file line.

I wasn't going to do it.

Chapter 42

Monica

People in movies, apparently, obtain reflexes in moments of stress that the rest of us dream will happen to us. We dream that when we're at the edge of the cliff, we can jump to safety or to rescue, magically stronger and faster than we'd been an hour earlier. We're entertained by the idea that we could be that capable when it's necessary, and our daily incompetence is simply due to the fact that we're not challenged enough.

That never happens, of course, because life doesn't happen on the edges of cliffs. It happens in bathrooms and hallways. It happens when a fire alarm goes off, and all the avoidance slips away like a silk nightgown. For me, it happened by the second whoop of the siren when everything clicked together.

Go time.

Every choice I'd made had led me there. If I denied it, I'd be the walking dead.

Humanity scurrying and shouting. Parts of a machine spinning and thrusting. Patients wheeled down the hall. A nurse demanding I go left, me doing it, then flipping back as soon as she turned away. A security guard shouted to me. I gave him a thumbs up and continued. I grabbed some coat slung over a chair as if I'd turned to retrieve my things, and again, I turned another corner when his attention shifted.

There would be cameras, and they'd see me. I didn't waste my time trying to dodge them. I would get caught, and I would take my lumps. Shame. Prison. A destroyed career.

Patalano's hallway was clear. Declan must have taken care of that. A fire drill was a diversion so obvious that the police would have planned for it. Even the stupidest mobster would have dismissed it, yet they were gone.

I walked into his room. It was dark, and he was alone, lying on his back.

Everything was exactly what I expected, as if I was walking into a familiar place. The whoosh and hum of the machines was drowned out by the siren. The machines were bigger than the ones in Jonathan's room, with more dials and gauges. Patalano's face was hidden by tubes going down his throat and a bandage on his head. His neck was kept stable by a plastic apparatus, and the eyes taped shut.

I waved my hand in front of him. Nothing happened. I don't know what I was checking for or what about that mattered. He was brain dead. His body was a life system for a functioning heart muscle. End of story. I focused on the machines. There had to be a switch or a plug. Right?

There were switches and plugs everywhere and nowhere. All the wires ran behind a two-ton apparatus and disappeared. Fuck. Why did I think it would be simple? I flipped any switch I could get my hand on. Though the thing whined, I had no way to tell if what I was doing was having the necessary effect.

"That does absolutely nothing," came a voice behind me. I recognized it immediately. Jessica.

"Get out," I said.

In two steps, she was at the machines, flipping everything back to the way it was. "You don't move a girl in a vegetative state and care for her for ten years without learning something."

"Get out!" I shouted.

"Listen," she shouted back. Our voices were covered by the fire alarm, but for how much longer? "Find his catheter."

I froze for a second, battling everything I believed about Jessica and analyzing what I saw in front of me. She was trying to help me. Was it love? Or was she saving the goose and the golden eggs? Did it matter? I found the tube coming from the center of the bed and ending in a sealed bag under it.

She saw me look at it. "Put a kink in it. It'll back up, and he'll die of septic shock in an hour."

A few drops of yellow liquid flowed through the tube. Jessica put her hand on my arm. She wasn't going to do it. It was all me.

He loved me because he thought I was *good*. Would he love me if I ruined myself for him?

The fire alarm stopped. The silence was overwhelming. I heard the forced breaths, and if I listened closely, I heard the fluid running through the catheter and the beating of a superfluous heart.

"Do it," Jessica whispered.

Do it and risk my own life. Do it, recognizing that Jonathan hadn't done it to Rachel because he must have believed something bigger, deeper, more spiritual lived in our bodies. Do it, and lose Jonathan even if he lived.

With a bend of my knee and a twist of my wrist, I kinked that thing, and the fluid running through it stopped.

"Run," Jessica said and was gone.

I became aware of voices, the squeak of gurneys, the rustle of human activity. I backed out of the room, watching that tube fill up. In my ignorance, I hadn't silenced my phone. When the *bloop* of a message came in, I jumped to turn the thing off. When I did, I saw it was from Brad.

—*We have a heart. Coming from Ojai. One hour.*—

Like a kid diving for the piñata candy, I went for that kinked catheter and smoothed it until the liquid flowed. I ran out as though I was coming back from a fire drill, slapped open the stairwell door, which was packed with people coming back from the drill, and backed into a corner, breathing in gasps as if my soul had been saved at a minute's notice. I waved away anyone who looked concerned. I just needed a moment to collect myself. Breathe. That was the scariest thing I had ever done.

"Ma'am?" Two police officers, the woman and man I'd seen outside Patalano's hall, approached me.

"Yes?" I answered.

"Can you come with us?" the lady cop asked.

My heart sank. They'd come for me. Despite unkinking the catheter, I'd tried it. Attempted murder. Someone had seen me and pointed me out. When they unraveled everything, they'd see my prints all over the place. The video. My seemingly meaningless appearance in the hall the previous night. Of course.

I was finished.

Chapter 43

Jonathan

I heard a fire alarm, but apparently it was on a lower floor. Nothing to panic about. My family laughed with relief, even my father, who I believed didn't actually understand levity. I stayed still and silent because I didn't have the wherewithal to do anything else. A room crowded with people who loved me, and I'd never felt so alone. I wanted Monica to come back. I felt childish wanting her so badly, but I felt scraped down to a nub without habit or discipline, no expectations or social cues. Just the core wants and revulsions unfiltered by a personality built up by half a lifetime's worth of experiences.

I was scared to die.

My body was uncomfortable.

I wanted Monica.

Past those three overwhelming sensations, I had only sensory inputs and petty feelings. Even the slight excitement that followed the end of the fire drill didn't move me. There was some happy news amongst my family, like an unlikely Dodger win or an upcoming wedding. People scurried in wearing sage green and pink, shouting orders. My mother came to me, smiling, and kissed my cheek. She stroked it until Dr. Emerson, the silver-haired one who came in and out of my room seventeen times a day, pulled her away. Her face was replaced with his.

"We have a heart. It's a match. We're prepping you for surgery."

They handled my body like a jacket they were mending, and I felt humiliated and shut down but hopeful.

"Monica." I choked the word out to a nurse I didn't recognize. She looked up and past me to someone I couldn't see. There was a conversation I couldn't make out.

She said to me in a voice designed for clarity, "We'll let her know."

"Where is she?"

"We don't know. Just keep still now." She lifted my head and strung something around my neck. It was happening too fast. I'd already let Monica walk out of the room. I'd let it happen because I was weak, and now I'd lost control of the situation entirely. That couldn't happen. They couldn't wheel me away and cut me open again without me seeing her. They'd done it last time, and look what happened.

"No!" I swung my arm. It must have been truly pathetic because they just strapped it down as easily as if I was made of bone and rag. I said her name to myself over and over, but she didn't appear.

Chapter 44

Monica

I tried not to fidget even after they took my phone.

I was raised to think cops believed fidgeting meant lying. I wasn't lying much. I wasn't with the mob or associated with any kind of underground business, which was what they kept implying. I didn't know anyone they asked about. I was just me. One of the thousands of tall, skinny, struggling artists in that intestinal tract of a city.

"I wanted to look at him," I said. The guy cop tip-tapped into a laptop, and the lady cop leaned her elbows on the table. The break room stank of stale coffee, non-dairy creamer, and sugar glaze.

"Why?" she asked.

"Because my husband's up on four waiting for a heart transplant. This guy's brain dead with this nice heart, and I just wanted to say a prayer that he died. I know that makes me a bad person." I left it there. That was about as much lying as I thought I could get away with. I could have told the truth, but they weren't looking for someone who'd screwed with his catheter. Their questions told me they were looking for a true assassin.

"That your ring?" she asked.

I held out my hand. "The diamond is his sister's."

"The other one's unusual."

"Quickie marriage to a dying man who I'd really like to see."

"Wait outside, please." They led me to a row of chairs they'd set up for people they were questioning. A stocky guy with black hair went in next. Fuck, how long could it take? I couldn't stop fidgeting. After twenty minutes, I looked at the clock.

Ten minutes to three a.m. Did the morning count? I waited for ten minutes, hands still, suddenly not fidgety at all. When the second and minute hands hit the twelve, I closed my eyes and put my fingertips to my lips. I don't know how long I held them there. They pressed my skin until the lady cop came out and handed me my phone and ID.

"You can go."

I ran like hell.

Chapter 45

Jonathan

It was bright. The voices around me spoke like robots to each other and with fake kindness to me. They narrated what they were doing, but all I knew was I was strapped to a gurney, staring at the ceiling, with no way to see what was happening around me.

"Okay," said a man somewhere behind me. "I'm Doctor Chen. How are we doing today?"

"Ask yourself half the answer."

"Right. Okay. I'm going to put this mask over your face. You need to just breathe and count backwards from ten."

"Wait." He bent over to look at me. Asian guy. Mid thirties. Cap. Hissing gas mask in his gloved hand. "What time is it?"

"Uhm..." He seemed put-upon by the question. "Three."

"Exactly three?"

"One minute til." He started to lower the mask again.

"Wait." I looked around the room as far as my position would let me. Five people stood around me wearing the light blue uniform of doctors and nurses, hands up with their palms facing toward their shoulders. More scuttled in the background. I didn't think I could be loud enough to be heard over the ambient noise. "Unstrap me. One hand."

Dr. Chen cleared his throat and exchanged some silent communication with the other doctors. "Mister Drazen—"

"Please."

"You shouldn't be moving now—"

"Please!" The plea came louder than I thought I was capable of.

Dead silence followed. The clock ticked, and though I couldn't hear or see it, I was aware of it in the beating of my fucked up heart. I had maybe thirty-five seconds.

"Mister Drazen," said Dr. Emerson, "you need to calm down."

"I'll calm down. Just do it. Please. Half a minute."

I couldn't see his face past the mask, but his eyes stilled. He glanced at an instrument before turning back to me. "No flailing."

"No. No flailing."

He nodded to someone, and I felt movement at my left wrist. I didn't realize how tense I was until they let it go. Overwhelming gratitude flooded me, and a helix of fear unwound from my torso, though my limbs. When it reached my fingertips, I slowly raised my hand.

"Can you tell me when it's exactly three?" I asked Dr. Chen.

He looked at the wall clock, and I noticed the rest of them standing, in silence, all looking in the same direction. Chen counted down. "In four, three, two..."

I put my fingertips to my lips.

Chapter 46

Monica

I couldn't sit in that room anymore. I was used to dealing with pain and worry by myself; I wasn't accustomed to group stress. When Dad died, Mom withdrew, aunts and uncles took off, and I basically dealt with it alone. Having sisters who were mine only by dint of a forced union wasn't the dream come true I'd imagined. They had personalities and needs I didn't know how to meet. I didn't know how to ask them for what I needed because what I needed was to be alone.

So I quietly withdrew. Declan wasn't in the cafeteria anymore. He was upstairs with the women, sitting by his wife but not touching her. They spoke sweetly to one another which, all things considered, was an improvement.

I felt hopeful. They did nine of these a year. That was good. It was a lot, apparently. He would walk out of that hospital, and we'd figure out what to do. I walked into the back parking lot, just seeking an open space under the sky, with a spring in my step. I was a little dreamy, hoping he'd want to stay married and move into a house with me. The heart would last ten years, but maybe we could squeeze in another two. Or maybe another one would come and buy us twenty years together. It seemed like forever. I saw Jessica's Mercedes then her, lowering the trunk lid. She saw me and waved but went for the driver's door. The wave was all I would get. I got to her just as she was pulling out.

"Hey!" I tapped on the window.

She lowered it. "Yes?"

"Thanks." Thanking her for telling me how to kill someone felt ridiculous. "For helping." Still ridiculous. "I got a call on the way out, and I put the tube back the way it was."

She just looked at me as though I was nuts. "He have a heart or not?"

"He's in surgery. Do you want to stay? I mean, not for me, Lord knows. The family? They kinda consider you one of them."

"No, but thank you." The window crawled up, and I stepped back as she pulled out.

I heard the squawk of police radios behind me, shocking me out of my reverie. Close. Coming for me. I turned around and found three uniformed cops running toward me, fists on holsters.

I put up my hands.

A black and white came for me, sirens on. I put my palms on my head and got on my knees. Okay, they knew. I'd tried to kill Paulie Patalano. Fuck. Okay. Okayokayokay. Just submit. Just shut up and let them take you in and call Margie and let her work on it.

The car stopped, and the three cops blew past me, practically knocking me over. I cringed. There was yelling. *Get out of the car.*

I wasn't in a car. Obviously. I took my hands off my head and opened my eyes.

One cop had his gun trained on the driver's seat of Jessica's Mercedes. Another opened the door. More stood behind car doors.

The woman who had guarded Paulie Patalano's hallway stood over me. "Not today, girlie."

"I was just—"

"Save it. Nothing to see here." She shooed me.

I got up and backed away. Walking fast, head down, I navigated a newly formed crowd until I ran into a man who grabbed my biceps.

"What was that about?" Will Santon asked. "You kneeling."

I didn't want to tell him. I wanted what I almost did in that room to disappear forever. "I grew up in the ghetto. That's what you do when the cops run after you." He seemed to accept that and released my arms. "But it was Jessica. What could she have done? My God."

Maybe they thought *she'd* been the one who twisted the catheter then fixed it. Maybe she was going to take an attempted murder rap for me. That made no sense. I had to consider for a moment if I would let her.

"We've been working on this for weeks," he whispered and smiled. "Once we stopped having to follow *you* around."

"It wasn't her," I whispered back.

"Yes, it was," he said with satisfaction all over his face. "She killed Rachel Demarest."

"But..."

"Play with enough tubes, and a someone in that condition's getting pneumonia. Trust me. We've been chasing her for weeks."

I watched as Jessica had her hands cuffed behind her.

Chapter 47

Monica

More waiting. I felt as though I'd spent the past weeks doing nothing but waiting.

The cafeteria was quiet for once. I stared at my tea, trying to absorb Jessica's arrest. That had been Jonathan's plan. It had been what my curiosity had kept him from executing. I seemed so petty now. I looked at my watch, checked my texts for word from Margie, and took out my notebook.

I opened it to the last page, the only one left blank. Much of what I had in the notebook wasn't suitable to be put to music. I had drawings and staff notes, compositions for multiple instruments with no idea if there was even a possibility of matching words.

"Monica." Brad sat across from me with a prepackaged yogurt cup and plastic-wrapped toast.

"Brad." I closed my notebook. "Thank you for that text. It was...it saved my life."

"I'm sure you're exaggerating." He unwrapped his toast. "You're off the hook for dinner, you know. But I hope we can still be friends?"

"Of course. You still need to yell at me for what I did."

"I'll give you an earful." He bit the toast, wrinkled his nose, and went for the yogurt. "What are you doing here?"

"Margie said she'd text me when he got out." I looked at my phone, checking to make sure it was on for the hundredth time.

"How long has it been?"

"Six hours, give or take."

He stirred his yogurt. "That's long."

I took a second to absorb what he said then snapped up my phone and texted Margie.

—*any word?*—

"If she forgot to text me, I'm going to beat her senseless," I said more to myself than Brad.

A text came back.

> —*Dr came out an hour ago. Issues with*
> *the aortic valve. Bad—*

"Fuck." I didn't say good-bye to Brad.

Chapter 48

Monica

That fucking waiting room, the same as every other I'd seen when they wheeled him from unit to unit. As I exited the elevator, I realized what a home they had become with their greyed colors and worn seats. I knew that no matter what happened, that would likely be the last day I spent in a waiting room worrying about Jonathan.

They were all there, like a red-haired baseball team. Even Fiona had stopped blowing by long enough to hold her mother's hand. They looked at me, eyes shaded from green to blue and back, as I stood by Margie's seat.

"Sorry I didn't text you," she said. "I have other things."

"Don't worry about it. Did you hear about Jessica?"

"Yeah." She waved it away as if she couldn't care less. Her mouth was tight, and she looked drawn and panicked. I never thought I'd see Margie so flustered.

Next to her, Deirdre stood. They all stood and looked at a set of swinging doors. Through the window, I saw an older doctor with silver hair take off his cap and pull down his mask. He turned to another doctor, a woman, and opened the swinging doors. Another followed. An Asian man, snapping off his gloves.

Three of them. One. Two. Three.

They came to us, and the older doctor put his hand on the woman's shoulder in a gesture of…what? Condolences? Professional commiseration? The Asian guy cleared his throat. What was that? Gathering strength?

Hope dropped out of me and flowed down an emotional drain, leaving black despair in its wake. Shit. Three doctors. If one took a blow, the other held the family member down, and the third called security.

Wasn't that how it was? I glanced at Declan. He must have seen the panic on my face because he smiled. Then I became that sister.

The horizon is
A moving target,
A straight line
Defining a round world.

Chapter 49

TWO YEARS LATER

Monica

The crowd wasn't for me that night. There was a relief in that. No pressure. I fluffed my dress and tucked my hair into place, fixing the web of pins and curls. The lights on either side of the mirror washed out my face, but I noticed it was rounder, healthier, happier than even that morning.

The dressing room at the Wiltern Theater wasn't the cleanest I'd been in during the previous months, hardly the most glamorous. The table was new but had the same half-eaten fast food crap that I'd known musicians to eat my whole life. The couch was worn but not ripped, the mirror was clean, and the counter had been wiped and replaced some time in the last decade. But I wasn't there for the dressing room. Darren blew in, sweating and panting.

"What the fuck?" I shouted. "You're in the middle of a show!"

"We're between sets. I had to make sure you were here." He pinched half a dozen French fries and stuffed them in his mouth.

"I'm here. I'll be out to do your encore with you, then I'm outtie."

"Is that what you're wearing?" He pointed at my wedding dress, a sleeveless silk and satin number that hugged me on top and went wild on the bottom, folding in on itself in twenty yards of lace and polish.

"It's dramatic. Everyone knows I got married today. When I get up on that stage—"

"They'll think you're nuts for doing a song between your reception and your honeymoon."

"I am. And I love you. It'll be a show that lives in infamy. Get out," I said.

"Your husband's roaming the halls looking for you."

"Get out!"

He grabbed his burger and kissed my cheek before slipping out. The door didn't click closed, and I rolled my eyes. Boys, even the sweet, bisexual ones, were careless. I took a deep breath and closed my eyes.

My name is Monica. I stand almost six feet tall. I walk like an ocean wave, and I sing like a storm. My voice is a force of its own, and I let it loose like a hurricane. I am safe. I own what I make. I am a creator. I am an artist.

I felt movement behind me and knew from the scent it was my husband. He put his hands on my neck, where every nerve ending in my body was now located, following his touch as he stroked me, like the little magnet shavings under plastic I'd played with as a kid. When the pen moved, the shavings moved, and I arched my neck to feel more of him.

He kissed me at the base of my neck. His lips were full and soft, more than lips; they were the physical manifestation of every taste of longing, every tingle of desire, every scorch of ambition.

"We said we weren't going to do this until we were out of the country," I said.

"Do what, goddess?" he whispered, and I groaned in response, opening my eyes to watch him in the mirror as his mouth caressed my neck and shoulder. "No one knew where you were until I asked for Monica Faulkner."

"You have to give the name change a little time." It was a lame excuse. The fact was I'd been too busy touring, recording, and taking interviews to do simple tasks like changing my name. I could have done it at any time, and he knew it. We'd stayed married in the eyes of the law, but to us and the world, that day was the day. Next came the name change. We finally could call each other husband and wife in public.

"Take your hair down," he said.

I smirked. "I don't think we have time."

"I won't wait."

Demanding Jonathan.

He'd left that operating room a different man. A person doesn't just walk away from a heart transplant and continue as before. He was confused about who he was. He was vulnerable, testy, physically weak, and overly cautious. He was also sexually vanilla, which I tried to accept. I didn't think it would last, but with each passing day, I feared my kinky Jonathan would never return. I stood by him, helping him manage his recovery. I loved him. I hated him. I wanted to beat and kiss him. But I needed him as much as he needed me.

Though we'd agreed our union wasn't genuine because of the circumstances surrounding it, we never suggested our love was anything but real. I renovated my place on the second steepest hill in Los Angeles and rented it out to one of Brad's colleagues. Jonathan bought a house in the Hollywood Hills, and we moved into it. Two years, we said. If we could live together for two years, we'd get married for real. If we couldn't, I was taking my ass back to Echo Park.

I inhaled deeply and put my hands in my hair, lifting my arms out of the way. He slowly unzipped the back of my dress, touching my spine as he went.

Six months after the transplant, Jonathan had roared back like a lion. Almost overnight, he became more aggressive, more demanding, more kinky, and more dominant than he'd ever been. A year later, he got me an engagement ring of my own, a round canary diamond the circumference of a nickel. He'd gotten on one knee all over again, and I realized the reason he'd returned to sexual ferocity was because he was happy.

I unpinned my hair, leaving in the one, pencil-thin braid I'd demanded. As it fell over my back, my dress slipped off.

"You're magnificent," he said, twisting my hair in his fingers. We faced the mirror, him in the blue shirt and tie he'd changed into after the reception, and I bare-breasted with a white lace garter. "All day, I wanted you."

"I am yours."

"Apparently not, *Ms. Faulkner.*" He loosened his tie, snapping it through the collar. "Hands behind your back." He must have seen me glance at the clock. "I have control of the time. Just do what I ask."

"Yes, sir." I cast my eyes down, submitting completely, and put my hands behind my back. Already a rush of fluid surged between my legs.

I would sing at Darren's encore and help his career, but if I had to be late, I would be late. Jonathan wasn't half as busy as me. He'd sold a bunch of assets, more than I could count, and started the Drazen Foundation for Arts Education. It took up about as much time out of his week as a typical DMV job. My co-chair duties took up a few minutes every morning, usually while I was tied to the bed.

My husband clamped my arms together hard enough to make me gasp and wrapped his tie around the elbows. "Look at yourself." He pulled my hair back until my head faced forward. Tying my arms at the elbows had the effect of jutting my tits forward. The nipples were tight and erect. The garter had tiny blue bows at the suspenders, my "something blue" for the occasion.

"What you see is mine. Do we understand each other?"

"Yes, sir."

"I don't think you do." He held me at the bicep. "Step out."

I stepped out of my wedding gown, and he picked me up and carried me to the couch, placing me so my head was over the arm, my arms draped below, and my lower back was on the seat. He opened my legs and unsnapped the crotch of the garter. Then he stood back and observed his handiwork.

I'd really thought he was dead. When those three doctors came out, I wasn't ready for them to say everything was fine. After what I'd been through, bottling it all up to keep enough control to kill Paulie Patalano, I lost it. They really had needed a third doctor to call security. Declan thought he'd played the funniest joke on me. Shitty hobby, as Margie said. When I had explained it to Jonathan, he bought my house from Declan and cut him out all over again. But the transplant put his father back in the good graces of the rest of the family.

With my pussy on display, tits sticking out, and my head facing the ceiling, I saw Jonathan in my peripheral vision. He picked up a cup of fast food-approved carbonated beverage. He peeled the plastic top off, straw and all, and peeked inside.

"Jesus fucking Christ. What's the world coming to?" He shook the cup. I heard the contents swish around. Crushed ice. Bane of my husband's existence. He put it down and picked up something off my makeup table. Then he came to the couch, pants open, dick out, and kneeled between my legs with a tube of lipstick jammed between his teeth like a cigar. He pulled it out, leaving the cap in his teeth. He spit it on the floor like a watermelon seed.

"I'm going to write something down so you remember it, goddess. I know you're busy being a superstar, and you forget." He put the stage-red lipstick to my left breast and dragged it across, then between them, then moved it over the right.

Carefully, he wrote on my rib cage, wearing the lipstick down to nothing. When he was done, he checked his handiwork. I glanced as far as I could to the mirror and saw what was written on me.

Jonathan crouched over me, smiling, then put a hand on the arm of the couch, leaning over me. "Got it?"

"Yes, sir," I whispered.

"That's *your* name." His gaze was meaningful, harking back to old conversations about the last woman to carry that name. Jessica was serving time for a murder she'd tried to pin on Jonathan. I hadn't wanted her name, but he'd convinced me that the name was *his* and now was *ours*.

"I'm sorry, sir." I tilted my hips so that his erection touched my wetness. He moved slightly until the head of his dick touched my opening just enough to make me ache for it.

"Those crowds out there, they don't own you. I do. I marked you with my name. This is who you are now." He moved so his dick rubbed my clit ever so slightly. I jerked to feel more of him. "No, no. Don't make me pull up the extension cords and tie you down tighter. I'm not done explaining." He put his face to my cheek and ran his open mouth along my jaw. "That name is your bond to me. It's your collar."

"I'm sorry, I—"

"Shh. Tell me who you are."

"Mrs. Drazen."

His cock pushed into me, sliding in with no resistance, every surface of my body a firing bed of sensation. All the way, until his body slammed against my clit, moved, and pulled out. "Who are you?"

"Your wife."

He went in again harder. Then again, grunting with the effort. He fucked the breath right out of me then stopped. "What's your name?"

"Oh, Jonathan."

"Nope. That's *my* name."

"Mrs. Drazen."

He slammed into me. "I don't think you believe it."

"My name is—"

He fucked me for real then, putting a hand on either side of my head and taking my cunt repeatedly. He pressed his face to mine, rocking. I was close, so close he could sense it. As was his way, he slowed down, dangling me over an ocean. And I let him, because he owned me.

"Look at me."

I did. His hips stroked me, stretching me, the friction between us a white heat. I was so close. I felt the undertow of my orgasm on my legs. I wanted to get pulled under, I wanted to drown in it, but he was holding me back, a life vest I didn't want.

"What's your name?" he whispered.

I gasped a few times, lost in the sensation between my legs. "I forget."

"Perfect."

He moved once, twice, three times, and I exploded, sucked down by the undertow, pulled out to the never-ending sea. I clenched him as if my body wanted to break him and fit the whole of him inside me.

"Ah, Monica." He came right after, growling my name then grunting as he never had before the surgery. I loved seeing him in those moments, overcome with his own pleasure, his connection to me complete and unbreakable.

"I love you," I said.

"And I you."

"Can you untie me?"

He reached around me and loosened the knot. "First you decide to work on our wedding night, and now you nag me to untie you."

"You're a horrible brute," I said, feigning offense. "I'm staying at my mother's."

He leaned up, and I stood. My new name was smudged on the bottom. Jonathan helped me back into my dress. My hair was a wreck, and my makeup was worn off.

"Shit," I grumbled.

"You look beautiful."

"You have lipstick all over your shirt."

He looked down at himself. "I look like I've been shot."

"By the cheerleading squad."

He laughed. "It's dark on the plane, and I'm going to be naked and fucking most of the way to Paris anyway."

"Really? What if I have a headache?"

"I'll fuck it right out of you." He buttoned his jacket, covering the lipstick stain.

There was a knock at the door. My assistant, Ned, a huge guy there more for my protection than assistance, said, "Ms. Faulkner?"

I pressed my lips between my teeth.

"Who?" asked Jonathan. "No one by that name anymore, Ned."

"Monica?" Ned called. "You're on, whoever you are. Three minutes."

"Coming!" I straightened myself, rubbed mascara from under my eyes, and fingerbrushed the bird's nest on my head as Jonathan watched. It was hopeless. I looked as if someone had just fucked the shit out of me.

"I brought this for you," he said.

He pulled a long chain from his jacket pocket. My lariat. I hadn't worn it because it didn't make sense for a wedding. But as it stretched across his hands, drooping between them, the encrusted berries on either side swinging and sparkling in blue and green, I wanted it around my neck.

"Thank you." I looked at the ceiling, exposing my throat. He reached up, looping it around me not once, but twice. When I looked at him, he pulled the jewels, snapping it tight around my neck.

"You ready?" he asked.

"Yes." I kissed him as if for the first time—his lips the symbol of vulnerability in safety, pain and pleasure, passion and contentment—until Ned banged on the door and called me by my first name.

Jonathan and I smiled as he opened the door. We walked through the cinderblock-lined hallways with Ned in the lead, another security guy in back. Strangers who didn't expect me, techies and runners, roadies and Darren's klatch of fans, all stopped and stared for a second. I smiled at them because they'd made me who I was, and I held my husband's hand behind me.

Darren stood out there with his band, sweating in the spotlights, his sticks twirling in his fingers. It was hot, and I felt the lipstick inside the bodice of my gown reminding me of my name. I went out when called to sing with them.

Each breath, each note, each word, no matter the song, was about one thing only.

Jonathan.

Jonathan.

Jonathan.

THE END

Acknowledgements

It's possible, if you pay attention to such things, that you've noticed a lack of acknowledgements in the back of my books. This goes back to the serial format. I felt that I needed a sense of immediacy. I didn't want to give you the impression I was done. *Tune in next week for another exciting episode...*

Well, it's time, because this song was the product of many voices.

I asked my husband for permission to write erotica, and he said okay. He's never read these books, but honey, if you're reading these now, maybe I'm dead. And if so, I love you. You are my king, my alpha and omega, my silent inspiration. You make me feel beautiful.

My children had nothing to do with these books, but I love them.

Cassie Cox is my editor. Thank her, and her boss Lynn McNamee (who edited *Submit*) for the fact that you can read these at all. They kept me readable without changing my voice. Eva and Jenx did proofreads in record time – thank you. Author gold.

For insight into the art world, thanks to Jenny Hagar. For the "typical" journey from lounge act to superstar, thanks to Nicole Kristal. For medical stuff, thanks to Dr. Alan Nayes, who I have possibly misunderstood repeatedly. Obviously, boo-boos are all mine.

I used a number of betas throughout: Stephanie, Julia, Nikki, Violet, Becs, thank you. My God, what crap I would have released without you.

Speaking of Violet....baby, thanks for sending that long missive about how I should write erotica. I don't know what inspired you to send it, as it was unprompted, but man, if there is a universal will, it was speaking through you.

Thanks to The Book Snob for deepening *Sing* with a simple line in an email.

I've formatted these books myself, mostly, but there have been folks who have helped with parts of the process, especially the print versions which have happened with the aid of Heather and Jolea. Erik has been instrumental in getting the later books to function at all. I swear Erik, I'm gonna learn Sigil. Scout's honor.

Renee Barratt helped with the cover of *Tease*. The hand looked geriatric until she showed me her little trick.

Gary, Anne, and Aria, tolerated a lot of crap from me at work, as I wedged my actual job responsibilities in between promotional tasks. Without that job, I would have died financially and artistically, and for whatever it's worth, it's been the one job I didn't want to actually leave.

We're almost to the end here....

My fellow writers, thank you for sharing your experiences, wisdom, and sympathy. Thanks for tolerating my surprise at my modest success. Thanks for not chewing me out when I deserved it and always staying supportive. The communities of II, The Eclective, and the EWF have been my havens.

The book blogging community is a committed society of book lovers. They work jobs and have families, and yet, they find time to tirelessly support this new wave of literature. I can't mention every blogger who has gifted me with a positive review, but I would be remiss if I didn't mention the women who talked me through tough times, suggested new ways to promote (I'm looking at you, Evil Bloggess), and carried me when I was down. Fifty5cent book blog, Jessy's Book Club, Nikki at Bookaholics, Sinfully Sexy Book Reviews, S&M's Book Obsessions, and Lorie Economos…a glass of wine to you. Or, in the case of Mistress L….here's a Twinkie.

Cafecito Organico/Helio coffee, Curious Palate, Pipers, and of course, Starbucks on Venice Boulevard….thank you.

Christy Wilson set up my Wiki so anyone could register and add to it. Go contribute to it! We need you!

Last.

Some of you have been with me from the beginning. You've waited for each new episode. You've discussed plot turns endlessly. You've distributed bonus scenes at my request.

You experienced this serial as it was intended. You never judged the way I released these because you sensed that this wasn't just a novel that I chopped up. It's a true, structural serial, and you guys have been as much a part of the final product as any of the abovementioned. Thank you so much for just reading and experiencing the story I envisioned, in the way I envisioned it.

Until next time, and there *will be* a next time…farewell.

coda.

The Submission Series
Book Nine

Chapter 1

Jonathan

I brushed my thumb against her nipple, bending it, then I leaned down to suck it. She wove her fingers through my hair. I tasted the shower water on her, the tinge of soap. Steam still fogged the room.

"Jonathan," she whispered, "I'll miss the plane."

"No, you won't."

I drew my tongue down her belly, flat and tight, stopping at the navel bar she still wore for me, then traveled down between her legs. I bent one of her knees and put it over my shoulder, giving my mouth access to her.

"I haven't packed yet," she said, but I knew I had her.

I opened her lips with my thumbs and licked her clit slowly, tip to taint and back again, tasting the fresh, clean skin and clear, rushing fluids.

"Pack fast," I said. She'd be gone for a week. I wanted her before she left.

"I have to pack the Theremin, and it's oh, God." She moaned when I sucked her, hitching her other leg over my shoulder. "Delicate. Jesus, what is with you lately?"

I stood and wiped my mouth with my hand. She sat spread-eagled on the bathroom vanity, wet and ready. She was mine, and I loved her.

"What's with me lately?" I was in my underwear, which I didn't bother taking off as I pulled out my dick. "Maybe I'm bored."

"You could work again."

"I could." I slid in nice and easy.

As I fucked her on the vanity, I had a feeling that something wasn't quite right. Something was missing. She was wet. I was hard. Her tits bounced when I thrust, and there was enough nudity between us to get my dick inside her.

But her arms. I didn't know where they would go next. She moved in unexpected ways. I put my arms around her, holding her together, and I leaned in close to kiss her, dragging my stubble over her cheek and the sensitive part of her neck.

She whispered, "Ouch."

I felt powerful. I'd been fucking her for months with this borrowed thing in my chest, but when she said ouch, I wanted to more than fuck her. I wanted to tear her apart. I lost my shit at the thought of it, coming in her the way I had been since the hospital, without control or intent, just because I was ready.

Monica came a second after I started, and we gripped each other, quivering. The steam had barely cleared from the mirrors when I kissed her shoulder and realized I had a problem in my arms.

• • •

I stretched out in the sun, with my scarred chest to the sky, and felt that thing beating. The July heat baked me, muggy and sticky. I was sharing sweat with a stranger's tissue and grateful to be alive, yet I was in a state of constant bewilderment, thinking, *How the fuck was I pulled from death for this?*

And who was I? I'd eaten and enjoyed blowtorch-spicy food, but suddenly I found it intolerable. I felt a new pull to run that I knew, intuitively, came from the same place. I jogged in the morning, and if Monica was away, I jogged at night. I loved it. I loved the burn in my throat and the fully energized exhaustion when I'd pushed myself too hard and too long. But I'd never wanted to run before. The desire wasn't mine; it belonged to the heart, which had grown in someone else. Was I still wholly me? I pondered it too often and for too long.

"Hey," Monica said, stepping into my sunlight. She wore a pale blue dress and clunky bracelets. "I'm going."

I patted a place for her to sit next to me.

"I can't," she said. "Lil's waiting."

I flipped my sunglasses up so I could look her in the eye, and with that gaze, I let her know I was entitled to a minute of her time. "Goddess."

"I'll call you when I land." She bent to kiss me, and when her lips hit mine, I held her head there an extra few seconds. She smiled and trotted away.

I had a problem. She was going to Caracas for three days to open two shows with some madhouse band, and I wasn't going with her because of doctor's orders. The impulsive side of me wanted to follow her and let the team of highly-paid specialists kiss my ass, but I stayed behind. There was no need to rush. Three days wouldn't change anything.

When I'd met Monica, I'd known what I was. Who I was. I knew what I was made of, and I knew how to get what I wanted. I'd still been in love with my idea of my ex-wife, but my goddess had cured me of that. I'd thought being happy was what had made me demand control in the bedroom, but I was wrong, or at least only partly right. All the soul-searching in the world had led me to a false conclusion.

I'd been dominant because I knew myself. In knowing myself, I had the confidence to bind and hit and hurt, because I'd know when to stop.

When we got home from the hospital, Monica and I eventually made love again. Still, I wasn't myself. I was mostly me and partly someone else. An alien piece of meat had been lodged in me, and I didn't know what it would do. Would it beat right for me or for the person it was meant for? Would it skip a beat at the sight of some strange woman? Would it break over a different past or a lost present? I kept imagining it jumping out of me like a frog from a frying pan, slapping on the kitchen floor with a *splat*, and beating on the tiles while squirting yellow plasma. Once, I dreamed it bounced out of me and landed in the pool to swim with Sheila in a trail of curly red blood. I laughed in my dream, but when I woke up, I ran to the bathroom mirror to make sure I had a scar instead of a hole.

I'd felt like a foreigner in my own skin, dragging around a sack of muscle and bone held together with medicine. Even after the doctor appointments dwindled and life returned to something that looked like normal, I hadn't adjusted to being two people in one body, and my wife knew it. She was drifting away like a bottle bobbing in the surf, tide by tide. She wasn't Jessica. She'd never leave for someone else, but she'd leave with distraction and indifference. At the thought of the lost intimacy, I felt a blade of ice cold rage so thick, I had no room for a reaction or an emotion. My head was clear. The anger had pushed out all the clutter. She was mine to lose, but she was mine.

Chapter 2

Monica

I missed two things.

I missed my freedom, and I missed slavery.

I was caught in a nether region where I couldn't come and go as I pleased, and I didn't feel protected.

I was being unfair, and I knew it. What man could be expected to keep up Jonathan's intensity for any length of time? No human could be a raging lion after having their heart ripped out.

So though we burdened each other with many things, I never burdened him with my longing for my dominant Jonathan. That man was gone, so I loved the man who'd replaced him. He was everything I'd almost lost in that fucking nightmare of a hospital. He was funny and thoughtful, gracious and wise. He was still the best lover I'd ever laid my hands on.

"Hello?" Jonathan's voice was thick with sleep. The sun was just coming up over Caracas, tainting the sky brown.

"I'm coming back early," I said as I walked across the tarmac toward the Gulfstream.

Jacques waved. His copilot for the day took my rolling suitcase and stowed it underneath the plane.

"Really?" Jonathan sounded as awake as if he'd had a gallon of coffee. "I have something for you."

"But I have to go right into the studio," I said. "Jerry wants me to work on 'Forever' for this sampler idea he's—"

"I'm sorry?"

"I'll walk in the door the same time as if I'd stayed here. I just wanted you to know what I'm doing with your plane."

"Well, thank you."

"Don't be mad."

"Goddess," he said, and I heard something in his voice I hadn't heard in half a year. It stopped me on the steps up to the fuselage door.

"Yes?" I was shocked by the small sound of my own voice.

"I don't give a fuck about the plane."

"It'll be fast. I'll be home by lunch."

"Text me where you're going to be."

"Why?"

"What?"

Fuck. I'd promised myself I'd never forget what Jessica had done to him, yet there I was, serial-bailing and giving him attitude about it. "It's the same place as always," I said, backpedalling as I snapped my seat belt. "I'm fine."

"Maybe you are," he said, then his tone changed to sound more pensive. "Maybe you are."

He hung up, and I was left with an oddly shaped emptiness.

Jonathan loved me. I never questioned that. His love was in everything he did. I heard it in his voice and felt it when he fucked me. Even when he took me like a stranger and reveled in hurting me, there was love in his abandon.

I also didn't question his commitment in what he'd thought were the last moments of his life. I was worthy of his love. I'd earned it, and he'd earned mine. We'd earned the easy part and the hard part. Most couples don't face life-and-death tests of their love until they're old and grey, or until they had children in middle school, but he and I had been put through the fire unprepared and come out stronger.

Yet we'd missed the basics, and they weighed on me. I constantly forgot that we loved each other because of the daily misunderstandings and confusions.

Like buying our house, which had been a series of misspoken desires, concessions, and bitter words left unspoken. Like water flowing downhill, it had been chosen via the path of least resistance. I didn't even remember choosing our real estate agent. I just remembered her showing up.

"So," she had said pertly. Her name was Wendy. It suited her. " I understand you want to get moving on this before Mrs. Drazen goes to Paris?"

I sat next to Jonathan on his couch, frozen in shock. "Paris? I didn't say I was going."

"You're going. It's a huge opportunity." He'd turned back to the agent, who wore a decal of a smile. "She's the opening act for—"

"Nobody," I interrupted. "I'm not going. So anyway, no."

Like any real estate agent in Los Angeles, Wendy had been perky, perfect coiffed, and blandly unthreatening. She'd come highly recommended for her discretion, her taste, and her ability to seamlessly manage massive amounts of money.

"What kind of house are you looking for?" she asked.

"Kind of house?" I asked, stalling.

Jonathan had been out of the hospital for a month, and we'd spent it managing a heart transplant. Appointments. Doctors. Medical procedures I didn't understand. Big pills in little boxes. A diet and exercise regimen that made me shudder. And Jonathan himself, my husband, felt shaky and unsure. I woke up most mornings feeling unqualified to live my life.

"Era," Jonathan said impatiently. I heard the rasp in his breath. It was late afternoon, and he needed to rest. "Something modern. Fifties. I'm sick of leaded glass."

"I, uh—"

"Did you have a neighborhood in mind?" Wendy interrupted me, making eye contact with Jonathan.

"The hills," Jonathan said. "Beechwood, maybe."

"Really, I think the ocean—"

"Great. How many bedrooms? Or do you want to go by square feet?"

"Big," Jonathan told her. "This house is cramped."

"Cramped?" I interjected. I thought his house was palatial, but I'd grown up with eleven hundred square feet, and I didn't like being bulldozed.

They both looked at me, and I felt ashamed. Then I felt ashamed for feeling ashamed. I wasn't embarrassed because Jonathan and I disagreed on the style or size of the house; I was embarrassed because we hadn't discussed it.

"Wendy, I'm sorry," I said, standing. "We're obviously not ready to discuss this. Can we get you to come back some other time?"

"Of course!" she'd chirped and was gone in a flutter.

"What was that?" Jonathan asked.

"We weren't ready to meet with someone about this. Not until we can agree on the basics. I didn't…" I drifted a little then came to the truth. "I've never bought a house before. I've never met with an agent. I didn't know what was expected."

He'd looked tired, as usual. He'd always looked tired in those first months, which was why I didn't talk to him about anything important. I'd tried harder after the non-meeting with Wendy. I agreed to stuff and put my foot down on others, and we bought a big fat compromise of a house that I lived in but didn't love.

I hadn't wanted to exhaust him. I thought it was the best way to help him get better. I hadn't had a period in months from the combination of anxiety and Depo-Provera. But when I got sick and thought I might be pregnant, I didn't tell him because I didn't want to start an argument about children. No stress. That was all I wanted.

When he'd gotten back from the hospital, he couldn't really walk. He just didn't have it in him. He had a staff of people and a huge family, so he didn't need me, yet I'd been surprised by how much he did need me. He needed to talk, and in those conversations, he laid out our future like architectural plans, pointing at the lines and angles I needed to see. I rarely disagreed with him. He was prone to frustration with his body and the exhaustion of small tasks, and I was still in a stunned state. I was functional, competent, and emotionally broken. But I'd thought I was handling our situation well. I was the picture of maturity and capability. I even laughed sometimes, when it seemed appropriate.

"Children," he'd said one night, on his back in the bed. The lights were out, and the flat latte color of the Los Angeles night sky lit the room. "When can we start?"

"You mean start having sex again? Your doctor said anytime." I leaned over him, half-sitting. His bandage had just been taken off, and the scar on his chest was still pink.

"Fucking with intention."

"I've never known you to fuck without it."

He smiled and touched my lower lip. "When does that shot wear off?"

My Depo-Provera shots rendered me infertile and nearly menstruation free for two to four months at a time. "Right after Valentine's Day, I guess."

"No more shots."

"Jonathan, I... I think we should talk about that again."

His expression became wary.

I froze, afraid of upsetting him. "I want children. You have to understand it's... this is hard to say." I touched his chest, brushing my fingers over the scar. "Everything seems so precarious."

"You'll stop feeling like that once I can walk more than ten fucking feet. Soon."

"Let's revisit this then. Please. I just need to know you're strong enough to handle running out in the middle of the night for chili chocolate ice cream."

"Who makes that? It sounds disgusting."

"It's delicious."

He pulled me to him, and I laid my head just below his chest. His heart beat in my ear. It sounded perfectly normal, a functioning organ capable of sustaining his body until something else broke. But it wasn't beating with life. It was a ticking clock, and it would stop too soon.

I'd gotten another shot in early February. I reasoned that he didn't need to know. I'd put him off. I couldn't do it much longer, but we were taking it one day, and one white lie, at a time. I'd need the next in June or so, and we could revisit then. Or not.

But it always came up, even when it didn't. When we talked about the house, we needed a bigger room just for the elephant, and after I dismissed Wendy the realtor, the animal only got bigger.

He'd leaned on the arm of the couch and crossed his ankles, the same posture as the first night I'd gone to see him at his office, when I threatened him with a lawsuit. "Whatever we get should be the exact opposite of what I had before you were in my life."

"I think that's reactionary."

"That's a big word that means nothing."

"Don't build us on top of what you did or didn't do before. How's that for a definition?"

Who were we, standing half a room apart with our limbs crossed? How did any of this matter? How had it become important? If he wanted to pass the next ten years in a big modern house overlooking Los Angeles, who was I to say otherwise? Wasn't that a small price to pay to be with him?

"I want you to go to Paris," he said. "You've never been."

"Who's going to watch you if I go? Who will make sure you don't forget to do what you're supposed to?"

"If you want children to take care of, that can be arranged."

"I don't."

"Then you don't need to baby me."

And that had been that. We got a house by default. The style he wanted and the location I wanted, because on paper, it seemed like a compromise. It had been more of a treaty.

Chapter 3

Monica

I ate a lunch of chicken fingers and half a radicchio salad in the engineering room. I shot the shit with Jerry and Deshawn. We talked about promoting the sampler, getting beer thrown at me in Caracas as a sign of respect, the roaches in the hotel, the excellent food. Half an hour later, we were back to work. Executives drifted in and out to listen to me. Eddie even showed up for fifteen minutes.

My phone was facedown on the baby grand piano; its sheen let me know when the glass lit up with a call or text. But I couldn't take a text. We were trying to get the last two words of the song right. *Forever fuck*. It had to sound like a powerful curse but be muddled, and on key, and gravelly and transcendent, all at the same time. My feet hurt, and my brain and eyes were so exhausted, the foam egg-carton pattern on the walls seemed inverted.

I couldn't possibly take a text, even from my husband.

Only when I was done did I check it.

—I want to see you—

The text had come twenty minutes earlier, while I was in the middle of recording "Forever." The song was based on a poem I'd written while Jonathan was in the hospital, and I had been so angry, I imagined myself in an eternal, raging battle with death.

—Where are you?—

Ten minutes later.

—You were supposed to be out two hours ago—

I scrolled through Jonathan's texts. Jerry and the sound team packed up. I was going to have to deal with my husband. I had my career, and he knew what it entailed. He didn't have the right to harass me while I was recording.

I took a deep breath and called him from outside. "Hi." The parking lot behind the studio smelled like sweaty asshole and stale cigarettes.

"You're out?" Jonathan asked.

"Just finished up."

"I have a surprise for you when you get home."

Home. A house on the beach that already had too many painful memories. Medications. Falls. Fights. He'd been sick and pissed. I loved him. I'd never leave him, but some days, I felt as though we were coming apart at the seams.

"The guys are going to dinner. I'm a little hungry," I said. The silence seemed eternal, and though I imagined him staring into space with the phone at his ear, when I heard a car door slam, I knew he hadn't been inactive. "Jonathan, it's—"

"Stay there."

"Not tonight, I—"

"This sounds to me like you're telling me no." The calm, arrogant dominance in his voice was like a slap on the ass, because I hadn't heard it in six months. "For the sake of clarity, goddess, when it comes to me, that's not in your vocabulary. I don't hear it."

I said, "Yes, sir," with all the sarcasm of a spoiled adolescent and immediately regretted it. Luckily, my husband had already hung up.

Chapter 4

Jonathan

This shit stopped tonight.

I parked in the back and went into the building. A couple of doors were ajar, and I could hear the laughter and mumblings of men. I heard her three doors down, her voice humming, piano strings getting hammered one by one, slowly.

I slipped into the engineering room and looked at her through the window.

She sat at the keyboard, scribbling in a notebook, then considering the keys again. Her back was straight, neck as long and white as a swan's, her ebony hair braided and twisted onto the top of her head. A goddess. She'd waited. I didn't know what would have happened with us if she hadn't.

The engineering booth was empty and dark, and I watched her like a movie. I saw her bite a fingernail. Close her eyes. Tap a finger then burst out with a word in one long note. It was *you*. She hit three keys, then three different keys, sang the word again in a different register, and wrote it down.

I felt as if I hadn't seen the length of her neck in months, nor the delicacy of her wrists. I knew every inch of her skin, every curve of her body, yet that day, when she'd said *no* to me, I anticipated the prospect of showing her why that wouldn't wash any longer with no little delight.

I went back into the hall, closing the engineering room door.

Chapter 5

Monica

His scent cut through the dank musk of the studio before the sound of the door closing reached my ears.

"Hi," I said without looking up from my notes. "Can we go meet those guys? Jerry wants to lay out a plan for Wednesday." His fingertips grazed the back of my neck, and I shuddered, closing my eyes halfway.

"No," he whispered.

"I'll meet you at home later if you want."

"Stand up."

I looked up. He stood over me, hand at the back of my neck, face broaching no arguments. I didn't know what my expression said, but my mind went utterly dark for a second. I stood, reaching for my bag. He gently took it and laid it back down. I started to object but didn't get past the first syllable before he had his fingers to my lips.

"Unbutton your shirt," he said.

We gazed deeply at each other for longer than usual, and I knew even before my fingers touched my shirt that he wasn't interested in a standard sweet encounter. He brushed his thumb over my lips, across my jaw, and lodged it under my chin, forcing me to look at the dusty fluorescent lights. I undid my buttons in a businesslike fashion while he spoke.

"I haven't told you this in a long time, so I want to remind you. You are mine. Any time. Any place. Without questions. You get on your knees when I say. You spread your legs when I say. You open your mouth and take whatever I put in it. Do you understand?"

He must have felt me swallow against the heel of his hand. He was back. I didn't know when or how, but this wasn't the sick Jonathan who got pissed at his handful of pills. This wasn't the guy who let me top him, or the man who made love to me fearfully and gently. That man was a good husband.

He was difficult, because he felt as if his body wasn't his own, but a good life mate by any standard.

But for as long as I'd been married, I hadn't felt safe. Until then, staring at the ceiling, unprepared to hear the voice of my king again. My insides vibrated like a piano string, and I shut my eyes tight against tears.

"Yes, sir," I said.

"Pull your pants down."

I worried about the door. Was it open? And the door to the engineering room. Anyone could walk in.

This was a simple matter of trust, which I'd forgotten how to do. *Trust him. You're safe with him.*

I opened my pants and wiggled them down. I wore lace and garters, which felt scratchy and uncomfortable under jeans, but I wore them because I'd promised I would, even if I'd promised a different man. He slipped his finger under the straps. His touch had gone electric, exactly right, like when we first met. I felt it through layers of skin and muscle, down to my bones.

"All the way off."

I stepped out of my pants.

"Why are you crying, goddess?"

"I don't know."

"What's your safe word?"

I blurted a laugh to the ceiling. "Fuck. I forgot."

"Do you want a new one?" He slid his finger under my bra, pushing it up and releasing my breasts. My nipples were hard candies, ready for him.

"Yes, sir."

"Your choice."

"*Invictus.*"

He pinched a nipple and pulled it to the point of delicious pain. "'Out of the night that covers me, black as the pit from pole to pole, I thank whatever gods may be, for my unconquerable soul.'"

"Jonathan..." His name was a prayer.

"Turn around."

I faced the piano, putting my back to him. He slid his hands over my neck and under my shirt collar, pulling the shirt down my arms and drawing his hands over my skin.

"I'm going to ask you something," he said, pulling my long sleeves halfway off. He twisted the sleeves around my arms, wrapping them and tying them tightly at the elbows.

He paused long enough for me to say, "Sir?"

"Are you happy?" he asked.

I heard the distinct clack of his belt buckle. I didn't answer. He slid his belt out of his pants with a *whook*.

"I asked you a question."

"Yes, sir."

"Is that the answer?" He gripped the back of my neck.

"It's confirmation that I heard you."

With a sharp push, he pinned my face to the shiny black piano. "Are you happy?"

"Can you be more specific?"

"Sure."

With a thwack that was as hard as it was unexpected, he slapped my ass with his belt. I screamed.

"Too hard?"

"No, sir."

It was. A fierce burn settled where he'd hit me, and I already wanted more. I wanted him to tear me apart. In the breath's worth of time it took for my body to register pain, I cracked. I didn't want to go to dinner with Jerry and the guys, and I didn't want to go home. I wanted to hurt, and hurt deeply. I wanted to feel pain, and safety, and surrender; to lose myself and my will. I'd forgotten how much I needed that, but like a woman waking from a dreamless sleep, the reality of who I was came back to me. I swore I wouldn't say my safe word until I was near death.

"Behave then, before I gag you." He whacked me again and again.

I grunted but didn't cry out, even when he hit the sensitive area at the backs of my thighs.

"Now"—his breath rasped with effort—"tell me, goddess, are you happy?"

His last stroke was so hard it felt like a blowtorch on my ass. He fisted the hair on the back of my head and brought his face close to mine. "To avoid misunderstandings. Are you *happily married?*"

I swallowed. He put his belt down in front of my face and squeezed my ass. The pain was overwhelming. I could barely see through it, nor could I form words past the gushing arousal between my legs.

"Answer me," he said. "And the truth. Are you happy?"

His face was foggy through my tears, but his voice was clear enough to focus on.

"No," I said. "I'm not."

As much as I broke down into tears and hitched sobs, he seemed unfazed by the news, as if he'd already known. And as if he didn't give a shit about my happiness. He brought his hand over my burning cheeks and laced a finger in the crack, down to my opening.

I was soaked. Dripping. Gushing readiness for him. I wished he'd asked me for the truth after he'd fucked me, because how could he now? I told him I'm miserable and expected a body-ripping, passionate screw? Crazy, magical thinking.

He slipped a finger inside me. I'd fucked him a hundred times in the past six months, but that finger cruelly jamming into me, his palm lying against my scalding ass, was the best thing I'd had in half a year.

"Thank you for telling me the truth," he said. "But you're wet. And crying."

"I'm sorry, sir."

"Poor goddess." He pulled his finger out and slipped it onto the hard nodule of my clit. My eyes shut. My mouth opened. My cunt was awake with anticipation as he continued. "Even in love, you need pain."

"I love you," I whispered.

He drew his hand back and slapped my ass with full force. I bit back a cry.

"Don't talk," he growled. "There's been wholly too much talking between us, and not nearly enough."

I nodded.

He folded the belt in two and said, "Open your mouth." When I did, he put the belt in it. "Bite."

I bit the leather. It was still warm from hitting me. Had he ever been this cruel and hard? Had he ever been this *dominant*? I couldn't remember. I couldn't think.

Then Jonathan put his hands on my hips and let his cock touch where I was wet. I bit the belt as if I wanted to swallow it. He didn't ask for permission to jam his dick into me in one stroke, making me grunt into the tanned skin. He didn't ask if my happiness was required. He just fucked me. He fucked me as if I wasn't even there, slapping himself against my burning ass cheeks, a frame of pain for the pleasure between my legs. He pulled my cheeks apart, stretching them, pain everywhere, and drove into me with everything he had, using me mercilessly. I lost myself in him, in the hurt, in the rising tide of my emotions. I'd told him I was unhappy, and the weight of the misery fell off, leaving an empty place for him to fill with his cock and his searing belt.

I grunted with every thrust. It was coming, the rush of pleasure.

My grunts turned to squeals, and he slowed to barely moving. "I didn't say you could come."

I hadn't had to ask permission for an orgasm in six months. I hadn't even thought of it. He removed the belt.

"I'm sorry, sir," I gasped. "May I come?"

"When?"

"Now?" I paused for a hitched breath. "And later, if it pleases you."

"No." He slowed, letting me feel every inch of him. He opened my cheeks again, right where my legs met my ass.

I was red and sore, getting his whole length. I choked out a half sob, half moan.

"No," he said, slapping my ass. "The answer is still no."

"I don't think I can stop it."

He pulled out. I gasped. As much as I expected him to continue fucking me, I didn't expect what him to quickly guide himself into my asshole and mercilessly push forward.

"No!" I shouted.

He yanked my head back by the hair. "What?"

I couldn't repeat it. Safe word or no, he'd stop, and I knew, more than anything, that I didn't want him to stop. "Nothing. Please, go on."

He pushed the rest of his cock into my ass without preamble.

My soft weeping turned into face-soaking sobs. "God, oh God, it hurts."

"Pain is the point, isn't it?"

"Yes, sir."

"Your ass is mine, whether I warn you or not. Do you understand?"

"Yes."

He yanked my hair again, pulling back until I faced him. "Yes, what?"

"Yes, sir."

The first few strokes were murder. I felt torn apart, ripped from the inside. We'd done some gentle, well-lubricated anal in the past few months, but not like this. Not as a beating.

"You've been a bitch, goddess. That's over. From now on, you step when I say walk. You eat when I feed you. You come when I allow it. If I so much as look at your knees, you get on them and open your fucking mouth."

I grunted. He reached around me and put his palm on my throat. He pulled me back, and though I felt as though I was falling, I trusted him and put weight on my aching legs, shifting backward. He sat on the piano bench, and with my back to his front and his cock in my ass, I sat into him.

"Spread your legs." Not giving me a chance to obey, he yanked my legs apart, squeezing my ass cheeks together and tightening me around his cock. "All the way. I want your cunt out."

I bit back a cry of pain. I spread my knees, on tiptoes to the floor, fighting for balance. My elbows were still tied behind my back, and when it looked as if I'd fall, he pulled me upright.

"Reach back," he said. "Spread those gorgeous cheeks apart."

I did, fighting the constraints of my knotted shirt, cursing the stinging skin on my ass as much as I blessed it.

"Now come down, all the way. All the way. That's it. Bury me in you." He reached around me and slipped his middle finger in my cunt, gathering wetness, and dragged it to my clit. "You're not coming until I say. You're going to hold back by concentrating on one thing and one thing only."

"What, sir?" I groaned, the pleasure in my clit pushing against the pain behind it.

"Pleasing me. So fuck. And fuck hard. Go."

I moved up his length and back down, his shaft sliding against my anus, friction hot against the dry muscle.

"Faster."

His cock beat my insides, shredded me, while his fingers took my cunt three at a time. The heel of his hand kept a constant pressure on my clit.

"Come on, goddess. I'm not pleased."

I pulled my cheeks wider and slammed down on him harder, my knees aching, my arms on fire, and my ass beyond pain. Yet the pleasure between my legs grew, pressing against the agony and winning.

"That's good," he growled. "Very good."

"Thank you." I gasped, relieved, relaxed now because he was content.

I heard his breaths getting shorter. I was close, but I didn't care. I wanted him to have what he wanted. I wanted him to be satisfied. I beat down on his cock, mindless of what I was doing to myself.

"I'm going to come," he said.

"Thank you," I squeaked, more tears streaming.

"Come with me."

"Yes. Oh, yes."

He grunted, but it was more than a grunt. In the second before I lost myself in pleasure, I noted how vocal he was. More than ever. He released, truly, fully, losing control, pulling my hair until I thought he'd tear it out. I was washed away in the pleasure of his hand on my clit, the torture in my ass as my orgasm clenched it around his cock in an undulating rhythm. I came forever, lost in it, in him, his satisfaction, in the pain. I was gone, my identity washed away in complete submission to his pleasure and his will; without ambition or desire of my own, I was simply enslaved, caged, collared. Nothing. No one. Not a feeling of dissatisfaction in my belly, only humility and a feeling of complete, overwhelming gratitude.

"Goddess?" he whispered when I stopped twitching.

I tried to answer, but I was blubbering. I took a few breaths to calm down. "Yes, sir?"

"Are you okay?"

"Thank you."

He untied me. I put my aching arms on my knees, and he pushed me gently forward, his dick slipping out of my ass. I sucked in a breath.

He pulled me into his lap and kissed the tears running down my cheeks. I held him and wept fully. The emotional release poured out of me as he rubbed my back and kissed my face and neck. My awareness of the world around me—my body, the chair, the room, the building, the time of day— was brought about by the softness of his lips and the way he whispered, "Goddess, goddess, goddess."

"I haven't been what you need," he said softly.

"You couldn't be. I understand."

"That's over now."

"Thank you."

He put his hands on my cheeks and brushed my lashes with his thumbs. I let my eyes flutter closed.

"You can't leave me until I destroy you," he said.

"If you destroy me, I'll never leave."

"Regularly." He took out a monogrammed hankie and held it up. "Blow."

I blew my nose. He pinched and wiped for me, as if I were a child. He kissed my lips, owning them with tenderness and confidence. I let his tongue into my mouth, its soothing warmth exploring me as if for the first time. The tenderness with which he kissed me was in such contrast to the beating I'd just received that I broke down in tears again. He held me and rocked me in the soundproof studio for what seemed like hours, saying sweet things in my ear. I felt so good, so calm, so loved.

"You'd better cancel dinner," he said. "You're going to need some serious aftercare."

"You think the guys would notice if I ate standing up?"

"Come home, and I'll feed you in bed."

"Yes, Jonathan. Yes to everything."

"And you shall have everything."

Chapter 6

Monica

Sometimes, I felt as though I wasn't in love with a man. Sometimes when things were tense, or we fought, or we made love, or I was away for too long or in the house for too many weeks, or even when he kissed me on the back patio, I stopped seeing him as a man. I stopped seeing him as even human. I felt as though I'd married a time bomb.

I thought once, as my plane crept down a runway away from some dipshit town, that he was more human in that ticking time bombness than he'd been as a normal man with a normal heart. More human in his mortality, his vulnerability, his lack of control.

Wives care for sick husbands who come back from war. Husbands stand beside wives with illnesses that deteriorate their bodies and minds. We read about their strength and dedication, their stand-by-your-manness. But no one talks about the adjustments and the sacrifices. Grieving for the husband who doesn't exist anymore isn't feel-good news. We're supposed to be chipper and upbeat and never admit to a single soul that we miss the men we thought we'd married.

I felt like a piece of shit for missing the hard, bruising sex. It was different with Gabby. When I'd wanted to go out but had to watch her, I'd felt burdened. I admitted it to myself but did what I had to do anyway. I always felt like shit about that too. But with Jonathan, I so ecstatic he was alive that I didn't even realize how much I'd missed him until he asked me if I was happy.

"What's wrong?" Jonathan asked in the back of the Bentley.

He'd just fucked my ass raw in the studio, just hurt me badly, and I'd begged him for every stroke. I'd never felt closer to him than in those minutes of pain. But on the way back, after I came down from my high and we had a bathroom break, I remembered why the last six months had been so hard.

"Nothing."

He stroked my arm with his fingertips. Perfect pressure for the gathering of electricity, as always. "Nothing?"

I shook my head, more at myself than at his disbelief. Nothing, my ass. Something. Everything. "That was a lot of exertion back there."

Exertion wasn't just a word but a keyword. Code for unreasonable fear. Secret speak for death. Terror in a few breaths of syllables and the tongue rubbing on the back of the teeth.

"You've been told a hundred times—"

"I know, please." I dismissed him. "I know."

He grabbed a fistful of my hair and turned me to face him, and my scalp became a center of pleasure. "You're shutting down."

I couldn't deny the truth. Not after he'd torn me open. For those minutes in the studio, when he commanded me, I'd forgotten to worry about him, and he was again my master and king. When he pulled my hair, I wanted to be ripped apart again, just for the release from thinking about him dying.

"I'm not," I said. "I'm just—"

"Open your legs."

I was pissed he'd ask at a time like this, and relieved. I spread my legs across the leather seat. Not far enough for him apparently, because he pulled my head back and yanked my knees farther apart. I gasped when a bullet of arousal shot through me.

He pressed four fingers between my legs, where the panels of my jeans met. "I am not going to die fucking you." He scratched the fabric, and I felt the tease through the layers.

Was this the time to answer honestly? Shouldn't we talk over dinner or in bed? Or across a desk surrounded by pens and blotters and serious things?

"You might. You could."

"I won't." He pushed against my crotch, and I pushed back as if I had no control over my body.

"You might," I gasped when he undid my jeans. "And you deny it, and it's a lie you tell yourself. I'm tired of walking around and pretending it's not a problem, because it is. It's a big problem. It's all I think about."

He slid his hand past my waistband until the tip of his middle finger reached my clit. He barely pressed on it, just rotated around the slip of skin at the top. "You never told me that."

"I have to be strong for you. You chase me out of the house to work, and I think it's because you don't want me to see you weak. And, oh God, Jonathan, I'm going to come."

"No, you're not." He reduced the pressure and intensity until I could only feel the outer edge of his hand's heat. "Pull your shirt up. Let me see your tits."

I yanked up my shirt and bra, and he leaned down and sucked on a nipple so hard and fast, it hurt like hell. I bucked under him.

"I'm going to die before you," he said, taking a last nip before putting his face to mine. "Way before you. You want to spend the time worrying? Or fucking?"

Which? Was that the only choice: this dichotomy of soul-eating pain or soul-revealing pleasure? I waited too long to answer apparently, because he circled his fingertip over my clit again, barely touching it. I groaned. I wanted to say fucking, to tell him what he wanted to hear, but when he had me like this, I couldn't tell one of the thousand untruths about my feelings. I couldn't say what would make him happy for the sake of saving him from stress.

"Which is it, goddess?"

"I'm going to come."

He brought his finger down my folds, to where I was wettest, leaving my clit kissed by nothing but the damp air in my jeans as he brought the rest of me to life. His outer fingers touched the welts he'd left earlier, setting them on fire.

"Which is it?" he asked.

"Fuck me or let me come," I whispered.

He pulled his hand out of my pants. The loss was painful.

"You are not stopping," I groaned. "Don't even—"

He held my face, putting his nose to mine. "You only talk when your cunt lets you. From now on, I control when you talk. And today, you talk."

The car stopped in front of our house, and the gate clanged closed behind us.

"You're a son of a bitch." My body arched toward him, making a lie of my words.

"Before I was in the hospital, you could hold yourself together. Now you're calling me a son of a bitch for doing what it's my right to do."

I glared at him, hating him and loving him at the same time, pain and pleasure always hand-in-hand with my king.

"Button up," he said, pulling my shirt down.

I closed the fly on my jeans, and he opened the door. The late afternoon sun blasted my face, turning Lil's form into a rectangular silhouette.

We didn't speak as we walked to the house. A modest thing by Drazen standards, it had a private beach in the back and the whole of Malibu in front. It was an old house built at the crest of the modern era by an ambitious architect who was way ahead of his time. It didn't have a porch, but a small overhang shaded the wide front door. He disabled the security system and put his hand on the knob but didn't turn it. Lil drove away, the sound of the engine giving way to the evensong birds and the breath of the freeways below.

I started to think about everything I could be doing. Over the past six months, my brain chemistry had changed so that when I was upset, my thoughts went to music and the business of making it. One ass fuck in the studio wouldn't change that.

"Come on. I have things to do," I said, knowing that wouldn't go over well. I reveled in my defiance. Fuck him with his new heart and old ways. If he wanted to talk, he could take me to dinner.

He swung the door open but didn't leave room for me to pass. I crossed my arms. He smirked. I felt the tightening of my cheeks as I almost smirked with him. What game was I playing? I wanted to get to work, and I wanted him to fuck me.

No, I didn't want him to fuck me. I wanted him to either rip me apart or let me make music mourning the loss of my wounds. If this defaulted to a vanilla middle ground because he thought he'd made his point, I would lose my shit.

"Take your clothes off. All of them."

I rolled my eyes. Lightning quick, like a man who had done nothing but work on his reflexes for the past six months, he grabbed my hair and dragged me to my knees. My safe word was *Invictus* and I probably still had a tangerine option, but the insides of my thighs tingled when he leaned down and growled in my ear.

"Unbutton your shirt."

I reached for my placket and carefully, without fumbling, undid the buttons one by one.

"I'll do what I have to to get you to talk to me. So first..." He yanked my hair, and I gasped. "Take it off. And the bra."

I shook both off until I was bare-breasted at the front door. How would he get my pants off? What did he intend?

He let go of my hair. "Stand up."

I got on my feet. He stood in the doorway, framed by a house I'd agreed to with a shrug, his hands at his sides. One of his fingers twitched.

I crossed my arms. "Are we going in or not?" I leaned on one hip, breasts out as if I didn't give a shit one way or the other how naked I was. "I'm tired, and my ass hurts. Can we just—"

"You're really pushing it."

I tapped a single finger on my bicep, a tic of impatience. Even though his beautiful green eyes didn't leave mine, I knew he saw it, and even if his mouth didn't smile, I knew I was pleasing him. We needed this, and we needed it to go down exactly the way it was going to go down.

He put a finger on my lower lip. "Open your mouth."

I didn't.

With his other hand, he cupped my jaw and exerted pressure, slowly opening my mouth. God, I wanted his cock in it. I wanted to taste the soft skin as it slid to the back of my throat. I relaxed my mouth, and he put his fingers in. First one, then four, pressing my tongue down.

He pulled me to him, speaking softly and firmly into my face. "I don't mind repeating myself. This is my mouth, and when I say open it, it opens."

I couldn't speak, but my eyes agreed. I was putty in his hands.

"Get your pants off while I explain my position."

I unbuttoned and unzipped while he held my jaw open. I couldn't swallow, and drool formed over his fingers.

"Do you remember the hospital? The week before the first surgery?"

Remember? How could I forget? I got heart palpitations thinking about it. Any time I smelled alcohol or something beeped, my chest felt as if it had been encased in a clenched fist.

"That week, we had rules," he said. "Should I remind you?"

I nodded as much as I could.

"Get your pants down." I wiggled to slide them down while he spoke. "The rules were: only the truth, even if it hurt. We would never protect each other from each other. And no judgment."

I got my pants down to my knees. I was twisted, fighting the tight jeans, the pressure of his fingers, and the memory of lying next to him in the never-dark Sequoia Hospital.

He removed his hand, which was wet with spit that dripped down his arm to the elbow. "All the way off."

I leaned to get my shoes off. He held my elbow when I almost fell then resumed watching my clumsy and twisted operation until I was completely naked before him. He was perfectly calm, perfectly commanding. Only the huge bulge in his pants indicated how involved he was in what was happening.

I stood with my hands at my sides. "I remember."

"I want that again."

"It's hard when you're telling me to get my clothes off."

"You know what, Monica, you don't even know yourself. Look at you. I haven't seen you this relaxed in months. The only time you let your worry go is when you give me control. And your worry is what keeps you from being honest."

I swallowed. Blinked. A torrent of wetness welled behind my eyes. "I don't want to break the scene."

"Stay still. Stay naked. Speak your mind."

"I almost died with you a hundred times. That recovery room, they had you in this induced coma, and you looked dead. There were bags of blood. Bags hanging over you, and you were all opened up. And, I'm sorry, I haven't said this because you're the one who went through it." I swallowed a gallon of tears. "I don't want to see you like that again. But I think about it all the time. I dream about it. I see it when I close my eyes. I want you to live, so I do what I think will make you happy, and I always get it wrong. Stay or go. I give you attention or none. It's always wrong."

"What about your happiness?"

"It doesn't matter. Not as much as yours. It's not life or death."

"It is, Monica. It is."

I shook my head. "You can't convince me of that. We can do this hurtful honesty thing all day. You're the priority, and I'm okay with that. Deal with it."

He nodded, looking down for a blink, then at me. He reached for my wrists. "These go behind your back."

I did as instructed.

"Now get on your knees."

I bent them. With my hands behind my back, it was hard to balance.

"Do you need some help?" he asked.

"Yes."

I thought he'd take me gently by the elbow, but he dragged me down.

He was right. I was relaxed, totally submitting and trusting him, loving every bit of discomfort he dished out.

"Spread your knees apart."

I did, too slowly for him. He kicked them wide.

"Do you remember your safe word?" he asked, unbuckling his belt.

"Yes." A tingling rush went down my spine with the promise of his dominance and the way it made me forget how fragile he really was.

His cock was out in the next second. "Open. Your. Mouth."

I parted my lips enough to breathe, and before I could open my throat or prepare, he put his cock between them and pushed my head into him. I choked on the mass of his dick, but the scent of his soap, the taste of his skin, the shape and thrust of him brought a wave of pleasure and a strong desire to please him.

"Take it, goddess. Take it all. Not one inch should be left."

He pushed forward again, fucking my face mercilessly. He pulled out, letting me breathe and making eye contact with me. Checking on me. I was safe. I gasped, chest heaving, and opened my mouth again.

"I want you to think about something. While I take your mouth, I want you to think about how its purpose is my pleasure. To fuck." He stuck his dick down my throat, all of it in one stroke, and pulled it out as violently as he'd put it in. "To talk." He jammed it in again before I could utter a word. "Whatever I say."

He began in earnest, treating my throat the way he'd treated my ass an hour before—as a receptacle for his soap-scented cock. He moved my head by my hair, pulling out to let me breathe but no longer than necessary. My hands were behind me, so I couldn't wipe the drool off my chin or move my hair from my face.

"I'm going to come down your throat." He was so strong, so solid, so commanding with a wisp of hair over his forehead, his monster cock dripping with my spit, hanging in the foreground of my vision. "You're going to swallow every fucking drop. Do you understand?"

I opened my mouth as wide as I could, looking up at him through my hair. I wanted to tell him to fuck me anywhere he wanted. To make it hurt. Make it uncomfortable. I wanted to forget everything in our way. The hurt, the stress, the worry. I wanted to break the cycle again, and be nothing more than under him.

But he didn't give me a chance to beg for it. He cupped my jaw in his other hand and stuck his wet cock in my waiting mouth to fuck my throat. He could live forever. He could pound my face like this in an eternal grind, never sick, never dying, never at risk. No. This dominant beast was built to fuck and to hurt and to live.

He pulled out long enough to let me breathe then shoved it back in, coming with a bark, his balls pulsing against my lower lip. His hair-pulling violence turned to stroking and caressing as he filled my throat, slipping out for a breath, and sliding in again.

"Goddess," he whispered. "Mine mine mine…"

My arms and knees ached. My throat was sore. Thank god I didn't have to sing the next day. Not that he'd care. Not this Jonathan, my Jonathan, with his come coating my throat as I swallowed, looking up at him. He smiled at me, and when he picked me up and carried me though the door, I forgot to worry about him at all.

Chapter 7

Jonathan

I could see this would take some time. It had taken me months to figure out we even had a problem; it wouldn't take me that much less to solve.

The flip side of the loyalty I loved was her stubbornness. She'd fully engaged in her submission when we started out because it was new and exciting. She'd discovered things she didn't know about herself, and she'd watched me discover my own boundaries as well as hers. Then I got sick, and her world flipped. She had become distrustful, and to her, the stakes were life and death.

All that made me want to fuck her harder, to drive submission back into her. While my dick was out, she was obedient and subservient, perfect as usual. In the doorway of our house, her mouth open, her chin slick with spit, waiting for me to come down her throat, she was a goddess. But once it was over, she would close her mouth and not talk about what was bothering her. She was going to simmer and worry and seethe, holding it all inside in an effort to protect me.

It was cute. Sweet, even. In a way, her protectiveness made me love her more than I'd thought I could love anyone. She was a mother lion, even with her hands behind her back and her mascara running down her cheeks.

And as if cued, as I carried her, I had a vision in four-dimension Technicolor, clear as reality and sharper than the truth: my heart blew through the scar in my chest, and I dropped her. The vision went *whoosh* when the heart flew out of me, *thup* when it landed on the floor, and *clonk* when I dropped her. I didn't hear myself fall, because I was dead.

This had to stop, but I didn't know how to do it. I didn't know how to shut it down. I shook myself free of the afterburn as I laid her on the bed. It faced the Pacific ocean, and the constant crash of the waves would make a nice backdrop over her screams of pleasure. She'd wanted to live on the beach, and I'd given her that, but I'd never given her myself. That was going to change. I couldn't live like this.

"I missed you," she said, and I knew what she meant.

"You barely knew me." I rolled her onto her stomach. I wanted to tie her up, but I couldn't. I had in the studio, but I'd kept thinking as I stroked her back, *what if the heart rejects me and she's tied down?*

She tucked her hands under her thighs. "How much do I need to know you to love you?"

"Put your hands on the headboard," I said, pulling her hair from her face.

She stretched her arms and turned to face the big glass doors onto the patio. The beach on the other side was private, and that slice of sunset was ours alone. Her eyes were blasted light brown in the dying sun, and they followed me as I stepped back and looked at her.

She was long and beautiful, with hair like a turbulent ocean. She was my songbird, my goddess, my slice of control in a world of chaos.

Ten years with her was better than sixty with anyone less.

I picked her legs up by the ankles and bent the knees, spreading them apart. Her cunt was wet, and her ass was welted pink. I looked back up at her face. Her eyes were closed tightly, wrinkles in the skin around her wet lashes, and I remembered how hard I'd hit her. Six months' worth of frustration. I'd never hit her out of anger, only arousal, but maybe the two had gotten mixed up somewhere.

"This hurts," I said, hovering my hand over her ass.

"Yes," she said, eyes open into the sun again. "Thank you."

She wasn't trained to thank me for spankings. No one had told her it was how a submissive was supposed to please their master. She simply thanked me because she'd gotten something from me she couldn't give to herself. How could I not love her?

"Wait here." I kissed her cheek and went to the bathroom.

I snapped open the medicine cabinet. I had a shaving salve and a lubricant. Abandoned hair things. Toothpaste. Band-Aids. Monica had a pale pink box of who-even-knew under the sink. The movers had taken everything and brought it from my house to this new house, and my wife and I had been too distracted and too vanilla to note where we kept the salves for her poor, welted ass. I'd been a sorry excuse of a dominant.

I laughed at myself and put the lubricant back. That wouldn't work.

I snapped it open. Little half-used tubes of whatnot clacked around.

Perfumey stuff that would burn. Zinc oxide would be fine for a small area, but her whole bottom needed attention. I clicked open a smaller box. Ah. Sunburn ointment and Neosporin. Perfect.

I checked a little velvet bag with a drawstring. I didn't know what I was hoping for, maybe the home-run of ass lotions or a magic unguent that would make her able to sit for more than five minutes without flinching. I just opened it and slid out a white plastic stick. A pregnancy test.

The nerve to my heart had been cut during the transplant, so I couldn't feel it stop and seize up. Couldn't feel the squeeze in my chest. But I knew it was there.

I turned the plastic wand. Not breathing. Not thinking about the fact that I'd been snooping into something that had been inside a bag, inside a box, inside a cabinet.

Not pregnant.

I wasn't relieved. I wasn't disappointed. I just realized how much I wanted a different result and how little control I had over it.

I slapped everything back in its place and went into the bedroom. She was still there, facedown, hands touching the headboard, bathed in the sunset. It would be dark in a few minutes, so I turned on the little lamp by the bed.

"I found these in your stuff," I said, holding out the tubes.

"I think the Neosporin's expired."

I flipped the tube. "Next month."

"Yes, sir."

I sat on the edge of the bed. "Ass up."

She shifted, arching just enough to get her pelvis off the bed.

"Goddess, when I say ass up, I mean ass up." I put my hand under her and jacked her up until her ass was in the air.

She groaned. I spread her legs under her and pressed down on her lower back. Perfect. I kissed a raw welt, and she squeaked in pain.

"None of that." Though my words were cruel, I didn't want her to hurt right then. She'd earned her pleasure.

I squeezed a lump of the sunburn cream onto my finger. It was cool to the touch, and when I put it on the pink skin, she breathed easily.

"Now," I said, "we have a problem. Fucking you in the ass isn't going to solve it."

"Yes, sir."

"First off, we need to drop the sirs and thank yous and all that shit until

I say otherwise. We're off scene. Verbally. But the ass stays up, or I'll welt your welts."

"Fine."

"I want you to talk to me." I dragged a mound of clear cream over the curve of her ass, watching it get smaller in the seam between her and me, disappearing into a cool coat.

"I'm fine," she said. "Everything is fine. I think, just… I think I needed this. What you're giving me now."

I ran my fingers on the inside of her thigh until there was no cream on them, and I slipped my middle finger between her legs. Her eyes fluttered closed.

"You're not fine. You're wet as fuck." I put my fingertip on her clit. "You're so close I shouldn't even touch you. But fine? You're not fine."

"I am. I—"

"You don't tell your husband you're not happy and an hour later tell him you're fine because he fucked you hard enough."

I slid two fingers inside her. Wet didn't describe her. She tightened around me, and my dick stretched my pants. I pulled my hand out and ran it over her clit again, front to back, touching every surface, waking it up.

"Jonathan, I can't talk to you like this."

"You don't talk to me, period."

"I want to come."

"You'll come." I gingerly spread her ass cheeks. She looked as if she'd been fucked by a battering ram. Bruises were rising already, and she was deep red around the edges. I'd need to leave that part of her alone for a while. "Tell me." I kissed her lower back while stroking between her legs. "Tell me how it's been for you."

"I don't want to. I don't want to upset you. I just want you to be okay."

"I am okay, except that you've been closed to me." I put three fingers in her, and she bucked. "Stay still. You can take your hands off the headboard."

She tucked them under her.

I slowly removed my fingers. "Tell me one thing you think of that makes you worry."

She sighed.

I put my hands on her thighs and kissed her clit. "Tell me."

"I love you."

"That's not what I asked."

She paused. "And I wonder if you've taken your rejection meds."

"I know you've been checking the bottles."

"When I'm here."

"Exactly." I gave her a long stroke with my tongue.

She groaned but stayed still. Such a good woman. "I told you I'd stop traveling if you wanted."

"I don't want."

"Why?"

I sucked her clit because it tasted good and because I wanted to please her, but mostly because I didn't know how to answer her question. She'd just accepted my encouragement and never asked why it was there. I felt the muscles of her thighs tremble and tighten.

As if she spoke best on the edge of orgasm, she continued. "You throw me away. We have such a short time together, and you kick me out. Jonathan, if you don't want me, let me go. Don't stay out of obligation. Not for ten years of misery with me."

I pulled my face away. "Oh God, Monica. You can't mean that."

I'd intended to torment her for as long as it took, then bring her to orgasm with my tongue until she begged me to stop. But she broke me with those words, and I changed the plan. I got on my knees and pushed her onto her back. Her hair made a ladder across her face, and I brushed it away. Her eyes were wet, and her face was creased from being pressed to the sheets.

"I mean it," she said. "That heart has ten years in it, and you can't spend them with the wrong person just because you got married under pressure. It's wrong."

"Would you have married me if I'd asked you under any other circumstances? If I'd taken you up to Mulholland and asked you under the stars, with a ring and a few nice words?"

"I would have said yes."

"Why?"

"I love you is why. But that doesn't mean you're obligated to stay now. Because you wouldn't have asked. Not for a while." I must have had a look on my face or made a sound that hit a button, because she blinked, and tears ran down the side of her face. "I'm not trying to make it about me, and I'm not looking for reassurance. But if you deny it..."

"I'm not denying it. I would have asked you... I don't know when. After a few birthdays. There are no rules for the way it happened."

"I want you to think about it," she said.

"About what?"

"About if this is what you really want." Her voice was sober and cold. "If I'm who you really want to be married to."

"Goddess…"

"No, I mean it. If you want to be together but not married. I just want you to have what you want. I want you to be sure."

I almost answered. I almost reassured her and told her how I felt about her. I almost made metaphors with the sky and stars, weaving threads of certainty into a gauze of confidence. But even if I got her to believe it for a second, she'd wake up wondering if I'd lied to appease her.

So I kissed her cheek. "Will you stay?"

She nodded, and I felt the insecurity in it. She'd never been insecure with me, and it unmoored me at the same time it filled me with a feeling I hadn't had in a long time.

I unbuttoned my shirt. She reached up and helped me, pulling it off and throwing it across the room. I got my pants off and stood over her naked body. Her magnificent tits were goose bumped, nipples hard, skin golden in the lamplight.

"Spread your legs for me."

She did it, hitching up her knees. There was so much between us. I would have married her in an instant, under any circumstances, and as I wedged myself between her legs, I knew my job wasn't to reassure her with pretty words or gifts but with actions. She'd believe it, or I'd die trying.

I put her hands over her head and leaned on them. "Look at me."

Her eyes went wide, looking up at me. "May I come?"

I pushed against her with the rhythm of slow torture. "Quiet now, goddess. Don't ask again."

Her face went from pleasure to constricted concentration as she tried not to come. I fucked her harder. She pleaded with me without saying a word. Her face begged for release, her beauty crunched into pain.

"Say my name," I said.

"Jonathan."

"Monica."

"Jonathan." She cried it, sobbed, breaking herself into pieces to say it.

"Come, my wife. Come for me."

She came in two strokes, arching and twisting. I held myself back until she'd finished, and I drank in every cry, every moment, every shudder.

My purpose in life had been simple up until then. Live. Just live. Now I had a resolution. Love her until she believed it.

Chapter 8

Monica

Love was easy. Love, the way everyone else defined it, was the fun part. But every hell, every conflict, every bit of miserable anxiety in those first six months had been born of nothing but love. I'd thought that was my new life. Ten years of it at least, until his heart gave out and he had to find another. Then another ten. Or more. Or less. Or not. Or maybe. I was playing Russian roulette with God by being away so much, but I thought he wanted me away, and he thought I wanted to be away. I didn't know whether to jump or crawl those first six months, then he came to the studio and fucked me like an animal.

The morning after he'd reclaimed me, with my ass aching and my cunt as sore as it had ever been, I woke up forgetting to wonder about his pills and his life. Just for a second. In that crack in my wall of concern bled something else I hadn't thought about since Sequoia. It had needled me every time I saw Declan and disappeared behind the buzz of death seconds after Jonathan's father left the room. Now that I thought of it, while in Jonathan's arms with the sound of the ocean outside, I couldn't go another second without telling him, even if it meant it was our last together.

His eyes were closed, light lashes casting darker shadows. His chest rose and fell under me, and his scar was hard white beneath my hand.

"Jonathan," I whispered, hoping he was asleep.

"Yes," he answered, eyes still shut, as if he was wide awake and had been listening to my thoughts.

I got my knees under me, the pain of every movement reminding me of how many times he'd brutalized me and how consistently I'd begged for it. "I need to tell you something."

He opened his eyes. Had they always been that green? Or was it a trick of the light and my fear of losing him?

"Okay, go ahead." He stroked the top of my breast.

I pulled his hand away and held it in my lap. I paused. A hundred years passed, and he said nothing. Not a word of encouragement or doubt. I could have hanged myself in the amount of time he'd wait. As always, he was a patient man in all things.

"When you were… I mean, you weren't yourself," I started, "and you were dying right in front of me. I thought you were second on the list for a transplant. It was like… I thought that was it."

His brow creased as if he didn't understand what I was talking about. God, there were so many little details, and I wanted to tell this story fast and dirty so I could get it over with.

"You hate your father already, so it's not like this will make it worse. I went to him because I wanted something."

"What did he want in exchange?" His voice was hard and cold, and the implications of his assumptions justified the tone.

"Forgiveness from you. Enough to get your mother back to him."

He put his hand over his face and rubbed his eyes. "That's what that whole thing was about. I barely remember it. I was in and out of consciousness ten times in a minute." He patted my hand then rubbed my fingers. "What did you want?"

I balled my hand into a fist. I didn't want his affection. I couldn't bear to feel it stop when I put the pieces together for him. "So I saw Brad's list. I didn't understand how it worked. So I thought what I was seeing was… you were second, and I thought it meant you were going to die. It seemed like a guarantee. And Paulie Patalano was brain-dead and right on the fourth floor." Unable to stand the weight of his gaze, I looked in my lap, where his hand rested in mine, our fourth fingers still circled by the cheap silver key rings. "I thought your father could get me access to Paulie's room."

He moved his hand away, placing it at his side. I wished he'd slapped me in the face. It would have been somehow kinder.

"Did he?"

"He did. He's very clever. And everything you said about him is probably right. But I was the one who went in Paulie's room. I was going to do it. I was going to end him so you could get his heart." I didn't mention Jessica's part. What I'd done was my choice and my responsibility. Now wasn't the time to diffuse it with Jessica-shaped shadow play. "I knew what it meant. I knew that if my plan worked, you'd have a heart that you thought was stolen.

You never would have felt right about yourself. I knew I was condemning you, in a way. And us. I knew you wouldn't forgive me. I was ending us. And I should say I'm sorry, but I'd do it again if I thought it would save your life."

"You didn't do it though."

"Brad texted me while I was in the room. He had a heart from that poor guy in Ojai. The one who jogs and hates spicy food apparently. So I didn't have to go through with it."

He took my hand again and rubbed each finger as if considering their ability to do harm. "God saved you."

"You believe in God? You believe he'd step in and save me? And he'd kill someone to do it?"

"God was in Brad's text. I believe that. But swear to me, I mean, I don't think that circumstance will recur, but swear to me you won't ever consider something like that again."

"I won't let you die if I can prevent it. I don't feel right about it, and I won't pretend I do, but it's like how a soldier must feel when he kills the enemy. I'm sure it doesn't feel good, but there wasn't a choice. And if it comes to me not having a choice again, I'll do it again."

I searched his face for distaste or foul rancor, and I found none. Then I looked for disquiet or emotional blankness, and I found none of that either. I couldn't read him, even when he took my arms and pulled me forward onto him. I rested my head on his chest.

"I have to tell you," he said, "I'm scared of death. But you? You put death to shame."

"Do you still love me?"

"Yes."

"Are you going to leave me?"

"No."

"Do you forgive me?"

He took a long time to answer. I told myself it didn't matter, that his forgiveness was beside the point when I had his love.

"I fear you. I am in awe of you. I can't forgive you for something you didn't do."

I'd thought I was committed to him before. I'd thought I'd given him my whole heart and that I owned him completely. But I hadn't. Maybe I'd spend the rest of his life realizing I'd never owned him, loved him, or committed to him fully. Maybe it was a matter of the changing acoustics of an ever-expanding heart.

I kissed his scar, and he stroked my hair. I worked down his body and took his cock in my mouth. I wanted to eat him alive, swallow his forgiveness, absorb his compassion. I wanted to become him, to own his pain and kindness, his sadism and his maturity, holding it to myself in a drum-tight skin of gratitude.

Chapter 9

Monica

I usually had a dream. I was in Sequoia, but it wasn't Sequoia. The hallways were narrower, the lights dimmer or blindingly bright—endlessly white and long. Doors everywhere, some locked and some ajar. In my right hand beat a throbbing, pulsing heart, dropping blood on the bleached linoleum. I only had as much time as the blood in the heart, and I needed to get to Jonathan's room with it or he would die. Sometimes the hospital was empty, and I couldn't find the room. Sometimes it was populated with people who didn't know what the hell I was talking about or where I should go. Once, I dreamed the halls were lined with chicken coops, and Dr. Brad sent me in the wrong direction on purpose.

Jonathan always died. I always woke up in a state of grief and misery, and he was either next to me or I was in an empty bed, looking for a way to call him without worrying him.

The night after he reclaimed me in the studio, with every inch of my body stinging and alive, I expected to have that same dream, as surprising and terrifying as it always was. But it didn't come. And not the night after, when he made me wait twelve minutes before touching me. Nor over the next week as he broke me, pushed me, hurt me until I was a puddle of emotional satisfaction. I never had that dream again, as if my subconscious was suddenly okay with the whole arrangement of my life and my conscious brain was the only troublemaker.

He hurt me, but he didn't bind me. When I asked him to, he spanked me for questioning him, but he still didn't tie me up.

I mistrusted this in quiet moments, but I let it go. He was too good, the same man he had been. Still wise and kind, still generous and funny, but with an added helping of scorching cruelty in bed. He'd scared the dreams away, and I was safe at night, but in the day, I still carried my anxieties. Even when I forgot to worry, I reminded myself that I hated grey and pale pink, that copper and blood had the same smell, and that the heart machine in the hospital made the same beep as the timer in the coffee shop. My brain did its due diligence, creating panic as insurance against death.

Jonathan had been more productive. Six weeks after he returned from the hospital, he started forgetting his anti-rejection meds because of the complexities of dosing, and his immune system started slipping because he wasn't getting enough nutrients. Shortly after Valentine's Day, he found out I'd been staying home to watch him. He'd sliced the air with his hand and said simply, "No."

He hired help.

Laurelin was a nurse, which I normally wouldn't hold against her. But I wasn't behaving normally. She came to the house to interview in the afternoon, after a long line of women and men who'd spoken to Jonathan about what he expected, what he needed, and what they could do. They'd all smelled sanitized. I couldn't sit in the interviews, because the hospital stink caused me so much anxiety I wanted to throw up. I told Jonathan I had to practice, but I peeked in on every interview, and every time he said one of them was no good, I felt relieved.

But Laurelin didn't smell like a hospital. Nothing about her reminded me of Sequoia. Her hair was the color of scrambled eggs, and her belly was rounded with the beginnings of her second trimester. She'd worked in the infectious diseases unit at Hollywood Methodist but couldn't continue while pregnant. She smiled a lot, which they all did, but she seemed to be made of sunshine and she smelled of rosewater. When I met her, I felt as if a blanket had been thrown over me on a cold night, and I couldn't imagine she would let anything happen to my husband.

"Her," I'd said. "You need to hire her."

"Really? Why is that?"

"She's pregnant. She's going to take good care of you. I can feel it."

"What does taking care of me feel like?"

"It feels like the only right and good thing. And she smells nice. And you like her, I can tell," I said.

"I think she might be bossy."

"I'll take that as a yes."

So she was hired, and she'd been the bulwark against my needling that she was supposed to be. I could travel and work without worrying, and without Jonathan worrying that I was worrying. Maybe it had been a bad idea. Maybe Laurelin had made our need to communicate less urgent.

Four months after she'd been hired, and two weeks after Jonathan reclaimed me, Laurelin shuffled in wearing jeans and a sweatshirt even in the late June warmth. Her code for the front gate worked three mornings a week.

Jonathan had left his little blue book on the counter for her. It was pliable leather with ruled cream pages and a black ribbon marker. In it, he kept notes about his diet, his exercise, and if he was late or early taking his rejection meds.

"Hi, Laurelin! How are you feeling?" I asked.

"Not bad." She pulled Jonathan's blue book and box of meds toward her. "I've skipped just about every complication I could." She put on a glitter face, swinging her blond ponytail from one side to the other, then popped open the box of pills that had a day of the week and a time of day in each compartment.

"How much longer?"

"Seven weeks," she said, brows knotted about what she saw in Jonathan's little pill box. "What's this?"

"What's what?" I didn't look at her, just the teapot as I filled it.

She looked at her watch. "It's ten, and he hasn't taken his morning treatment."

I didn't say anything.

"Monica?"

"Yeah?"

"Where is he?" She flipped to the last page of the book.

"He's on a run."

She snapped the book closed. "Well, we're going to have to have a little talk, the three of us."

I felt chastened. I shouldn't have. She worked for Jonathan, and thus, she worked for me, and it wasn't as if I were the one who had missed a handful of pills. That had been my husband, wanting one more tumble before his run, then breakfast, then his cubicle of meds.

Laurelin hummed and pulled the blender to her. She had packets of vitamin powders and access to the fridge, so she set up his Shit Shake for that day and the two following.

I felt as if I'd been let off the hook. I hadn't been able to resist him that morning. He wanted a tumble. No pain, no scene, no demands, just a one-two-three bite of vanilla cake. Delicious. Not something I wanted every day, but a good interlude between the usual screaming, bruising games we played. I must have been smiling, because when I looked up, Laurelin was staring at me and smirking.

"I know you're still newlyweds—"

I slapped my hands over my ears. "La la la! Stop it, Laurelin!"

She ripped open a packet of powder and dumped it in the blender. "You can get on with it after he takes his meds."

"You know how responsible he is," I said.

"Generally."

"Can you not give him a hard time? I'll take care of it from now on."

She poured milk in the blender and shook it, peeking in the top. "You're away too often to keep that promise."

She was right. But I knew when I was away, he was perfect. When I was around, he let things slip.

"Well, consider me chastened. I'm going to lunch. You can berate my husband when he gets back." I kissed her on the cheek and ran out.

• • •

I spotted Darren halfway down the block from Terra Café. He looked taller by a few inches, possibly because Adam, who walked beside him, was only five eight. Darren keened a little to the left, bumping his boyfriend affectionately, and Adam nudged Darren with his elbow.

"You're late," I said.

"Oh, Miss Hotshot's on a schedule." Darren gave me jazz hands while Adam kissed my cheek.

"The line in this place is nuts. So this five minutes counts." I wagged my finger at him as if I meant it, which I didn't. Not even a little. I couldn't have cared less if he was late.

"Did you finish the EP?" Darren asked.

"Yesterday. It was great. I mean, all of it. Every track I feel good about."

"How many?"

"Six."

"Nice." He looked at the menu. Organic fair trade lunch, gourmet cakes and pies, vegan, free-range, grass-fed, gluten-free, cruelty-free, flavor-challenged, and the descriptions of what wasn't added, wasn't done, or wasn't offered took up half the board.

"You look different," Adam said, looking me up and down. He'd really grown on me with his sharp mouth and cutting sense of humor. If you could take a joke, he was the guy to hang around, and if you beat him to the punch, even better. Thin-skinned weeping willows need not apply.

"I'm the same."

"Just richer," Adam snapped. Darren elbowed him, and Adam laughed.

I shrugged. "There's that. But you're still buying your own lunch."

"But no," Adam continued, "seriously, something's changed since the last time I saw you."

Darren cut in. "The last time you saw her, she was in a hospital cafeteria. She hadn't eaten in weeks. It was a fucking nightmare."

They'd come to visit a few days after Jonathan had his transplant. I barely remembered it. No, I did remember it. It was Christmas. Darren had brought me a piece of holiday cake, and I'd eaten it down to the last scrapings of frosting. The cake I remembered, the conversation, which probably centered around physical damage and medical procedures, was lost.

We sat at a cramped spot by the window and put our number on the table. I'd seen Darren a lot since the hospital. He was the only one I'd told about the horrors of Sequoia. The recurrent dreams. The heart-gripping fear whenever I heard a machine beep or saw an innocuous color combination. I told him about how I went miles out of my way to avoid the hospital compound and turned off any TV show with scenes in a medical facility. I even refused to use white sheets in the house because the sheets in the hospital were white.

He'd been there for me in the middle of the night when the door alarm beeped and I freaked out because it sounded like a heart monitor. He gave me directions when I got lost in West Hollywood because I couldn't find a way to get where I was going without passing Sequoia. He'd heard about all the dreams of endless hospital hallways while Jonathan died in a room I couldn't find.

"When is Jonathan going back to work?" Adam asked. He traded real estate insurance products, so anything that happened in real estate was hugely interesting to him. I always had to make sure to only tell him things that had been announced publicly.

"He's selling most everything," I said.

"Really?" He considered his iced green tea latte. "He need more money?"

"Shut up." I flicked a few drops of condensation from my cup at him.

"Sorry."

"I mean, who wants to run an empire on borrowed time?" I said. "At this point, it's either sell it all or go back to working like a dog. And that's all you're getting out of me, Mister Corporate Raider."

Adam rolled his eyes. "You going to tell her?" he asked Darren, biting the straw of his emerald-color latte.

"Tell me what?"

Darren pressed his fingers into his eyes as if he still had sleep in them.

"You are an unbelievable chickenshit," Adam mumbled.

"Fuck off."

"Okay." I held up my hands. "Listen, this is cute, but if you guys haven't talked about this already, I'd be happy to step outside while you—"

"Easy, it's not a big deal," Darren said.

"Really?" Adam seemed put off.

"I'm moving out of Echo Park."

"You're moving in together!" I squealed joyfully. "That's awesome!"

"Yes, but that's not it. We did something impulsive, and we're just sticking with it before some asshole makes it illegal again," Darren said.

I heard something about assholes at the end, but not really, because I'd scraped my chair back to run around the table. I plopped right in Darren's lap and hugged him. Adam got in on the action until we were a pile of happy limbs.

"Just say it so I know I'm not hugging you for buying a pot farm," I said.

"We got married!" Adam said.

Three tables of people twisted around to look at us then broke into applause. I stood and clapped too, and Adam pushed his lips onto Darren's cheek. My ex-boyfriend blushed. I sat when the applause died and our food arrived.

"So," I said, "why now? Or then? Or when?"

"Yesterday," Darren answered. "The deal was, when I had a foothold as a musician—"

Adam interrupted between taps on his phone. "And I was not holding my breath—"

"Oh, fuck you."

"It's got nothing to do with your talent, and you know that, honey."

"Whatever. That was the deal. I've been working at Redlight Studios pretty regularly, and Harry and I have been working on some really broad, commercial stuff."

"Yeah," I said. "I know all this. Why are you stalling?"

"I don't want you to compare this to what you get, because you, I mean you're getting a different kind of deal."

"Oh. My. God. You got signed."

"It's nothing," he said. "It's music for a video game. *City of Dis*, if you've heard of it."

"I have."

"Well, it's a good gig and good money. And I didn't even mention it because who cares? But it just got us noticed enough that we're getting signed by Beowolf Records for a really small thing—"

Adam dropped his phone on the table. "And this is why I said, 'Marry me now, or I'm done with you.' Nothing is a big enough deal for him. He'd accept my proposal after his fifth Grammy, maybe."

"Are you guys having a party or something? I want to give gifts and get drunk. You owe me that."

"When we get a place not in the slums of Los Angeles, so sorry," Adam said. "Something nice on the west side with a big enough yard for a reception."

The look on Darren's face told me there had been some contention over either the size or the location, but I said nothing. I'd get it out of him later.

My phone rang.

"Let me get this." I slid the phone off the table and walked outside.

Jonathan and I had made a new deal after he reclaimed me. If he called, any time, any place, I picked up. If he called during a show, I had to pick up in front of the audience. The only way to avoid that was to tell him when I would be on stage and when I would be in the studio, then he'd only call if it was an emergency.

"Hello, goddess," he said.

"Hi." I felt warm and giddy.

"I think we should cancel on Sheila tomorrow."

"Why?"

"I noticed you were walking straight. Can't have that."

As appealing as the thought of him making it hard for me to walk was, he needed to be at Sheila's tomorrow. "We can work around it."

"Since when are you so eager to see my family?"

The rule of never lying to save each other pain was still in effect. I couldn't travel thinking he wanted me gone, and he couldn't chase me out to save me from being around him. We were to be direct in our insecurities and our desires, even if they would hurt.

"I want to go," I said, telling the truth but keeping a tiny lie to myself. "I happen to love almost all of your sisters as much as Margie."

"Truth?"

"Truth."

"Come home."

"May I finish lunch?"

"Hurry. I want to fuck you blind."

Fluid rushed between my legs. I almost buckled at the knees. We hung up, and I dialed Margie while leaning against a parking meter.

"Yes?" she snapped.

"He's trying to wiggle out of tomorrow."

"You have one job, Monica. One job."

"I can do my best, but—"

"For the tenth time, he is not going to have a heart attack when we yell 'surprise.' You're going to give yourself an ulcer," she said.

"The doctor said no stress. That's stressful."

"Is he taking all his rejection meds?"

"Yes."

"Eating right?"

"Yes."

"Is he exercising?"

I sighed, frustrated. She was building a case, and the jury would find in her favor. "Jogs miles and miles a day."

"Is he not taking care of himself in any way possible?"

"He's a model citizen."

"So what's the problem?"

"I love him, and I don't want to lose him. That's the problem. When are you going to tell him about the Swiss thing?"

"Tomorrow I'm going over to your place to get some things signed. I'll bring it up then. Be scarce."

"Okay." What I said with that "okay" was that she'd better do it or I would blurt something out in the bedroom. We'd agreed that it should be presented as business, and Margie was business, but after one more day, it would feel like withholding.

"What did you get him for his birthday?" Margie changed the subject.

"I wrote him a song." As soon as I said it, I knew the song was wrong. It was about a flat compromise over a house. I'd written it before he'd reclaimed me, and I suddenly hated it.

Margie's sigh was audible over the traffic. "You're a good wife. It's almost sickening."

Chapter 10
Monica

The morning of Jonathan's birthday, I woke him by putting his cock in my mouth, and he twisted me around and put his mouth on me at the same time. He didn't even say good morning before I came, groaning with his dick down my throat.

"Monica, you didn't ask."

"But, wait, we're in scene?"

"Get up and stand by the window."

I had to write him a new song, and dinner was at five. I was already cutting it close. I wasn't a particularly quick songwriter. Since we'd both collapsed without fucking the night before, this could go on for hours.

But I couldn't hesitate. I wasn't afraid he'd beat me harder. I was afraid he'd think I didn't want to play. So I stood, already naked, and faced the back patio. I wanted to do this and do it hard, then write the song, because I had no idea what I wanted to write. I had no idea what to say except everything.

"Put your hands on the glass."

I leaned forward and put my fingertips on the back doors. Behind me, I heard his belt buckle clink and his fly zip as he put on his pants.

"Whole hand. Come on, Monica. Commit." He spanked my ass playfully.

I put my whole palm on the glass and stretched my back.

"Open those legs." I did, and he pressed on my lower back until my ass was all the way up. "Good."

"Thank you."

He nonchalantly went out the back door and looked out over the ocean. The salt breeze blew his hair back. Then, as if noticing something for the first time, he played with the bamboo stalks in the patio's stone planter as if they were strings on a harp. Then he stood in front of a pot of rattan. It looked just like any other potted palm in Los Angeles. He'd had it brought in a few days ago to block a sliver of view from the beach. He'd insisted on rattan, and from what I'd heard on the phone, he had to go see it personally. I'd had no idea what his problem was. I didn't know if it was some obsessive pickiness he'd inherited from his new heart that hadn't yet had the opportunity to show itself or if it was something I simply had never known about him.

But my king wasn't impulsive. He bent one of the leaves and snapped out his pocketknife, which also just happened to be in his jeans. He cut off a branch and stripped off the leaves.

He stood right in front of me on the other side of the glass door, as if he were in a different room, as if I couldn't see him. He rolled the cane around in his hands, then across them, inspecting it for I didn't even know what.

He walked back in the house with the switch. "Now," he said from behind me, "I think we've talked about your orgasms before, and who owns them."

"You do." I looked out the window. Without him in front of me, I felt exposed, my breasts hanging, ass up.

"No one can see you." He slapped my ass.

"Yes, sir."

"Do you believe me?"

"I want to."

He swatted me with the rattan switch, lightly, as if testing. Then he did it harder. It was no thicker than a pinky, and that second time, it made a whipping sound before it landed with a *crack*. Then he did it a little harder.

I sucked in my breath.

"How is that?" he asked.

"Good, sir."

He cracked it again, at the topmost fleshy part of my ass. The sting was incredible, searing me. I felt as if my flesh was opening. Then he did it again, an inch or so below the last stroke. I let out an *mmm* sound, biting my lips. And he did it again. There was a rhythm to it, a slow build as he worked his way down to my knees, searing pain leaving blossoming pleasure in its wake. Two taps to aim, one to awaken the skin, and one to make me scream in pain, and it went *thwap thwap* thwap THWAP. *thwap thwap* thwap THWAP. *thwap thwap* thwap THWAP.

• • •

In the little studio in the guest house, the piano keys went *tap tap* tap TAP. *tap tap* tap TAP as I searched for the notes. I shifted in my seat. Jonathan had given my ass and thighs plenty of aftercare, but I wouldn't be comfortable for a couple of days. I'd think of him and his mastery of me whenever I sat or walked, which was the point.

I had only a few hours, and I was slow. Slow with words and clunky with melody. I missed Gabby. She made things work in minutes. I'd write a poem to the snap of my fingers, and she would tap out the rhythm and embellish it until we had a song. Not every song was good, but at least I knew what I was dealing with before ten minutes had passed.

But by myself, I had a hard time. I thought the work was good in the end, but I wasn't producing well under pressure. I didn't even know what the song was about, except time.

Ten years. It had been impossible to talk about that length of time without impaling myself on it. It was so far off, and tomorrow. It was a lie, because it could be so much more if he took care of himself and played by the rules. Even after his heart gave out, if the doctors saw he ate right and took his medicine, he'd get another heart if it came available. It had been done. And was it really ten? Because there was a very healthy guy in Wyoming who had had his for a record-breaking twenty-five years, and there were new advances in anti-rejection meds every day and and and.... .

None of that would matter if he was dead. So I'd planned for that eventuality by girding myself, day after day. It would hurt. I would be in the hospital again, crying over him, alone, vulnerable, and scared. A shaft of ice already stabbed my spine whenever I passed Sequoia Hospital, and the knowledge that one day soon, I would go back for the same reason froze me in panic.

All I did was pray for him. The first six months of our marriage had been one big prayer without end, amen.

I couldn't get control of it by running or staying, and he wanted children. Children. I'd lost my father, and it had crushed me. But Jonathan wanted to have children and disappear when the oldest was nine. Or eight. Or who even knew. Left with a hopeless mother who had lost the love of her life. No amount of money could cure that.

And now, six months later, with his breath in my ear and his sexual dominance reestablished, was anything solved? No. Nothing was. But God damn if I was going to sing him a birthday song about a house because it was the only thing we could agree on.

He was better than that.

We were better than that.

I had a few hours to write him a new song. Not about how much time we had. Not about all our failings, but about what we meant to each other. About how fulfilling and worthwhile those ten years could be, if I stopped squinting into the distance at the end of them.

Tap tap tap TAP. *tap tap* tap TAP.

Chapter 11

Jonathan

Jogging. Herbal tea. Rabbit food. Jesus Christ, how had I survived six months without making my wife beg for mercy? I stood in the driveway, looking at our house from the street, for the hundredth time. It was deep in and behind a wall of roses, but who could see? From what angle? If I fucked her on the back patio, were her shaking tits visible from the public part of the beach? Could they hear her scream next door?

The low-slung, mid-century glass box was so well-designed and so well-placed that unless we kept the lights on and fucked against the window in a certain part of the bedroom at night, we couldn't be seen. I'd known that from the second day. But it *felt* as if we were exposed, and she liked that.

That morning, before she'd slinked off to the guest house to tap on the practice piano, I'd taken her against that window. Her handprints were still on it, like two frosted starfish. She'd put her hands against the glass when I told her to, ass out, legs spread almost but not quite wide enough. I'd stuck my fingers in her.

"No one can see you," I'd said then slapped her ass.

"Yes, sir."

"Do you believe me?"

"I want to."

I'd caned her hard and thoroughly until my arm ached and she was a groaning mess. It was her way of telling me she trusted me but needed that shade of doubt. It brought her so close to orgasm, I barely had to touch her with my dick before she came.

I might even learn to like this house.

"What are you doing in the middle of the street?" said a voice from behind me.

I didn't turn around. I knew my sister's voice better than I knew my mother's. "You should call before you show up."

Margie was hanging half out of the window of her Mercedes and waving for me to get out of her way into the driveway.

"I'm a newlywed, you know," I said.

"We had an appointment." She pulled in, and I followed on foot, letting the gate close behind me.

I opened the door for her when she stopped. "We did. I forgot."

She got out, yanking her briefcase free of the passenger seat floor. "You shouldn't have fired your assistant before you were finished with your business."

"I'm sick of calendars and commitments."

She made a thick sound that could have been interpreted as a *harrumph*, except that was too passive-aggressive for my sister. If she had something to say, she'd never let a vocal tic replace a well-placed barb. I led her inside.

"You want something?" I asked, opening the fridge.

"Nice place," she said, putting her briefcase on the island bar. "I almost went to the old one. Up in the hills." She snapped the briefcase open.

I got her a glass of water with no ice, and she thanked me as if she'd actually asked for it. But she didn't have to. I knew her at least that well. I opened a bottle of water for myself. I was off Perrier. Carbonation was on the No Intake list.

"Is it what you expected?" I asked.

"I expected a house cut in half with masking tape," she answered, taking papers out and laying them in neat piles on the granite.

"Did I make it sound that bad?" I had leaned on Margie the most since the surgery. I'd never talked about my emotional life before, but I had to now or I'd break. Margie was my valve, because she was honest and straight, and she knew when to shut the hell up.

"For two people suffering from post-traumatic stress? I think you're doing great. Not that I have anything healthy to compare you to." She clicked a pen and handed it to me. "Sign where I put yellow tabs. Initial on the purple."

I started from left to right, signing away about ten years of my life. The business I'd rebuilt for Dad in repayment for silence over Rachel. Twenty-two to thirty-two—over a billion and a quarter in assets in a managed trust. He could have it. Sale of the hotels, except K, where I met Monica. I wasn't ready to let that go. Another half a billion in real estate to a trust Margie would manage and share. After all the sales, my responsibility would be to do nothing but take care of myself.

"You think you might get bored?" Margie asked when I was halfway through the stacks.

"Yes. But I don't know what to do about it."

"There's this thing I heard about. You might be interested. Could kill some time. Definitely burn through some cash."

"Go on."

"In Switzerland. They're really close on an artificial heart."

"No."

"It's made from tissue. It doesn't need an external battery," she said.

"No."

"They need a lot of money for development, but you have it."

"Am I speaking the wrong language? No."

"Why?"

"I don't like the Swiss. The cheese offends me."

"Nice answer. Got a reason that makes sense?"

I put down the pen. I knew my mouth was set because I felt the tension in my jaw. "What would be the point? To get my wife's hopes up when it won't work? Then I die anyway? The sooner she starts coping with it, the better."

She pushed the pen toward me. "Finish up."

I got back to signing at the tabs. Full signature for yellow. Initials at purple. "I have the Arts Foundation to run. That'll keep me busy."

"Yeah. And you don't have to waste your time hoping for anything. You don't have to build a future."

"I'm the one who wants kids."

"That's not a future if you're dead. That's called a legacy."

I checked the details and flopped the last contract closed. "Just like a lawyer to get hung up on semantics."

"Just like a man." She restacked her papers, clacking them against the counter. "You just want to piss on the world one last time like it's a fire hydrant you'll never see again. I don't blame her for holding out on you."

Coming from anyone else, I would have been enraged. But Margie's love was so unconditional, I didn't know if she could ever say anything to make me truly angry.

"You know this is not about legacy," I said.

"Not consciously."

"It's about Monica."

"The everlasting gift of your DNA? Way to woo a girl."

I laughed. I had nothing else for her. I couldn't even explain myself to myself.

"It's nice to see you laugh, little brother. I thought they'd transplanted your sense of humor there for a while."

"Are you staying for lunch? I could stand to be insulted for another hour."

"Sorry." She plopped the papers in her briefcase. "Some of us have to work."

"I have a thing," I said. "For the birthday dinner later. I need you and Sheila to help."

She raised an eyebrow at me while she snapped the case closed. "A thing?"

"You'll like it. It involves jewelry."

"I hate jewelry."

"You'll like this."

Chapter 12

Monica

I exited the studio in the mid-afternoon, completely unsatisfied with my work. I went into the kitchen and, seeing as Jonathan wasn't around, reached for his box of pills.

I didn't know where I'd picked up the habit of thinking it was all right to count someone's meds. From living with Gabby, maybe. Jonathan had Laurelin to monitor him, make sure his medication was taken, and help him mind his Ps and Qs. That didn't stop me from peeking in his little plastic box with the days of the week on it.

Too many sets and subsets of pills. No wonder he needed a medical professional.

"Stop it," I told myself, snapping the box shut.

I pushed it back into the corner between the toaster and the fridge, but it was too late. The medicines had a smell, and they brought it all back. The inevitable images of him dying in that fucking hospital, his heart breaking right out of his chest. The colors of the hospital lounge carpet, the paint, the cafeteria, the recovery room, all of it flashed before me. I closed my eyes as if that would block out the smells and colors of those weeks.

"He's fine," I said to myself. "Stop it."

"Stop what?" Jonathan came in from the patio, slick with sweat and ocean water. He'd been jogging.

"Stop tracking sand all over the floor. Look at this mess!"

"Why?" He grabbed my waist and pulled me into him. "Afraid it'll scratch your back?" He pushed me into the kitchen island and bit my neck at the curve.

"Don't leave a mark!" I pushed him away, not that it did anything. "We're going to Sheila's and—" I couldn't finish when he stuck his hand between my legs and yanked my pants down by the crotch. "We just did it," I groaned. I could have ended the California drought with what flowed between my legs.

"Define 'just.'" He unceremoniously pulled up my shirt and grabbed a nipple. My body went on high alert.

"I'm still sore."

"That's how I like you."

I pushed him away for real. "I don't want to use my safe word for stupid bullshit, Drazen, but back off. I'm making a snack. What do you want?"

He smiled, taking the hint but not believing me. "You, with butter and jelly."

"I have a baguette left from last night."

"Fine." He pulled my shirt down.

"You should have protein. An egg or something."

"There's enough protein in my morning shake to create an entire mammalian species."

I kissed him gently. "You should try the bread with the chimichuri."

"Hell, no." He opened the fridge and leaned into where the condiments hung out. His running pants hung low on his hips. "I see you looking at me," he said, still rooting around the back.

"You've gained weight."

"These are my fat pants." He smiled, shutting the door and putting the goods on the counter.

I unscrewed the cap on the hot sauce and ripped off a piece of baguette. "Try." I dipped the bread into the sauce, but I got as little as possible. I wanted my husband to get over the spicy food thing. I knew it embarrassed him. I held it up. "Come on, I made this with my own hands, with my mother. Think of the generations of women who have perfected it for the sake of this one moment in time."

"Not to be dramatic."

"I'll get a samba band in here if you like. *Cha cha chadda.*" I swung my hips to the rhythm, with my piece of bread out.

He grabbed my wrist and held it still. I froze. Had I insulted his masculinity or something?

He locked eyes with me then tore them away. He kissed down the inside of my arm, my wrist, and took the bread in his mouth. He chewed. I waited. He had zero change of expression, and I smiled a little.

He swallowed. "I feel like my face is burning from the inside."

"Well, you look gorgeous."

He let my hand go and screwed the top back on the chimichuri. "You're just seeing a free man."

"Oh, right, Margie came today. Did you get rid of everything?"

"I gave up every hotel from A to J. I kept the one where I met you. I'm sentimental like that."

"Did she tell you about the Swiss thing?"

He froze. I swallowed. Was it more complicated than I thought? Was it too expensive an investment?

"Yes," he said.

"And?"

"I'll think about it."

"Really?"

"I—"

I had an explosion I couldn't control or foresee. All my pent-up feelings went off like controlled detonation, except the building didn't collapse but took off like a rocket. I threw my arms around his neck, wrapping my legs around his waist.

He was thrown back a step catching me. "Jesus, Monica."

"Happy birthday, baby." I kissed him seven times. I couldn't stop, but then I had to talk. "They're so close they just need a push. I know it's a lot of money but it's worth it when they figure out the rejection thing it needs its own special rejection meds which they're also developing and then a healthy testsubjectwhois—"

"Whoa whoa."

"Young, with no secondary problems."

"Monica."

"It's you. You. Especially if you fund it, then they have to make it you. And it lasts forever. You'll have to get hit by a bus when you're a hundred and ten."

He loosened his grip until my feet hit the floor. "Do you know what the odds are of it working?"

"Great!" I stuffed the bread back into the bag. "The odds are great. I mean, I don't know. I didn't ask. But the odds of the one you have lasting even twenty years are worse, since they're, like, zero."

I felt like a giddy schoolgirl. I wanted to sing and dance, and my smile was totally involuntary. I could barely contain myself. I felt as if the past seven months might be erased, put away in some jar in the china cabinet where we could ogle how cute and silly it all had been.

Jonathan leaned against the counter, clicking the ice in his water glass and staring into it as if it were a problem. I felt crazy and childish in comparison. I cleared my throat, choking back the relief and trying to find that worry again. But it wouldn't go away. I was over the moon, and he was still on the earth.

I breathed deeply, trying to calm down. I was overreacting for sure, but it was his heart, his life, his chest. If he was somber over it, then I could take it down a notch. I moved the bread bag three inches. I touched a pan, shifting it on the stove. I smiled as I turned a knickknack a quarter way around. My mother had given it to me. It said BELIZE.

"I thought you were going to eat something," Jonathan said.

"Fuck it." I stood in front of him. "I want you for a snack." I dropped to my knees and yanked down his sweatpants.

"Okay, Monica—"

I gave him big eyes from below. "You don't want me to suck your cock?" I felt him harden in my hand.

"I'd love a blowjob, thank you. I have to take a handful of pills. Then I'm going to shower. So I need you to go upstairs, take your clothes off, and be ready for a quick go before we leave. And when I say ready, I mean mouth open and hands behind your back."

"Yes, sir," I said through a smile.

"Your legs should be open all the way this time. I mean it. We're on a tight clock."

"Yes."

"Have I mentioned how much I love being married to you?"

"Not today."

"Let me finish up here, and I'll show you."

Chapter 13

Jonathan

I loved being married to Monica—at least, I did once we had reestablished full participation by both parties. The weeks following my visit to the studio, minus the constant medication, had been exactly what I'd wanted from the honeymoon we never had.

Things would get back to normal soon, whatever that was. I still couldn't find a taste for the food I used to like. Anything spicy tasted like poison, and I craved sour foods as if I were pregnant. I thought less and less about having a strange piece of meat inside me. My chest didn't feel as heavy with attention as often. I was in a routine with Laurelin, the medicine, the nutrition, and my odd addiction to jogging which made the team of doctors happy.

Normal. For somebody.

But at least I could still make plans for Monica's body and execute them. If I couldn't eat the spicy chimichuri, which we apparently had a never-ending supply of, at least I could spoon-feed her while she was on her hands and knees.

I'd overheard her fielding calls from the people she worked with, putting them off, apologizing. She was an artist, and she'd need to get back to it soon. We still hadn't talked about how to manage that part of our lives because when we did, I'd have to admit for the first time that I didn't want her to travel so much. I didn't know what to do about that.

The visions of my heart leaving my body persisted. Sometimes it flopped around the floor and squirted blood; sometimes it only came halfway out; and sometimes, when I scratched the itchy scar, my fingers went through the soft tissue and touched the foreign, beating thing, and in response, it detached and slid into my palm.

Monica was always there in those waking dreams. In the easiest ones, she was simply horrified. In the worst of them, I was driving and killed her when I died at the wheel. But traveling? I was convinced the heart would stay on the ground if I flew, as if it weren't tethered to my body but to the state of California. I'd ruin her trip and probably her life. I was never scared of my own death. I'd dealt with that already, but its effect on Monica would be shattering.

None of it was rational. None of it made sense. And my nearly physical ache for children made the least sense of all the crazy nonsense I believed. Knowing that didn't shake the fear or the longing away.

I'd managed to wiggle out of traveling until we drove down to Sheila's place in Palos Verdes. The June sunset left the sky palette-knifed in orange and navy, and the temperature hung between inoffensively cold and completely generic. With the top down and Monica next to me in the Jag, twisted in her seat, the weather was perfect.

"Are you going to sit like that in front of my sisters?" I asked.

"Hey, if you wanted me to sit straight, you should have been a little gentler."

"You didn't marry me for my gentle ways."

She poked me in the ribs and I laughed, but she sat straighter.

"Is there any country in the world you haven't been to?" she asked.

"Probably."

"Any one you want to go to?"

"Iceland. But I'm not cleared yet."

"Yes, you are. You haven't asked Dr. Solis at all. We could send a bunch of shit shakes ahead and make sure whatever cardiac unit there was knew you were coming."

I didn't answer right away. We were communicating, but I shouldn't answer rashly. I pulled off the 110, slowing my car and my thoughts. "The thought of it is…" I knew what the honest answer was, but it was hard to speak aloud.

"We can do everything to make it less scary—"

"I didn't say I was scared."

"Well, I am." She took my hand, looking out her side of the car. "Anyway. The food's really bland there. You should like it."

I reached under her arm and tickled her. She squealed and twisted away. What was I going to do with her? Besides spank her raw and love her senseless? At some point, I would keep our honesty promise and break it to her that even if I funded the artificial heart, I wouldn't test it. But her relief and happiness were too precious and delicate. I hoped some other obstacle would present itself in the meantime. Blood type, body size, anything.

I went through the gate and parked in front of Sheila's house, pulling the emergency brake. "About the Swiss thing…"

"Yeah?"

"If it's not what you think or if it doesn't work out, you're going to be disappointed."

"It'll work out. I know it."

She didn't wait for me to come around. She just opened the door and got out, bouncing as if it were someone's birthday.

Chapter 14

Monica

Jonathan followed me, flipping his keys in his palm, spinning them around a finger, flipping again. Spin. Flip. Spin. Flip. All in the rhythm of his gait, like a perfectly tuned instrument of movement and sound. He wore a white shirt open at the collar, sleeves rolled to the elbow, and jeans that fit as if custom built for him. Jogging miles every morning had toned his legs and added grace to his gait.

I rang Sheila's bell. The door was wide enough to fit two adults walking abreast, so I didn't know how he was supposed to get in without seeing everyone. But it hadn't been my job to hide everyone. It had been my job to get him there on time.

He slipped his hand across my bare shoulder and grasped me by the back of the neck, saying nothing and owning me completely. I relaxed right into the warmth of his hand.

The door opened. Sheila wore a pair of skinny jeans and a lavender hoodie. Bare feet. Hair brushed for a change. "Happy birthday!"

"Thanks." He kissed her on the cheek, leaving his other hand on me as if I'd run away.

Was the party off? Had something happened? Where was the big opening salvo? Sheila stepped out of the way. Jonathan guided me in the door, and I greeted her. Looking over her shoulder, I caught sight of the buffet and felt more than saw the presence of other people.

After Jonathan stepped in and the door closed behind him, the shout of "Surprise!" came all at once, at incredible volume, from an impossible number of people. They appeared from the hall, behind the couch, the patio, as if a switch had been flicked.

Jonathan stood in the doorway a second then clutched his chest and stepped back. Mouth open, eyes wide, as if in shock and surprise at the pain.

I went blind, reaching for him, everything shut out but the sounds of the beeping machines, the stench of alcohol, the shadowed lines of the blinds falling across his white face in the afternoon.

Hands on me. Strong arms, and the sounds of the room pierced the veil of terror.

Laughter. A few dozen people laughing hysterically, and a collective *awwww*.

Jonathan held me up, looking at me with a smile.

"You asshole!" I said.

"Come on," he said. "It was funny."

"No, it wasn't," I whispered softly so he'd know I was serious. I dropped my register and changed my inflection to sound like him when he didn't want an argument. "Don't ever do that to me again."

"I think it was that bite of chimichuri." He rubbed his stomach and smiled.

I didn't laugh. Didn't smile. Didn't give him anything but ice cold anger.

He looked pensively at me, pressing his lips together, before he said, "I'm sorry."

I was still shaken. I couldn't forgive him. Not yet, and luckily I didn't have to, because Leanne put a drink in my hand.

"Thanks," I said.

"He's a fucker." For a fashion designer, Leanne usually dressed in clothes that were no more exciting than the average plain Jane's, and to be honest, she was kind of a slob. But that day, her jeans were rippling with shades of blue and the creases in her hands were deep indigo.

I swished the drink. It was a yellow, juicy thing with ice. Behind me, Jonathan gladhanded and laughed.

"What happened to your hands?" I asked.

"We're doing denim tie-dye in India." She indicated her jeans, which went from deepest indigo to pale sky in irregular patterns.

"Hm," was all I said.

"Not perfected yet, obviously. And it's messing with the sideseams." She grabbed her belt loops and yanked up her pants.

"God, I wish you'd brush your hair," Margie said to Leanne from behind me.

Leanne's bracelets jangled when she extended her silver-ringed middle finger at her sister. They tormented each other for a few more seconds,

Drazen-style, and I twisted around to look for Jonathan. I found him chatting with Eddie and another guy, perfectly happy, no chest pain, arms gesturing without stiffness. He wasn't having a heart attack.

As if summoned by my attention, he looked at me through the crowd and winked.

Asshole.

Gorgeous asshole.

I excused myself and went to the kitchen. Staff buzzed around, slapping the oven open and shut, speaking the language of waitstaff I knew all too well. Eileen Drazen stood by the sink in sensible tan pants and a jacket, throwing her head back as if she'd just taken a pill. She sipped whiskey and turned around.

"Hey," I said. "How are you doing?"

I reached in the cabinet for a glass. She and I had met under terrible circumstances, and once I understood that, and she understood that I wasn't after her son's money, she was still made of ice. But at least she was only cold, rather than cold and dismissive.

"Fine. You?"

"I'm getting over the psychotic break I nearly had a few minutes ago." I filled the glass from the fridge door.

"Yes. On the scale of inappropriate jokes, that was deep in the red. You should make him suffer for it."

"Where's Declan?" I wanted to avoid him. He'd laughed off the three-doctors incident as simple misinformation, and I didn't have a fact to hold against him. Sure, he *could have* innocently told me three doctors exiting the operating room meant the patient had died because he'd thought it was the case. To a certain extent, it was true. But it had been two doctors and a patient advocate. So that was explainable. And he *might have* not known that the anesthesiologist was expected to sit through the entire transplant to manage the induced coma and, thus, would exit with the other doctors. Sure. It was all plausible. But his smile of satisfaction when I dropped? That was totally subjective and completely real.

So like the rest of his children, I simply didn't trust him.

"My husband's around." Eileen waved her ring-thick hand. "Everyone is here somewhere. I lose count of all of them."

"Have you seen Leanne's jeans?"

I said it to get a reaction, and she shuddered as if it was scandalous. My mother-in-law was such a backward prude that sometimes I wondered if it was all an act to protect a burning sexuality.

"I think they're cute," I said, sipping my water.

"You would," she said without reproach. "I've learned to stop concerning myself with my children's tastes. They get away, and then, poof, they're not your responsibility. They're just people who invite you over for holidays."

I nodded.

"How many does he want?" Eileen asked.

"Ten or more," I said, putting my empty glass in the grey bus pan.

Eileen barked a little laugh. "Men."

"Yeah."

"They figure if they have the money for a staff, they can breed to their heart's content."

"You didn't want eight kids?"

"I wanted seven. Though the eighth?" She shrugged with a smile. "He'll do. It was nice to have a boy. Broke up the catfights over who used the last of the conditioner."

I laughed. "Really? With all your staff? You ran out of conditioner?"

"Your husband was pouring it down the sink," she said. "The joker. No matter how much Delilah bought, he dumped it or hid it."

I caught sight of Eddie in a tan suit and red tie.

"Ed," Eileen said. "Nice to see you." They double-kissed.

"You too, Mrs. Drazen."

I rarely saw Eddie Milpas in his social setting. He knew Jonathan from college, but to me, he was the guy in the engineering room who made everyone else nervous. So I nearly burst out laughing when he called Eileen Mrs. Drazen.

"Come to check on the catering?" Eileen asked.

"Came to steal away this lady," he replied, cocking his head toward me.

"Do we have to talk about business?" I asked.

"If you'd call me back—"

"My cue to leave," Eileen said. Without another word, she was gone, leaving me with Eddie and the constantly moving catering staff.

"I'm sorry," I said. "I was going to call you on Monday."

"Which Monday, exactly?"

"This coming—"

"Look, I know you have other things on your mind. So I'm not going to sit here and watch you fidget."

I crossed my arms. "I'm not fidgeting."

"Can I give you a piece of friendly advice?"

"No."

"Professional advice then. One hundred percent free. Get yourself an agent to filter your damn calls."

I laughed softly at the irony. That was exactly what I'd been trying to do when I met Jonathan.

Eddie continued, "If I wasn't friends with your boyfriend—"

"Husband."

"You'd miss out on the opportunity of a lifetime if I didn't happen to be at this party."

"Okay, you've got my attention."

"Your EP is releasing in a few weeks. Right about then, Quentin Marshall is doing another charity song. Single cut. Wide distribution. Like the Christmas one for the drought in Australia. Everyone's on it."

"Everyone?"

"Everyone. Omar. Brad Frasier. The Glocks. Benita. The list will knock you over. They have a space for a girl act like you, but here's the thing."

My heart pounded. That did sound like something groundbreaking for my career. Being associated with big names like that could get my name out to people who had never heard of me. It could give me credibility and standing. And if it was a little after the EP came out, even better.

"Okay," I said. "Tell me the thing."

"They have to herd all these cats, and that means it could record on a dime any time between the fifteenth and the thirtieth, and the big names? Well, they call the shots. They get there when they get there. The less-established artists have to be ready to go."

"I'm ready."

"Can you fly to New York tomorrow?"

"Tomorrow? New York?"

"Quentin Marshall? Hello?"

My throat went dry. I wanted to go. I wanted to get on a plane immediately and sit in the studio waiting for The Glocks to show up. I wanted to hear Omar sing in a studio. I could learn so much from that guy. He had a sound no one could emulate. If I could watch him, I was sure I'd pick up some tips.

"I don't know," I said.

"You don't know?"

"I have to ask Jonathan."

He put up his hands. "Fine. You have until tomorrow."

"Tomorrow is Sunday."

"Music doesn't take the weekend off."

"Okay. I'll call you by tomorrow night."

"Noon. That's the best you get. I have a line of people who would scratch your eyes out for this opportunity."

"Monica," Margie said, poking her head in. "We need you at the piano."

I glanced at the counter before following Margie. The catering staff hovered over a cake, lighting thirty-three candles. It seemed like enough fire to burn the house down, but that was the point. A man who almost died at thirty-two deserved every single flame.

Stop.

I needed to stop obsessing over the transplant. I'd given my worry a wide berth, as if it was insurance against something bad happening, but I'd let a healthy concern metastasize into a cancer. I had been perfectly happy letting it take over my life until I dreaded singing "Happy Birthday" because it sounded like a dirge.

I knew where the piano was from my last visit, when Sheila had insisted I play. I'd thought she was trotting me out like a trained monkey, which I resented for a few seconds, but once my fingers hit the keys, I realized what she'd done. I'd played "Wade in the Water" for his family, and music did what music does: it brought us together and gave us something to talk about. It was a way into our shared humanity. I'd loved music before I loved my husband, and it would outlast the two of us.

As I stroked out a scale in the parlor with thirty people in attendance, I let myself love it again. I caught Jonathan's eye across the room. He was fingering an apple with his nephew David. I knew the positioning. Split-fingered fastball. David, at ten, was too young for that. I shook my head at Jonathan and took my hand from the keys long enough to wave my finger "no no" at him. He smiled, winked, and showed David the whipping motion that would get the ball to split, along with his nephew's young tendons.

He's not teaching our kids that.

"Up tempo, people!" I cried just as the cake appeared.

"Happy Birthday"—well, there's not much you can do with it when everyone's singing and not listening to the piano. I smiled. Fuck it. I gleefully let everyone else set the tempo, and I sang along in the dragged out rhythm. No one knew why I was smiling, not even Jonathan, who came up and leaned on the piano.

Sheila brought out the blazing white confection and placed it on the piano as we sang, "*yoooooooouuuu!*"

His face lit golden and his smile a true thing, from his beautiful candlelit green eyes to his borrowed heart, he blew out his candles. Or tried. No one could blow out thirty-three candles (and one for good luck) in one breath.

"Nice effort," I said, standing.

He put his arm around me, and we blew together. I clapped and faced him. I wanted a kiss, but he glanced at the cake, then at me, then back at the cake, then at me, as if he was trying to tell me something. I looked down at it, thinking we'd missed a candle.

And we had. One little bugger was still bopping along, but I didn't blow it, because inside the ring of candles sat an open, frosting-caked velvet box, and inside the box was a ring.

"Jonathan?"

He plucked the candle out of the cake. "That was the candle I hold for you." He blew it, and the flame popped up again.

Thirty people and ten kids said, "*Awwww.*"

He pursed his lips in a smile. "I didn't know there would be so many people here."

Margie took the candle from his fingers. It still burned. It must have been one of those parlor trick candles, and it was sweet.

"What are you doing?" I asked, still confused. He guided me back onto the piano stool, and I sat. "We're already married."

"Not properly," he said, picking the ring out of the box. "Not on my own power and not for the right reasons."

Were there dozens of people in the room? I couldn't hear them. I couldn't see them. Only this man, this king, getting on his knee in front of me.

"Jonathan, you don't have to. I…"

"You going to give me your hand or not?"

"I can't." I put them in the corners of my eyes as if to press the tears away. "I'm using them. Hang on."

"Get on with it!" a male voice called from the crowd.

"Shut the fuck up, Pat!" someone else said.

Jonathan touched my left wrist, and I brought my hand down. I didn't wear the borrowed diamond anymore. Just the key ring wedding band.

"Will you marry me, Monica?" I sniffed back a bunch of tears, and before I could answer, he continued, looking at me. "Will you have a normal engagement with me? Will you get to know me on any given Tuesday?" He shook his head quickly, as if making it all up on the spot and discarding an idea. "Can we plan a real wedding and argue over seating arrangements? Can we find the things we agree on naturally? Flowers. Invitations. Whatever is important to *us*. I want us to be right with the world. I want us to take our time, because you're worth it. We are worth it. Nothing skimped or rushed. You deserve all of it. Everything."

Doing it all over. A second chance at a mask of normalcy. He wasn't rethinking or going backward. He was giving me a gift.

"I love you," I whispered through my tears. "I want you. Everything."

He slipped the ring on my finger. The diamond was huge and the color of sunshine.

"A canary diamond," he said. "For my songbird."

"Gross, Uncle Jon!"

Jonathan turned around toward David, who had a face like kneaded dough at the thought of icky grown-up love.

"Yeah, gross," a laughing, adult voice called out.

Jonathan glanced at me for half a second, and I saw mischief in those eyes. I didn't have a moment to tell him not to do whatever it was he was about to do, before he scooped up a swipe of white frosting from his cake and flung it at his tormentor.

"Quiet, Patrick!" Jonathan said.

Impulse moved my arm. I scooped up another bunch of frosting and flung it at my husband and fiancé, coating the bottom half of his face in a buttercream goatee. "Be nice to the guests!"

He blew, spraying me in vanilla, and everyone laughed and clapped. David, seeing the world as only a ten-year-old could, recognized an opportunity when he saw one. He mashed his hand in the cake then flung it at both of us. Jonathan, not to be out-immatured by a ten-year-old, whipped around and threw a mess of it at his nephew, with half of it getting on Eddie.

"Hey, asshole!" Eddie shouted.

"Language!" Sheila called, too late.

Her son threw another handful of cake at her. The young pitcher had great aim, getting his mother in the face with white confection.

"You!" Sheila said with a pointed finger.

I shut the cover over the piano keys just in time, because all hell broke loose. Cake flew everywhere. Laughter. Squeals. My god, the cake must have been huge. I was covered. Jonathan was covered. Everyone I could hit with a lump of cake was covered, and we were all laughing through beards of white frosting and fruit filling. The kids were licking the floor. Eileen slipped on a wad of cake and laughed, and her granddaughter put a handful down Eileen's shirt. Leanne fell when she tried to help Eileen up, and Jonathan, my beautiful king, put his arms around me and kissed cake off my lips.

"Goddess," he whispered, even though in the chaos, he didn't have to. No one was paying attention to us.

"Yes, Jonathan. Yes. I'll marry you."

"Let's take our time." He kissed my cheek, sucking frosting off.

Our time.

He was giving me permission to stop counting the months and years. Permission to let it happen as it would, to stop using worry as a paper-thin bulwark against the tides of fate. This was our time. However long it was, it belonged to us.

• • •

The staff had made short work of the mess. Clothing had been stripped off, some laundered, some left in bags, some rinsed and worn wet. Sheila had loaned me a pair of pale blue velour sweatpants and a white shirt with a neck so wide it fell off my shoulder. It was probably the best party I'd been to in my life.

"I love this on you," Jonathan said, pressing his lips to my bare shoulder. We sat at the piano in the empty parlor as I played a soft jazzy thing.

"It doesn't go with the ring."

"I can't wait to see how that looks on you naked."

"It's beautiful. I love it." I did. I had a hard time keeping my eyes off it.

"I'm not trying to take away our marriage, goddess. You need to know that."

"I know."

"But it was hasty."

I sighed. Yes, it had been hasty, and for all the wrong reasons, but I hadn't thought about it that deeply. I hadn't thought about anything deeply in the past six months, because it hurt. I had the feeling I wouldn't be able to avoid it anymore.

"I got you a birthday present," I said.

"What do you get the guy who has everything?" He brushed his lips on my shoulder and drew his fingertips along the back of my neck.

I smiled, and a ball of hitched breaths gathered in my throat. He thought he had everything. I had no idea I'd married such an optimist. "I was supposed to play this for you in front of everyone, but you stole my limelight with this big stinking rock."

"They had a bigger one, but it was imperfect."

"It's not the size of the boat."

"Yes, it is. It's a buoyancy thing, see." He motioned with the flat of his hand, swaying it. "Too small and it sinks."

I laughed, and he laughed with me.

"Do you want to hear your song or not?"

"More than anything."

I took a deep breath. "I want you to know, I wrote one before, and it was all about what we've been through in the past six months. And I hate it. It was… I don't know. It was ugly, and it dwelled on things that weren't important."

"Can I hear it?"

"No." I hit the first notes definitively and found my opening tempo. "It's short."

"Sing it twice."

"You ready, Drazen?"

"I'm ready, Drazen."

I sang it quietly for an audience of one. I wasn't confident enough that it would survive me belting it out. Not until I did a few hundred rewrites.

How fragile it is
And how real it all feels
I can touch it, taste it
Hold it like a baby forever
But that's not the deal

I am your ever
You are my after

I am your altar
You are my prayer

Where do I end
And you begin
Because I'm untied sometimes
And we're a dandelion seed in the wind
I'm a seed or a flower.
Or I'm a breath or a wish

I am your heart
You are my beat
And I am your voice
And you are my song

"Happy birthday," I said, letting my hands slip off the keys. "Many more. Many, many more."

He kissed me, then I kissed him. His skin smelled like cake, and his tongue tasted of salt water. We wrapped our arms around each other, connected at the mouth, as if we were passing a common soul between us.

Chapter 15

Jonathan

She was most perfect in nudity. I left her standing there, hands at her sides, in front of my chair so I wouldn't have to move to watch her change. I put my elbows on my knees and folded my hands together, leaning forward. She was an arm's length away, but I didn't reach for her.

"Look straight ahead, Monica."

I knew what it did to her when I kept her in stasis. I'd known the first night when I'd sent her upstairs naked, and I knew now, after my birthday party, with the canary diamond heavy on her finger, that her body was changing before my eyes. In trying to stand still, she was acutely aware of my gaze on her. If she stood still and I kept my concentration, she'd be soaking wet and very close before I even touched her.

Her nipples hardened in the cool night air. The triangle between her legs was a promise of compliance and unyielding pleasure. The ocean outside the open balcony door would be the background noise to the melody of her cries.

Slowly, I reached my hand forward and touched her belly. It quivered like the undulating ocean behind me. I drew the finger down between her legs and stroked inside her thigh. Her body reacted involuntarily, and I took my hand back.

"I'm not going to fuck you," I said. "You're already bruised everywhere I want to put my dick." I kissed her navel then pulled away.

"My mouth is in great shape," she said.

"So is mine." I stroked her gently, awakening her nipples. "What if I laid you on that bed and pulled your legs apart. Just the tip of my tongue on your cunt. If I was gentle, would you come, do you think?"

"Yes. I would."

"Do you like your ring?"

"I love it."

I stood and wedged my foot between hers, pushing her legs apart. She was used to it and spread them without a stumble. I went behind her. She was framed by the ocean, the curves of her ass blue and black in the evening light. I got on my knees, close to her so she could feel my breath. I waited until the tension was so taut it felt as if it would break like rock candy.

I brushed my finger inside her thigh. She was painted in angry bruises there too. I'd stopped feeling guilty about inflicting damage; I knew the difference between hurt and harm.

"I'm sorry about the party. About worrying you. I was joking, not thinking."

"I'll die if you do that again."

I brushed my fingers over her soft wet lips, slightly touching the dampness.

"I just..."

"Go ahead," I said.

"That hospital. The smells. The colors. You. It claws at me. In my sleep, I hear the doctors whispering. I dream you're dying in a room I can't find. When I think of it, I just think of you in pain. It hurt me. And I'm sorry I'm being self-involved."

"You're not being self-involved." I kissed the small of her back.

"I dread it. I know I'm going to have to go back there with you, and the dread hangs on me."

I rested my cheek against the curve of her spine and put my arms around her waist. She didn't move her hands, ever obedient when in scene. I could hear her lungs through her rib cage as they let out short, sharp breaths.

"I didn't give you permission to cry," I said gently.

"I'm sorry."

I pulled away from her and stood. "On the bed, goddess. Facedown. Hands under your thighs. And face the window."

She did it, and when she automatically put her ass up in ready position, my dick went completely rigid. I pressed her ass down until she was totally flat against the bed. She watched me peel off my clothes. I put pajama bottoms on so I wouldn't distract her.

"Wait here."

I went into the bathroom for lotion. The last time I'd done that, I'd seen her negative pregnancy test. I thought about that thing every time I went in there. The burden of it was so heavy that I often went down the hall to piss.

"Are we still in scene?" she asked when I sat at the edge of the bed.

"No." I put a blob of lotion in my hand and closed it into a fist to warm the lotion.

"I want you to fuck me."

"Nope."

"Why not?"

"Because it's my birthday, and I can do whatever I want." I put the lotion on her back and slowly dragged my hands down from her shoulder blades to her waist.

Her eyes fluttered closed. I put more weight on the heels of my hands and moved them back up to her shoulders. She groaned.

"What were you and Eddie talking about?" I asked. She stiffened. "Relax. It's just a question. Did he upset you?" I worked my hands over her shoulders and down her biceps.

"No. But there's a thing in New York. I don't think I can make it."

"No?"

She made a noise in her throat that was a cross between "no" and "that feels nice."

"The last two weeks have been good, goddess. Really good." I focused on her shoulders for a second then moved back down her body. I stopped at her ass, which, in all its beauty, was welted and tender. I pressed my thumbs into the sides of her spine and moved back up.

"Mmm."

"You are everything. My everything. There's nothing I'd change about you. And that includes your talent and ambition."

"I don't want to be away from you," she grumbled.

"I'm bound to you wherever you are. You know that, right?"

She opened her eyes and looked at me through the web of hair. "Come with me."

"No. I have things to do here."

"Like what?"

"Hush." I moved the hair away and kissed her cheek, then I grabbed the lotion and moved to the end of the bed. "You need to make your life happen. If I hadn't been sick, you'd come and go as you pleased. As *we* pleased. That's what I want for you."

The insides and backs of her thighs couldn't be touched. Her ass either.

What a gorgeous mess. I'd planted that bamboo thinking I might use it, but I had no idea how effective it was. I gave her feet and calves attention, rubbing away her worry and stress.

"We need to live fully, goddess. We both need to live as if we could die tomorrow, and we have to plan for a future where you're a hundred and ten."

She moaned. I'd promised her my mouth, and my dick wanted hers, but when I finished rubbing her feet, she was fast asleep.

Chapter 16
Monica

I called Eddie from the back deck while Jonathan had his run, and I told him I was going to New York. Laurelin dropped into the lounge chair next to me in her sensible little sneakers and zip-up purple fleece.

"You're going again?" she asked.

"Yeah. New York. It's a big deal, kind of. Why?"

"I have a week away coming. Jerry is taking me to—"

"You can't!" I sat up straight in my chair, tingling with adrenaline. "No, I mean. You can but not now. Please!"

"Don't worry." She put her hand on my shoulder. "I'll set him up. He'll be fine."

I wanted to support her, and I wanted her to have a nice time. I wanted Jonathan to be fine. But the reality of him being alone wasn't making it from my brain to my mouth. No, worry was taking a detour through my heart instead.

"You know what?" I said, leaning back in my chair. "I'll just stay home. It's not that big a deal."

Laurelin leaned back and put her foot on the little glass-and-metal table. She must have thought I was schizophrenic. "You know, if this was my house, I'd never want to leave either. I'd just sit here and gestate all day."

I laughed, and she smiled at me.

"I think you can go," she said after a minute.

"Nah."

"I think you *should* go." I didn't answer, just tilted my head a little, and she continued. "I'm not going to be here forever, and you all need to learn how to function. I mean, these issues? The pills and the way he has to log everything? They aren't going anywhere. It'll always be this way. And you hovering over him because you're scared, I get it. But at some point, you have to let go."

I set my jaw. "I'm not letting him go."

"You know what I mean."

I did. I knew she meant I had to stop mothering him, but I'd taken it the exact wrong way because it served my immediate purpose. If I acknowledged that I knew what she meant and that I'd heard it, I'd have to admit she was right.

Chapter 17

Jonathan

I ran far away. Far enough to be out of Monica's earshot and then some. I made it to the crowded part of the beach and trotted to the street, trying to shake a feeling that if Monica went to New York, things would get disorganized and neglected.

I'd had a mitt when I was about eleven. It was a Rawlings Gold. The best. And I wore it in just the way I liked it. One spring afternoon, I was dicking around with my cousins in the yard, tossing the ball around and trying out new curse words. We went inside to play video games, and I left my glove in the grass as I'd done dozens of times.

It never rains in Los Angeles, unless you leave your glove out. Then it pours, and the leather hardens. Stupid negligence can turn into disaster. I got another glove, but it was never the same. My hand grew before I could wear it in right, and I always felt an acute loss I couldn't explain.

I didn't want to treat Monica like a baseball glove. I didn't want it to rain on her while my back was turned.

"Quentin?" I said when I got through to my friend. A dozen seagulls screamed at me when I interrupted them on a bench.

Quentin Marshall answered in his Aussie clip. He was a rock star specializing in charity work, and I'd written his foundation a few checks over the years. "Drazen! How are you doing? I heard about the heart, mate. That's tough stuff."

"It keeps life interesting."

"Bet it does."

He paused, and I heard a siren in the distance and the belch of a city bus. Typical New York ambient noise.

"So what can I do for you?" he asked.

"You invited my wife to sing with you for something?"

"Yeah, I hope that's all right? She's got a great set of pipes. And the cause could use your help as well. There are kids dying of dehydration every day."

"You can always count on my help. But if Monica decides to go, I want you to do something for me."

"Just say it, and you got it."

How was I supposed to phrase this without sounding like a sicko stalker? I meant no harm by it, of course, and it wasn't as though she hadn't traveled before, but I felt differently than I did months ago, even weeks ago. "If there's anything she needs, or if there's something special you think she might need, even if she doesn't know what it is—can you make sure she gets it? I want her taken care of."

"That's it?"

"That's it."

"Mate, I will treat her like a precious flower. On my honor."

"Thank you."

"My pleasure."

We hung up. The ocean pounded the edges of the rocks into smooth stones, a millennias-long process I witnessed for a few minutes before I got up and continued my run.

Chapter 18

Monica

I'd been away from post-surgery Jonathan before. I'd flown to places I'd never been to and experienced them through hollow eyes and a worn-down heart. I couldn't say my trip to New York was any different. I was still worn out; I was still dragged home by tight-twisted strands. I was still worried. But something had changed. The worry wasn't colored a dark grey, and my thoughts of Jonathan weren't painful. I didn't feel guilty. I felt alive, vibrating, humming with potential, and I missed him. I missed his company, his laugh, his touch. I missed his enfolding presence beside me. The guilt left a vacuum in its absence, and nature, in its abhorrence, filled it with hope.

I flew commercial. I wanted to be surrounded by people. I wanted to feel the hum of life in the comings and goings of people: the babies crying; the pilots and stewardesses in their neat little packs, rolling suitcases whirring behind; the bright colors of the snack stand in the artificial lights; and the carpets worn where people walked.

I didn't make up a story when I told Jonathan I didn't need his plane. Instead of saying something facile about scheduling, I tried to express my need, as intangible as it was, and he understood, and agreed, and asked if I was going to fly coach.

That didn't seem necessary. Marrying a Drazen had its privileges.

He'd laughed and held me, offering his team to set up the flights. As close as we'd been in bed, or at play, or when he was rubbing my back and telling me how much he loved me, when I explained why I wanted to fly commercial and he understood, I felt truly married. He understood me. I could tell him even the worst nonsense, and he did more than agree. He became a part of me, tapped into my thoughts, a partner.

I'd thought I knew what that meant, but I didn't.

I was so high, I chatted incessantly with the guy next to me about music and dance. He was a French choreographer, and of course he gave me a definite "I'd be happy to fuck you" vibe even after seeing my ring. But I didn't care. I wasn't sleeping with him. I could still enjoy the conversation. I was married to a king, after all. I didn't have to concern myself with what other people wanted from me.

A bodybuilder in a suit waited for me at the gate with a handwritten sign that said "Mrs. O'Drassen."

"Hi," I said. "Are you Dean?"

"Yes, ma'am." He took my bag. "I'll drive you to the hotel to drop your things. I'm hired out for as long as you need me, so you can call any time."

"Great. There's a dinner tonight. In Hell's Kitchen. Can you take me there?"

"Absolutely."

I'd never been to New York, and I couldn't believe how crowded, tight, old, and yet shiny, spacious, and vibrant it was. And this was just from the window of a silver Rolls Royce.

Jonathan had set me up at the Stock New York, the sister hotel of the one I used to work at, citing the hotel he'd just sold as "too grubby." Everything was perfect. The room was huge, slick, with precisely designed proportions and windows that let onto a little patio that I wanted to sit on with my husband.

Jonathan was in the process of transferring his hotel on the Lower East Side. Hotel D, on Avenue D. His fourth and a huge risk. He shook his head whenever he talked about it. He'd said it was too small for me. Too old, too trendy, too loud—he had a million reasons why I should stay at the Stock. After few minutes of listening to him, I knew why he was keeping me away from D. He didn't think it was safe. Who even knew why. He'd been known for putting beautiful hotels in up-and-coming neighborhoods like canaries in a coal mine. Maybe this little bird hadn't gotten out.

The Stock had every imaginable trend-forward trapping. Wool rugs with barely discernible patterns that looked as if they'd been through a war zone in exactly the right places. Maple and mahogany paneling. Blackened brass chandeliers with frosted glass shades that curved in ways that were surprising and yet inevitable. Good-looking staff in sharp uniforms.

I was wrung out from the flight, but I shook it off by taking a coldish shower, and I left before I missed Jonathan more.

"Ah, I know your face!" Omar said when I showed up for the pre-studio dinner.

Hartley Yallow and the Trudy Crestley were already there, and the table was huge.

"I know yours too," I said. Everyone knew Omar's face. He had classic South American good looks that came from an Argentinian mother and an Italian father. His voice, however, was something no genetic pairing could predictably create.

I sat down, and we ordered. More people came. I could hardly keep up with the names, because even though I knew them all, I was overwhelmed and in love with that moment. Ivan Braf showed up with his wife, and I envied her presence. I wanted Jonathan next to me, even if he didn't say a word. It wasn't that I wanted to steal moments before his death; I wanted this moment to be complete, and without him, it wasn't.

But it was good. Very good.

Quentin Marshall showed up with the guys from The Breakfront. "Monica Faulkner," Quentin said in his thick Aussie accent. "So happy you could come. Now we all have to take our game up a notch." He wagged his finger around the table.

"Oh, I don't think—"

"We need her on the chorus," Omar said, pointing his fork. "Flat out."

"*You* were on the chorus," Quentin replied.

"I—" I couldn't finish a denial.

"There's no point having her here unless you showcase her voice," Omar argued.

"That's true," Quentin replied.

"Hang on!" I said, putting my fist down. I didn't watch for their reaction, because I knew I didn't have a second before they'd interrupt. "Even if all this is true, it's irrelevant. My name won't sell the record, and the point is to *sell the record*. Nobody knows me, so showcasing me gets you nowhere."

"She has a point," Trudy said.

I nodded to her, and she nodded back.

"Fine!" Quentin proclaimed. "We rehearse tomorrow and try it out. Once Victory Spontaine gets in, whenever that is, we decide once and for all." He clacked the ice at the bottom of his glass. "My drink is empty." He twisted in his seat to look for a waiter.

I hadn't realized until that moment that the rest of the restaurant found our gathering very interesting. Black rectangles hovered over heads, and little phone flashes went off. The dinner was publicity. I hadn't thought of that. I wished I'd worn lipstick or done something with my hair.

Omar, who was next to me, leaned close. "I'm fighting for you to get the chorus."

"Why?"

"Because you have the most unique voice I've ever heard."

I swallowed. "Well, my point stands."

"If we want to sell the record, it has to be a *great record*. That's the number one priority."

I couldn't believe he was saying that to me. Omar D'Alessio. Holy shit. I couldn't believe he was even talking to me.

"You're pretty great, Omar."

"I never said I wasn't." He put his arm around me. "But there's room for another."

He kissed my cheek, and I felt accepted as a musician and artist. Jonathan was the only thing missing from that moment. I wished he could have seen it.

Chapter 19

Jonathan

Laurelin puttered around the kitchen, putting ingredients into two blender jars that were meant to hold me for two days. She put measured portions of vitamins, greens, milk, powdered puke, and dried shit into a healthful grotesquerie of layers that would be in the fridge for my reluctant consumption.

I didn't have to think about it. I just had to blend it and choke on it. She'd already taken my blood pressure (one-ten over seventy), drawn blood (a monthly task), and hooked me up to an EKG (looked good). The meds for the week were set out so I didn't have to count them. The privilege of money. I could pay someone to keep me from the mundanities of my illness.

"Where's he taking you?" I asked.

"We're driving up to Monterey," she replied in a singsong voice. "Donny is staying with Grandma, so it's kind of a last hurrah before I get huge."

"Good for him."

"I have everything you need here until Wednesday. Then you follow this list on the fridge to make new. I'd make them for you for the whole ten days, but the ingredients are perishable."

"I wish they'd perish," I said in passing just to make a joke. I was looking at the news on a tablet and was on humor autopilot.

"Oh stop. Be cheerful." I looked up at her to see her holding up her finger. "Twenty years ago, you'd be the one who perished. And when you complain, people think you won't do with you're supposed to when they're gone." She winked and went back to arranging my fridge.

"Are you trying to tell me something?"

"Attitude is everything." More lilting vowels to express something serious. "You missed a few days in your log." She flicked her wrist at my little blue leather book. "You need to take it with you everywhere. Even if you're going to a restaurant."

I rolled my eyes and immediately felt like an adolescent or worse. I ran through the international news as if the tablet was on fire, trying to not feel over-mothered. I hired her to do this. I couldn't get mad about it. "Okay," was all I could get out.

"What is this?" She took a plastic container out of the crisper and held it at my eye level.

I looked at it then back at the tablet. "Monica's Brazilian chimichuri. Her mother was over the other night. The two of them ate it like… I don't know." I waved my hand. "They slather it on everything like they're trying to scald their faces. It's blowtorch-hot."

"Oh, that sounds good."

"Does spicy food bother you? With the pregnancy?"

"Nope."

"Take it then." I scrolled through the financials. "We have two."

"Really?" She peeled the top off and took a whiff. "Oh my God, this smells so good." She put it under my nose, and I pushed her away. "Oh, I forgot. Well, I understand. Donny doesn't like spicy food either." She put the container in her bag of medicinal crap.

"Donny's three," I said.

Laurelin shrugged. "He's a good boy." She patted my shoulder. "Like you."

I didn't want to fuck my nurse at all. Not even a little. But I wanted to spank her. Hard.

I turned back to my tablet and tapped the local news, missed, and hit entertainment, which I couldn't care less about. But I let it load, and probably because Monica's name was associated with my account, or the wifi, or because it was the top entertainment story of the minute to people who weren't married to her, her picture was front and center.

Her and some swarthy guy. His arm was around her. He was kissing her cheek at a restaurant, and she was smiling, looking at the ceiling. She looked happy and carefree. In her element. And on his face? That was a simple prelude to fucking her. I couldn't take my eyes off the picture and that look in his eye. His fingertip was on her shoulder as if testing his right to touch her.

I knew my wife didn't have cheating in her heart. But I also knew men, and that asshole had her body on his mind. He wanted to fuck her. My wife. Mine. I wanted to take his skin and peel it off him. Rip him apart.

"Mister Drazen?"

Laurelin's voice sounded a million miles away.

"What?"

"Are you all right?"

I tore my face from the screen and looked at her. Her brow was knit, and she was packed to go.

"I'm fine."

"I think I should take your BP again."

"No, no. I'm fine. Let me walk you out." I smiled, but I knew no joy reached my eyes. I hustled her to the front door.

"Mister Drazen," she said when we got there, "really, you need to avoid stress."

"Stress is part of life. Don't worry. I'm good."

She left. I went upstairs and paced. Looked at my watch. Did some math. I couldn't keep Monica enclosed. I couldn't keep men from wanting her. She only got more beautiful every day, and men were disgusting creatures who cared for nothing but the daily mounting pressure in their ball sacks.

I trusted her. With every cell in my body, I trusted her. But when I thought about how I'd almost lost her, how she hadn't been happy and I'd just kept letting shit slide, I wondered what would have happened if I hadn't gone to the studio that day and reasserted myself.

She could be away. She could travel. Her career was necessary to her happiness, and more than anything, I wanted her to be happy.

So why did that picture bother me? We'd reestablished ourselves. I trusted her. She needed to do her job and make her art. What was the problem?

The problem was that we had a disconnect, and that disconnect was me. She'd come back to me fully, but I hadn't broached my side of the distance. I hadn't gone to her with an open heart the way she'd come to me.

That was going to change.

Chapter 20

Monica

The balcony had room for two, maybe three if everyone liked each other. It overlooked a tiny cobblestone street in Chinatown and onto the tops of the beat-down signs in Cantonese. Manhattan had many of the same structures as Los Angeles. They were straight up from the ground at ninety degrees, had corners, straight walls, windows, and roofs. Some buildings were made well and some were sad. But the whole proportion of the place was different. It couldn't be absorbed by car; it could only be experienced on foot or bike. Then the flower boxes, cornerstones, and cobbled streets took on their natural life.

I had no business being on the balcony off the studio, since Omar and Trudy were smoking and I wasn't about to even try it.

"It gives me my edge," Omar said. "Biggest secret in music is how many of us smoke."

"The other type of smoke, not such a secret," Trudy said.

She was a guitarist and could smoke her brains out for all I cared. From Omar, well, I admitted to being a little disappointed. I took so much care with my vocal chords. I could tell when there was a forest fire in Flintridge based on how my throat felt.

"Does he do this all the time?" I jerked my head toward the inside, where Hartley had abandoned his drums to throw up last night's party.

Trudy smashed her cigarette underfoot and blew a cloud carelessly. It landed in my face, and I resisted the urge to wave my hand in front of me.

"Constantly," she said. "But he never pukes. I think it's a flu or something."

"Oh." I tried to not look more worried than any normal person would. Normal people got the flu and just suffered through it. But I had a husband on immunosuppressants, and a flu could kill him.

"Quentin's looking for another drummer." Omar shrugged. "Or Franco can do it."

"Nope," Trudy said. "He's down with it too."

"What is it? A percussionist's strain?" I joked.

"All those guys hang out together. It's like incest without the sex."

I didn't know what came over me, but the words shot out of my mouth before I'd even thought about the logistics. "I know one. He can be here tomorrow. He has something today. He's really good."

"Do I know him?"

"He's from LA originally. So probably not. He's super-hot in indie circles."

"Not that husband of yours, is it?" Omar smiled a half moon of perfect white piano keys. It was the third time he'd mentioned Jonathan that day, as if he was trying to gauge my reactions.

"The only instrument Jonathan plays is me."

"That can be good or bad."

"He's a maestro, trust me."

I went inside. I'd wanted to learn from Omar, and he'd taught me a few things, but I was starting to feel as if it all came with a price. Maybe that price was simple flirtation and attention or maybe he expected more, but I was getting irritated with his off-color comments and sultry eyeballing.

Everyone was filing back into the studio. There were fifteen actual musicians. Some kept klatches of preeners and hangers-on. Others traveled alone. Add to that the engineers, press, security, and agents, and the room was as hot as a sweatbox and smelled only ten percent better.

I couldn't believe there wasn't a drummer among us, but it was worth a try. I found Quentin in the middle of eating a slab of crunchy fried fish, surrounded by people I didn't know.

"Hey," I said, trying to slink into the tiny room unobtrusively and failing.

"Faulkner! Everyone out!" He made shoo-shoo motions with his fingers, and everyone shooed. He closed the door behind them.

I hoped I wasn't stepping out of the frying pan with Omar and into the fire with Quentin.

"Sorry," he said, rooting around his leather messenger bag. "Not a big deal, but I didn't know what this was, so I didn't want to give it to you in front of everyone." He handed me a long, blue velvet box. "This was at reception with your name on it."

"Thank you," I said, taking it.

He slung the bag over his shoulder. "I have to find a drummer."

"No one in this building can do percussion? It's a house full of musicians."

"You have no idea how hard it is to find a good one."

"I kind of do."

"Evan Arden's in the bathroom puking his guts out, and he's on bass. If I can't find someone within the hour, we're all going home for the day." He made motions to leave but was so slow about it. He glanced at the velvet box then back at me. "Sorry, not trying to be nosy."

"Not trying?"

"Even straight guys like a little sparkle. Come on. Don't hold out."

I smiled. What could it be? Jonathan never disappointed me, but I was afraid it was a diamond-studded leather collar or a bracelet with the word SLAVE in emeralds. That might require a little more explaining than I was willing to do.

I held the box at my eye level and cracked it open so only I could see. Whatever it was, it didn't sparkle. I didn't know if that excited me or scared me. But it looked harmless enough. I opened it all the way.

"What is it?" he said, hand on the doorknob.

"It's a Sharpie." I turned it toward him. Indeed, right inside the bracelet box lay a black Sharpie. I could see from his expression that he was disappointed, as if he'd expected an actual bracelet in the bracelet box.

"What's it for?"

"I have no idea." I opened the little card that had been folded inside the lid. It was typed.

Keep this with you, goddess.

I closed it slowly.

"He's more of a romantic than I thought," Quentin said.

"You know him?"

"We have a long history of feeding children together."

"Is that why you hired me?" I said before I could catch it. That was a completely unprofessional thing to ask, and it made me look like an insecure ingrate.

"I hired you because Dionne Harber couldn't make it. I don't regret it." He winked at me and got away with it.

"Thanks. And I'm sorry, I didn't mean to imply my spot was bought."

"It wasn't. Trust me."

He left with a smile. I opened the velvet box again. Shook it. Looked under it. Turned the card over. Nothing special. I got my stuff ready to go.

Typically when I traveled, Jonathan and I spoke once a day, and our conversations were short and mostly about his medicines and appointments. But that was the old us. The miserable us. The couple treading water in a sea of doubt and unsaid truths. I didn't know or understand the couple we'd become, and I didn't think there was much precedent for it.

So I didn't know what he intended with the permanent marker, and I didn't know enough to be excited or anxious. I was only curious as we laid down some tracks, and I played my theremin for everyone in the studio while we waited for two other people to decide if they were too sick to continue.

"We're doing a small thing at a club after," Omar whispered in the hall outside the bathrooms. "You're invited."

"Thank you. I think I'm just going to bed."

"Alone? I bet we have the day off tomorrow." He put his hand on my wrist.

"You know I'm married, right, Omar?"

"Where is he?" He spread his arms, indicating the whole of the studio, New York, the world about us, where Jonathan wasn't.

Was he drunk? Who would make such an implication? What person in their right mind would assume my husband's presence was required for my fidelity?

The answer came to me in the tightness of Omar's jaw and the tension in his fingers. He was on something. Some white substance whispered in his ear that he was a god and entitled to whatever he felt like having.

I sighed. I'd really admired him. He sang like an angel, but he'd just been in the studio thirty minutes ago. I recalled the moments of inappropriate laughter and long space-outs when I'd thought he was preparing, but he'd been stoned the whole time. I knew how many artists worked stoned. I'd always told myself it was their thing and not my business, but suddenly I felt as if it was most certainly my business.

"My husband's home," I said, "waiting for me to call."

He looked at me as if he didn't believe me.

"Look," I continued, "I know what you've probably heard about me, and it may be all true. But this scene, the drugs, and the other shit? The partying until all hours? The fucking around? It's not my thing. And if that means I'll always be small time, well, it's okay."

He didn't move, as if stuck in that moment. "You think I got where I am because I party?"

"No, I—"

"No?"

I didn't think he'd coasted. Not at all. But he wasn't interested in hearing it. I'd insulted his talent and his manhood, and he was walking away with at least one intact.

"Break it down," he said firmly, his jaw still grinding. "You just said you'd be small time if you didn't party. You know what, girl? I've done everything I could to support you. I lifted you up the minute you got here. And this is the attitude you throw me? You think your pussy is dipped in gold? Well, fuck you."

He turned on his heel and went down the hall just as Rob Devon cut the turn and ran into the men's room as if his belly were on fire. In seconds, the hallway was silent again.

I dragged myself out the door, and Dean waited for me in the Rolls. I'd walked into the studio wrapped in confidence and love, and I was walking out feeling as if my expensive ride was an ugly appendage, a street sign pointing at my gold-plated cunt. God, I must make such a scene with this stupid car.

"Mrs. Drazen," Dean said by way of greeting.

"Hi, Dean."

"Back to the hotel?" He opened the back door.

"Yes, thanks."

I slid into the pristine comfort of the Rolls. It envelops you, that luxury. The money. The sense of well-being. That was the point, wasn't it? When the car started, there was no jolt, no rumble, just movement.

I called Jonathan as the streetlights streaked across the night sky, then stopped seamlessly at a stop sign, then started again.

"Hello, Monica," he said, and I wanted to cry.

"Hi."

"I see you're on your way back to the hotel?"

"Is this Dean telling you everything, or do you have a tracking device on me?"

"Yes to both. How are you?"

"Do you know the Rolls doesn't even obey the law of inertia? Like when Dean stops at the light, my body doesn't go forward a little. and when he starts again, I can feel it moving, but it's not like I feel my back against the seat. Did you know that?"

"I never noticed."

We went through a busy part of town, and I curled into the seat, watching the Saturday night crowds walk the streets. People crossing stared at the car, big packs and smaller groups, dressed for big things and made up for the lights and sounds, a single wave in an ocean of revelry.

"Did you get my present?" he said.

"Yes. I love it. How did you know I needed to write my name on all my tags?"

"Are you all right?"

"What time is it there?" I asked.

"Sun's just thinking about setting."

"Is it hot? Is it gloomy? Tell me things."

"It's nice. It's mid-June. Same as always. The marine layer burned off, and I can see… let me look… one two three four five clouds out the kitchen window. One is shaped like a rabbit. One is shaped like a guitar. It makes me think of you."

"What about the other three? What are they shaped like?"

"Big white turds."

I laughed. "Did you take your medicine?"

"Yes, Mom."

"And drink your shit shake?"

"Yes."

"And did you go for a run?"

"Yes. You never answered my question. Are you all right?"

I sighed. I knew he could hear it. I wanted him to. "I feel, I guess, not lonely. Not alone. Just separate. Separate from you, and separate from everyone here. It's… I can't pin it down. I guess it's not a bad feeling as much as it's a weird, disconnected feeling. Uncomfortable. I don't know."

I could hear him breathing, and the lawn mower outside our house, and the birds in Los Angeles.

"Would you believe me if I said I know how you feel?"

"Yeah."

Dean pulled up to the hotel. A doorman in a snazzy uniform was ready to open the door before the car stopped without a jolt. The inside of the hotel looked gilded and soft through the glass windows, as if the lights were colored gold.

"Do you have your marker?" Jonathan asked.

"Of course. I'll treasure it always."

"Hang up with me then and call back on the tablet. I want to see you."

Dean opened the door for me, and I hung up.

Chapter 21

Monica

I'd kicked my shoes off and dropped my bag before calling Jonathan from the iPad. He picked up on the first ring.

"How is the hotel?" he asked.

"It's a parody of itself." In the screen of the tablet, I saw he'd moved out to the side patio that overlooked the twinkling grid of the city. "Or a farce. I can't decide which." I pouted at him from the edge of the bed.

"I'll tell Sam you said so."

"I wanted to stay in D." I snapped the drapes open. Manhattan was dark and vibrant and closed tight in a granite-and-clay-brick embrace.

"It's in Alphabet City. There's piss in the doorways from the seventies. I already don't like you spending days in a studio in Chinatown."

"A little grit's kind of nice."

"Nice?" He leaned forward in his seat.

"Yeah, nice." I opened the patio door, holding my tablet out so he could see me.

"Turn the camera around," he said. "Show me the view."

I did, then I showed him the street below and the building across Lexington. "Not much to speak of," I said. "Except, yeah, New York's kind of fabulous."

"Go back inside."

I turned the tablet and looked at him in his dying-daylight rectangle. He was looking directly into the lens, which was right above the screen, and though the mic was tiny and tinny, I knew I was hearing his dominant voice.

"Put the tablet on the desk so I can see you."

I leaned it against the lamp. Seeing him inside that rectangle with our backyard behind him was somehow ridiculous. In the top right corner of the screen, a small box showed what he saw as I stood there. My face was off screen. I was only visible from neck to knees.

"Take your clothes off," he said casually yet firmly, as if asking me to pass the salt. As if it was no more than a courtesy to ask for what should be available to him without question.

I pulled my T-shirt over my head and watched myself take off my bra. My breasts bounced out, and I saw my hard nipples in the screen. Jonathan was impassive, tapping his thumbs together as if keeping a rhythm. I peeled off my pants, down to the lace thong I wore for him in his absence. I let him see it for a second, but he twisted his hand at the wrist in a "get on with it" motion. I got my thong off and stood before the tablet, naked neck to knees.

"Are you wet?" he asked.

"Yes."

"Check for me."

I put my hand between my legs. I saw it slipping down my belly in the screen, saw the way my knees bent a little when I spread my legs to accept my fingers.

"I'm wet," I said.

"Put your fingers in your mouth. And let me see."

I bent to look at him, lips puckered around my fingers, tongue curled around them. The pungent, sordid, sexy taste of my cunt filled my mouth. His eyes warmed with arousal.

"Go get the pen," he said.

I plucked it off the desk and showed him.

"Put the pen in your mouth. Get the desk chair. Sit in it, and put your feet on the desk. I want to see your beautiful cunt."

I wheeled the chair over, placing it in front of the desk. He waited, fingers laced together on the iPad screen. He was casual and intense at the same time, as if he didn't have to worry about me doing what he asked. He was just going to wait.

I put my feet up on the desk, exposing myself to him. I could see myself on the little corner of the screen, the soft part of me, the place where I was split in two, the fold of sensation between the smooth mass of skin, and I was shocked by the sight of it.

"That's mine," he said. "You understand, my wife, that everything I see there is mine?"

"Yes."

"You're wet, and that's mine too. No matter where you are, I own your cunt."

"It's yours. It's only for you. It's so wet for you."

"Mark it," he said.

It took me a second to understand, even with the Sharpie in my teeth. Then, seeing my thighs against the wet flesh between them, I knew what he meant. I popped the base free of the cap and leaned over, pressing the pen tip to my left inner thigh. I glanced up at him.

He gave a slight shake of his head. "You start on your right, at the knee."

I switched and pulled the skin to make it taut for the marker. Like his fingers, the Sharpie was firm and purposeful; like his tongue, it was damp and warm.

"Wherever you are," he said low and steady as I wrote his name, knee to crotch, "I own you. I own your filthy mouth. I own your dirty mind. When you get wet thinking about fucking, it's mine. Every drop from you. I own your every thought. You are my property."

I looked back at him. My breath was short. When I saw myself, the flesh between my legs was now exposed, wet, and swollen. "Jonathan's" marked my inner thigh, and a bolt of pleasure ran through me.

"This is crazy," I gasped. "I'm going to come."

"Not until you finish the other side."

"Okay." I didn't know if I would make it.

"No touching."

What was I supposed to put on the other side? I couldn't think. I glanced at him. A shadow of a smirk crossed his lips.

I started with the letter "P" a few inches from my center, the pen tip becoming him, his body, his intention, his attention. The tingling was a wall of sensation as I spelled "Property" down my leg. As I put the leg on the Y, the pressure had built up so much, I knew I didn't have long.

"Look at yourself," he said.

"I'll come if I do."

"No, you won't. Not until I say."

But I didn't. I just looked at the marks between my legs. I was owned. Property. Without desire or ambition, a slave without responsibility or longing. Free.

"Look, Monica," he said sternly, and I looked.

Jonathan's Property.

"Yes," I said, flooded with a tsunami of an orgasm that pushed at the walls of my control. "You own me. I am your subject." I could barely speak through the throb. "You are my master."

"I'm going to put my cock inside you, everywhere, and I'm not going to ask first. You're going to spread your legs and submit yourself. Your mouth. Your cunt. Your tight little ass. I'm going to hurt you. I'm going to crack you open and suck you dry."

"Oh, god, when you talk like that." Every word rushed me to orgasm, but like the door at the end of the hall in a movie, it got closer and farther at the same time. Juice dripped over my ass. How long would he do this? "I am yours," I said, because I wanted to say, "Let me come."

"Put your fingers inside yourself."

I slid two fingers in me and groaned.

"Shh. Over your clit. But don't come yet."

I didn't know how it would be possible. My clit was swollen and soaked. I touched it gently.

"Would you like to come?" he asked.

"Yes, please."

"Move your fingers very slowly, and don't make a sound. I want to see how your body moves."

I moved my finger in circles.

"Slower, not enough to come. Not yet."

But it didn't matter. I was on the edge. The dam burst, and I came, first bending over, mouth open, face rigid, then arching my back until I was leveraged on the edge of the desk and thrusting my pussy at the camera. When I came down, looking at him with my hair disheveled and my hand cupping the throbbing mass between my legs, I smiled.

He shook his head. "You are in so much trouble."

"I'm sorry, I couldn't—"

"No talking. When I see you, be ready for the spanking of your young life."

He winked and cut the call. I was left staring at a dead iPad.

I wanted to go home. I wanted his arms around me, his sharp scent, his cruel hands, and his unforgiving mouth. I held my phone as if I was testing its weight. I could book a flight right now and show up naked on our doorstep.

But what if the tightness in my stomach was the flu? Everyone was getting it. But it didn't feel like any flu I'd ever had, because it was just tight.

No more, no less. Like a butterfly's torn ligament. But if I had it, I couldn't go home.

Between my legs, the words *Jonathan's Property* was scrawled in Sharpie. I was his, and I wanted to go home to him. Could I go home the day after tomorrow for a weekend? And if so, should I? I could have the flu. I could be carrying it. No, I couldn't go. I couldn't risk his health, because complications were a cotton candy funnel rolling around the edge of the drum. It looked like nothing, then not too much, then an insane cloud of pink sugar before you even blinked, and we were back to dying at Sequoia.

I couldn't go home if I was sick.

The phone buzzed in my hand. It was Quentin.

—*Omar's got it. We're off for a week*—

I could go now. Tomorrow.

—*Ok got it*—

I tapped the phone to my upper lip, looking out over Lexington Avenue. So many people everywhere, in a city that never sleeps.

—*Do you have the number for a doctor who keeps late hours?*—

—*Sure. You all right?*—

—*I'm fine just want to see if I have this flu thing. I want to go home and can't be sick. Pls don't tell Jonathan it's a surprise*—

An address and number came through. I believed I was being diligent about my husband's health, but I knew that no matter what the doctor said, I was going home. I'd rather talk to Jonathan through a wall than a phone line.

Chapter 22

Jonathan

I cut the call because I was frustrated and I couldn't show it. Watching her come thousands of miles away wasn't good enough. Her willful obedience drove me to distraction, and her accidental disobedience made my palms sting with the longing for her ass under them. I wanted to mark her with my own hand. Make her come with my body. Fill her with myself, and there I was in my kitchen, with a dick hard enough to crack the granite countertop.

This wasn't working. A thousand times this wasn't working.

And why? Because I didn't want to travel. Because the thought of being too far from Sequoia froze me solid. And a plane? I couldn't get the image of my heart jumping from my chest out of my mind, and the thought of isolating myself on a plane made that image play and replay until the organ squeaked out a puddle of blood in the leather seat.

But being away from her wasn't working either. She was getting recognized for her talent, and that meant she was becoming desirable to a certain kind of asshole. She was trustworthy. I didn't have to assert myself. I didn't have to lay claim on her. I was an intelligent man with a wife who had laid down her life for him. I knew she'd never betray me. I could feel the fidelity in her heart.

But I did need to assert myself, and the thought of men who wanted to fuck her breathing the same air as her made me boil. I was a child. An unreasonable, hateful brat.

All true. And so what?

I was hungry, and the fridge was empty of anything I wanted. I snapped out my box of pills and the last jar of chimichuri.

If staying close to her and keeping those men off her meant I got on a plane and went where she went and did what she did, then my anxieties about traveling would have to just shut the fuck up. I took a handful of pills and choked them down with warm tap water. Then another, swallowing more frustration than vitamins, more anger than medicine. My body was going to reject this heart just because my mind was rejecting everything I'd held on to for months.

That picture with Omar. If I trusted her, why had it burned me? Why did it feel like a punch in the gut?

Because I'd left her alone. I'd deserted her. She didn't need a leash. She didn't need a reminder of her vows or commitments, but I'd assumed she didn't need or want my presence. I'd accepted that because it was convenient for me. I didn't have to go anywhere if I made it her fault I wasn't going. I'd been responsible for that picture and the state of our current discontent.

I ripped open a bag of bread and jammed a piece in the chimichuri. The oil and flakes of parsley dripped off it. The peppers were invisibly green in the mix, and I didn't give a fuck. I ate it. Cringed. God, that chemical burn. How could I have eaten stuff this hot and not needed a skin graft after? How could this not be damaging tissue? I smelled flesh burning and knew it was in my mind. I curled up the bread and scooped out more, eating it before the burn from the last bite had dissipated.

I didn't swallow. I kept it in my mouth, nurturing it, letting it hurt me, rejecting whatever weakness this new heart had brought, because they were reactions to something that had happened to someone else. They weren't me. I had the opportunity and responsibility to reject the changes I didn't want, and goddamnit, this was excellent chimichuri.

I ate it, leaning over the counter, until the last flake of parsley was gone and my eyes ran with tears. And as if all the new traits I'd gained feared I'd leave, I had the desire to go for a run.

"That, I'm keeping," I said as I dropped the empty jar into the sink. "I like it."

I laced up my sneakers and took my phone, because this run had a purpose. I had no more excuses. In the middle of the run, as I was whipping wet sand, I slowed to a walk and called Dr. Solis.

"He's with a patient," his assistant said. "Should he call you back?"

She'd presented me with the perfect opportunity to bail. His call back might not go through, or maybe I wouldn't pick up. If he called back late enough, I wouldn't be able to get Jacques online for a flight plan.

"I'll wait."

"Is this an emergency, Mr. Drazen?"

"No. Yes, but no."

I faced the darkening ocean, watching the last of the sun dip into the horizon. I heard the birds overhead and had a flash of my heart jumping out onto the wet sand before a wave came in. The weight of the heart was enough to dig it into the sand and create a wake of ripples as it fought, still beating, to stay on the beach against the pressure of the water. I stared at the spot, feeling an emptiness in my chest as two seagulls came down and plucked up my heart, fighting for the fresh meat.

"Fuck you," I said. "You're not real."

"Jon? What's the trouble?" Dr. Solis said, jarring me.

"I need to travel."

"So?"

"Cross country."

"Tell Patty the city. She'll notify the nearest cardiac unit and text you a number. Is that what this was about?"

I swallowed. No, that wasn't what it was about. It was about a paralyzing fear that I didn't recognize because it was so foreign. It was about my wife and how I'd abandoned her because of that fear. It was about regret, and forgiveness, and worthiness.

"Yeah," I said. "That was it."

"Good," he said and hung up.

Damned doctors. Hold a human heart in your hand and the everyday courtesies go out the window. I laughed to myself. I was going to New York.

Chapter 23

Monica

"Can you explain this one more time?" the old doctor asked with an accent so deeply New Yawk, he sounded like an old Irish cop in a black-and-white movie.

The office was in the eighties and Seventh Avenue, with old cabinets, ancient metal and glass syringes in frames, and photos of a family, then a family's family. The certificates and diplomas, if observed closely, were from the fifties.

I sat on the leather-surfaced examining table with my hands folded in my lap. "My husband is immunosuppressed—"

"I got that part." The doctor moved his half-moon glasses to the top of his bald head. "I'll be happy to help you, but if you're not actually sick..." He pivoted his hand at the wrist.

"I can't bring the flu home."

"Do you have any symptoms?"

"My stomach is a little ishy."

"Vomiting? Diarrhea?"

"No."

"So go home."

I made a face and twisted my shoulders. I don't know what I was trying to express but discomfort and awkwardness.

"Do you not want to go home? Does he beat you?"

"No!" He did, of course, but that wasn't what the good doctor meant. "I'm worried. If I get him sick, it's not like a normal person getting sick. He had a heart transplant."

The doctor up held his hand. It was surprisingly big, like a wrinkled leather dinner plate. "I'll tell you what. You're a nervous wreck. I can see that. And your blood pressure's through the roof. You gave Bernice a urine sample when you came in?"

"No, I—"

"Do that then. We'll check your sugar. Check for antibodies. If there's anything irregular, I'll let you know. You might be carrying a virus, and you might not. There's not much more I can do."

"That's fine. It's great. Thank you!"

"You're very cute, young lady. If I were about sixty years younger, I'd be the older man in your life."

I laughed, and he helped me off the table with his dinner-plate hands.

I gave my sample and waited.

What would I do if my results came back with some sign that something wasn't a hundred percent? Like elevated blood sugar? That could mean my body was fighting something, or it could mean I ate too much bread with lunch. Would I stay in New York to keep Jonathan safe? Or would I go home and tell him to stay away from me?

I'd been sick only once since the surgery, at the end of February. A cold had kept me out of the studio, and as frustrating as that was, it also meant I was relegated to another bedroom until Laurelin cleared me to touch my husband. I cursed her. I yelled at her. I told her that I was leaving for Corfu in three days and I was entitled to see Jonathan before then.

And she reminded me that by infecting him with a cold, I'd send him back to Sequoia Hospital faster than if I hit him over the head with a two-by-four.

That shut me up.

I was smiling about it when the good doctor appeared from behind his shellacked wood door.

"Mrs. Faulkner?"

I didn't correct him. "Yes?"

"Congratulations. We've found the source of your ishy stomach."

Chapter 24

Jonathan

The night I decided to shed the yoke of love I carried for my ex-wife, I'd felt so unburdened, I laughed. When I let go of my fear of traveling, I didn't laugh quite as hard, but I walked home quickly, smiling the whole way.

"Mira!" I said when I saw her. "Pack me some things, would you?"

"Sure, sure. How long for?"

"Few days." If I stayed longer, I could have the hotel launder them or buy new. It didn't matter. Nothing mattered but getting out of this old skin of a house and into my wife's arms.

"Business or pleasure?"

"Pleasure! A little chilly. Los Angeles in November-ish."

She smiled widely. "Yes, sir. When are you leaving?"

"Immediately. Go. Jeans and shirts. Two sweaters. Go." Ailing Mira trotted upstairs as I remembered something. "Mira!"

She leaned over the banister. "Sir?"

"Two leather belts. One narrow, one wide."

"What color?"

"Doesn't matter."

She nodded and went upstairs.

I got on the phone. "Jacques?"

"Hello, Mister Drazen."

"I need to go to New York."

"When?"

"Now."

I was greeted by an unusual pause.

"What?" I said.

"I'm calculating how long it will take to get there."

"From where?"

"We just got into Chicago."

"With the plane?" I started my own calculations.

"For the Prima Culture conference. You—"

"Signed off. Shit." I stood in the middle of the living room and rubbed my eyes.

When I'd stopped flying, I'd freely loaned the plane to anyone on my staff who needed it for business, and months ago, my executive group had requested it. So the Gulfstream was in Chicago, which was three flying hours away. An hour getting a flight plan approved, half an hour prep. Three hours in the air. Redoing it all once he hit Santa Monica, and the last, most unmovable of obstacles was pilot exhaustion. If he flew into Chicago today and came right back, he wouldn't be able to legally pilot the plane to New York.

"I can get back, but then I can't take you," he said.

When did I decide to start hiring such law-abiding staff? Was I going to have to jog to New York? "Is Petra with you?"

"She's with the baby."

I'd hit some nerve; I heard it in the edge in his voice. Petra had given birth to their little boy, Claude, weeks ago. Jacques had been manning the plane on his own, which was completely legal and fine up until then. At that moment, it had become a pain in the ass.

"Do you have a nanny?" I asked, knowing the answer.

"She's breastfeeding, Mister Drazen. I'm sorry. She can't pilot to New York and back without feeding him."

I thought there might be answers that had to do with latex nipples and breast pumps, but I knew nothing about them. Jacques probably would have suggested it if it had been a possibility.

And did I need to go, really? What would happen if I waited a day? Exactly nothing. No lives or livelihoods were at stake. But having decided I wasn't afraid, that I was ready to go anywhere with her, I couldn't wait another second.

"Listen," I said, "I'm being a nightmare of a boss, and the fact that I admit it isn't going to soften this. I need you to get home, and I need Petra to fly that plane. Get a freelance copilot or a nanny, on me, but I need to go."

"Mister Drazen. We won't hire a nanny. That's not how we do it."

What I enjoyed about Jacques was that he'd never asked me why I suddenly had to go anywhere. He just flew the damned plane. In return, I couldn't ask him what kind of stupid fucking rule prevented him from taking care of his son while Petra sat in the cockpit.

I plopped back on the couch, and put my feet on the coffee table, stretching my legs, tensing and releasing.

"How long in the air between here and New York?" I said. "Five hours? Six?"

"Yes. But—"

"I have an idea. Just hear me out."

Chapter 25

Monica

I snapped the hotel room door shut and ran to the bathroom, stripping as I went. The mirror in the deluxe suite went from floor to ceiling seamlessly, and it made me look sickly skinny. So when I got in front of it and turned to the side, I felt the same, or worse, because I was knocked up, and to me, I still looked like bag of bones.

"You have to start eating," I reprimanded myself. "Someone else is counting on you."

I surprised myself. What was I doing? I didn't want a baby. I just wanted to make Jonathan as comfortable and happy as possible for however long he had. That was it. Not raise children into orphanhood.

I breathed heavily and tilted one leg. Inside the thigh, the word *Jonathan's* became visible. I was marked, written on, branded with his name. I closed my eyes and asked myself what I wanted to pray for.

Was I relieved? Disappointed? What would change? Would I throw caution to the wind and let my sons and daughters go through puberty with a brave and dead father? What was I agreeing to?

I didn't know. But I knew things were going to change. If we were having a baby, then fuck it, I'd just deal with it.

A smile stretched across my face as if it were someone else's face. I felt the muscles tense and expand, felt the swelling in my heart one felt when one smiled with joy. I felt as if deciding to deal with it had cracked open part of me, and that smile spilled out.

I opened my eyes. This was awesome. When did it get awesome? Had I been holding on to the desire for his children without realizing it? Had it crept under the covers with me? Had it been in my diet? The air I breathed? When had this glee snuck into my heart?

I pressed my eyes shut against tears. I didn't want to cry. I didn't want my body to have any confusion. The burst of emotion came from a place I didn't know existed. Some string of code in my DNA, some hormonal rush that was more biological than logical.

I was overjoyed. Thrilled to bursting. I jumped up and, still naked, ran to the tablet. I couldn't wait to tell him. The metal and plastic were cold in my hand as I woke the device, then I stopped. I wanted to hold him. I wanted his reaction to myself, to own it the way he owned my orgasms. I wanted to feel his strength and his warmth around me when he found out.

Instead of calling him, I made reservations to go home.

When I put the tablet down, I saw the Sharpie on the desk. I picked it up, went to the bathroom, and stood in front of the mirror. My body looked the same to me. I turned every which way and saw no difference. His name between my legs was barely visible when I stood, just a few unreadable hashes of black. I popped the cap off the marker and pressed the tip to the skin below my navel.

"Upside down and backward," I said. I looked in the mirror. That just confused things.

Right is left and up is down. I drew a J with my right hand and, convinced I was doing it correctly, continued until I'd written *Jonathan's baby* across my abdomen.

Then I laughed so hard I lay on the bed and cried with joy.

Chapter 26

Monica

I couldn't contain myself. It was twenty minutes to boarding, and I fidgeted around the terminal, wishing I'd taken the Gulfstream. I picked up the phone. As much as I wanted to call Jonathan... I didn't. Not yet. I wanted to see his face and hear his breath. I wanted him to hold me so close I could feel that motherfucking heartbeat.

"Mom?"

"Monica, are you all right?"

She was wide awake, and it was four in the morning in Los Angeles. If I'd called at noon, she would have been sleeping. That was Mom. I'd learned to accept it.

To say my mother's attitude about me had changed after I'd married Jonathan would be a gross understatement. And now she'd be the first person to hear the news from my lips.

"I'm pregnant." Silence. I didn't realize how quickly I'd been circumnavigating the terminal until I slowed down. "Mom?"

A woman rolled over my foot with her square bag and gave me a dirty look. Fuck her.

"Monya."

"Are you all right?"

"Am I all right? Are you asking if I'm all right? My only daughter marries a dying man in the hospital, nurses him back to health, and gets pregnant with his baby, and you ask if I'm all right?" I started to reply, but she cut me off. "How can I not be all right? I'm so happy I cannot even speak. My God, a baby. A *baby*."

"Thanks, Mom." I was glad I'd told her, but I didn't feel the explosion of joy I'd hoped for. The reveal was kind of a letdown. It needed to be Jonathan, but in front of me.

"Where are you?" she asked. "How far along? Do you have the sickness?"

"I have no idea, but I had kind of a little period a couple of months ago, so the doctor figures two months. And I'm not sick at all. I mean, there was a little flu going around, so—"

"Do you have it? You can't catch anything."

Between the worry in her voice and my flight number being called, I lost track of the conversation. "I know, I know. My plane's boarding. Just don't say anything to anyone. I haven't told Jonathan yet."

"You can't tell him."

"What? Why?"

"Anything can happen." Her voice took on that mysterious, awed tone it got when she talked about the inscrutabilities of God. "You have to wait until you're twelve weeks. You don't want to disappoint him."

"Disa—"

I realized what she meant in the middle of the word. She'd miscarried a few times and had just bled the babies away without ever bothering my father with the gory details. She was who she was. The fact that I was a different person completely, healthy and young with every reason to carry a baby to term, didn't matter. She would worry about stuff because that was what she did.

"Okay, Mom. I won't tell." I painted the lie white and called it a day. "I have to go."

"Call me when you get back."

"Will do."

I walked up to the gate and boarded the plane, a little disconcerted. I'd dreamed of doing things like flying first class from New York to LA, booking at the last minute without a thought to the extra cost. But once I could, I didn't give it a second thought. Taking money for granted seemed to be an unavoidable symptom of actually having money.

I got the window and leaned my head into it as soon as I sat. I watched New York get as small as a Lego set, with pieces scattered around the outer boroughs and stacked beautifully on the erection-shaped island in the middle. The evening air was crystal clear, even on a weekday. I'd been shocked at how little pollution there was, and as we flew away, chasing the setting sun, I prepared myself for the soup-thick air of my home.

Should we bring up a baby there? Los Angeles, with all of its silicone reality and blind eyes to real problems? The poverty we swept under the rug, the crumbling school system, the undercurrent of violence and ferocity that coexisted with my little hipster world and was completely foreign to Jonathan's. Should we go somewhere cleaner? More real? More wholesome? More sincere?

I didn't even know what I wanted from having children. I didn't know what questions to ask. I needed Jonathan to even continue thinking about it. Past his excitement, the happiness I knew my news would inspire, he'd have ideas. I wanted to hear them, all of them. I wanted to hear his dreams for the future, and I wanted him to talk far ahead. Ten years. Twenty. Thirty, even. Because I was having his baby, and goddamnit, by hook or crook, he was going to live.

Chapter 27

Jonathan

Petra stood in front of my plane in her uniform, carrying a bundle of navy blankets. Both my pilots were complete professionals, but Petra made most professionals look like part-timers. Jacques stood next to her, also in uniform, but tired, as if he were the one who had been nursing a newborn.

"You flying?" I said to him after Lil let me out of the car and handed me my bag. "You look too tired to drive. Can Lil give you a lift?"

"He'll take you up on that," Petra said with a smile as she handed me the bundle she carried.

"Claude," I said as I held him. He still had the squishy pink look of a newborn. He looked angelic in the mid-morning light. "Nice-looking kid, Jacques. Lucky thing your wife has strong genes."

Petra pressed her lips together as if she was trying not to smile. "If he roots, come and get me."

"Roots?" I asked.

Claude waved his hands around, not knowing what they were for or if they were even his. I gave him my finger, and he clutched it.

"Tries to latch on to your breast."

"Ah. I'm sure I have a bad joke somewhere, but it flew out of my head."

"That happens." Jacques picked up my bag. "I'll help you up. Lange's gonna copilot. He's running through the terminal as we speak."

"I owe you for this." Worse than owing him, having that baby in my arms made me feel like a petulant, spoiled ass who couldn't wait a day to see his wife.

Jacques shrugged. "You're usually pretty easy. And you know, it's nice to see you getting around again."

I would have questioned him on how obvious it was to everyone that I wasn't myself, but it didn't matter. The baby wiped it all away. I picked a piece of crud from his eye, and when I pulled my arm back, Petra put the diaper bag around my shoulder.

"He needs to be changed fifteen minutes after a feeding. I nursed him in the car, so you'd better get to it," she said. "You know how to change a diaper?"

"I did it for my nephew once."

"Great. If he cries, you swaddle him tight. I'll show you how. He doesn't use a pacifier, but you might let him suck on your finger for a minute when he's wrapped. And you hold him and bounce him. Not much rocking, just bouncing. The noise of the plane will probably put him to sleep, but if not, he'll scream. That's on you, sir. I can't come out of the cockpit for fussy. Only hungry."

"Were you saying something? I was distracted." I smiled at her to let her know I was kidding.

"We have half an hour or so of flight prep. If you play your cards right, he'll sleep through it."

Jacques started up the stairs and indicated I should follow.

This would be the longest flight of my life, and I was ready for it.

Chapter 28

Monica

I slept a little, all wrapped up in my first-class-approved blanket. I woke close to landing at the same time of day as I left, chasing the sky from blue to yellow. The city below was grey, blanketed in thick brown smog, and we were descending right into it.

I hadn't been dreaming, but when I woke, my mind was in mid-question. What would it be like to be pregnant? Would I be sick? Active? What could I eat? Could I fly? Could I fuck? I didn't even have a doctor. I'd just run to the clinic for my last Depo shot. No way I could do that for this pregnancy. Jonathan wouldn't allow it, and I didn't want to. I wanted the best, even if I didn't know what that meant yet.

I hustled through baggage and to a taxi stand. If I knew Jonathan, he'd be in bed still, but I wouldn't make it home before his run. I sat in the back of the cab, tapping my fingers and wondering how much of a surprise I wanted to deliver. I'd snuck back without using any of his staff, so he had no way of knowing I was home. It could be too much of a surprise. Not quite thirty people jumping out from behind the couch and yelling "Happy Birthday!" but not a stress-free event either.

Stop worrying. Just stop it.

I turned on my phone. I could call him. But what if he came home from his run, and I was just there in a total non-shocking kind of way? Then I could tell him. I ran alternate scenarios through my head. In bed, naked. In the kitchen, making eggs. I could write him a note and leave it on the banister. I could call first and tell him to wait somewhere in the house. I considered everything as the cab slid onto the 105 freeway toward home.

Chapter 29

Jonathan

I'd gotten the baby to sleep without much trouble. He'd sucked on my finger while I sang him a few off-key verses of "Collared." Thankfully Petra couldn't hear me give her son evil ideas, and he couldn't understand a word of it. They only spoke French to him anyway.

The plane started down the runway. I put my feet on the seat across from me and slipped out my phone. I wanted everything to be perfect when I landed. I needed to know where she was, who she'd be with, and how close she would be to the hotel.

"Quentin?" I said when he answered.

He was somewhere loud, a club or restaurant, and I couldn't yell with a sleeping baby in my arms. I just hung up and texted him.

—Is Monica with you—

—I have no idea where she's off to—

—You were supposed to watch her—

—Sorry, man. Didn't work out that way. Haven't seen her since last night. The sessions broke down. Starting up again on Tuesday—

Damnit. I couldn't hold Quentin responsible, and that was the problem. He owed me nothing, and now Monica was MIA. How did I know she wasn't being attacked by that singer? Or dead in a ditch? Or getting roofied in some dirtshit club?

I should have hired someone to watch her. I should have sent drones or bugged her purse. I had been so busy proving what a nice, reasonable guy I was that I walked right into this. Fuck that. Never again. I was neither nice nor reasonable when it came to Monica. The next time she went anywhere without me, I was planting a locator chip under her scalp.

I called my wife. She wasn't dead.

"Jonathan? Where are you?"

Would I blow the surprise? I had to think fast. "I'm on a plane. I'll be back in a few days. Where are you?"

"No! Oh, Jonathan! I'm home. In the house."

"No!" I immediately looked at the baby. He was sleeping like a doll. "Don't move!" I hung up. "Petra!"

Calling to her from the seat wouldn't work, and it would wake the baby. I reached for the intercom. Couldn't get it. Shifted. The plane sped up. It was going to take off in seconds. I couldn't reach, nor could I put the baby down. I hit the intercom button with my foot.

"Mister Drazen?" Petra asked. "We're taking off—"

"No. Stop. No take off. I'm going home."

"Oh, *merde!*"

I'd never heard her swear before. It was cute, and I braced myself for what was about to happen. The plane slowed down. I leaned my head back, and Claude rolled his eyes open then screamed. After the plane stopped, the cockpit door clicked open.

Petra peeked out. She was back to her normal level of professionalism. "Everything all right?"

"Yeah, I just… don't need to go anymore." I found myself yelling over the baby. I stood and rocked him.

"You need help with Claude?"

"No, I got it. I owe you for stopping the plane."

"My pleasure. I'd rather go home."

"Me too."

Chapter 30

Monica

I ran to the door when I saw the Bentley across the drive. He got out with a bag, leaving Lil half out of the car when he said something to her with a wave. She got back in and drove off.

He turned to the door, jacket under his arm and bag over his shoulder. His hair was a little disheveled, and his cheeks were scrubby with two days of beard. His shirt was open to the second button, and his sleeves were rolled to the elbow, revealing his taut forearms and strong wrists. And his hands. Those hands. Like the marble statue of David, he was an altar to the aesthetics of perfect proportions.

"Hi," I said as he strode to me.

"What's this about?" He looked stern, but under it, he was pleased to see me.

"You were supposed to be home."

"I was. But let's cut the supposed to's. If you came home to get laid, you shouldn't be wearing clothes. So let's fix that."

He reached for me, just touching the red scarf around my neck, but I backed up.

"I want to try something different."

"Really?" He stepped forward again. One more step, and we'd be in the house.

"I want you to do what I tell you," I said.

He stepped forward again. I backed up, and we were inside.

"Like how?" He slammed the door shut.

"Like I'm in charge."

He dropped his bag and jacket with a thud. "I told you I don't bottom." His arm shot out and grabbed me by the waist.

I pushed him away. "Today, I'm the boss."

"You want to start a limits list? We won't get laid for a month."

"You have to just trust me." I pushed him backward, and he fell into a chair.

"Monica"—his voice got serious—"really. This is not going to work."

I put my hands on the arms of the chair and leaned forward until my nose was an inch from his. "You smell like baby powder."

"And you smell like you want to piss me off."

"Trust me." I placed his hands on the arms of the chair, laying them flat. "I won't tie you up or hurt you. That's mine. But I want you to stay still. That's all." I pulled my scarf off.

"Better watch it with that thing," he said. "I know how to use it."

I got behind him and tied it around his eyes.

"Monica?"

"Jonathan?"

"I'm not turned on."

"You will be."

I peeled my clothes off quickly. I'd showered but taken no effort to scrub off the Sharpie. I was still marked with his name and the location of his baby. I took a deep breath. He tapped his finger, mouth set in a tight line. Not turned on. Almost frightening in his stress. He really didn't like taking orders. But he would love this. I turned my naked back to him, facing the Mondrian over the fireplace, and crossed my arms over my abdomen. I didn't know how long I would last. I felt like a bottle of soda someone had shaken but left sealed.

"Take the blindfold off," I said. I heard a rustle behind me.

"You have a great ass."

I turned, fully nude, and after half a second, I moved my arms to my sides. His eyes worked their way from my face, to my tits, hardening them without even touching them, and down my body until he stopped where I'd written *Jonathan's baby*.

"Really?" he said.

"Really."

He laughed. Not a laugh of humor or derision, just delight. Pure, childlike delight. I had to laugh with him. I got on my knees and crawled to him, still laughing, and he kissed me all over: my cheeks, my forehead, my neck. His hands went everywhere, as if touching all the parts he loved, then he kissed my mouth, long, hard, and deep.

"Thank you," he said, breaking the kiss for half a second before putting his lips on me again.

"No problem." It was the least I could say, a joke of miniature proportions.

"You know you wrote it backward, right?"

I leaned back and looked at my abdomen.

"Is it because you have your doubts?" he asked.

"No. I did it in the mirror."

He pushed against me until my back was on the wool rug, and he was over me like an unclouded sky.

"Are you happy?" he asked.

I put my hands on his cheeks. "I didn't think I would be. But I don't know. I'm just elated. I feel like I'm walking on air."

He put my hands over my head and kissed me. "I want to say thank you over and over. I find myself at a loss for words otherwise."

"Don't speak. Just fuck me."

"I want you, I love you, you're mine." He said it all in a string, as if it was one thought. "Do we need a bigger house?"

"This is plenty of space."

"We have to ask Sheila what schools to apply to."

"We can worry about that later."

"The wait lists for preschools are four years long."

"That's obscene."

"I have to set up a trust and fund it. Tomorrow I'll call Margie and have it done."

My face wasn't supposed to tighten, but I feared it did, so I just spoke my mind. "The Swiss thing. You need to promise me you're going to fund that. Before the trusts."

"The trust is easier."

"I don't care if the kid grows up poor. I care that it has a father."

"Hope is deadly."

"Maybe. But tell me you don't have a little bit now? Or some reason to hope you're not taking a bunch of pills just so you can fuck me harder and more often? Don't you want to try? I mean, look, think of it this way. Maybe you'll save someone else."

"Monica, you don't know what this does to me. The idea of leaving you alone. I've been, I think, afraid to make you happy because of what we both know is coming."

I brushed my finger across the scruff on his cheek, this living man, blood beating through him as he scratched and clawed to be reasonable, sensible, and mature while still living life corner to corner. I'd thought I understood his struggle, but I didn't. I thought he just wanted to live or die. I thought he just wanted to be in the moment and not worry, but he'd carried the weight of his own life alongside the weight of mine.

"All I want is for you to try," I said. "Let me and the baby know we're worth you fighting for your life."

He smiled ruefully. "You make compelling arguments. When we met, I thought you were studying law."

"Because I threatened to sue you?"

"It was cute. You were so sexy, the way you tried to back me into a corner. I wanted to bend you over that desk and spank you raw. The minute I laid eyes on you, I wanted to fuck you until you begged."

"Do it now."

He kissed the space between my breasts. "You came when you weren't supposed to. I had plans, but I don't think I can follow through on them."

"Don't you dare."

He put his ear between *Jonathan's* and *baby*. "I can't hear anything. When is he coming?"

"She's coming in late January. And I'm coming today. I'm still me. Do everything. Don't make me beg. Or make me beg. Whichever. Just make me."

He got on his knees and pulled my legs apart. His name was still visible, and Jonathan looked at me everywhere, as if searching for something inside himself, bathing me in the scalding water of his gaze.

He smirked and put his eyes on mine. "I'm thinking. Can I destroy you when you're carrying my baby?"

"Yes, you can."

He slapped the inside of my thigh. It stung like hell because it was unexpected. I gasped and bit my lip.

"I'll decide what I can and can't do," he said. "And I'll decide what you can do. Do you understand?"

"Hurt me," I whispered.

He slapped the inside of my other thigh, and yes, it hurt. And yes, it was demeaning, and yes, I pulled away. I thought I might come from that alone.

"No more demands, goddess. I have ways to hurt you that aren't as much fun." He pulled the red scarf off the arm of the chair. "No talking. No whimpering. No crying. Not a peep out of you. Just yes and no."

"Yes." I couldn't imagine, as he kneeled above me, his knees keeping mine apart, that the word *no* would exit my lips.

"Put your hands over your head and grab the table leg."

I did it, stretching to reach the leg of the heavy sideboard.

"I haven't tied you up since the surgery. You've noticed?"

"Yes."

He leaned over me and wrapped the scarf around my wrists, attaching it to the sideboard as he spoke. "I was nervous. I kept dreaming the heart would leave me. Probably all the talk of rejection going to my head. But I worried that it would happen while you were tied up, and you'd be trapped until someone came." He leaned back and checked his work by pulling me toward him until my arms were completely extended. "I know it wasn't sensible. But it was there." He stood and reached for something in the bag he had been about to take on the plane. His blue book. "You got away with a lot in the meantime."

"Yes," I said.

"Open your mouth." I did, and he put the book in it. "Hold this for me."

I bit down on the leather. He stepped back, and the book blocked my view of him. I heard the clink of his belt and the rustle of clothes, but I couldn't see him. I could only see the damn book.

"The rules—and you can tell me what you object to when I take the book out of your mouth—the rules are this. I'm going to do what I want to your body. You're going to have your safe words. If you worry about the baby for one second, you use them. And if I worry, I'm stopping the scene. It doesn't matter if those worries make sense. And when you start showing, we're renegotiating."

He pulled my legs up and bent my knees until my ass was off the rug, then he took the book out of my mouth. He was naked and perfect from his scar to his huge cock. Lithe and strong. Nimble and taut.

"Yes or no, Monica." He slapped the book on his palm.

"Yes, sir."

"Good." The book landed on my ass with a *thwack*. I chirped and held my cry. He paused then smacked me again. Paused, letting me feel the delicious sting. "Yesterday, you forgot that I own your orgasms. That means I say how and when you come." *Thwack*. "Every time." *Thwack*.

"Sorry."

"You don't sound sorry."

"I'm not."

"You were getting three. Now you're getting four for lying. Count with me."

The book landed between my legs, flat on my engorged clit, and I bit back a scream. It hurt, stung, burned in the opening notes, and the echo was pure pleasure.

"How many is that?" he asked.

"One."

He smacked it again, and I twisted away at the same time as I wanted it again. He straightened me and spread my legs, exposing me to him.

"Count."

"Two."

"You okay?" he asked.

"Yes."

Thwap. Harder than the others. I held back a scream.

"Breathe," he demanded.

"Three!"

"Last one."

He did it again, and it hurt bad, but it left a rush of warm, pre-orgasm quiver in its wake. How had I ever lived without that? How had I ever had an orgasm without the counterpoint of pain?

"Four," I said through my teeth.

He put the book aside and slid his fingers in me. "You're soaked." He drew his wet fingers over my clit, and it burned. That burn, not his touch on me, nearly put me over the edge into orgasm. "And you're close. What am I going to do with you?"

Begging him to fuck me might cause an indefinite delay as I was told to think about what it meant to make demands out of turn, so I said nothing. He moved his hand over me, setting my soreness on fire.

He leaned over and slid his dick into me. I gasped from the pain and the rawness, which had brought every nerve ending into high alert. I was sensitive at every range of the spectrum, and he was stretching me open, putting his whole length into me. I strained against the ties from the pain and the pleasure.

I expected him to take me like an animal. But he didn't. He shifted slowly, making sure I felt every inch. He pushed against my clit, angling himself so he rubbed against it, slowly, slowly, in a tortuous rhythm.

"Please," I whispered.

"You wanted something?"

"Faster."

He didn't go faster. If I'd had a metronome to count by, my bet would be on slower.

"Why?" he asked.

"I want to come."

"Really?"

"Please."

He pressed into me, breathing the words into my cheek. "You are so good. But you have to wait."

"I can't."

"Do you know what happens when you rush? Things don't go right. They're not full. Not complete. If I let you come now, you'll be conscious. You'll say thank you and start thinking about music before you even close your legs."

He pulled out slowly and pushed back in. I moved my hips into him to speed it up, but he adjusted and made it worse. I groaned.

"If I let you come now," he continued, "you'll be satisfied. But you deserve better than that. You deserve to have your mind erased."

"I have a snappy comeback. But I can't breathe."

He moved as if we were underwater. The pressure built, and stayed, and built again, never breaking. What should have taken a second took several. My brain told me I was coming, but I didn't. I stayed in the netherworld between knowing I was going to come and actually doing it. The ultimate mix of pain and pleasure. A tug-of-war between two matched opponents.

Chapter 31
Jonathan

If I'd told her to add two and two, I didn't think she could have answered. It did occur to me to ask for a little simple math, but we were treading a wire-thin path as it was. If I pulled her back too far, I'd confuse her body and ruin the orgasm. She wouldn't be able to have a good one until her body came down fully and her over-stimulated nerves recovered, which could take hours. That was never fun. It made everyone cranky.

But I wanted to see how far I could go and how much pain this caused, because there would be a time, soon, when the bruises and contusions wouldn't wash, and I would derive no pleasure from hurting her. It was one thing to break and push a consenting adult. It was another thing to spank and grab a pregnant woman until she was black and blue. I would have to find other ways to dominate her or we would both wind up unsatisfied and discontented. Controlling her orgasms to the point of pain was a possibility. She was suffering, and she loved it almost as much as I did.

She was giving herself to me in that microcosm of her pleasure, and especially her pain, because in the macrocosm of her love, she was giving me what I wanted most: a family, a home, roots that were mine completely. Nothing borrowed. Nothing temporary. Through all her doubts and legitimate fears, she was taking a leap of faith into the net of my happiness.

I would live for her, for the family she was about to give me, for the home she'd agreed to create. My orbit around her was going to get tighter and tighter until, for better or worse, we fused into a single sun.

A tear dropped from the corner of her left eye, and I kissed it, still shifting with a slow, grinding rhythm. I had to pull her over the edge. It was the perfect time. Another second would be too late. I gave her no permission to come but got up on my knees and thrust deep and hard. Her eyes opened wide and rolled back with the second thrust.

I had complete control over her.

What that did for me, there were no words. Just a peace. A sloughing off of life and its pressures and worries. I existed only in this corner of the world, and it was mine, fully under my purview. The rush of euphoria that followed was submission in itself, to the act, to her, to the power she'd given me.

"May I come?" she whimpered.

"Yes."

I took her. Made her mine. I saw the tide coming in her, and I encouraged it. When she was midway, I'd slow down to make it last, then I'd let go and fill her with me.

It was a good plan. But I looked down as she started to cry my name.

I didn't know what I was looking for. Maybe I wanted to see our connection point when I came or see her cunt pulsing around me. But that's not what I saw.

I shriveled up. Stopped moving.

My name rang in my ears as I looked at my dick, seeing something horrifying, like the death of joy, and I couldn't hear my name anymore. Maybe she was screaming in her orgasm, or in pain, or in blame, I didn't know, but I couldn't form a sentence or command.

The streak of blood on my dick was unmistakable.

I only had one word in my head.

"Tangerine."

Chapter 32

Monica

"What?"

I was pulled so far out of my orgasm that my body went rigid and my mind was soaked in adrenaline. He might as well have screamed *Stop* in my ear. I yanked my hands against the ties with a motion so violent, I heard stuff clatter and clunk as it fell. He got up on his knees, and I saw the fullness of him.

His cock was streaked in red. It wasn't supposed to be. Not unless something was broken, and we weren't doing broken. We were doing celebration. This was wrong. Everything was wrong. I pulled again, even as he reached up to get the scarf undone.

"Monica! Stay still. Give me a second."

But all my yanking and pulling had tightened the knot, and he growled as he tried to pick it loose and failed.

"Say it's from hitting me," I begged. "Please say it's from—"

"I don't know what it's from. Just stay still."

I couldn't. I had no control over my body. I yanked and pulled, trying to slip free, but my husband knew knots like he knew ice cubes and sore bottoms. If he'd set up the knot to keep me from slipping out, I wasn't slipping out.

"Jonathan," I said without anything else to say. Him, I just wanted him. I wanted to say his name to gather strength. He got up, and I had a full view of his beautiful, bloodied cock. "Don't leave me."

"I'm not." He walked away.

"Don't leave me here!"

But he did. He walked away, and I didn't know why I felt so bereft. Some need to run away, coupled with the inability to even lower my arms, made me panic. I could feel something dripping down my leg. And he wasn't there. He was going to the fucking kitchen.

Then I heard knives clack and his footsteps coming back toward me. I calmed. Barely. He came back a bread knife and leaned over my hands.

"Stay still," he said. "Please. I don't want to cut you." He put the knife to the scarf.

"What's happening?" I asked.

"I don't know." His concentration stayed on my bound wrists.

"I don't want to lose it."

"Me neither."

"It's from spanking me. That's all. You hurt me worse than I thought. Let's not do that again, okay?"

"Sure." He laid his hands on my wrists, pressing them apart and making the fabric between them taut. He sliced the scarf open with a *snap*.

I got my arms under me and started to get up, but Jonathan pushed me down. I resisted. He pushed harder.

"Hold on. Gravity," he said.

"That doesn't even make sense."

"I know, I know."

He put his arms under my shoulders and my knees and carried me to the couch. I was sore where he'd hit me. That was the reason for the blood, but he seemed worried, and I wanted to respect that. I didn't want to be dismissive or call him silly, but his knotted brow and the taut line of his jaw made me want to stroke away his fear.

He leaned over me and caressed my cheeks. "Can you wait here while I get dressed and get you some clothes?"

"Why?"

He got up and plucked his clothes off the floor. "We're going to the hospital."

I got my elbows under me to sit up, and with only one arm in his shirt, he rushed to push me down.

"It's nothing, Jonathan. I'm sure of it." I said it to calm him, but I wasn't sure if I believed it out of anything but necessity.

"Then humor me. Lie back."

I did, and when he saw I'd obeyed, he trotted upstairs. I looked down at his name inside my thighs. I was drawn on like a cinderblock wall in gangland. Jonathan's dominion over me was written in black Sharpie, his territory marked in permanent ink.

Was I losing the baby? And so what if I was? What was the big deal?

I didn't even want to have children right now. I wanted nothing to do with it. Jonathan was going to die after a tortuous wait for a second heart before the kid was in high school. What kind of selfish bitch creates a child to go through that?

All I had to do was go back to the me of a few days ago. Nothing had changed.

Except everything. Having carried that baby knowingly for two days, I'd had a cellular alchemy. The shape of my brain and my heart had shifted, grown. I wasn't the same person. I wanted that baby. I wanted it so badly, and I didn't even know it.

I wanted this to be nothing, an embarrassing symptom of rough sex play, but the twitch in my abdomen, the tightness told me otherwise.

Jonathan came down the stairs dressed, with a dress over his arm.

"Do you think they can save it?" I asked, my voice breaking on "save."

"I don't know." He sat on the edge of the couch. "Arms up."

I raised my arms, and he put the long, modest dress over me. He snapped out a pair of simple cotton underwear and slipped them over my ankles then drew them up my legs and over me.

"I was supposed to get rid of all that underwear," I said.

"Sometimes you need it." He stood beside the couch.

I heard the crunch of tires on pebbles outside. "Is it Lil?"

"Yes. I texted her." He put his arms under me and picked me up, carrying me toward the door. "I don't think I can drive."

"Thank God for her." I looped my arms around his neck, and he carried me out.

"Sir," Lil said as she opened the back door. "Mrs. Drazen, I hope you're all right."

"I'm sure it's nothing." I didn't know why I said that. As the minutes passed, I started to think that was some whitewash of hope on a steaming pile of tragedy.

Jonathan held me tight and somehow got me in the car without putting me down. I shifted down and put my head on his lap.

Lil looked into the back. "Sequoia?"

"Yes."

"No!" I said, rigid. I looked up at Jonathan. "No. Anywhere but there. Please. I can't."

"It's the best obstetrics unit in the world, Monica."

"I don't care. I can't go back there. I can't. Let's go to Hollywood Methodist."

"It's a different ward entirely."

"Do you know how far out of my way I go to not drive past it? And it's on Beverly, so yeah, I'd rather be late than see it. I'd rather go to the urgent care clinic on Sunset. I'd rather see the witch doctor in Silver Lake than go anywhere near that hospital. It smells like death. It's hell. Nine stories of fucking hell, and I won't go."

Jonathan looked at me for a second then back at Lil. "Drive."

"Jonathan!" I said as Lil closed the door. I tried to get up, but he pulled me down.

"Listen to me," he said. "I know how you feel. Believe me, I get it. But that was enough blood to scare the hell out of me, and it wasn't enough to convince me this is completely over. If we lose this baby because we went to a second-rate hospital or nowhere at all, because we were scared... well, I'd like to know how you're going to forgive yourself. Because you're going to have to teach me."

I looked away from him. His gaze was going to break me. It was a wall of resolve. He was doing what he wanted to do, and I had to go along. From my angle on his lap, all I could see was the grey-blue glass of the sky, streetlights, and telephone poles zipping by. A speck of bird or plane.

He was right.

Fear was fungible, and death was forever. Overcome one to face the other. Blah blah. I didn't want him to be right. I wanted to fall down a hole of despair or climb a pillar of hope, and reason and rationality were distractions from the choice.

Reaching for the hope, I touched his face. "I'm sure it's fine. We're just overreacting."

"I hope so."

"Didn't Jessica miscarry? What happened?"

He turned toward the window. "We were throwing an event at the house. Some fundraiser for the artist co-op she was in. She just takes my hand and brings me into the house. Doesn't break a beat. I'm following her, and I can see the blood inside her stockings. I picked her up and carried her to the car, but it was too late. It was a mess before we even got there. So much blood. I never saw her cry except in the front seat of my car. The pain was so bad, and you know, I asked her how long it had hurt before she told me."

"Could they have saved it?"

"The doctor wouldn't guarantee anything, but just said that next time we should come right away."

I relaxed into that, watching the fancy streetlights of Santa Monica turn into the more urban, less fussy designs of the west side of LA. "I had pain yesterday, but I thought I had the flu."

"Let's see what happens."

"If we lose it, do we try again?"

"I don't know."

That didn't help. If he pulled back from getting what he wanted most, what he'd *always* wanted most, then I didn't know who he was anymore.

"Did you try again with Jessica?" I flinched from my own question. It sounded petty and mean. Our situations couldn't have been more different. But I wanted to know what to expect from him. Did he give up or truck on?

If he heard the question as cutting, he didn't show it. "We both got checked out. I was fine, but her uterus had a shape that made it hard for her to go to term. We were fine, but it never took again. In a way, it improved things between us for a while."

I cupped his face in my hands, and he looked down at me then leaned over and kissed me.

"This won't end us," he said. "I swear, if it's the last thing I do, I'm keeping you."

The car stopped.

"I'm ready," I said. "If you stay by me. I'm ready."

Lil opened the door, and Jonathan carried me through the sliding glass doors into Sequoia Hospital. Hell on earth. I closed my eyes, but the smell was still there, and the ambient noise. When something somewhere beeped, I clung to him.

Chapter 33

Jonathan

I'd called ahead while gathering our clothes, and I was able to carry her right up to the second floor. We were offered a gurney outside the elevator, and I put her on it, insisting even when she clutched me. She weighed nothing to me. I could have carried her ten more miles, but I knew hospitals better than I wanted to, and she needed to be on the gurney.

We exited onto the maternity ward. The first thing I heard was people laughing, and I looked down at Monica to see if she heard it. I thought it would relax her. Maternity wards were gentle places with better results than the parts of the hospital she'd been stuck in for weeks.

Her eyes were clamped shut, as if she were a child who didn't want to see anything scary. I was about to make some wisecrack about ocean views and a full buffet. Describe the dancing girls and rare art she was missing. Anything to calm her down. A chuckle. Even if she slapped me and told me to shut up, it would have been preferable to seeing her coiled in dread.

"Mister Drazen," a young woman in blue scrubs said.

"Are you Dr. Blakely?" I asked. It had taken Dr. Solis seconds to recommend this young woman with the flat brown ponytail above all others.

"Yes. Dr. Solis told me you'd be coming." She looked at Monica. "How are you feeling?"

"Fine," my wife lied.

"This way, then."

The nurse, a muscular woman in her forties with a military cut, asked a battery of stupid questions. Monica answered them with her eyes closed.

"Mister Drazen," Blakely said as she stepped into the exam room in front of the gurney, "Dr. Solis says you're immunosuppressed?"

"Yes?"

"You shouldn't be in a hospital."

Monica opened her eyes. "Go."

"I'll text you our findings," Blakely said as they moved Monica from the gurney to the table.

Monica seemed so helpless, so separate from her mind and will, so corporeal as she stretched across the table. Her dress hitched above her knees, and I saw the Sharpie script of *Jo* and *erty*.

I wasn't abdicating responsibility. Not the medical part. I knew my limitations, but I wasn't turning my back on her. I wouldn't let her sit, alone and hurt, while I protected my immune system. "I'll stay, thank you."

"Jonathan, please," Monica said. "She's right. I'll be okay if you keep your phone on. Really, I'm not freaked out. You need to go."

But she was freaked out. From the ends of her hair, through the writing on her thighs, to the tips of her toenails, she was terrified. I hadn't known her that long and I had plenty to learn about her, but I knew goddamn well when she was lying about her comfort to protect me. We'd both done that enough to get PhDs in it.

"I'm not going," I said then turned to Dr. Blakely. "This is my wife, and she needs me. I don't want to hear, from either of you, that I should go home and live in a bubble and wait for a fucking text telling me what's happening with my family." I sat in the seat next to the table and held Monica's hand.

"He can wear a mask outside maternity," the nurse suggested as she tapped on a computer keyboard.

"Will you?" asked Monica.

"Fine."

Dr. Blakely sat on a stool at the end of the table. "You're not my patient. Dr. Solis will chew you out if you get sick. Let's get these underpants off."

Monica picked up her butt, and the doctor helped her slide out of them. The nurse started to pick up Monica's dress but glanced at me once she saw the words *Jonathan's Property*. I wanted to mention it or make a tension-splitting joke, but I didn't want to embarrass Monica. The nurse put crinkled paper over Monica's abdomen. The doctor spread Monica's legs, and I thanked God Solis had recommended a woman.

"Well, no question of paternity," she said, looking over the paper. "The baby has to work on his handwriting though."

The joke wasn't that good, but I was glad she'd made it. The tension fell off my wife as she laughed.

"All right." The doctor smiled behind her mask. "Let's see what we have here."

Monica cringed, and I heard a squishing noise. I squeezed her hand.

"Plug is in place."

More tension dropped off Monica. Maybe she was right. Maybe the book had been the wrong tool. Maybe I would have to start getting proper toys. I had to stop using whatever was on hand if it made her bleed.

The doctor put the sheet back and put her Monica's legs down. The nurse wheeled a cart over.

"I'm supposed to tell you jokes," I said to Monica. "Something clever and funny to take the edge off."

Blakely and the nurse said things I didn't understand, and they exposed Monica's abdomen. So much like my own experience as a patient. Experts talking about me as if I wasn't there, huddling together before approaching me with an approved line of bullshit.

Blakely squeezed clear gel on Monica's abdomen as if every patient had the baby's ownership scrawled backward on the mother.

"I'm waiting," Monica said. "I know you have a few thousand jokes in there."

"Knock, knock."

She laughed as if that were the entire joke, which it was. I didn't know any knock, knock jokes.

The ultrasound screen went live as if it had been fingerpainted in shades of grey. We watched as if it were the seventh game of the world series, but we had no idea of what we were seeing.

Silence. Too long. Shouldn't we be hearing a heartbeat? I'd had sonograms when I was in the hospital, and I always heard whooshing. I squeezed her hand. The doctor slid the wand over Monica's abdomen while tapping keys.

"Okay," Blakely said. "Well, that explains it." She pointed at a black oval. "This is the ovum, and typically we have a little peanut-shaped blur in there, and there isn't. It's empty."

"What does that mean?" Monica asked.

"Well, it's a blighted ovum. Meaning the egg was fertilized and made it to the uterus, but the cells stopped dividing. Either the cells were reproducing incorrectly or there was some other technical malfunction. Your body kept doing its job though, so you have an ovum and the beginnings of a placenta." Blakely shut off the machine.

Monica went white, and something in me did too. I wanted to throttle this young doctor. I wanted to choke her until she admitted she was wrong, that she'd misread the images. It was all a big mistake. There was a baby in there, right as rain and thriving.

"I was traveling," Monica said. "Did that do it?"

"Probably not."

"We're rough in bed, the two of us." Monica was past sense. Her hand had gone cold, and she was babbling. "I shouldn't say this, but you're a doctor, right? I mean, sometimes, it's just, well, like I said we get rough and—"

"I saw the bruising, and no, that wouldn't cause this. I'm sorry. The good news is, you're in perfect shape. You should be able to conceive again without a problem."

I stood. "Thank you, Doctor." I held out my hand. Those people had to leave immediately. I got it. I'd heard it. I needed to be alone with my wife.

"Not so fast," she said. "Let me give you a quick rundown, then I'll leave you alone. You have tissue in your uterus that your body needs to get rid of. It's messy and painful, and it could start today or next week. Most patients opt for us to remove it by dilating the cervix and scraping the uterus. That shortens the—"

"No." Monica pointed her chin up. "I'm not evicting the baby."

"Mrs. Drazen, I'm sorry, but there is no baby."

"Don't you tell me there's no baby!" She was pure kinetic energy. A blur. Her limbs were still but poised to shake the earth free of its orbit.

I put myself between the two women.

"There is a motherfucking baby!" Monica called from behind me.

I felt the same as she did. I felt all her anger and denial, but I couldn't allow myself to get lost in it. "Is there anything else, Doctor?" She had to get out before we were escorted out.

Unfazed by Monica's denials, Blakely took a card out of her pocket. "Call me if the pain is really bad. I'll prescribe something."

"Pain?" Monica's voice shot from behind me. "I can take pain. Just try me."

I took the card. This was it. So much had changed in the past four hours, I felt numb. I hadn't even had a chance to process flying to New York, then not flying to New York, then the baby, now the lack of the baby. It had been a day of miserable false starts, ending with the promise of pain for my wife. "Thank you."

"Have her take it easy, if possible. It's going to hurt."

Chapter 34

Monica

Take it easy. What kind of bullshit was that? How was I supposed to take it easy? Was I supposed to sip piña coladas by the pool and wait for a miscarriage? Like la-di-da, let's take a jog and have a good laugh and watch TV and forget that my whole life, everything I thought I wanted, changed in the past two days. I'm supposed to pretend that didn't happen?

Well, fuck you, Doctor. Fuck you with a big bag of fucking fucks.

Once that fucking fuck of a doctor and her little nurse were gone, I flipped them a double bird, because fuck them and fuck that machine and fuck that room and fuck that hospital and fuck the lie I fucking wrote on myself.

"And fuck you," I said to Jonathan when he twirled my underwear.

"You should get the D&C," he said, looping the cotton panties around my ankles. "Let the doctor end this. She suggested it for a reason."

"No."

"What if you're in the studio when you start cramping?"

"Fuck the studio. I hate this hospital. I hate everything about it. It's a rat shithole. Everything is beige and pale pink. The decorator should be shot. And they could run fucking potpourri through the vents, and it would still smell like bleach and death."

He slid my underpants back on, and I let him, because I was too mad, too confused by my tangle of emotions to get dressed and get off the table. Jonathan pulled me into a sitting position.

"Don't fight me," he said, opening the door.

His voice was as definitive as ever, telling me my behavior before I had a chance to question it. I didn't know what he meant until he put his arms under me and picked me up, carrying me out the door and down the hall. I put my arms around his neck and rested my head on his shoulder.

"You don't have to look," he said, and I knew what he meant.

I closed my eyes and focused on his leather scent, pretending that bleach and medicine didn't hover around the edges, ignoring the ding of the elevator and the whispering of nurses and doctors in their parallel language. It was so familiar and so foreign, because though the sounds and smells were the same, this time I wasn't worried about Jonathan, or even myself. I was just angry, and disappointed, and touching the edges of grieving the loss of something I hadn't even wanted twenty-four hours ago.

"I'm okay," I said into Jonathan's ear as he carried me out of the elevator and across the lobby.

"I know."

"I'm not upset anymore."

"I know.

"You can put me down." I opened my eyes. He filled the frame of my vision.

"Nope. You're my wife, and I'll carry you where I like."

Lil waited in the roundabout, parked in the red zone as if it were a marker for Bentleys. She opened the back door, and Jonathan poured me in.

I didn't say anything the whole way home. I sat on Jonathan's lap, wrapped in him, my head on his shoulder. Somewhere on the 10 freeway, I felt a twinge, and it started. The doctor had been very explicit about what to expect, and I didn't know if I'd thought I'd be immune, or I didn't care, or if I simply underestimated what she'd meant by pain and bleeding.

But by the time Jonathan carried me to the door, I felt as if I'd been stabbed in the stomach.

"Monica?" He swung the door open.

"I think I should go to the bathroom."

"Are you all right?"

"Yeah."

He looked concerned, but he let me down, and I ran to the bathroom off our bedroom. It had a shower, and a bathtub, and a door that locked. It was a super fancy little corner of the world, and it had a view of the ocean, because what else did a girl need when her body was ridding itself of a blight. Right? I peeled off my pants and sat on the toilet, hunched in pain so bad, I felt as if my guts were being pulled and tied into a knot at the end of a balloon.

There was a soft rap on the door.

I couldn't do this in front of anyone. Not even him. Not even the man whose chest had been open before me. Not even the one whose bleeding heart I carried every night in my dreams. I was doing this alone, whatever this was.

I grunted when the air went out of the balloon and the stretching and knotting started again.

"Monica," he said through the door, "I'm calling for pain killers."

"I'm fine!" Why did I say that? I wasn't fine.

"You were with me in the hospital," he said. "You have a distorted view of pain."

"Don't take this the wrong way," I said, barely able to breathe. "You are the love of my life, but get the fuck away from the door."

"No, I will not leave you." He used his dominant voice, and I didn't give a single shit. "Open it."

"*Go jogging!*" I screamed it not because I wanted to scare him, but because the pain intensified by an order of magnitude. I put my head in my hands, and the blood started.

Chapter 35

Jonathan

The door was locked. Not that I gave a shit on a practical level. A bobby pin could fix that. I could knock the door down or unscrew the knob. I was sure the staff kept a chainsaw somewhere in the garage. Or hedge clippers. I could have broken that lock with my spit, to be honest. That was how wound up I was. I put my fist on the door for one last threat, but before I pounded it, I heard her hiccup then sniff. As badly as that made me want to get into that bathroom, I imagined a sudden bang on the door would only startle her. What would be the point of that?

"I'll tell you what," I said.

No answer. Just breathing.

"I won't break this door down. But I'm staying right here." I sat with my back against the door, my forearms on my knees.

She groaned, and I heard her pregnancy ending in a rush. She made an N sound that stretched out like a rubber band.

"Monica?"

"Women have gone through this for centuries, okay? Generations. Just… if you're going to sit at the door like an eavesdropper…" She stopped, and I could only imagine why. "I'll let you know when I'm through."

The last word ended in a squeak. If I broke down the door, I could hold her hand. Or bring her a painkiller. I could be *doing something* instead of sitting against the door and imagining what she was going through. I felt trapped and incompetent. I wanted to grab my fitness as a husband back.

That was it. I wasn't leaving her alone.

Bobby pins. I needed just one to open that door. I went to her dresser. The surface was cluttered with a picture of her parents, a crochet runner, a calendar. I opened her nightstand drawer. Old pictures. Sunglasses. Pens. Little notebooks. What the fuck? Where were her bobby pins?

It hit me hard, deflating me. The bobby pins were where they belonged. In the goddamned bathroom.

I stood by the door, ready to break it down, and I heard her on the other side. She was humming the "Star-Spangled Banner" of all things. I put my hands on the door. She groaned the lyrics, and I heard a sickening splash.

I couldn't take the door down. I couldn't do that to her, but I couldn't leave her either.

She was the heart patient, and I was the lonely young woman trying to grasp onto anything I could to make something happen. Would I have gone into Paulie Patalano's room to pull the plug? Maybe. Maybe I would have. Because if this kept up for weeks and was a matter of life and death, yeah, I'd take that door down with a chainsaw even if it scared the shit out of her. I'd take the door down and shove it up someone's ass.

But it only *felt* like life and death. It wasn't.

I put my forehead to the door just as she sang "...*and the home of the brave.*" "Brava," I said.

"Go away," she replied so softly I could barely hear her.

"Is 'America the Beautiful' next?"

"Not until the seventh inning."

"I'll wait out here all day."

"I wanted this baby, Jonathan. Once I found out, I did. But before that... do you think not wanting it... it's so stupid."

"You didn't miscarry because you didn't want it. You didn't scare it away."

"We'll try again. Right?"

She needed that hope. Hope was her power, her way of coping. She'd do reckless things to keep it alive. She'd murder and betray. She'd be brave and strong, all in the name of hope. If I could take her hope and let it feed me, I might have a nourished life, no matter its length.

"Yes, Monica. We can try again. Right away. Once you're better."

Another groan, and she started the "Star-Spangled Banner" again.

I put my hands on the door as if that was at all soothing to the woman on the other side. The song passed, and silence followed, interrupted by a few sniffs, a few breaths, a few hummed bars of something I couldn't identify. I sat at the door and listened. I didn't know how else to care for her but to make that door into my love, touching the wood as if it was skin, comforting her through it, making her safe with space and matter between us. I didn't know how much time passed before she spoke.

"Are you there?"

"Yes."

"I can't flush. I just… I can't."

"Do you want me to do it?"

A long pause followed.

Chapter 36

Monica

This was ridiculous. Everything about it. Me on the toilet for over an hour, cramping as though it was my job. The crime-scene-worthy mess. My compassionate and gorgeous husband standing outside, asking me if I'd like him to flush the baby.

I should just do it. Then I could run into the shower, do a quick clean up of the floor and outside of the bowl, and exit looking fresh. I knew this would continue for a few days, but not like this. Not to the point of non-functionality. I felt finished. I felt as if the worst was over. I felt empty.

"Monica?"

I couldn't do it. It wasn't a baby. It was tissue that had formed because my body had fooled itself into thinking there was a baby, but it was a terminated mission. My uterus just hadn't gotten the memo. So I should just flush instead of being a cliché of a woman who'd just had a miscarriage.

"I'm unlocking the door," I said. "Just wait until I call you to come in okay?"

"All right."

"And I'm warning you, ahead of time, it's not pretty."

"Consider me warned."

The bathroom was huge, and it had a separate bath and shower. Blood dripped on the edges of the toilet from when I'd cramped so badly I'd moved away from the seat. Otherwise, the room was as pristine as Jonathan's staff could make it.

I unlocked the door and turned on the shower. It was hot in half a second. I didn't know how he did that, but money got rid of even the smallest inconveniences of thermodynamics. I stripped, stepped in, and clicked the door shut.

The water flowed over my face, scalding hot. I wanted it hotter. Second-degree burn hot. I wanted to sterilize myself from the baby that wasn't a baby. I wanted to forget the feeling of something real and human dropping from me to its death.

When the water flowed over me fully, a stream of red-stain went down the drain. It was too much. I didn't think I could stand it. I was broken and useless. What had felt real, wasn't. And now I was expected to—

The door clicked open, and Jonathan stood in the shower entrance, fully dressed.

"I'm sorry," I said. "I forgot to call you."

He stepped into the shower, water slapping onto his shirt, sticking it to his skin. Darkening and flattening his hair. He put his arms around me and pressed me to him. His lips brushed my shoulder, and his hands pressed against me as if he wanted as much of himself touching as much of me as possible.

"I love you," he said.

"I—" I choked up the rest of the sentence, because I felt lost and empty, and he was still there. He was my sky. Through blood and breath, sin and sorrow, I was his sea, and wherever the horizon was and the world ended, we were there, together.

What had I done to deserve this? Repeatedly and often, I'd failed to deserve him. I'd resisted him, tried to deny him a family, then I'd failed to carry his child. I wasn't worth him getting his clothes wet, but I needed him. I needed him so badly. To fail for him and to try again, because having been pregnant for those hours, I couldn't see any future past giving him children.

I clawed at his back and pressed my face to his shoulder. He rocked me under the hot water, sodden and strong, even after my legs couldn't hold me.

"Come on," he said, shutting off the shower, "before I flood the floor."

He carried me for the third time, his feet squishing on the marble tiles. The bath was running, and the lights were dimmed. He laid me in the tub.

"I'm sorry," I said.

"For what?" He leaned over the tub, his clothes still soaked, and submerged a sponge. He didn't even roll up his sleeves; he just got them wetter.

"For letting the baby go."

"You know I'm not going to accept that apology."

"I feel like I failed you. And hours after getting you all excited. God, I'm such a fuckup."

He put his fingertips to my lips. "Stop."

But it was too late. My eyes filled up, and the skin behind my face tingled. "I can't. I can't stop thinking that—" I heaved a breath. "That it's my fault. That I killed it."

He soaped the sponge. "If that were possible, there wouldn't be any unwanted pregnancies."

I was Teflon, immune to logic, sense, and evidence-based reality. I couldn't shake the feeling that I was somehow at fault for this disaster. I couldn't answer him with the straight fact that despite the pure reason of his assertion, I was poisoned. Blighted. My body wasn't fit for a child.

He put the sponge between my thighs and cleaned off the last of the blood. His name was still there, and he rubbed until it was gone while I laid my head on the side of the tub and cried.

What shame. Lying in a tub with my legs spread, weeping while my husband scrubbed our baby from between my legs. But despite what the scene may have looked like, I wasn't ashamed. I was open, raw, and comforted.

"Thank you," I said. "You're good to me."

He put his hand flat on my abdomen. "You wrote something here too. It's darker." He ran his wet hand over my cheeks, wiping away old tears to make room for the new ones.

"There was a shower in between."

"I'm going to have to work to get it off."

"I don't want to look."

"Don't." He picked up a scrubby thing, tossed it, chose something softer, and put soap on it. He was all business. I looked at the ceiling as he scrubbed.

"Do you want to hear the last stupid thing that went through my head?" I said.

"If you're willing to hear my stupid thing after."

"I thought, 'This happened because I wrote it backward.'"

"That is stupid."

"What was your stupid thing?" I asked.

"That next time we should tattoo *Jonathan's baby,* and it'll stick."

I laughed through my tears. That was Jonathan, a poet in love and a realist in life, thinking superstitious nonsense, just like me.

"Are you cold?" I asked when he put the scrubber down. "Your clothes are soaked."

"I feel trapped in a bag."

"You do look a little vacuum-packed."

He laughed, and I laughed with him. He stood and peeled off his clothes, getting down to the pure magnificence of him. I didn't know if I could every be away from him again. I needed him.

"They're going to restart the track in a week," I said, holding out my arms.

"I think you'll be okay by then."

"Come with me."

He stepped into the tub without answering.

"Jonathan," I said as he leaned his back on me, and I wrapped my legs around his waist.

"I heard you."

"Please. Don't leave me alone. Don't make me choose. I can't do it anymore."

He leaned his head back and kissed my cheek. "I own you, and I take care of my property. Every minute of the day."

"Say that means you'll travel with me."

"It means wherever you go, I'll be by your side. I'm going to take such good care of you, you're going to get sick of me. You're going to tell me to stay home, and I won't."

"Thank you," I whispered, laying my cheek on his shoulder. We stayed there until the water got cold.

Chapter 37

EIGHTEEN MONTHS LATER

Monica

"Today?" Laurelin cried as she zipped my dress. "You agreed to do a show *today?*"

"Tonight, actually." I held up the strapless top with my forearm.

"You're supposed to get swept off your feet to a foreign land." He face was red with irritation, and her fists were tense. She was quite the romantic, our nurse.

"I am. After the show. Two songs in my wedding gown. Darren and I will blow the roof off the place, then I'll go on my honeymoon." I kissed her cheek, and when she tried to push me away, I kissed her harder.

"Come on," she said. "Let me get this on you."

Laurelin struggled to get the zipper up, cursing. Her pale blue gown hung on her like a sack, as if its lack of efficiency made her body repel it. She, Yvonne, and three of Jonathan's sisters were my bridesmaids, and they tittered around the waiting room, drinking tea and fussing with their makeup.

My hair was braided, of course, and twisted into a bun. Leanne had fashioned a veil of twisted tulle and beadwork, knotted it into the plait, and let it fall to the floor. I wasn't into finery, but the dress was gorgeous. Rock star gorgeous. Underneath it, I had a custom-made lace garter set with enough hardware and straps to suspend me from the Eiffel tower. I couldn't wait for Jonathan to see it.

I hadn't let him have me in two weeks, which hadn't been easy for either of us. But I wanted to be wild with desire on our wedding night, and I wanted to torture him as much as he tortured me.

During the weeks after my miscarriage, I couldn't. I had been bleeding drop by drop, and I felt so raw and hurt, I couldn't let him near me. I hated my own skin. Then, one day, as we were getting on the Gulfstream to New York, the rawness left, and I wanted nothing more than his body inside me. He was gentle at first, but once he realized I was all right, he went back to the rough bastard I always knew.

He'd barely left my side since. Where I went, he went, and if he had to travel, I followed him. We brought Laurelin if we had to, and she brought the baby and her husband and kid sometimes.

Jonathan with a baby was magic. He opened up. His sense of humor turned to silly faces and funny noises. And yet, I couldn't give him one. There was nothing. Not even a threat or a tickle. Just us. We started talking about adoption, because he only had so long and I wanted joy for him before his heart gave out.

"Any word from Mr. Gevers?" Laurelin asked, as if reading my mind.

Andre Gevers was a Dutch man, and the first recipient of an artificial heart made by what we privately called the Swiss Project. Jonathan had funded the research, and though he still promised nothing as far as allowing an artificial heart to be used on him, if it worked, I knew he wouldn't say no to a life.

"Stable. The fake heart seems really happy in there." I held my hand up with my fingers crossed so tight, I nearly pulled a tendon.

"Two weeks doesn't mean it won't be rejected," Laurelin said. "I'm not trying to be negative, but medical research… there are a lot of failures before something sticks."

"It's going to work. He's going to be an old man."

"Gevers or Jonathan?"

"Yes."

"My brother was born an old man," Margie said, appearing next to me in the mirror, wearing a feminine-cut tuxedo. She was the best woman. We'd been at a loss for men, so she, Sheila, and Fiona were groomsfolk, along with Eddie and Darren. "Your dress isn't as puff pastry as I feared."

"You look perfectly marriageable yourself." I said.

"That's what I'm told." She handed me the loose bouquet of flowers. "You ready?"

"Thank you, Margie. For everything. I've always felt taken care of with you around."

"My pleasure. Now go."

All my sky-blue girls waited at the exit, and I followed them through the stone hallway and into the courtyard. The security detail followed us, as visually conspicuous as they were silent. I didn't know if I'd ever get used to being famous. It had been a year since my EP hit, and seven months since the full album. I was already having daily wrestling matches with my belief that I was a freak and a fraud, and Darren and Jonathan had to pull me away from them.

In the middle of the chaos and changing expectations, there was Jonathan, always at my side in public and always my master and king in private. We'd planned a wedding between plane rides, concerts, family functions, the management of a handful of hotels, and enough lovemaking to make my whole life a honeymoon.

Jonathan's divorce made him ineligible for a wedding in a Catholic church. Fortunately, Episcopalians were less strident, and St. Timothy's was more than happy to do the honors. The church was a huge stone edifice crusted with stained glass and surrounded by old trees in the center of Los Angeles. I got to the narthex, where my mother waited in a dress she tried to look modest in. It didn't work. She was too beautiful, and she carried it like a cross. She kissed me on the cheek and held me. I was overcome by the seriousness of it all. Yes, I'd been married for two years, and yes, this was all a big redo for the sake of his family and tradition, but those stones and brass fixtures had seen generations of brides. And the pews, from what I could see, were full of people.

"So much for an intimate event," I mumbled.

"Oh, please, Monya," my mother said, "you had no chance of that."

She took my hand, and we were hustled to the back of the line.

St. Timothy's had a huge organ, and at the first note, a hush fell over the congregation. I waited at the end of the line with my mother as the bridesmaids and groomsfolk walked down the aisle. David and Bonnie were right in front of me with the rings and a basket of rose petals.

"You ready, Mom?" I asked as Margie and Laurelin went.

"I hoped I wouldn't have to give you away. I hoped I'd meet someone to replace your father."

"No one could replace dad."

The music changed, and I took my mother down the aisle so she could give me away. I was so excited I wanted to run, but my mother took it slow. Too slow.

"Come on, Ma."

"You only do this once," she whispered.

I felt like a kid held back from the tree on Christmas morning. I knew what Jonathan looked like. I knew what his tux looked like, how it fit, how the white tie blended with the white shirt and how the line of the sharply cut black jacket made a perfect triangle from his throat to his waist, like an arrowhead to… well, I admit I was thinking of my wedding night.

Cameras had been confiscated. I couldn't look at all the people watching me. But I felt their eyes on me. Felt their good wishes.

Once I got halfway down the aisle, I could see Jonathan, because he'd stepped toward the center to see me. Margie tried to pull him back, but it was a wasted effort. Jonathan did what he wanted, when he wanted, and how he wanted, and he apparently wanted to watch me rush down the aisle.

Could my heart continue to melt every time I saw him? Would the day come when he had no effect on me? When I took his presence for granted? I couldn't imagine that. He was so straight, so perfect, carrying the formal suit as if it was the most natural thing he could put on his back. The man I'd met had returned, slowly but surely. His sudden visions of his heart rejecting him were gone, and my dreams and fear had collapsed under the weight of our intimacy. He was stronger, fitter, more dominant than ever, and he was my perfect life mate.

"Hey," I said when I reached the altar, and he took my hand. "How are you doing? You look nice."

"Nice? I'm surrounded by cross-dressers, and they all look better in a tux than I do."

I put my fingers over my mouth to stifle a laugh.

As the congregation sat behind us, Jonathan leaned over and whispered in my ear. "I own you. I'm going to take a belt to you just because I can."

"Jonathan, we're in church." I shut out the white noise of the church, the ministrations of the bellicose bishop in his sixties, and the rustlings of the choir.

"This is just a building," Jonathan said so low I could barely hear him. "Worship is later. I'm going to tie your legs over your head with that pretty veil, and I'm going to beat and fuck you so hard the words, 'Oh, God,' are going to summon the heavenly host."

His words went right between my legs. We stood at the altar as people talked about us, as a service was said in our honor.

I didn't know if there was a mic somewhere that could pick us up, so

I turned and spoke directly in his ear, my breath to him, my vocal chords disengaged. A butterfly couldn't hear me. "I'm singing later. Be gentle with my throat."

His hand twitched. I was expected to know he was aware of all my needs, including my need to sit at a meeting, walk in front of people, or sing. He knew when to be gentle and when to score my skin because he was inside every part of my life, and any lack of trust warranted a delicious spanking.

"Good thing you don't sing with your ass," he whispered back.

I spit out a nervous laugh that every mic caught, and Jonathan's smile broke into a chuckle. The bishop looked at us, and the congregation stared. I waved and curtsied.

The bishop looked motioned us front and center.

David held out the red pillow with our rings. They'd been designed as tight coils, like key rings, to remind us of our first wedding rings and the circumstances they'd been given under. But they were gold, and they fit right, which would be a nice change. Jonathan and I positioned ourselves across from each other, and he took the smaller ring.

The bishop cleared his throat. "Mister Drazen, repeat after me. I, Jonathan Drazen—"

"I, Jonathan Drazen,"

"Take thee, Monica Faulkner—"

"Take thee, Monica Faulkner." Jonathan was smiling, the ring hovering over my finger, and I could practically hear the gears in his head turning.

"To be my wedded wife," the bishop said.

"To be my wedded wife," Jonathan said before he turned to the bishop. "You know we memorized this, right?"

"That would be the first time in my forty years of officiating weddings."

Laughter floated up from the congregation, and I put my head down to stifle a big giggle.

"We thought it was kind of important," Jonathan said.

"Get on with it then."

"Where were we?"

"Having and holding," the bishop said.

"Thank you," Jonathan squeezed my hand and continued. "… to have and to hold from this day forward, for better for worse, for richer for poorer, in sickness and in health, to love and to cherish, till death do us part." He dropped his voice, as if expressing seriousness, but also to create a web of intimacy around the words. "I own you. Like the sky owns the stars. You are mine." He slipped the gold key ring on my finger.

"You memorize yours too?" the bishop asked, looking at me over his half-moon glasses.

"Yes." I picked up the ring. "You ready, Drazen?"

"Yes."

"I, Monica Faulkner, take thee, Jonathan Drazen, to be my wedded husband, to have and to hold from this day forward, for better for worse, for richer for poorer, in sickness and in health, to love, cherish, and to obey till death. Your name is written on my heart."

I heard the murmurs. Jonathan and I had kept the word obey in my vows because we knew what we meant. He was my master in the bedroom, and I obeyed his commands. We knew the limitations between us, and these were our vows. We neither explained nor excused them.

And thus, both standing on our own two feet, before God and our families, with the news media waiting outside, we were wed.

Chapter 38
Jonathan

She was most kinetic in stasis. With her energy contained by my will and her desire to please me, she was a sizzling box of energy, and the longer I kept her there, naked and still, the closer to her skin her arousal came.

She stayed still for me, the streets of Paris below, on the first night of our honeymoon, her nipples hard in the chilled air. I was behind her, which was all she knew. She didn't know when I'd move or what I was doing. I could hear her heartbeat, and her breath, which she tried to keep even but failed.

She was mine. I owned this body, this heart. I wanted to put my fingers and tongue inside her, my cock, everywhere all at once. Every act of ownership felt incomplete to the totality of my love. I'd married her for the second time only a day before, and I'd marry her a hundred times more, but our bond was in our consummation. I was hers, and she was mine, and we only came close to the expression of the depth of it when I broke her patience, her resolve, her expectations, soothed her heart, and broke her again.

I came around her, fully dressed, to watch her naked body as it shifted, to watch her eyes try to stay focused ahead. She was so good, objectifying herself for me, becoming an owned thing so we could play the games that were an expression of our deeper truth. She owned me. I was an object for her pleasure.

I sat in the chair in front of her and brushed my fingertips across her breasts. She shuddered. My plan was to get her on her knees and take her throat, then it could go one of three ways, with every step leading to a new game plan, depending on her level of obedience. Every plan led up to the both of us quivering together. But as I ran my fingers from her breasts to her belly, something changed.

Something about her.

I kissed her navel, pulling the diamond bar with my lips.

She'd gained weight since starving herself in Sequoia. On our honeymoon, she was a little heavier than when we'd met. I knew what her body looked like and what it felt like. My hands and mouth discerned her shapes in all their perfection. And as she stood by me, groaning as my tongue traced circles around her navel, I perceived a change as subtle as the sea.

"Monica," I said.

"Yes?"

"I don't want to alarm you."

She stiffened. "Are you okay?"

"*Shh*. I'm fine. As are you." I looked up at her. She looked straight ahead, as she was supposed to, and I stood so I could look her in the eye.

"What is it?" she asked, meeting my gaze.

"I don't want you to get excited for nothing." A senseless desire. No matter what I did, I was going to get her hopes up. I was going to risk causing her disappointment and pain. I couldn't protect her from that. The greatest gift I could give Monica, a wedding gift for our life together, was hope.

She broke the silence. "Tell me, or I swear I'll—"

"You'll do no such thing."

She set her mouth in a tight line and put her hands on her hips. Scene over.

I took her by her chin and risked her dashed hopes. "I think you're pregnant."

Chapter 39

Monica

He was impossible. From the minute he'd run across Paris for a pregnancy test, to him cancelling everything on my behalf, to the doctor's appointment where I couldn't understand a word they were saying, he was the most impossible man I had ever met.

"I'm fine!" I said in the square across from the doctor's office. It had a church, and a statue, and pigeons everywhere. The sky was the color of the sidewalks, and the air was so wet it stuck to me. "I'm not even a little sick. I feel better than ever. I could run a marathon, so back off."

"The doctor said you should take it easy," he said. Mr. Easygoing in a blue polo, houndstooth scarf, and a wool coat was taking control of the situation. It calmed him to be in charge, which was fine, up to a point.

"That's totally not fair. You could tell me he said I have to wear a clown suit on Tuesdays, and I wouldn't even know."

"A clown suit? Even you couldn't make that sexy."

I crossed my arms and turned to face him. Pigeons flew up in the fog. The square was just starting to get crowded with the lunchtime rush, and we were ignored.

"You should have gotten me an English-speaking doctor," I said.

"I got you the best."

"Well, I felt left out. I felt like you all were talking about me like I wasn't there. And of all people, you should understand how shitty that is."

He stepped forward and cupped my cheeks. "Do you remember that heartbeat?"

The whooshing sound, like an angel walking on a heavenly treadmill, had come through the sonogram loud and clear. I admitted that a tear fell from my eyes. Maybe two. Maybe I'd wept right there.

"So?" I said with a choke.

"What language was that?"

I shook my head. No language obviously. I wanted him to get to his point.

"It was our baby's," he said. "It was the language of life. Who cares what the doctor and I said? Who cares about how I want to take care of you? You want to fight about something? Let's fight about what you're having for lunch."

I smiled and turned my face into his hand, kissing the palm that was warm despite the December cold. "I want one of those ham croissants with the sour cheese."

"And a salad."

"Fine."

"And after, you take one of the prenatal vitamins."

I made a yuck face. The doctor had given me bullet-sized vitamins that smelled terrible. But I'd take them. Jonathan was my inspiration for keeping up a regimen. I'd take them every day on a clock, but I didn't have to pretend to like it.

"I could lose it again," I whispered.

"You won't. I have a feeling this one's going to stick."

He gathered me in his arms, and we held each other in a Parisian square, rocking back and forth for blissful minutes.

Epilogue

Monica

I woke up alone, and I panicked. I had that heavy feeling from sleeping longer and harder than I was used to. I felt drunk, hazy, and worried. The baby was supposed to be next to me or in the little cradle next to the bed, and Jonathan was supposed to be in the next room, but god damn if I couldn't smell him in the sheets.

"Jonathan?" I mumbled.

Was I still dreaming? Or was the air actually thicker? I knocked a glass of water from the night table. Cold water splashed on my leg. Not a dream. This was real.

How had I slept? I shouldn't have. The fact that I hadn't slept in three days notwithstanding, no decent person should sleep when their baby was as sick as mine was. Light flickered at the corner of the bedroom, under the bathroom door, and voices... no, a single voice. My husband, singing. God, he was terrible.

I opened the door.

The bathroom was washed in candlelight, and he was running the sauna with the door open, so I walked into a hot cloud. Jonathan was in the tub with little Gabrielle, all of three weeks old, face up on his thighs. I crossed my arms.

"You're not supposed to be around her while she's sick."

He ignored me and nuzzled the baby. "Can you say good morning to Mommy?" he cooed.

Gabby snorted then sneezed.

"Jonathan, I'm serious. At least wear a mask. You're immunosup—"

"I'm sterile enough for an operating room, and she's not contagious any more."

He wielded an ear thermometer. I took it and crouched on the side of the tub. The little screen said 99.1.

"Oh," I said, "that's good. Do you think it's over?"

"I don't know." He dotted the baby's nose. "Are you going to let Mommy sleep, little girl?" She made an *ahhh* sound, and Jonathan turned to me. "She says yes, but she's reserving the right to change her mind."

"When did you learn to speak baby?" I ran my finger over his cheek, stripping away the water droplets.

"I live in Los Angeles."

We'd had a trying few days, with Gabby posting a 104.5 fever. Her pediatrician had come over late in the night, gotten it down to 101, and gone home. We could call him any time, but he said the ER wasn't necessary just yet. A few hours later, we were woken by the night nurse. The baby was spiking again.

It wasn't the nurse's fault, but dismissed her anyway. The worry and responsibility were ours, and though we had the resources to hire out the exhaustion, we decided to own it. These were our moments of aggravation and pain; we wouldn't pay someone else to stand in for being together as a family. So we stayed up all night and cared for Gabby in shifts that didn't happen, because neither of us rested. I did the night nursing, or Jonathan gave her a bottle, grumbling about wearing gloves and a mask. We were still working out a routine that my body would accept, but those moments with her were so precious, I didn't care what time of day they were.

Gabby wiggled, still not knowing what her arms were for, grabbing at air with her tiny fingers. She had a full head of black hair, and though her eyes had the blue cast of a newborn's, they'd turn a shade of brown.

I submerged a big yellow sponge in the warm water and squeezed it over my daughter. Water fell over her chest and round belly, shining as if she'd been lacquered.

"I want redheaded babies," I said.

"We can try again, but unless both parents have red hair, it skips a generation."

"Why?"

"Dominance. It's in your genes."

"You're a jerk."

Gabby opened her mouth and turned her head, squeaking. She was just learning to cry. She could scream, squeak, sneeze, and smile, but we hadn't gotten to full-blown crying without a full-blown fever.

"Uh oh," Jonathan said. "She's calling Mommy."

I peeled off my shirt and underpants. My body was still misshapen from the pregnancy, but my husband eyeballed me as if I were the only woman in the world. Slowly, my figure was returning as if his kind attention was teasing it out.

I picked up the baby under her arms. She loved the water and jerked her tiny legs angrily when I took her out.

"Patience, little girl," I said.

Jonathan held his arms out for me. He was still magnificent, wearing nothing more than a scar and an erection that would go unattended until the baby was down. I got into the tub, sitting between my husband's legs. He wrapped his arms around me, and I positioned baby Gabrielle at my breast.

Jonathan rubbed my back, kissing my neck as I nursed. I was in some heavenly place where I was cared for physically and emotionally, turning this warm tub into a slice of well-being.

"Mister Gevers called," Jonathan said.

"Oh, did you thank him for the bunny and flowers?"

"Yes. He wants us to come out there. He wants to meet the little girl."

"I'm not travelling with a newborn."

"It's not that hard. I did it for ten minutes once."

"He and his wife can come here again. I'm not going anywhere yet." I leaned into him, and he wrapped his arms around us. "Not until I'm good and ready."

"Yes, mistress." He kissed my shoulder.

Little Gabby nursed her little heart out. I was so in love with her, more in love than I'd ever thought possible. I leaned my head against my husband's chest, letting the soft warmth of the water envelope me, and somewhere in my half-sleep, I became a part of it, growing into a universe where I was loved and where I loved. Where I was needed and where I was allowed to need. In our tight realm of three, I dreamed myself expanding into this tiny, infinite universe, perfect in its balance and stability.

I opened my eyes when Jonathan tucked my hair behind my ear and kissed my neck. So perfect was the silence, and our baby, sated and sleeping in my arms, mouth cocked open, the edges pointed in a smile.

Flesh of my flesh, love of my love, broken and tied back together with the strings of my heart, these are mine. And whatever life may bring, whatever tests and tortures, I am complete, and competent, and ready to go to battle in their defense.

But for now, there is only peace.

THE END

If you liked this series,
check out these other CD Reiss books:

Shuttergirl
USA Today Bestseller

I never forgot her. Not for one minute. Not from the last time I saw her, at seventeen, to today. I measured all women against her and all women came up short.

But being with her was unfeasible in high school, and it's taboo now.

I see her sometimes, but I've never spoken to her. She runs, or I run. We're in the same town, on the same block, in the same building, and the gulf between us is just too wide to cross.

Until tonight.

He was my high school crush, back when I lived in a world that didn't want me. He was the perfect boy, and I was the outcast kid from the other side of town. And when he held my hand I thought I could fit in, just a little. I thought I could be his and he could be mine.

Then he left, and my life fell apart.

Now we are the king and queen of opposite sides of Hollywood. And we haven't spoken a word to each other.

Until tonight.

The Corruption Series
USA Today Bestseller

Theresa Drazen wants to know one thing.

Is there something wrong with her?

Because from what she can see, she has money, brains, a body that does the job. Yet, she keeps getting shelved. Most recently, by her fiancé who happens to be the DA.

And she'll get over it, really. No problem. She'll just have a nice, short encounter with a mysterious Italian named Antonio who may or may not be involved with some kind of alleged criminal activity...blah blah...

Let's call a spade a spade.

He's a mobster.

Let's face a few more facts.

He's hot. He's smart. And if anyone breathes on her the wrong way, he's got no problem beating their head in.

Just about everything about that turns her on.

Yeah. There's something wrong with her.

About the Author

To keep up with what I think is sexy today, see **CD Reiss on Facebook**
Email me at **cdreiss.writer@gmail.com**

If you'd like to be notified of new releases, which are run at a discount during the first days of launch week, sign up for the mailing list by visiting the facebook page (click on the rainbow envelope button up top) or my website at **cdreiss.com**. I'll also be sending out bonus scenes, when appropriate, but only to people on the mailing list.

And, of course, if you have any feelings about this book you'd like to share, kindly leave a review.

CPSIA information can be obtained
at www.ICGtesting.com
Printed in the USA
BVOW08s1410070917
494259BV00001B/12/P